GOLD

BY
JACOB WASSERMANN
Author of "The World's Illusion"

Authorized Translation by
LOUISE COLLIER WILLCOX

NEW YORK

CONTENTS

CHAPTER   PAGE

I   ULRIKA MAKES HER ENTRANCE   3

II   THE GOOD SERVANTS: EYES AND EARS . .   14

III   TINDER IN THE DRY WOOD   25

IV   AND ULRIKA TELLS   35

V   ULRIKA ACTS FEARLESSLY WHILE ALL TREMBLE   48

VI   MONOLOGUE AND DOMESTIC STORM . . .   62

VII   ULRIKA DRAGS THE SECRET FROM ITS KEEPER .   73

VIII   AND IT WAS NO DREAM   88

IX   COUNSELLOR WOYTICH VISITS THE MYLIUS'S
HOUSE   100

X   THE CONQUEROR AT THE FEET OF THE CON-
QUERED   112

XI   JOSEPHINE   125

XII   "MON HÉROS QUOIQUE PETIT"   142

XIII   A CHAPTER WITH NO SPECIAL INCIDENTS . .   157

XIV   ULRIKA BALANCES ACCOUNTS   169

XV   JOSEPHINE'S FLIGHT   183

XVI   CRYING OVER SPILT MILK   206

XVII   MARRIAGES AND LEGACIES   217

XVIII   YES   229

XIX   DEPARTURE WITH BAG AND BAGGAGE . . .   243

XX   ACCUSING GOD   257

XXI   A WONDERFUL TRIAL   265

XXII   UNEXPECTED RESULTS OF A PEDAGOGICAL UNDER-
TAKING   275

XXIII   A RUSTIC IDYLL   289

XXIV   THE WITCHES' MULTIPLICATION TABLE . .   294

CONTENTS

CHAPTER		PAGE
XXV	THE WAX PEAR	302
XXVI	FANNY GOES WANDERING	310
XXVII	HOW DO YOU DO, MY LITTLE DARLING?	324
XXVIII	THE GUEST AT ECKERN	337
XXIX	ULRIKA APPEARS	350
XXX	ALL SORTS OF LETTERS AND WRITINGS	362
XXXI	OBEDIENCE	372
XXXII	A SHORT INTERLUDE	381
XXXIII	THE CYCLE OF TIME	385
XXXIV	A VAIN OBLATION	402
XXXV	THE MOUNTAIN	415

PART ONE

CHAPTER I

ULRIKA MAKES HER ENTRANCE

To many people in Vienna, the great fire at the Ring Theatre, on a December night in 1881, seemed a sinister omen. There were prophets who looked upon the accident as the forerunner of far more tragic catastrophes. For weeks a guilty sense of discouragement reigned all over the city, in all the various strata of society.

It was with the greatest difficulty that Frau Christine Mylius had succeeded in getting one orchestra seat for the first performance of "Tales of Hoffmann." She had been told that the demand was so great that hundreds were being turned away. But as it was to be a surprise and a birthday present for her daughter Josephine, the fifteen-year-old girl's first visit to the theatre, she had spared neither trouble nor money, and finally on the very morning of the unhappy day, a speculator had brought her a ticket, demanding an impudently high price and assuring her of the insuperable difficulties, with wordy complaints of his efforts.

Christine had had to go about the business secretly and alone. Not only did she want to keep the matter from Josephine herself, since it was to be a surprise, but also from Josephine's father and brother and older sisters; the first because he regarded such extravagant expenditures most unfavorably; and the latter because they were never free from jealousy of the favourite, Josephine, and might easily spoil her pleasure in the gift by their sullen discontent.

Of course it was more or less uncertain whether Josephine herself would be glad. The self-contained temperament of the girl, her shy solitariness and withdrawn ways with people led one to fear that a gay evening at the theatre might not lie within the realm of her desires; that she might even prefer

3

to avoid, rather than to reach out toward the common
diversions and pleasures of others. But it was just for this
reason that Christine had decided upon her plan; she wanted,
for a few hours at least, to lift the child from her customary
surroundings, to brighten her mood and raise her spirits. To
her mother only was Josephine confidential; toward every one
else she was silent and cautious.

But Christine was agreeably surprised. After dinner the
father had gone out; Esther and Aimée had disappeared to
their own room; and the seventeen-year-old Lothar had been
taken by his schoolmate, Robert Elmenreich, who lived in
the same house, to the Gymnasium.[1] She took Josephine
by the hand, led her to the console between the two windows,
where a little casket stood, and told her to raise the lid. Inside there was an envelope inscribed: "For Josephine's birthday," and inside the envelope lay the theatre ticket. Josephine smiled a happy smile; even her eyes under her heavy
brows smiled; she kissed her mother's hand.

"Are you glad?" asked Christine.

"Very glad," was the answer.

Christine warned her to keep silence about it. The secrecy
should be maintained until evening; at supper, while Josephine
was still in the theatre, when no objections need be feared, she
would tell the others. Lothar should fetch her from the
theatre at ten o'clock and she could go alone. At six o'clock,
to prevent her sisters from unexpectedly interrupting her, she
went into her mother's room to dress. Christine helped her,
smoothing the folds of the new white dress and the ribbons into
place (and these, too, were a birthday present that Christine
had teased out of her husband), sewing up the hem, wiping off
the satin shoes, smoothing out the velvet cloak, and then
looked at Josephine, who, blushing, had become suddenly
pretty. Then she looked in the adjoining room to assure herself that there were no listeners or spies about, and started
Josephine off with a tender kiss on her forehead.

A few minutes after eight when no one was at home, as she

[1] Gymnasium in Germany is a college preparatory school or kind
of high school.—Note by translator.

sat in the living room by the lamp embroidering her husband's
initials H. O. M., Helmut Otto Mylius, on some linen handkerchiefs fastened in a frame, she heard the fire trumpet
sounding down the street. Hideous sound; she raised her
head and wrinkled her forehead. Quick horses' hoofs clattered
on the pavement; wheels rolled by; she got up and went to
the window. The hose-wagons tore past, and in the waving
flames of the blaze the helmets of the firemen glinted; excited
people were gesticulating and running in the same direction
as the fire engines. Suddenly the door was thrown open and
the maid rushed in announcing: "The Ring Theatre is burning
up!"

Christine never knew how she managed to slip into her coat,
throw a shawl over her head and rush down the stairs; nor
was she aware what streets she ran through or what she asked
the crowds as she passed or what they answered. As she approached the theatre she pushed, with every sign of horror,
through the massed people whose pale faces were lit up by
the flames breaking from the windows of the building. Christine's features were distorted, her eyes senseless, her hair fluttered about her forehead; the strength with which she pushed
through the crowd and shoved those aside who barred her
passage, was that of an insane person; broken mutterings and
breathless sighs broke from her lips: "For Heaven's sake, O
people, for the Lord Christ's sake, good people, let me through!
My daughter—Oh, have mercy—my daughter!" she pleaded;
and the breath rattled in her throat, like a dying person's.
She pushed her way through; felt her cloak torn off and her
dress ripped at the armholes; the hem of her dress was stepped
on and torn. At last with superhuman energy she pushed
herself through to one of the side doors of the theatre. Black
smoke poured out snakelike and evil-smelling; to right and to
left bodies were being dragged out, smothered, charred, unconscious; and inside, down the stairway waltzed a shrieking,
screaming mass of humanity, coiled about one another, clinging convulsively to each other.

Wildly Christine stared about her; her senses reeled; the
heat singed her skin; terror blinded her eyes; suddenly she

gave one piercing scream: Josephine! Like a ghost the face of her child had appeared and then disappeared. But Josephine had heard the cry; she raised her arm; she was being half carried, half dragged by a young person on whose shoulder her head rested. Christine parted the crowd that had gathered round her in a moment, almost with fury, uncertain whether she should weep or rejoice, made for the raised arm and caught her child sobbing to her breast. With her fingers she passionately smoothed the beloved head, and so they were pushed on by the stream of panic-stricken folk fleeing from the crowd, until once more they had space and air, and the young woman to whom Josephine owed her rescue offered to fetch a carriage. The sky gleamed purple, the whole atmosphere was like a black face hung over with a veil of moving sparks.

Josephine's dress hung in shreds; even her underclothes were not spared; a wide tear showed from neck to hip, and the white skin of her bosom gleamed through. Her cloak was gone, and to shelter herself from cold she pressed the fluttering shreds and tatters to her body. Her rescuer had gone, after warning them to stand in the same place till she returned with a carriage. Exhausted and shuddering, Josephine clung to her mother, who was leaning against the wall of a house, shuddering too, as she stroked her child's cheeks and whispered confused and tender reassurances; at the end of a quarter of an hour a cab stopped on the pavement, the young woman jumped out, motioned them to get in, took a rug from the driver, wrapped them up, and asked if she should drive home with them. Josephine now told her mother hastily, that in the worst of the tumult on the stairs, just as she was losing her breath and was about to give up and sink down to be trodden to death, this young woman had caught her, protected her from the hideous rush of screaming and groaning men and women, and with marvellous strength and presence of mind had cleared a passage. Without her she would have been lost.

Christine, unable to speak, siezed the hands of the rescuer and pressed them. In her glance lay her overflowing thanks and a dumb plea that she accompany them. As they drove

along, she stammered: "Such a debt cannot be paid in a life
time." The unknown, sitting slim and quiet, opposite her,
strangely with almost no damage done her, and without any
excitement, waved away the thanks modestly. Then Christine asked her name. She gave it. Her name, she said, was
Ulrika Woytich; she had only been a short time in the city
and lived with her uncle, a pensioned court official, Clement
Woytich. All this dropped quickly and fluently from her lips
as if these personalities were not of the slightest importance.
To turn the subject at once she asked if the gracious lady
came from North Germany, and when Christine said "yes,"
she nodded, satisfied, and said one always heard it in the
accent; said the fact that the family had lived here twenty
years did not matter, that such little points of difference in
speech always remained under all circumstances, and her own
ear had been sharpened to them by her residence in foreign
countries. She had lived two years in England and one in
Belgium.

Then she told of her experience in the theatre. Before the
curtain went up, as she looked over the parquet, from the first
row of the balcony with her opera glass she had been struck
by Josephine's face. So it seemed like a coincidence that she
should see her again on the narrow stairway, in the dangerous
crush, and her resolve to save her had been purely instinctive.
"But you must have had some presentiment of danger as you
left your seat?" she asked, as she turned to Josephine. "Why
did you do it?" The girl had to confess that this was true,
and she and her mother both wondered that Ulrika Woytich
had from the first observed her so closely. She said she had
been suddenly overcome by a violent beating of her heart, such
as she had never felt before. The orchestra had just begun to
play, but the tempting strains of Offenbach's music could not
quiet her; on the contrary she was frightened lest she lose
consciousness and hastened as quickly as she could into the
Promenade outside. While she was walking up and down, she
heard a sound like a downfall of pebbles and the glass roof
broke. Then every door burst open, and screaming people
rushed out; in an instant she was in their midst; but had it

not been for the heart attack she would have been imprisoned in the auditorium, where, shut in with the raving crowd, there would have been no escape possible.

"So you see you had a good angel inside you as well as outside," said Christine. "It is wonderful, Josephine, to be saved from all that horror."

Josephine smiled slightly and looked steadily at Miss Woytich with big, attentive eyes.

The cab stopped at the house door. A number of little anxieties had arisen in Christine's mind. First, she had no money to pay the driver, and he would certainly not be moderate in his charges, but would seize the opportunity of general misfortune to overcharge for his service. She did not even know if she had enough money to pay him upstairs in her money box. Helmut Otto still owed her this week's allowance; he always gave it at the last moment; she would have to go and ask him for five or six gulden and that was a ticklish business. Then there was the question as to whether he was at home yet. She looked up; the light was burning in the living room, but it had probably been burning ever since she left; everybody had rushed to the fire, for in the street around them they stood packed against each other. Probably he had gone too. Still it would be worse if he were waiting up there; then she would have to confess, in all the haste and flurry, that Josephine had been in the theatre; questions, arguments, reproaches were to be expected when she asked for the money for the cab; her everlasting care to hide these scenes from her children had been forgotten in her anxiety about Josephine. The girl's pale face expressed her unmistakable inward excitement; it seemed best to get her to bed at once without letting her see her father or brother and sisters.

As she thought over all this and, overcome, stared up from the cab at the lighted house, Ulrika Woytich guessed her embarrassment and informed herself by two or three skilful questions. She drew out her purse, fumbled in it with busy fingers and showed that she had exactly enough money to pay the driver. Then she lifted Josephine from her seat, put her arm around her, led her into the house, and guessing Christine's anxiety, begged that she go ahead to make sure that the child could be taken undisturbed and immediately to her own room, as her hands were hot and she seemed feverish. Christine ran up the stairs and Ulrika followed slowly with Josephine. As she went, she looked with interest at everything, the balustrade, the floor, the walls, even the doors, while she took the utmost care of her protégée.

Mylius was at home. He knew everything before Ulrika arrived with Josephine. Christine was not the kind of woman to shun a threatening storm, especially in her present mood. She told her husband in a few words what had happened and asked him for the money. He had not been to the burning theatre but had contented himself with the excited accounts which he had heard on the street; he had been waiting an hour for supper and was in a bad temper because of the delay. Christine's confession, the way she had broken into the room, her torn and dirty apparel overwhelmed him. He could not suppress at once his ill temper at the secrecy which had made Josephine's visit to the theatre possible. To all this was added his vexation over the expense. Despite the tyrannical rule he kept, allowing his family no freedom of action, he was often worried by a suspicion that all sorts of expenditures went on behind his back; little unimportant expenditures, and yet to be feared since all evil had hidden roots.

When Christine asked for the money which Ulrika had paid, for she wanted to pay the debt at once, he hesitated, turned round, shrugged his shoulders, shook his head, said they had paid too much, but finally, forced by the despairing and pleading look of his wife, he put his hand in his pocket and brought out his purse. Christine snatched the bill from him with a sigh in which a thousand suppressed complaints vibrated and hastened with heavy steps to Josephine's room. Owing to the girl's disposition she had a room alone while her two sisters shared a large one. Calling Theresa, the old maid, to heat water, the universal medicine in her eyes, she lit the lamp, pulled the curtains, and opened the bed. As soon as Ulrika and Josephine came in, she helped undress her daughter, while

Ulrika, whose quick eyes always noted the most necessary thing to be done, knelt down before the stove and lit the fire.

She was still doing it when the door opened and Esther and Aimée entered. Alarmed at the delay and yet bursting with secret joy at the excitement, they, like Lothar, had just gotten in. Their joy increased as they heard the story of their mother and Josephine's adventures; but at the same time they felt angry that Josephine had been allowed to go to the theatre, while the fact that she had escaped death by a hair's breadth and even now gave cause for anxiety seemed to make no particular impression upon them.

Lothar stood in the doorway, an amazed smile on his pretty boy's face. "How was it, Josephine?" he asked the girl lying there with closed eyes. "Tell us about it; it must have been frightfully interesting." Josephine did not answer, and Ulrika did instead. "You'd better try to be useful, young man," she said curtly and unconstrainedly, though not unpleasantly as she rose from her knees and handed him the empty coal scuttle. "Go into the kitchen and fill the scuttle; we need heat here." Lothar looked astonished, shook the wood-brown curls that framed his face coquettishly, but at her shining glance took his hands out of his pocket and obeyed.

Esther and Aimée stared at the stranger who even in the presence of their mother seemed so unconcerned and impressive and gave their brother orders. Christine explained to them in a few hasty words full of passionate gratitude. The girls were all the more surprised. They had crowded together in the window seat, for they were inseparable both by habit and a like sullen disposition. Nor was Ulrika inattentive to the harmony created by the pale, spring-like countenance of the twenty-two-year-old Esther with her brass-gold plaits close to the darker but bloodless face of the nineteen-year-old Aimée with the braided, copper, shimmering crown over her forehead. It made her curious. It made her think and pushed her quick mind to conclusions—their suppressed manner, timid glances, cold demeanour, and something strangely like watchfulness in their bearing. That she was on the right track was proved by the entrance of the father. Both faces took on a fixed, servile

expression which made them look like puppets; even Lothar
dragging in the filled scuttle and emptying it with unnecessary
noise into the stove, started as he noticed his father in the
room and suddenly looked as if he were too stupid to count
three.

"Good discipline at any rate," said Ulrika to herself.

Mylius had walked up and down the corridor for some time.
He did not know exactly how to conduct himself; whether
Josephine's condition allowed him to complain of the delayed
supper or whether it was wiser to contain himself until the
strange lady had departed. On the whole he thought it better
to keep quiet and act as if the meal were already over, so that
she might nurse no hope of being invited to it; for nothing
was more hateful to him than a guest at table. So he came
in, assumed a sympathetic manner, which gave his faded
smooth-shaven face a look of sour-sweetness, bowed to Ulrika,
and with indistinguishable mutterings, offered his hand. Then
he went up to the bed, wrinkled his forehead, glanced at Josephine, and looked enquiringly at his wife.

Christine thought that it was not good for the child to have
so many in the room. She drove them all out and told them
to begin supper and she would join them later with Miss Woytich. Mylius cleared his throat; the fearful thing was no
longer to be avoided. Esther and Aimée knew the sign and
were frightened; they admired their mother's courage. When
all was still again, Christine bent over Josephine and asked
her if she would like to be alone. Josephine drew her mother's
hand to her lips and nodded "yes." Then Christine and Ulrika
withdrew.

There was one picture in Josephine's mind that she could not
banish. While she was still in the Promenade of the theatre
and the first panic of the fleeing people from the auditorium
burst forth, she had experienced something which made a
deeper impression upon her than the devastating scenes after-
ward and her own danger. Among the first who rushed out
upon her, for she stood right at the entrance door, was a man
who held both fists high in the air; his mouth was wide open
but he did not scream; his eyes, glassy with fright and fury,

looked only to see how he could get ahead of others. He was a man with white hair and beard, well dressed, evidently belonging to the upper classes. He wore a gold chain over his snow-white waistcoat and a diamond stick-pin in his tie. It was easy to see that his face at other times might have an expression of benevolence; that his eyes were habitually kindly and benignant and that he had an imposing and poised carriage. But now there was not a vestige of all that. In place of it was the greed of a bird of prey or a wild animal, frantic to escape; an open, decayed mouthful of broken yellow tooth stumps, the wide open eyes of an insane man, the curved wrinkles of horror on his forehead. And this fury, this inexplicable fury, as if he wished to beat down with his fists all those who were striving in the race with him! All this Josephine had felt, pityingly and from a distance; but now it happened that he found himself completely barred on his way to the staircase by the mass of bodies. In his raving fear he tore out his pocket book, seized a package of bills with his trembling fingers and, his arm raised high, he offered them in flattering, whining, moaning tones. That was the horror of it! Money in this moment! It seemed more horrible to Josephine than all the rest; a manifestation of pollution and rottenness beside which the physical danger which threatened her, seemed hardly worth consideration. The whole seventy years that the old man must have lived became a lie to Josephine's eyes; all his white hair and dignity—lies! friendliness and smiling—lies! Money! when humanity was passing in torture! That any one should think he could buy his way free of the general destruction! This was hell. She remembered that under the burden of this scene, she had turned away from the thought of safety, and cold and profoundly impressed in the midst of the horror, she had said to herself: "What good is life to me if an old man with white hair can turn into Satan to save a piece of it?"

Her sorrow at the sight did not pass. It seemed to her she had looked too deep into the abyss of life, and now could never again be joyous. A procession of figures moved about in the air and each one bore wearily a burden of gold; flags hung motionless and stiff all made of gigantic gold certificates; the leaves on the trees were clicking like coins; the tapestry on the walls was all made of dirty ten-pound notes. And as she tried to free herself from these visions and to form a little prayer in the darkness of her soul, the door opened quietly and the joyous, well-featured face of her rescuer appeared. Ulrika wanted to assure herself she slept or see if she wanted anything. She only peeped in and her shining black eyes peered at Josephine's cot.

Josephine was frightened at first and her heart began to beat under the influence of her feverish dreams. Then she breathed deeply and nodded thankfully to Ulrika. Ulrika approached and dropped a sisterly kiss upon her forehead.

CHAPTER II

THE GOOD SERVANTS: EYES AND EARS

WHEN Ulrika came back into the dining room, Herr Mylius had just learned the full extent of the losses—that Christine and Josephine had both lost their cloaks in the general misfortune. He could no longer restrain himself and broke loose despite the presence of the stranger in lively reproaches of the frivolity Christine was guilty of. He rose, flung his napkin on the chair and his little, colourless eyes gleamed with anger. In a shrill voice he asked if they all thought him a millionaire. Dumb, submissive looks; no one was bold enough to believe it. Did they think he picked up his money on the pavement or won it with a lottery ticket? No one thought so. Did he not daily warn them to be economical? Did he not warn them, whenever it was a matter of personal expense to turn every kreuzer over ten times, and ponder whether it was absolutely necessary to spend it? Nor could it be denied that complete silence confirmed him. Was a living such an easy thing to earn? Would food, clothes, and dwelling produce themselves for six people and unluckily a servant too? Certainly not! One could see that! And three grown daughters! What was to be done with them? Who was going to start them out in life? What mad idealist would marry them without a dowry? And he had none to give. He had not carried things that far yet, and as far as he could see, he never would. Esther and Aimée hung their heads; they saw the hopelessness of their position. And a son, who had not in the least grasped the seriousness of life and whose teachers foresaw the worst for his future! How many years would he, the father, have to bear this burden? Lothar gazed unhappily at the troubled future and inwardly swore to do better.

As the scolding aroused no sign of contradiction Mylius' wrath calmed down by degrees. He was responsible for everything, he resumed; he had to furnish the money and plague himself; he was entitled to at least enough appreciation to restrain their extravagance beyond the point of ruin. Here he threw a stern look at Christine. To-day's mishap was only a finger pointing at Destiny. God wanted to warn them not to give in to evil impulses. Let them remember it in the future.

Scolding thus, he stamped about the table on his short legs. Christine begged him softly to quiet down. His meat was getting cold on his plate. (He alone had meat; the rest had only vegetables.) What had happened was exceptional and she promised it should not happen again. She had turned pale and her fingers played nervously with the chain of her key-ring. That he should depreciate her, the mother of his children with her fifty years, like a schoolgirl—in presence of those children, and in the presence of a stranger who had especial claims on their consideration—was very bitter. For the first time, she felt it with such bitterness; perhaps because of the stranger's presence. But she had to bear it; replies would only prolong the unpleasant wrangling. She had never defended herself; never sulked; never tried to influence her children by word, deed, or glance, or turn them from unconditioned reverence and silent obedience.

Then it appeared that Mylius again became aware with some compunction of Ulrika's presence. He stopped his promenade near her chair and said with the sour-sweet smirk which came to his face when he wanted to appear agreeable: "I beg pardon, honoured young lady; you will surely not take it amiss that a much-worried father should speak excitedly when it is a matter of the welfare or destruction of his family—a matter of order, exactitude, discipline; that what he has won by the work of his hands in twenty-seven years of servitude should be thrown thoughtlessly away. To-day I am sixty-two, my child; when I was thirty-five I was still a poor wretch in a province of Hesse, who did not know where he was to get his next day's dinner. True, we no longer have to fear hunger; still one has to look out for one's existence every hour. These are difficult times, and before one knows it, Fate may catch one in her claws; poverty, need, may catch us. So it stands."

"You are quite right, Herr Mylius," answered Ulrika, raising her candid look to him. "Even if I do not quite believe that the Lord burned down the Ring theatre to preserve your family from mistakes. Otherwise I heartily uphold you. My uncle, the State-counsellor, pointed out to me, as a child, that nothing was more to be condemned in people than the careless handling of money. Any one can spend; but earning is hard. And after all, the best thing in life is to own something. Who has nothing might as well let himself be buried; a dog is as much esteemed as he."

Mylius nodded approvingly. "That's true," he said. "You've never fallen on your head, lovely lady. To own something, that is the best thing in the world. One cannot express it better. It sounds like the motto on an old coat-of-arms." He sniggered and lit one of his evil-smelling cigars, in returning good humour.

"Spendthrifts hardly know how to express enough contempt for the economical," Ulrika went on eagerly. "But when things go badly, when the water rises up round their necks, to whom do they creep then? To whom do they whine? Whose praises do they sing? To whom do they promise the very blue out of the Heavens? The despised economist. He is master now and they have to thank him for the kick which he gives them."

"True, true," said Mylius, delighted, and Ulrika laughed.

While she talked, Esther, Aimée, and Lothar exchanged anxious glances. They were used to carrying the heavy yoke of their father; to murmur would have seemed outrageous to them; to throw it off was an impossibility and the thought was far from them; his authority was too firm, his person to inaccessible, his will, with which he had ruled them from birth, too firm. But that a stranger should come in, without rhyme or reason, and pull upon the purse-strings, roused their mistrust and doubt.

But suddenly they all noticed something odd, all three at once, led by the same instinct. There was a tone of deliberate intention, an undercurrent of mockery and impishness, that made them listen more carefully and look more sharply into that gay and clever face. The answering look frightened them; it seemed to promise such tremendous things. It was a look that said quite plainly: I am with you; I am forming an alliance with you; but let me do it my own way; I understand these things thoroughly.

They gazed doubtfully and tried to understand and dropped their eyes dazzled.

Christine remained untouched. She had a painful impression that Ulrika was being turned against her by Mylius; and a few minutes later, when she had invited Ulrika with a quiet gesture to leave the room with her and go to Josephine, she laid her hand on the arm of the young woman, as soon as the door was closed behind them and said hastily: "You don't really believe that I am frivolous? You don't think me so bad a mother and housewife as he made me out in his anger? I can assure you he does not really believe it himself. He is just and he cannot really complain of insubordination."

Ulrika replied softly: "To judge you is not my affair, but perhaps I ought to tell you that you appealed to me more, at the first glance, than any woman has ever done. I don't care much for women in general, but I honour you. I could wish for nothing more than that you would let me visit you often."

"Thank you," said Christine. "Those were kind words and I don't hear them often. Come, then. Come every day, or as often as you can. I shall be glad."

They walked along the entrance hall, where brackets were fastened along the walls adorned with pewter figures.

"One thing you must understand at once," Christine began again in a cautiously lowered voice, "otherwise you might come to believe that Mylius was really a sacrifice to his family. Things are not as he so pessimistically describes them. Any one in town would confirm that. His antique business is known all over Europe. H. O. Mylius; enquire about it if you want to. Of course I don't know whether there is a fortune in it, or how much it is worth. My husband never speaks of such things to me; it is against his principles and I have to respect them. I do not know if his gains are great; I never ask. But I do know that he denies me and the children even necessi-

ties. Such scenes as we had to-day are rare but not altogether to be avoided. Poor man! he can't help it. It is
stronger than he is, and I only explain to you because it can't
be hidden; and because, if in despite of it all you still want
to visit us, you may have to experience it again."

"It would be stupid, if I were to let myself be frightened
off by that," said Ulrika in her deep, trust-awakening voice.
"On the contrary, it seems to me that in many ways I can
be useful to you. In the first place, I have not always lain on
feather beds myself; secondly, I am a born lightning-conductor;
and, thirdly, I am determined to go through fire and water for
you—if you will only like me a little."

Christine pressed her hand, and they walked on tip-toes toward the sleeping Josephine.

Christine's shy explanation had been quite unnecessary.
Ulrika had lost no time. Her observations had given her the
certainty that she was not with poor people, not indeed in a
sinking ship. Herr Mylius's speech did not lead her astray; on
this point she had unquestionable meteorological signs.

At first indeed the home seemed to impress her as belonging to the lower middle class; and had the impression remained
she would have taken flight, for that was what she was determined to avoid. In such circumstances everything was so
narrow, so crowded, so exactly counted. Spaces were so low
and damp; there was no comfort, freedom, generous outlook.
Adornment and hangings were there only because they had
to be there—not because people prized them or cared for
them; there was something unloved and unlovely about such
things.

But Ulrika noticed that here the furnishings, while not
showy, were solid and stately; not things made by the dozen
or mere suburban taste. The carpets were the real things; the
linen was of the finest quality; the table furnishings were of
massive silver; the gold-framed pictures on the wall were origi-
nal old masters. Here and there she saw objects of unquestionable costliness; a Nippon figure, a bronze, a lamp, a crystal globe, a Chinese vase. It was possible that the old man
might have brought these up from his shop, with the intention

of offering them for sale later, and thus acquire cheaply a worthy decoration that must pass on. But Ulrika threw aside this thought; it was not in character with the man; he would lend nothing—not even to himself. He would never pretend. Everything with him was real and in the right place. Deception was hardly possible. Here was prosperity, dignity of possession, such as one rarely meets with a modest outer bearing.

Nothing escaped her sharp eye, though she knew so well how to control her glance that no one could have guessed how much she saw. She compared things with people; she guessed people's habits, qualities and kind from the things about them. She considered the two silent young girls, only a few years younger than herself; considered their inconspicuous, almost poor clothes and their depressed manner, as if they were mourning their strangled youth and the way they dragged through their days without a single outburst of rebellion; the son, with his face of a charming rascal, full of demands and secret desires, but bound by fear of his father who forced him along the prescribed way; and the youngest one, with the glowing, questioning eyes of a dreamer; the mother, tender, shy, softening, reconciling, veiling, a medium between the man and the children, but herself servile, with a look of bewilderment in her beautiful eyes; and lastly she considered the old man, with his tricky smirk, acquired doubtless in his business, when he bargained as buyer and seller; his birdlike movements of the head, his tyrannical bearing, and constant indignation against life's claims and life's desires and the treacherous anxiety back of all. "Something is the matter with that old man," thought Ulrika, keen for battle. "He has some secret. It may not be so difficult to find out what it is; and patience and cunning only are necessary to tear it from him and make use of it. It is possible that it is worth while," she went on; "it will give me an aim and in the end may be fun. Who knows where it may lead and what surprise may be in store? Evidently he is deceiving his entire family and plays the poor devil so that they may not know what riches he has heaped up in secret. It is easy to attribute that to him. They must go without and tremble, while he gloats over his treasure and laughs in his sleeve. If this prove true, my good man, your hour has struck and I'll light you home."

She laughed to herself, delighted with the plan, still distant but enticing, that was forming in her mind .

In the next few days she listened about a good deal. Mylius's business was in the Himmelspfort street; in casual shopping she led quite a number of shop-keepers in the neighbourhood to tell what they knew of Mylius. Her good manners helped her, her winning candour and openness, but above all, the humorous way she had with people of the lower class. Her other source of information was an old lady who had lived for twenty years in the same house as the Mylius family, and who, she learned casually, had formerly been acquainted with her uncle. The brother of this old lady and her uncle had been in the same cabinet some fifty years ago. Now the son of that dead brother lived with his aunt and was an intimate friend and schoolmate of Lothar Mylius. Ulrika paid a visit to Fräulein von Elmenreich, after having greeted her the day before on the stairs as if she had long been consumed by a desire to meet her. The connection was easily made. The reference to the State-counsellor delighted the lonely old lady, who poured out her reminiscences; she proved most docile and hid nothing from her young guest that could add to her knowl‹ edge.

The first results of Ulrika's researches were these. Both Mylius and his wife came from Hesse on the Rhein. He was the son of a Protestant pastor and had studied theology and the history of art. He had fallen heir to a small property which rendered it possible for him to travel to Italy and spend some time in Rome. Here he had changed his vocation and became an art-dealer. He returned home, settled in Frankfurt, and married. Christine came from an old, impoverished, patrician family and was born a Vollprecht; before the Revolution of 1848 her father had been the grand-ducal minister of state, a man of intellect and culture. When he died, what he left was inadequate to cover his debts and Christine had no choice when Mylius asked for her hand. Things did not

prosper much with the young household and Mylius decided
to leave that locality and settle in Vienna. He gave up dealing exclusively in pictures and threw himself into a general
business in antiques. That was in the beginning of the 'sixties.
At first it appeared that things were going none too well in
the new business, but one day he had the idea of buying up
the entire movable property of the recently deceased Count
Zieroten, the last of his family. He made favorable terms, and
since then he had worked his way up, slowly but steadily.
With the aristocracy he stood in high favour; people trusted
his taste, held his judgment as final in all doubtful cases,
turned to him for all delicate bargainings, and praised his
business probity. With the help of a select clientele, he had
managed to corner a market attainable by few. With the aristocracy of England and France and also among American collectors his name was well-known, and with a certain amount of
regularity he made shipments of untold worth to foreign lands.

The question as to whether he was really a rich man was
differently answered by different people. Some answered with
an unconditional "yes." They said he had at least a quarter
of a million secure. Gulden? A quarter of a million gulden?
Certainly, why not? A quarter of a million gulden. Others
questioned this and mentioned a smaller sum, seventy or eighty
thousand. Still others, for instance the glove manufacturer
Schlitteis, whose building was opposite Mylius's, went up to
sheer fantastic sums, and asserted he must at the least be
worth four to five hundred thouand gulden. Ulrika laughed
in his face and told him he was a gifted fairy-story teller but
of doubtful business acumen; a man with all that money would
find something better to do than to lie in wait in a dark hole
and bargain over bric-a-brac. Such madness she could not
believe of a rational man.

Fräulein von Elmenreich thought that he was a rich man
according to bourgeois standards, but owing to the peculiarities
of his business it was difficult to decide what his actual capital
might be. The value of his property was constantly changing;
he must often sell below value; speculation often erred and
expectations were deceived. Of course, it did happen that

certain objects increased tremendously in value; she herself in the year '73, the year of the great crash, had sold a Gobelin tapestry for two hundred gulden and to-day it was worth six times as much. Whenever she thought of it, she came near crying.

"To tell the truth, I never pass Mylius without a little fright," said the old lady. "Now and then I meet him in the dim light of the entrance hall. He says good day, I reply, and that is all. But these secretive money-men spread a kind of evil magic about them. They love the fetich of their cash box as a man with a heart loves the living, with the same surrender, the same passion. From such an ungodly love their blood turns thick and black, and one feels imperceptibly that their souls are shrouded in anxiety. There he goes, up the steps, like a ghost. What he has makes him tremble and what he has not makes him tremble."

"True," said Ulrika Woytich, "but I am not afraid of ghosts. I accept them. If they are too intrusive one gives a shove to their dry bodies and exclaims, 'Praised be Jesus Christ.' They can't stand that; they vanish. I never knew how to shudder; I shall have to learn like the man in the fairy tale who had to strip himself to do it."

As Ulrika was soon convinced, Mylius had the reputation of being a responsible man of sternly upright principles. At first things had gone none too easily for him, a Protestant alien, in the city of light-heartedness. His derivation and the people of his race were unfamiliar. They made fun of his precision and suspected his industry; if they were not shocked by his curt turning away from any pretensions, they were vexed by his correct conduct. But in the end, with his own quiet tenacity he had stuck it out and won ground.

Actual friends he had none, nor any familiar intercourse. His family life was considered unimpeachable, and people praised the good conduct and training of his children, the modesty and courtesy of his wife. Naturally some people pitied the daughters. They were never allowed to go to balls or accept invitations, and could only go on excursions when they cost nothing. Even the least little railroad trip had to be begged for. Josephine was the only one to whom this was no renunciation. Even in her earliest years, her piety was noticeable and striking. Many could not understand how a Protestant could be devout at all. Protestantism, they declared, was not a creed but denial and heresy; even Jews were better than Protestants.

Through her first talks with Christine, Ulrika found out that the child had converted her mother to her views. For quite a while Christine had accompanied her child to church, and she confessed that it was all very surprising to her, as she had been brought up in enlightened and advanced tendencies and had spent her time very differently in youth. Her grandfather had known Merck, the friend of Goethe; her mother as a young girl had moved in the Brentano circle and had corresponded with Arnim, Görres, and Friedrich Schlegel and their letters were treasured among the family archives. She still remembered with pride a visit of Wilhelm von Humboldt to her parents.

Her mental tendency, when she tried to put it into words, was the product, the echo of that deep, inward romanticism which had been swept away from German soil as by an ice storm and left another Germany to be sensed, quite different from that which had arisen under the thundering cannon before the walls of Paris. But the fundamental colour of her mind had long since faded; that former being had no reality now; it was only a dream from which she sometimes drew courage at great need, courage to become a pleader for her children, when it was important to give them pleasure or to flatter her husband into the fulfilment of their wishes. Otherwise a great stillness ruled her whole being; a sleepy, joyless stillness. And the same thing was true of the children too, except of Josephine, who led her own hidden life, which none could divine. Yes; a sleepy, joyless silence weighed upon them. When the windows were thrown open in the morning, they seemed to wonder that people passed in the street and that a world lay out there. Little by little this world took on an inimical and dangerous aspect. Mylius never missed an occasion to warn them against it, its temptations, rottenness, emptiness, and pitilessness. It all sounded true enough, and so there was all the more reason to keep very quiet.

And all this Ulrika eagerly discovered. There were signs and signals enough. The field lay open. First of all, to get the principal hindrances out of the way, an understanding with Uncle Clement was necessary. As a guest she was burdensome to the counsellor, even though she lived on money earned and saved in England, and occupied a small room in the mansard roof where the rats were riotous and the winds blew through the cracks of the windows. He had already gotten her letters of recommendation in Paris and she was to start at the earliest possible date and go as far as possible. And she had to coax and think up things to placate him to keep him from urging her, while she was giving her plan a serviceable form. But this hardly answers the question; what was her plan? What was enticing her? What drove her to gather up her strength and work toward one end? Did she want to find shelter in the peaceful little bourgeois nest and share a meagre living with those who were captives? Her hunger was not great enough, her ambition not small enough for that. Was she chasing an emotion, a whim, a sympathetic impulse, or was she just curious? It would never have occurred to her even in a dream to sacrifice either her plans or her time for sentimental reasons, for she certainly did not think little of herself.

Had her incomparable instinct discovered in this tiny world the possibilities of success and expansion which had escaped less penetrating eyes, such as you, my reader, and I, the teller of tales, have? Doubtless this was so, for upon one thing we can count. Ulrika Woytich was always to be found where great things were going forward.

CHAPTER III

TINDER IN THE DRY WOOD

ULRIKA thought it would be unwise in the beginning to visit her friends too frequently. She waited to be invited, postponed the visit, said that she did not want to be too intrusive, was amazed that Christine seemed put out, failed to come on the day she promised, waited to be invited again, insisted Josephine was not well enough to see visitors and that Esther and Aimée avoided her, had to be reassured and was finally persuaded. It was excellently planned. Not for a moment was she the wooer. She was run after; and as she showed such shyness and reserve, her value naturally increased.

To take care of Josephine she recognised as the most important thing to do. She must above all things win over this favourite child of Christine's. But with this girl, she took pains not to go too fast; she waited a long time before she assumed a more confidential tone, and she avoided punctiliously any feeling of a debt of gratitude from the sensitive child. The complete physical and mental exhaustion which Josephine suffered after the fire lasted longer than any one knew. She had grown shyer, more self-restrained, more inaccessible. She made an earnest effort to meet her rescuer cordially but she had no words at command, and she suffered to see her silence misinterpreted. Ulrika guessed her condition and tried to smooth it over. She had a way of allowing the person to whom she talked the final word or retort, or she attributed it to him, so that he might feel that he was carrying off the best part of the conversation—a very delicate way of flattering. She brought Josephine flowers. She knew how to go to the kitchen, and in five minutes turn out exquisite dainties with no more than a spoonful of flour, the yolk of an egg, chicken livers and a few spices. Then she would serve the results with the cunning pride of an Italian chef. It was

25

irresistible. Such odours had never before floated through the Mylius apartment. Theresa shook her head, Lothar sniffed and drew in the delicious smell; and then all the draughts had to be opened to let out all traces of the culinary extravagance before Mylius came home.

She tried, too, to lure Josephine to take short, regular walks, though she only succeeded once or twice, for walks according to the Mylius outlook on life were a luxury, permissible only to the aristocracy and actors, and Josephine really desired to keep the law which the inner life of the family ordered. She preferred to renounce the pleasant diversion offered by Ulrika's gay chatter. Often she listened in astonishment; for through some casual, haphazard word she would gain an insight into life that was utterly strange to her and which excited her imagination.

"You are spoiling that child, Ulrika," Christine would say, but one could look at her and see she was pleased.

Ulrika always said such a creature could not be spoiled enough; that Josephine needed love, warmth, and care like a flower in winter. She wanted to take her for a few days to the mountains, if possible, saying it would be good for her health and her mental condition and not very expensive. Christine harboured the idea with doubtful pleasure, but could not bring herself to speak to Mylius about it. It was easy to see that so unusual a break from the usual course would excite his most violent anger. Ulrika could not help reproaching her for such cowardice and weakness, but Christine answered solemnly that that was her life; her task was to avoid friction, to suppress discontent, and to smother all little family conflagrations. "It is a hard task," she added, "and one that I feel in every nerve of my body."

"Certainly: the personification of caution and protection; but whether your rôle will prove a grateful one only the future can teach us," said Ulrika dryly.

"Children must believe in their father as subjects believe in their king, and the devout in God," said Christine, "for when faith begins to waver, everything falls."

"Let's hope not," replied Ulrika, pretending fright. "Don't

paint the devil on the wall at once. So our little trip to the mountains is to be given up."

"Alas, it cannot be," said Christine. "At any rate, not now. Moreover I've talked about it to Josephine and she absolutely refuses to hear of it. She knows what battles and difficulties it would entail, and it would be unbearable to the child to consider herself the source of them."

Esther accidently heard the end of this conversation which took place in Christine's room and listened dumbly with wide-open eyes. Ulrika turned to Josephine who was waiting to have her read aloud to her. Josephine was embroidering by her window and gave her a friendly smile as she came in. It was past twelve when she began, and with real power and understanding she read passages from "Amaranth," from Stifter's "The High Woods," and Hamerling's "King of Zion." Then she laid the books aside and recited from memory and in English long poems of Tennyson, and Byron's "Farewell of Childe Harold."

At the last stanzas there was the sound of applause, and she looked around surprised as though she had not seen who had entered. She had heard though: it was Mylius who now nodded his head thoughtfully, and with raised eyebrows said admiringly that such a talent was worthy of all praise; did she know any other language beside English?

"I have fluent French and Italian at your service, and some Polish and Spanish at need."

But when had she had time to acquire all that? She must have expended measureless industry. "Oh, no," she said: "in the six years since I left my parents' house, I have met so many people from so many lands, I learned languages like play. When one has to bargain for every shilling with deceitful agents, or proud ill-tempered ladies and viscountesses, the sounds flow quickly enough from the tongue and grammar and syntax come of themselves." Of course she had studied too, but Fate was the best teacher.

"What a pearl," said Mylius, simpering.

"A pearl, possibly," she replied, laughing, "but, unfortunately, with no setting and still not out of the shell."

"All the same, accept my compliments," said Mylius. "A young person like you, it seems to me, is called into the world to make a success."

Ulrika blushed charmingly, flattered by the recognition he gave, and accepted it as due tribute.

"Now, what do you say of your father?" She turned to Josephine as Mylius left the room. "He is not the barbarian people take him for but a real cavalier."

"Barbarian? I don't understand," replied Josephine, wrinkling up her forehead. "It is nothing new to me that he knows how to behave."

Ulrika bit her lips.

The next afternoon when she came, Christine had gone out with Josephine. Esther and Aimée sat at a table in the living room, absorbed in a worn-out novel from a circulating library. The one who was through a page first had to wait for the other. They answered Ulrika's cheery greeting sullenly without raising their eyes, and Lothar, who was marching up and down the room with ridiculously big steps, his hands behind his back, looked grimly out of the corner of his eyes at her. Ulrika drew off her gloves, measured all three of them with an astonished look from her slim height, and with raised eyebrows, asked: "Well, what is the matter?"

"Nothing special," said the boy in a teasing, mocking tone and planted himself in front of her. "We have just made up our minds that Josephine is *not* to have everything and we nothing. She is already mother's ewe-lamb and now you are planning an excursion for her. What for? What are you mixing yourself up in our family affairs for? We simply won't allow it. Do you understand?"

He got no further. He got a blow and a box on the ears that made him sit down. Ulrika said indifferently, "If the other cheek complains it can have one, too."

The bewilderment of the boy was measureless. He rubbed his smarting cheek with his fingers and stared, overcome and furious, at Ulrika. But under her cool, sneering smile he became more and more embarrassed. At last he dropped his eyes, put his hands in his pockets, and shrugged his shoulders.

Now Ulrika began her real work of art. Taking him by the arm she asked if it had really hurt? He nodded. "That was skill," she laughed. Blushing he tried to free himself from her, but she clung to him and teased him about his manly resolution which had in no wise imposed upon her because, she said, she was half a man herself and knew how to protect herself; and she told him in a most genial way one or two comic episodes of the kind in her varied, wandering life. And Lothar was tamed! He listened to her with pleased, admiring eyes. They were walking up and down the room together now, and Esther and Aimée, hardly believing their own eyes, forgot to go on reading and looked on dispiritedly, turning their heads automatically to follow the walkers. From their sinister surprise at the quick secession of their brother, Ulrika surmised that she had broken down the first bulwarks of the conspiracy.

As she had progressed so far, little effort was needed to bring Lothar over entirely to her side. From day to day, she found time and opportunity to busy herself with him. She drew him out about his tastes and inclinations, and upheld them without ever becoming too definite. Even her surprise helped to awaken a spirit of opposition in him. When his utterances became too bold she warned him, but in such a way as really to rouse his spirit. She let him see how easy it would be to break through the iron laws that bound him, and at the same time strengthened his fear of going beyond bounds, so that in any case she could justify herself. She lent him pocket money, and threw up her hands in amazement when he confided that he had only twenty kreuzer a week to spend. "You can't make much of a splurge with that," she said sympathetically; and then she told him anecdotes of young lords and counts who threw money about as ordinary people do plum stones. She knew how to express disapproval of such characteristics and at the same time to paint them in glowing colours, and to mix in with her blame a seductive sigh for the forbidden fruits; and she had the pleasure of seeing the boy's slumbering longing turn into conscious desires. Then she would beg him to avoid evil and be an obedient son and a decent human being. He always promised heartily.

He was now her debtor, although the sum was only about two or three gulden, and he became more and more dependent upon her; and as she made a deep impression upon him as a woman, his service was willing and enthusiastic. His whole frame of mind was bubbling and seething. Every look, every word of Ulrika's nourished his discontent. The fetters, which he had hardly felt before, because they were forged when he came into the world, began to chafe; the rules and circumscriptions of his days awakened an ugly impatience. He wanted to get away from himself, away over the years, away from prudence; his blood was heated and all kinds of formless resolves crowded in upon him.

To hide all this dangerous process from Christine's eyes was not always easy for Ulrika. But she had all the tactics of a gambler who can throw others off by constant motion and witty speech. She succeeded not only in deceiving Christine but in making her believe that Lothar had changed for the better under her sympathetic comradeship, that he was more open, free, and conscious of his goal. There seemed to be every reason to praise Ulrika's pedagogical science. Sometimes Christine had to smile when Lothar spoke of his new friend in such exaggerated terms; and Josephine would smile then too and rejoice with her mother. But Esther and Aimée were not subdued in the same degree by Ulrika's perfections. Ulrika had a good deal more trouble with them than with the others. She seemed to knock against an unconquerable distrust—a distrust inborn and general and not directed against herself in particular. It seemed a sort of laziness, a sort of mental dozing. All her attempts to rouse the two from their sullen quiet failed. Ulrika thought over many schemes and finally seized upon the nearest and was surprised at the result.

One day, shortly after dinner, she found both sisters sitting over a novel. They were allowed an hour daily to give themselves up to this passion for cheap reading, and promptly when the clock struck they were obliged to stop at the most exciting passages. Lothar, in the next room, was drumming on the piano, as he had a half holiday. When he heard Ulrika's voice he appeared at once. Ulrika asked where their mother was; Aimée gave no answer; after a while Esther decided to reply and said her mother had gone out with her father; they had both gone to interview a creditor who had presented the same bill twice and their father had been very angry about it.

Coming up behind the two sisters and leaning over between them, Ulrika seized their book. She clapped the book to and read the title: "Slave Life in Europe" by von Häcklander. Then she laughed, put an arm round each girl and whispered that she had thought of something splendid, but it was a secret and she would have to depend upon their silence. They looked at her questioningly and she whispered so low, that Lothar, who was leaning against the stove and was jealous, could not hear, that the next Tuesday she wanted to take them with her to the Academy ball. She had thought everything out, and if they were only clever and would do what she told them, she could manage it.

In an instant the two sisters were transformed. Their eyes shone; life and hope came into their faces. A mask ball! They had never seen such a thing; that it was possible to go to one they had never dared hope! They had always had to content themselves with adventures in books from the circulating library. And though they realised it would be only a foolish pageant, whose false colours would deceive them, their imaginations were hot at the thought. That night they lay sighing in bed, waiting even in sleep to see how their great dreams would be shattered by reality. But consideration and also skill are needed for the impossible. Even in such matters human nature reveals itself and finds a way out through the darkness. While Esther's desires were all directed toward extraordinary events, confused agonies, and the joys of great passions, in which she saw herself as a yielding and sacrificing beloved, or as a high queen untouched by the worshippers who came, Aimée's whole thought was turned upon pictures of extravagant splendour and exotic luxury, and her imagination was so obsessed by feasts, excursions, and great entertainments that she had only to close her eyes, to glow inwardly and be a part of them.

The first question, of course, was where were they to get

the money. "Let me manage," said the temptress soothingly. "I have weighed everything; we'll take your mother into the plot, and if worst comes to worst, we'll manage a loan." She assured them that this should not be their only chance; she knew a source of money, awaiting only her inviting hand to be made to flow. Esther's and Aimée's faces were flushed with excitement. But how could they hide the fact from their father that they were out at night? Nothing was easier. Ulrika would invite them to spend the evening with her. And finally, what were they to wear? Hired costumes? Heaven forbid! They could easily turn some of their old rags into costly costumes.

So the work began at once and the hunting up of things. Lothar watched slyly, and from bits of talk here and there he guessed what was happening. Nevertheless he enquired in order that he might be formally admitted to the secret by Ulrika. Ulrika ran her hand through the mass of his curls and told him that if he were very good and would look after the fires well, for a barbaric cold had invaded the Mylius apartment, he would be let into the secret. He flamed up under her touch, but her demand that the fires be kept up made him hesitate. His father had forbidden any heating in the afternoon, and he had to be careful as it occasionally occurred to the old man to examine the coal bin. Ulrika replied sulkily that it did not suit her to freeze and she would shoulder the responsibility; and if Herr Mylius complained she would present him with a hundredweight or two of coal. Such rebellious speeches brought confusion upon the young family, but after a little hesitation Lothar overcame his scruples and triumphantly obeyed. Ulrika took an arm of each sister and wandered through all the rooms, peering into cupboards, laughing and rejoicing whenever she found a bit of fine material or silk or a fragment of lace.

Now it was twilight, and Josephine came home from the handicraft school and immediately after came Christine. Every one was embarrassed but no one wanted to explain. Ulrika knelt down before Christine and begged for a blind consent to what they were doing and a general pardon for all possible misdeeds. Christine softened, but said she must have a full confession at the coffee hour.[1] But to celebrate the day, Ulrika wanted to make the coffee herself with a double ration of coffee beans. She even made the daring proposition that they should use the beautiful, old, Nymphenburg set and decorate the dining room, and she laughed joyously at their horror. Finally all opposition fell before her amused teasings and paradoxical arguments, and the quiet, amazed Josephine was sent to bring the best china and set the table, while the others, even Lothar, played about in the kitchen, chattering and joking as they made the coffee. Even the sullen Theresa woke up and took part, not always willingly, in the gaiety. Lothar said he could not remember ever having had so jolly a day.

"And yet think, we are ripe for prison!" said Ulrika, as she stood surrounded by steam, the fur cap she had put on her head for fun falling over to one side. "If there is a Judas among us, we are lost. And we'll deserve it too; for we are rioting, carousing, and despising our Lord's commandments. There is a fire in the stove, some real coffee in the pot, and real china on the table. Such conduct cries to Heaven. The day of judgment must be near."

It struck five, and with the last stroke, as if so ungodly a speech must be punished at once, the latch-key turned in the house-door. Horror and fright—Father! Lothar peeped out, and his dumb withdrawal was a confirmation. Theresa made the sign of the cross; Esther and Aimée hid behind the cupboard. Lothar looked for a means of flight. Christine's face was all distorted. To return at such an hour was a break in his customary ways. All his habits, his comings and his goings, were as steady as clock-work. It turned out later that he had been obliged to do some work in a suburb; and with his usual economy he had gone a long distance on foot and was tired. His return brought him near home and he wanted a half hour's rest.

They heard him grumbling. He had discovered the best china and the decorated table. It was Josephine who had

[1] Tea time in England is coffee time in Germany.

to meet him. He began to scream at her; his voice broke; anger made it as shrill as a parrot's. Josephine escaped and held out her hands pleadingly to her mother.

All eyes turned to Ulrika, the instigator of all the mischief. To their surprise they found her perfectly composed. "Sit down all of you, round me," she said; "let's pour out the coffee; we don't want to have made it for nothing. Take down those cups from the shelves; we don't need the fine china; the coffee will taste just as good in these, and it *is* fine. Sit down; there's room for everyone; even for you, Frau Christine; sit around the fire; it's warmer there. I want to tell you the very beginning of Ulrika Woytich's way through life. Let Herr Mylius stay in there and rage. He need not bother us and if he comes and finds us, he can sit down with us. We won't let ourselves be disturbed."

Her words were so firm and assured that suddenly no one felt afraid but only waited with a certain excitement to see what would happen. Christine obediently sat down on the bench by the fire. Josephine sat beside her. Esther and Aimée drew up two chairs and leaned their heads together. Lothar sat down on the coal-box and swung his legs comfortably. Theresa, overcome by astonishment, stood at the window. Ulrika, in the midst, crouched on the kitchen settle, an amused cynicism in her face, and brushed rebellious locks of hair from her face, all purple with the heat of the stove.

Each one had a cup of coffee, and as they swallowed they listened to the racket that sounded from the next room.

CHAPTER IV

AND ULRIKA TELLS

"I AM twenty-five years old," she began, "but I have lived as much as if I bore fifty years on my back. You can't see it, for I still have strong bones, and it's easier for me to throw my spine back than to bend it forward. If I could be paid for the number of times I have slept on a plank instead of in a proper bed, I'd have a pretty sum from it, but the year is long, and if there are some days when one sets one's teeth into one's fist to live through the worst, then there are others when the sun always shines, and one feels young and strong and one knows one has two arms to work with and two eyes to see. Your little nestlings here know nothing of that. Your roast is brought in to you, all prepared; your shoes come new from the shoemaker, whenever the old ones are worn; and when the wind blows outside, at best, you think: 'Well, it's hard for those who have no shelter.' "

At her first words she heard steps creeping up. But she pretended to be entirely unaware, though she knew the attention of her audience divided; and she listened uneasily to the noise outside, well aware of its source. Then Mylius stood in the frame of the door. Under his threatening brows his little eyes gleamed like two phosphorescent flames; the ugly hatred in his face made Ulrika stammer. He looked at the group with stupid rage, his lips quivering; and beside himself, he brought out: "In the devil's name what does this disorder mean? Disorder inside and disorder outside!"

Ulrika looked at him quietly and said: "I am talking. Perhaps what I am saying will interest you; if so, you can listen, Herr Mylius, but I can't be interrupted. I got here first; first come, first served. Once I have finished, you can show me the door on account of my wicked presumption; that's

35

your affair; but I promised my friends to tell the story of my life and I am going to keep my promise, and you'll have to wait. There's a seat by your wife on the bench; may I offer it to you?"

Mylius struggled in vain for an answer. The cold-blooded courage with which he had been corrected and put in his place robbed him of speech. And the gay smile, glowing look, lively domineering manner—they were like a blow on the head to him. It was all new to him, it overwhelmed him; he did not know how to behave or how to save his authority and dignity. His four children stared into their empty cups, the daughters cowered, but Lothar was alert; Christine was embarrassed, and the maid at the window grinned slyly. That grin made him wild with anger. He wanted to break out again and scream, but Ulrika, who held him with her eyes as a snake charmer does its prey, began again. He pursed his lips together and resolved to be silent and withdraw. But as the deep-toned voice began again, merry and fluent, he felt forced, despite himself, to stand still; and then her words, forming pictures and tales, quieted his wrath, although he still knit his brows angrily for a while. It seemed all right to him to lean there, if he wanted to, on the door frame and without any further participation, listen to what was going on.

As Ulrika continued, a satisfied smile came over his face.

"I grew up in surroundings where the very dogs turned slowly to wolves," the tale went on. "My father was an Austrian officer. With a small salary and without the protection that advances blockheads and parasites, he dragged a weary existence through a half-dozen Eastern barracks. He married late; there was no money. At forty-three he became a major with fifty men ahead of him, and there he stayed. Can you imagine what a position such a major is in, in a wilderness of Jews and officials, especially when he is not a noble and has no fortune, but a wife and a herd of children? Lamentable figure!

"The Woytichs come from Poland originally. The blood of musicians flows in their veins. My father's father was one of Paganini's favourite pupils. Paganini the magician, whose like the world has never seen (you know about him perhaps), taught him all his magic and art, and loved him to his dying day. My father often told about it in his sympathetic moods, and that too had a part to play in my life. My father was himself a violin-virtuoso, though of the untrained kind; and sometimes during manœuvres he would play for his comrades in some Gallician tavern until morning, and then in wine drown his melancholy over his wasted existence.

"My mother, who died shortly after my father, was a beautiful woman, much admired and sought after in her youth. She was a strong woman too, and came of a strong race— a proof of it is that six children and poverty combined never broke her spirit. She knew how to enjoy life and people gossiped about her. There was a good deal of scolding and quarrelling too, between her and my father, so family life was not particularly pleasant with us. But when I recall her I see a proud and stately woman, and her memory is the purest pleasure I have in all that lies behind me. Perhaps she knew what she was doing. At any rate those should judge her least who carry on their meannesses in secret. Those whom the Lord God cut after a grand pattern disdain the crowd of cripples who always mix up good and evil so that it sounds as if they were bawling the *Te Deum* and *Gaudeamus* in one breath.

"In my fifth year I spent a whole winter in Vienna with my mother and my older brother Franz, who is now in the Embassy in Madrid. My mother was ill and had to go to a nursing home, and we two children lived with my uncle Clement and his Smirczinska, who is still his housekeeper. One day, I think it was about Christmas time, he gave me a sparkling, new, gold ducat. It was a wonder much discussed at the time, for giving isn't at all in his line. However, I got the ducat and many serious warnings with it, and every Sunday before church I had to go to his room and show it to him. Then he would hold forth about the value of the ducat—all one could buy for it; how it would increase of itself if it were only wisely invested, and might even become the foundation of a future fortune. Of course I did not understand, but the coin became a kind of fetich to me. I wore it on my breast, sewed into a little canvas bag for years; I fastened all my hopes and dreams upon it, and no temptation would have led me to spend it; no deceiver could have lured it from me, nor any thief be cunning enough to steal it. Not that then, or later, I adored money, as some people do, who would rather have their hearts cut out than provide a joy for some poor wretch with what they have gathered together. Really with me it was only a matter of that particular ducat; it was an image of help and reliance. Money, money, yes, money—as much as one could earn so that one would not have to hunger and to suffer; to look on humiliated while others sat at the heaped-up table. I knew all about that early in life. For meagreness was the kitchen-master at our house; there was something needed in every niche and corner; nothing was in good condition; our linen was worn out, our clothes positively ragged; our silver pawned, and debts upon debts! My mother bothered little about it, and as the years went on she went her own way more and more stubbornly. The management of the house slipped from my father's hands; we no longer had any servants except a boy who helped to cook and clean. One brother died of scarlet fever and a little sister of consumption, and I nursed them though I was only ten years old. But year by year more burdens were thrown upon me. Whenever we moved from one garrison to another, our mother went on a trip long before. Our debtors dunned me; I had to beg for mercy of the butcher and the baker or for an extension of credit. I had to see to it that somehow my father got his dinner and that the younger children did not miss school. I often sat up all night darning stockings, mending underclothes, with an English or a French grammar on the table in front of me. I don't want to boast, but I did some solid work before my seventeenth year; that I can assert before God and to all men. What came afterwards is a chapter all by itself.

"At that time my two brothers were already in the cadets' school, and my sister Anastasia and I were the only ones at home when something important happened concerning my father's fiddle. The violin was an old one which he had inherited from his father, the pupil of Paganini; and we knew nothing more about it. Later it turned out that our grandfather had deposited a very important document about the violin somewhere, but as he died very suddenly of a stroke and never in his life had spoken of it (presumably because he did not want the people round him to know the worth of the instrument or let it become an object of greed and speculation), nobody knew anything about it, with whom or where he had deposited it, nor even really that it existed. He had expressly left this violin to his younger son, and no doubt or trouble arose over that. My father had a right to it anyhow because he always cared for it and because he played so well.

"When he played on it, even the most unmusical of listeners recognised its beautiful silver tone. I myself, though I only heard it played two or three times, remember I was quite carried away by it. Once when my father was playing to some comrades, a young Hungarian officer by the name of Ribeny stepped up to him and asked him to let him look at the violin, as, he said, he knew something of violins and it seemed to him an unusually beautiful and costly instrument. My father handed him the violin; he looked at it a long time, turned it over and over, tapped it and listened to the sound, and then drew my father aside and said he would like to buy the violin and offered him three thousand gulden. My father laughed, said he treasured the violin, and did not wish to sell. Ribeny then offered four, five, six thousand, and though my father hesitated and the temptation was great, he turned down the offer.

"One day, however, he received a letter from his brother Clement that greatly excited him. I must tell you, Uncle Clement was twenty years older than he, and to-day is a man of seventy-six; to my father he seemed a kind of higher being, not only on account of his past and his position in life, but because as a young man he had been accustomed to obey him and submit himself to him in every way. Clement's word was like the law of a higher court. What Clement did was the pattern never to be destroyed. Uncle Clement had inherited all grandfather's furniture, and amongst this was a very ancient walnut secretary, a really fine piece such as is sometimes handed down from generation to generation in families. In making some repairs that were necessary, a secret drawer was found and there lay the document which showed without any doubt that the violin was a real Guarneri and that Paganini had himself used it and given it to my grandfather as a token of his affection. So the violin had an almost inestimable value as you can imagine, and a long, exhausting fight about it began that in the end cost my father health and life.

"I can't remember all the details, and none but the chief matter. I only understood little by little. I remember that every week two or three letters came from Uncle Clement and each one made a change in my father. At first his brother wished, then ordered him to send him the violin to keep. He said it would be safer with him, and it was a matter of course that as the representative and oldest member of the family it was his right to have the care of so great a treasure, which had been allowed to remain all this time with my father merely because they had totally ignored its value. Now, however, it would be both frivolous and unfitting for him to subject the rare instrument to the accidents and upheavals of his restless life (to say nothing of the chances of robbery or fire), without weighing the possible results to himself and his children.

"My father refused firmly. It was hard for him to be firm with his brother, but for once the matter was greater than the person. My mother begged him to get the instrument out of the house; to give it to some friend to keep and put off Uncle Clement. She felt that my father would be deceived by his brother or in some way brought low, and she hoped to force a sale of it; for the violin was nothing to her, and the money for it would have been a great consideration in our circumstances. But my father would not listen. The more his possession of it was fought for and threatened, the dearer the violin became to him. Then there were long nights of violent discussion between him and my mother, and I must confess that she nagged him and left nothing undone to make his hard life harder. Moreover he had difficulties in the service; he was embittered by all sorts of reprimands and warnings, things that had never happened to him before, and he began to fear for his pension—a thought that drove him to despair. The suspicion that Uncle Clement was behind it all was not to be turned aside, for he had formerly had a certain influence in court and military circles; and while my father, in his kindheartedness, disliked admitting so ugly a suspicion, his brother declared quite cynically in one of his letters that he was the sole source of the trouble. Soon after that he appeared himself and chose a day when my mother was absent. She often went to Cracow or Pesth.

"I can remember this day in detail. I can see Uncle Clement standing before me, as if it were yesterday; the way he stepped through the door, in all his lean length, his head bent forward, a stick with an ivory crook handle in one hand, while he rubbed his chin with the other and laughed in a singular, toneless way. I can see him in his endless, long, shabby frockcoat, the same kind he wears to-day, and high-cut velvet waistcoat. Father was very pale as he greeted him; I think they had not seen each other for a quarter of a century, for my father never travelled, and it was pitiful to see how he stood there before him. I had to call out to him: 'Man, where's your backbone?' Then they disappeared into father's room, and what had to happen happened. My father had been able to withstand the pressure of letters, but he was weaponless face to face with his brother. He gave him the violin. He demanded a receipt for it and got it, but it mysteriously disappeared. Uncle Clement also gave him three thousand five hundred gulden as part payment; the worth of the instrument ran up to some ten times that much, as Ribeny naïvely confessed to us later and as indeed we learned from various quarters. The same night my father, who till then had never touched a card, lost the whole three thousand five hundred gambling with the self-same Ribeny, strangely enough. His downfall was swift after that, and in six months he died.

"My mother moved with us girls to Czernowitz, where my brothers lived; she bothered very little about the housekeeping and we sank now into undisguised poverty. I wanted to go out in the world; I had plans and desired above all that my brothers and sisters should not suffer actual misery. Moreover the affair with the violin gave me no peace. My mother and I often talked it over. Embittered and vindictive, and yet without any means or outlook for reparation or restitution, we did not even really know what had become of the violin or what arrangements my father had made with Uncle Clement, so to bring suit against him was impossible. I was determined to look up the Court-counsellor and warn him that his brother had left four children, totally unprovided for, and also to find out where the violin was and to make good our claim to it, even though it cost me several years of my life. So I went to Vienna.

"Uncle Clement was thoroughly taken aback when his Smirczinska announced me one November evening. He asked gruffly what I had come for and what I wanted. I told him that sheer desire to see him had brought me. He noticed the irony, and said his house had no room for run-away nieces in it, and I had better find shelter elsewhere and a means of livelihood. I realized that I must not let myself be frightened, for if I appeared as a downcast beggar from the provinces, kissing his hand when he stepped on me, which was what he expected, my plans would disappear at once in dust and ashes. I refused to be abashed, told him in what difficulties my mother was; that Anastasia would be a positive disgrace as the daughter and niece of a court official, if she went out as a scullery-maid or hairdresser, which she would have to do if he did not help us; that in the eyes of the whole world it was his duty to help my brothers, of whom the elder had no desire to turn to a military life, and they were both suffered as mere charity pupils in the Institute. I told him that I, myself, would gratefully forego all help and would push my way through the world somehow or other; but I had sought him out for the purpose of making clear to him just what his position was and to remind him there were other Woytichs in the world beside himself who had perhaps fallen into misfortune not altogether without his help, and that I should certainly not leave his threshold until I was assured that he would bestir himself for his brother's children.

"He was completely upset by it. He looked as if he would like to swallow me whole or tread me to death. He walked up and down with his pipe in the corner of his mouth, looking like a gorilla in a cage. He said he would make quick work of me and hand me over to the police. I laughed in his face and told him he seemed to forget we were no longer living in 1850. He was furious and screamed: 'You toad! get out of here.' And Smirczinska wrung her hands and began to cry. I laughed. When this had gone on a little while, he changed his tone. He said he would like to think it over, to sleep upon it, and Smirczinska took me and my things up to the room in the attic. The next morning he sent me an old-fashioned folded letter with a ten-gulden note in it, and in a most formal pulpit style ordered me to go home without further delay. I spread his note on a piece of buttered bread and presented it to the horrified and speechless Smirczinska. Uncle Clement raged below and I laughed above. That was the beginning. He gained some respect for me. Against his will and step by step he let himself be dragged into negotiations. They went on for weeks and months. He tried to trick me, turn me aside, hush me up, feed me with false hope. I never gave in. Finally he declared he was ready to send my brother Franz to the Gymnasium and open a way for him in the consular service. But he resolutely refused to let him study music, for which he had remarkable aptitude. He did not want any gipsies in the family, he said; Severin, the younger brother, was to remain in the cadet-school, but he should be properly fitted out and receive a monthly allowance. My mother was to have a small contribution so that she and Anastasia could live decently. But all this was gotten only by unwearying effort, daily, hour-long quarrels, with abuse, raging, bargaining, and curses on his side and cold-blooded patience on mine; with cunning, pleading, threats, and scolding while Smirczinska, listening at doors and spying, almost passed away in her anxiety lest I should replace her in the favour of her master.

"It would have been hard to bring him as far as I did if he had not suspected that I had something else in mind than what I openly asked for. It was apparent now how cleverly

I acted in not uttering a syllable about the violin, although there were temptations enough to do so. He seemed to be waiting for it. He watched me. He felt an impending storm. How he rejoiced when he thought me unsuspecting; but when he thought he could no longer deceive me or keep me in uncertainty he would get wild again and threaten to throw me out into the streets. But I was earning a little money by giving lessons in drawing and languages, so I was quite unafraid of the worst and he knew it and it impressed him. Moreover I read and studied up in the attic like a student before final examinations. That increased his instinctive fear of me, for at bottom anything that touched upon books and culture was appalling to him.

"One day I was not a little surprised when he himself began to speak of the violin. He did so after unending circumlocutions and offensive allusions, to hide his real intention from me. He knew what I had come to him for, he said, but there was nothing in it and I might just as well get it out of my head, for he was not going to give up the violin; it was secure in his house, and he was never going to let it out of his hands. And as he said it, he stroked the cat that lay in his lap, laughed again in that odd, toneless way and nodded emphatically at me. He had it in his mind to keep it in his own possession for some time to come, he continued, at least for twenty-five years, for he was going to live to be ninety-five; he was assured of this by the condition of his body and the consistency of his blood, and no one could take it ill if he failed to give up such a jewel, but held it in reserve for his latter days. He had allowed the thing to be examined by experts, naturally, together with the historic document, and what they said had surpassed his highest expectations and the family might congratulate itself, though certainly not sooner than the year 1900. And he laughed again and squinted triumphantly at me.

"It all sounded like childish chatter to me and I thought he was just indulging in his usual sly trickery. But little by little I began to understand that he had some motive underlying it all; to let me know that he understood my secret scheme and that it would be useless to try to get ahead of him or bring him to a bargain. He wanted to relieve himself from the constant restraint and watchfulness and alarm me by the openness of his tactics. Also he wanted to get rid of me and he felt that nothing else was keeping me there. So he resolved, like many another diplomat when they have tried every other underhanded scheme, to turn to a deceptive candour.

"I asked myself what good the violin was to him? He seemed not to set any very great value upon money or display. He was no more miserly and covetous than most old men. He was not rich, perhaps not even well-to-do. His needs had been practically the same for the last fifty years, and he would probably be able to provide for them until his blessed end. Why had he taken so much pains to get hold of the violin and then contented himself with the mere possession of it? He had jumped upon it like a magpie on a bit of shining metal and then hidden it in his nest; for I did not doubt for a moment that he had it in the house right under his eyes. Why on earth did he not make some use of it, since he kept it from its rightful owners, at least to better their lot somewhat? I could find no answer to these questions. His was a disposition that I could not puzzle out, and I think it over in vain, even to-day. Some day I shall find out.

"Now a new war began; this time with cards on the table, so to speak. When he saw that his attempt to discourage me was futile, he became furious. He forbade me my place at the table. Nothing could have been more indifferent to me than that. I ate my bread and sausage in the attic. He sent me up exasperating notes, all written like a monk's illuminated manuscript. I never answered them and refused to open the door any more to Smirczinska. She spied on me, leagued herself with the master of the house, and brought him news of my every step and every conversation I had with outsiders. Then the old man began to be afraid I should do him some harm, and he sent for me. He cursed me and behaved like a devil; ground his teeth and screamed till the people in the street ran up. My self-possession and amused face stung him

more. He said he would not let me out of the room, locked
the door, and put the key in his pocket. When he seized me,
however, I made him sorry for it, and he never attempted it a
second time. I made him give up the key, too. The next day
no one would have recognised him; he was so friendly that I
was actually frightened. He said he had finally decided to
leave the violin to me in his will; he had formerly thought of
leaving it to the Imperial Treasury on condition that they
would give Smirczinska ten thousand gulden, but if I would
pledge myself to do the same the will could be drawn up at
once I replied that the woman would never get one red penny
out of me, and he said maliciously that he had suspected as
much and that therefore everything must remain as before.
It was like struggling with a werewolf, but I learned a good
deal about human nature, that I can assure you, for the man
was a combination of many men and a symbol and image of
many. And I had a good deal to do to build up a world
that was disintegrating, to overcome a powerful, sinister
something that ate into my very heart. I told him once that
since I had dealt with him I knew what Austria really was;
that now for the first time I understood the history of our
poor nation The glance he gave me I shall never forget. I
was almost sorry for what I had said. It was the first time
I really felt I had touched him.

"As in the Bible it says, 'I will not let thee go, except thou
bless me,' so I said to him, 'I will give you no peace till you
give me my rights.' I interrupted him day and night. I
threatened him with the law-courts. I sent him little notes
to terrify him. I persuaded people to come to him and ask if
he had any old violins to sell. I put newspaper clippings on
his table telling of murderous attempts on hard-hearted old
misers. I had some one tell him that I was trying to get an
audience with the Kaiser. This last worked like magic. He
came and begged for peace. We made a bargain. He saw
there was no other way of getting rid of me and I did not
want my life torn into tatters by him. He demanded that I
make myself a place in the world, either by marrying or some
other way—he did not care how—but somehow I was to

make a career; I had the stuff for it in me. And when I had managed this, definitely and without hindrances, he, on his side, after ten years, neither earlier nor later, would give me the violin as my own inalienable property, provided that I would then undertake his care and support. Moreover he was prepared to give me three hundred gulden to start out with. Well, I had confidence in my luck; three hundred gulden seemed a fortune to me. I consented and the conditions were all set down in writing, also that should he die before the ten years were up I should unconditionally inherit the violin. And then I left. I never saw him so joyous as when I said good-bye to him.

"Only six of the ten years have passed, but my circumstances have not as yet so changed that the compact could be carried out, and I don't see how they are going to change. I have not given up all hope, yet I see no prospect of making a career. However, Uncle Clement is alive and in good health and I believe he will last on into the next century, and that is two decades away. For three years I lived in the family of a Count Lippa in Bohemia, and they were hard years. Then I went west and did all sorts of things among all sorts of people, all kinds of fools and rascals and blockheads, and if I were given a choice I should always prefer rascals to blockheads. The latter go more slowly to destruction and moreover they bore one to death while they are going. But what I lived through in all those years I can't tell to-day. What is it they say in the 'Arabian Nights'? 'Scheherazade noticed the grey of dawn,' but night is coming on now, and that is just as much a signal to stop."

Ulrika arose laughing, and made a deep bow. Not one of her listeners asked a question or said a word, but by their eyes, which were fixed upon her in admiration and excitement, she knew she had won them, each in a different way, even Herr Helmut Otto Mylius, who was still leaning as at the beginning against the door frame.

CHAPTER V

ULRIKA ACTS FEARLESSLY WHILE ALL TREMBLE

ESTHER confessed to her mother their plan to go to the Academy ball. All the initial preparations had been made; they needed only Christine's consent and help.

She was frightened. Here was what she had always avoided, underhandedness and secrecy. But her protest was weak because she knew she had set a bad example with Josephine; moreover both girls had flung themselves so headlong into the scheme that they would not listen to protests. To get their father's consent would be out of the question, even Christine admitted this, so they were determined to undertake it behind his back, and stormily demanded that their mother help them to conceal their plan.

"It goes against me," said Christine in her shy way to Ulrika; "it is the first seed of discord and lying. I quite admit that the girls ought to have such little harmless pleasures; indeed that it is their right. They are no longer of an age to be kept like prisoners; I know it. But up till now I have managed to keep them reverent and obedient toward their father. That seemed to be my duty. It cost me a good deal, to be sure; I've often felt like a target being shot at from two sides. Still my conscience was clean."

It was hard for Ulrika to suppress her impatience. Such submission and self-restraint got on her nerves. "What for? and for whom?" she asked, shrugging her shoulders. She already dared a little contradiction and mockery over general matters. Christine listened to her opinion and was slowly accustoming herself to the idea that breaks might be made in the stony routine. She was astonished at the courage, the abrupt form of the opinions expressed. Without actually

noticing it, she was becoming slowly enmeshed and was drinking in the poison of rebellion as if it were medicine whose
powerful influence one only feels after a time.

But in this case she was defending holy ground, and Ulrika
recognised that she must be cautious. She chose therefore to
lay her trap in anything but a straightforward way. She let
Christine explain the methods of her up-bringing, and listened
with interest, and yet by cunning questions and with the skill
of an advocate, she made her waver. While seeming to agree,
she showed the emptiness of all these dogmas. She pulled the
characters of the children to pieces and showed how each one
was suffering under the lash of inner suppression. Her words
were so impressive that Christine turned pale.

Christine began to look at things differently. In order to
influence young people, perhaps it was necessary to give them,
if not freedom, at least some illusions of freedom. If one did
not, their hearts might harden and the gathered explosives
might burst all fetters, even those that were beneficial. Especially did Christine listen to her friend's judgment of Mylius
and admire the clarity of her vision:—he was a man of primitive endowment, who was hindered by work and civic ambition from recognising the little necessities of every day. He
shut himself up from them and his wrath was caused not so
much by their deception as by his discovery of the deception. Doubtless he hoped that they would deceive him a little,
for he was far too reasonable to believe that five grown people
should do nothing but dance to his piping, only he did not
want to be vexed by open contradiction. That offended his
egoism and disturbed his domestic comfort.

Christine had to laugh: "It is possible that you are right,"
she said. "But to think right is not always to do right; it is
not even always being in the right."

"Well, as one makes one's bed, one must lie," Ulrika answered. "You lie very uncomfortably, and why you should
point to your hard bed—according to the falsest of proverbs—
as a comfortable cushion, is beyond me. I am a simple creature and I don't understand the spiritual delicacies and distinc-
tions that would bring a nobly born person to bend under

palpable tyranny. Powerful natures are naturally superior to submissive ones, for they do what is useful themselves and what gives them pleasure, and bring their little sheep into shelter before one even knows whether it will rain or not, and the soft, patient ones are at least cared for. Well; it is well enough for those who like it."

Christine gave in. The room belonging to the two sisters became a sewing-room. Christine, Josephine, Aimée, Esther, and Ulrika ripped and sewed from morning till evening. Esther and Aimée could not sleep and their cheeks looked drawn and their eyes faded. So far they had not gotten the money that they needed to go to the ball, a matter of about thirty gulden. Christine energetically refused to borrow the money from an outsider; nor could she make up her mind to take it out of the household allowance; she would have to explain to Mylius when she showed him her accounts and he was to know nothing of it. She also hesitated to pawn anything, and it was difficult to know where to turn. While they were turning over this and that and telling each other their fears and anxieties, Ulrika kept perfectly still. Aimée fixed questioning eyes upon her as if begging her to speak, for Ulrika had promised they should have no trouble about the money.

Suddenly she began, as she smiled at them: "Do you know whom I am going to get money from?"

Nobody knew.

"And yet it is quite clear," said Ulrika in a nonchalant tone. "From Herr Mylius, of course."

There was general astonishment, even fright.

"What? From Father? Are you dreaming? Wake up, wake up, Ulrika!"

"I can't get it all at once, to-day or to-morrow," Ulrika went on indifferently, as she sewed; "I will not go to him and say: 'I need thirty gulden; the young ladies want to go to a ball.' That would be stupid. One has to take hold of these things differently. How I am going to do it I shall not tell at once. But I am never turned aside by a trifle; I shall get the whole amount; you may rest easy about that."

They listened breathless, wavering between doubt and hope. Ulrika looked critically at her work, crossed her left leg over the right, and began again with a sly smile: "The matter is very simple. Frau Christine has not the money; you girls haven't it; but Herr Papa will hand it out, only not immediately; and it's as necessary a climax as 'Amen' to the Lord's Prayer that Ulrika will have to be your prop in the meantime. No; don't interrupt me, Frau Christine, and don't say no, or I'll put down my needle and scissors and disappear, never to return. I'll use my little savings. There's nothing much in that. Are savings never to be used? Is that the law in the Mylius house? Are they to lie in the safe until one buys an old maid's wreath with them to hang over one's bed? What could I do better with them than lend them to my friends? I suppose that is just why they are not lost yet. I brought home twenty pounds from England and that is two hundred and forty gulden. What I spend for you will be reckoned in heller and pfennigs. Now I don't want to hear a word about it. Finale! It's horrid to talk about money."

Christine wanted to protest but was curtly broken off by Ulrika. "You are too high-strung. All the others agree with me, even Josephine. Don't you, Josephine?" She turned to her with a flattering gesture. "You think your mother is positively offending me when she turns a little friendly service into a debt of honour?"

"Forgive me, Ulrika; I did not mean that," Christine hastened to assure her.

Josephine was silent, and whether she was agreeing with Ulrika or her mother it was impossible to read in her face, which despite its dreamy charm still had something set and stubborn in it. In her eyes only one saw a gleam of eager penetration, as if she were trying to see through Ulrika's gay, alluring face; as if a hidden yet wakeful spirit in her was saying: "Who are you? What is it you are doing?"

She could not get away from the impression that Ulrika's recital of her childhood and youth had made upon her. Never before had she felt so powerfully what Fate was. It seemed as if a flame broke out in her heart and she would like to have

knelt before Ulrika, because it seemed so true to her, so cruel
and inexorable. She went to her room and prayed in her own
way; prayers?—rather formless demands and questionings,
torn from her inner distress. She placed herself opposite God
as if for a battle, and on her lips the very word "God" was a
word of wonder, a word to make one shudder. "God, you
created her and you created me," so she accosted the Almighty,
"why give me the light burden and her the heavy one? If you
dwell in her as in me, why surround her with such darkness?
Why am I myself and not another? Why should that be like
a brazen barrier—the being Josephine and the being Ulrika?"

In her naïve sorrow she gripped the very root of things.
It was not only the inner storm or the continued feeling of
thankfulness that bound her to Ulrika; it was an ever-fresh
doubt that she was fighting, that forced her to think of her.

She saw that things were changing in the house, that her
mother and sisters used other words, looked differently, that
the whole colour of their daily life was changing—at first
hardly noticeably, and yet day by day more definitely; and
she knew Ulrika to be the cause of it all. It did not seem to
be a wicked power, not something to be criticised, but it was
a dark, strange power, as if one turned from one's habitual
motions to entirely different ones and strained all one's limbs
painfully. Lights and shadows were no longer divided as of
old; solitude was not the same; talking to her mother was not
the same; work and sleep were not the same; and she had
hardly a thought left that did not turn, restless and teasing,
back to Ulrika.

Yet none of those about Josephine guessed her suffering, not
even her mother.

On the third day the silken dominos were all ready for
Esther and Aimée; one was wine red, the other the yellow of
a tea-rose. For each of them, a dress of Christine's that had
long hung in the closet unused, had been cut down. All the
accessories had been gathered together from old belongings
and skilfully and tastefully adapted. Ulrika had found an old
velvet dress among her belongings and remodelled it as well as
she could. By Monday noon she had it in shape and carried

it home with her. Then she came back to help the sisters, and by Tuesday noon the last stitch was taken.

This was the arrangement: at dinner Esther and Aimée were to tell their father that they were invited to Ulrika's to spend the evening; no matter what he thought, he could hardly question the harmlessness of that. In the afternoon they were to attend to their last small purchases, for they had to get suitable stockings and a few trifles for which Ulrika had already given them the money. After supper they were to go to their room and dress naturally, taking every precaution (perhaps Josephine would watch); then they were to get in a cab and go to number 10 Dorothea Street, where Ulrika would be awaiting them punctually at nine o'clock.

Everything went off as smoothly as possible despite the feverish excitement of the girls. Permission for the evening visit was given, though with some snarling and muttering. Mylius lay down for a nap; Esther and Aimée went out, and Josephine went with her mother to the dentist's.

Unfortunately, believing their mother at home and on the watch for them, the sisters left their dominos spread out on the bed in their room; and Mylius, when he woke from his after-dinner nap and found no one at home, fell into a bad humour, as he objected to their going out. Whether it was to spy about or just to give himself a little exercise, he went through all the rooms, and when he reached Esther's and Aimée's at once saw the two costumes. He saw that they were new and evidently for some suspicious object. For a while he stood and stared; suddenly he was enlightened: the proposed visit to the Woytichs' did not seem to him quite in order anyhow. So something was on foot; such things were happening and behind his back. It all pointed to luxury, pleasure-seeking, extravagance. He gave a low whistle, seized both dresses, folded them together, fetched a large piece of brown paper and made a neat package, which he took under his arm to his shop to lock up. And as he went down the stairs he grinned grimly.

When Esther and Aimée reached home about five and found their dominos gone, they suspected nothing. They thought their mother had put them carefully away. Still they waited her return somewhat discouraged, and it was half-past six before she and Josephine came in at last. To their horror Christine declared she had not taken the costumes—had not even touched them. Theresa was called in and questioned. She knew nothing. Aimée screamed: "Father! it can only have been he!" The whole house was searched, drawers thrown open, wardrobes emptied; under the beds they searched, in the kitchen, entrance hall, storeroom, maid's room; everywhere and in vain. Esther wandered pale and listless from room to room; Aimée threw herself on the sofa and broke into noisy weeping; and Josephine and Christine were busy trying to soothe her. When Lothar came home he suggested that Josephine should go to her father's shop and ask him outright. He could only send her away. He offered, with some embarrassment and haste that pointed to more than brotherly sympathy, to go himself to Dorothea Street and fetch Ulrika. Josephine was willing, though she hardly liked her errand. Her attitude toward her father was both restrained and shy. He was a stranger to her, though she met him with tender reverence and consideration. Although she always avoided rousing his wrath, every approach cost her real courage.

When she reached Himmelpfort Street, it was past seven o'clock and the building already closed. People knew that Mylius was in the habit of going between seven and eight to a coffee-house in Little Baker Street. There he had one cup of black coffee and read the German papers. Josephine did not want to turn back without attending to the matter; she went through Little Baker Street, stood a while at the entrance of the coffee house, and walked up and down waiting. Still she felt very uncomfortable when men turned back and stared at her. She went up to a window, where the curtain was not quite drawn and peered in. How taken aback she was when she saw her father sitting at a small table with Ulrika. They were sitting opposite each other and Ulrika was talking, with her free gestures, unperturbed manner, shining eyes and her usual gay, almost mocking smile. Her father was leaning back in his chair, listening, with a certain politeness, a certain kindliness that Josephine was unaccustomed to see in his face and which gave it a new expression.

She turned homeward, hardly understanding her own bewilderment. She could not quite make out what it was that was so unusual, so disturbing in what she had seen. Nor could she understand why she had not gone right in and declared her errand. To justify herself, she said that probably everything was all right now, and as her father and Ulrika were there together in friendliest converse, probably her sisters had nothing to fear. Then it occurred to her how small the whole matter was, and this increased her depression.

Strangely enough, when Josephine got home she found it impossible to tell what she had seen. She was angry with herself and yet her lips seemed sealed, as if a warning command bade her be silent. So she only told them the shop was closed, and that did not decrease the anger and disappointment of the sisters.

Josephine was always reserved in the family circle. She had learned by experience that one does not serve people by telling them everything, and that in general it is better to wait and watch than mix oneself up in their affairs. But in this case there was something definite in Ulrika's bearing that frightened her. She was literally afraid to betray her or to speak of her at all.

Just a few minutes after Josephine, Lothar came in with the news that Ulrika was not at home. A yellow old person spoke angrily to him and then shut the door in his face. He was angry and declared he was going right back again to wait for Ulrika in front of the house. He uttered his words breathlessly and was evidently in despair at not finding Ulrika. Christine noticed his restlessness and nervous look, but before she could ask him anything he had gone.

He had a dreadful confession to make to his friend. In his newly awakened desire for life, brought about deliberately and intentionally by Ulrika, hemmed in by lack of money, he had resorted to criminal means, and in an unwatched moment had taken a silver snuff box with an emerald on its cover from his father's shop. In his terror lest he be discovered

if he sold the thing to any dealer in the town, he had taken
the snuff box to his friend Robert Elmenreich, who gave him
all his savings for it—forty-eight gulden. Now as Robert was
himself in difficulties he demanded the return of his money with
most unpleasant insistence. Lothar did not know where to
turn to get it. The other threatened to pawn the box. Lothar
represented the danger of such a step and that he might be
arrested as an accomplice; then Robert, trembling for his little
fortune, declared openly that he was going to carry the snuff
box back to Herr Mylius and demand the return of his money.
Lothar knew his comrade well enough to feel sure he would
do as he said. He asked for twenty-four hours' grace and
Robert assured him of that much in the afternoon. Now
Ulrika was his last hope.

Impatiently he walked up and down Dorothea Street. Just
as he was about to ask for her at the house again, she came
walking rapidly toward him and stood staring at him in surprise. First he told her what had happened at home. She
shook her head, looked at her watch, and said she would go
right along home with him. But he held back. He begged her
to listen to him for a minute and slip with him into the shelter
of the door. She listened, foresaw disaster, drew him into
the house, and he confessed.

Ulrika was silent for a while. It was a good thing to let
the evil-doer writhe a bit. So it had come to this; perhaps
she wanted it to come to this. She did not keep any very
strict accounting with herself. It was an evil deed that lay
in the circle of combinations whose strings she pulled and
played with.

She asked him what he had done with the money he had.
Stammeringly he accounted for it; so and so much he had
spent at the confectioner's, and so much at the coffee houses,
and some for a forbidden book, and some for gloves and
cravats that he did not even dare show at home.

"And what else, you child?" said Ulrika; "think now."
Her searching look enchained him. Blushing and paling by
turns, he confessed that he had spent the night with a girl,

an usher at the Earl's Theatre to whom one of his school friends had taken him.

Ulrika laughed scornfully and her face darkened. "Are you angry?" asked Lothar with trembling lips.

Ulrika answered: "It is not very nice or very decent, for a fine youth like you to go to women who are paid for love. Fie!" With folded hands he begged her to forgive him, to stand by him in his need, for she was the only person in the world he had any faith in. If she were to turn him down, he would give up and shoot himself. Ulrika laughed at him. He was so handsome in his despair, so fawning as a broken sinner, that she comforted and consoled him as they walked along and promised to see what she could do, but now she had to go to Aimée and Esther and help them in their trouble.

As she walked along swiftly by his side through the snowy streets, she thought over her conference with Mylius from whom she had just come. She had spied out his evening shelter. She wanted to sit face to face with him, watch him, and lay her plans for the future, an undertaking that did not awake the shadow of a doubt in him. So she appeared at his table,—just a casual guest—was so surprised to see him there, sat down with him and used all her gift of speech to fascinate him and make him betray himself by word or glance. In vain. She might just as well have tried to move a hundredweight of heavy rock from its place. He had his usual sour smirk, nodded to her from time to time, pleasantly, sympathetically, or amusedly; showed indeed that her society was not altogether unpleasant to him, but she got nothing else for her pains.

Still she was content. She couldn't say why. But she had a tiny, sly, perfidious presentiment that seemed to warrant that the rock would not always stay lazily resting in the same place.

It was this that turned the scale for Lothar. After she had carefully weighed everything and just as they reached the Mylius house and were going up the steps she turned to the anxious, waiting boy and told him she would advance the forty-eight gulden, and he could get the money from her the

next day at noon, when he must bring her the snuff box which
she guessed was worth far more than the loan. "Really and
truly?" he cried relieved and raised his beaming eyes to hers.
She warned him with her glance to be cautious and in a
dictatorial tone she hoped that her kindness this time would
keep him from further foolishness. He promised eagerly.

At eight o'clock, punctual as ever, Mylius came home to
supper. Esther and Aimée rose; each stood behind her chair.
They looked at him; they were timid, pale, and silent. They
did not dare ask the question that had in it all the fulness of
life for them, all the brilliancy and wonder of a night of fes-
tivity. Esther's pleading eyes were turned to her mother.
Christine went up to her husband and whispered half-heartedly,
half-soothingly: "So you took the children's ball dresses?"

Mylius, pretending to be greatly surprised, answered with
lifted eyebrows: "Ball dresses? Have the young ladies ball
dresses? Well! well! tut! tut! Another little conflagration
on hand perhaps? Is the ball to be given in my house? I
had no notion of it. It surprises me greatly. True, I saw some
silly looking rags lying round and took them to my office.
Quite right. But nothing has happened to them; I took good
care of them, and when the ball takes place, it may be you
can have them again. Now I want to eat my supper in peace
and not be disturbed by your nonsense."

They knew, they had lived through it often enough, that
no appeal was possible when he spoke in this tone. The worst
results, cross questioning and punishment, the withdrawal of
pocket money, eating in the kitchen for a day or so, all this
would come afterwards. Esther and Aimée rushed from the
room, their hands covering their faces; Christine sat uncertain
and grieved in her seat; Josephine with her great eyes full of
questions, sat silently watching beside her. Occasionally a
stealthy glance fell on her father, and turned aside frightened.
She was waiting for him to speak of Ulrika in whose company
he had been only a quarter of an hour ago. Why should he
hide it from her mother? But he was silent. The usual quiet
comfort that he gave to meal times seemed to her hardly to be
borne. A hardly noticeable smirk played round his smooth-

shaven lips, but he was silent. Her sense of justice was disturbed. She wondered since he was so friendly with Ulrika—and she had seen it—why he treated her sisters so, since they were all playing the same game. Why did he not tell Ulrika that he had ruined their plan? This was not worthy of him. And why had not Ulrika who was so courageous and candid confessed the whole thing to him, so as to save her mother from humiliation. Why were things so hideous and confused when they might be easy and joyous, if people would only think a little about what they were doing.

Josephine lived and breathed in a clear, inner world, where there was no evil and no falsity and whose threshold had never yet been trodden by the realities of life.

The bell rang. Excited whispering was heard outside and then Ulrika came in with Lothar. After a slight greeting, Ulrika sat down at the table opposite Mylius. She crossed her arms and said, laughing: "You will give back the costumes; won't you?"

Mylius shook his head and answered: "I can't think of it."

Perhaps it was because at such moments his provincial accent, his broad Hessian speech was most noticeable, that Ulrika's sense of fun was awakened. She laughed heartily and said: "But I know you will."

"I am curious to see how you will manage it!" answered Mylius without raising his eyes from his plate.

Ulrika bent forward. "It is very simple, I hope; since I am dealing with an honest man. The costumes belong to me. I paid for the material and I paid for the opportunity to use them."

Mylius was silent, hardened.

"Do you understand me, Herr Mylius? I paid for them." Ulrika went on threateningly. "Paid; that word means something to you, doesn't it? Paid." She knocked with the nail of her thumb on the table and showed her perfect white teeth. A little intimidated Mylius answered: "Very sorry. Impossible to hand you the dresses. They are in my shop. I'll have to ask you to be patient until to-morrow."

Ulrika stood up. "That is going a little too far," she said.

"Impossible? That would be an edifying idea of justice! But I tell you I must have the costumes and at once. I need them and I need them this evening. I must put you to the inconvenience of getting them. I am sorry to trouble you, but a good deal depends on it; light, music, friendliness, joy; all things that perhaps you despise, but that are important to me. Perhaps they are worth only one indrawn breath of beauty, one happy thought, but at any rate they are mine and I never let myself be robbed of what belongs to me. What is mine I insist upon having."

Mylius did not reply. But as Ulrika stood there before him, her head thrown back, her black fur student's cap on one side of her head, her hair all blown by the storm and her quick walk, her cheeks flaming, her eyes gleaming, her full mouth half open, he felt himself forced against his will; more really by her mocking intensity than by her force and resolution. He rose, murmured something unintelligible, walked over to the window, rattled the keys in his pocket, laughed in a scornful, half-embarrassed way through the snow-covered panes and then in a gruff tone, said: "Well, if you insist, it must be so."

And he went.

Barely had the hall door closed upon him when Ulrika turned to Lothar and bade him call his sisters. But Esther and Aimée were coming already.

"Gather up everything you need and go to Dorothea Street," she hastily commanded them. "Wait on the steps till I get there; or no,—go right up into my attic. Here's my key. I will wait down at the door for your father that there may be no further hesitating and questioning, take the costumes from him and follow you as quickly as I can." The girls waved joyously to their mother as Ulrika shoved them out of the door.

Then she turned round to the table, cut a big slice of bread off the loaf and began to eat it. Christine, who had not let one word pass her lips since Ulrika had come in, gazed at her in shy astonishment and said: "You're a strange creature, Ulrika."

Ulrika replied as she ate: "Why? I don't know really what kind of a person I am. I never think of it. I only know I cry when I'm pinched and scratch when I'm pulled. The important thing in life is to make the people who think the whole thing, is theirs realise that one is here too. So long as I have lungs to breathe and a tongue to speak with, I'll let no one get the better of me."

Christine wanted to have the meat and vegetables warmed up for her but she refused, saying she had no time for it. She held out her hand to Christine, gave a friendly nod to Josephine, clapped Lothar on the shoulder and was gone.

When Christine and Josephine were left sitting alone in the room, for despite the cold, Lothar had gone to the piano in the drawing room and was drumming out a street song, Josephine went up to her mother and, leaning over her, said softly: "I am afraid, Mother, I am afraid."

Christine, who did not understand, looked at her, troubled, and patted her hair.

CHAPTER VI

MONOLOGUE AND DOMESTIC STORM

ULRIKA had not waited five minutes at the house door when Mylius with his ambling step came pushing through the snow. He carried the package of clothes under his arm. Seeing her, he started back, controlled himself quickly, beat the snow from the package, and said sulkily: "Ugh, cold weather to send an old man out in the night for such rags! At any rate you can't reproach me with lack of good will, my gracious lady."

"You brewed your own broth and now you must drink it," said Ulrika unconcerned. "Why didn't you put gloves on, anyhow? Have you none? Doesn't your business bring in enough? And what a thin, shabby coat you have on; haven't you a warmer one? Aren't your profits sufficient for a fur coat? Aren't you ashamed to let your own body shiver so? But if I have to pity you because your circumstances do not allow you any luxury, even that of sheltering yourself from the winter's cold, then I might ask why a man like you should grub all his life long? Why should he creep behind office walls, year in and year out, work harder than a coolie, if he can hardly make enough to get the suet for his roast? My pity doesn't belong to the old man, for you are not so far along in years or so fragile either, but rather to the man in general who has never managed to do anything well, who lacks talent perhaps, or luck. That's my honest opinion, Herr Mylius, and now good night; my feet are cold."

She wanted to go, but his look held her. He looked up at her for he was distinctly shorter than she, put his hands behind his back, his little lynxlike face drawn up into wrinkles, his glance keen, anxious, suspicious, uncertain. The questioning movement of Ulrika's head intimidated him, and he stammered out suddenly: "I have a couple of French business letters to write; might I ask your help? I should be very grateful."

Ulrika answered that she was entirely at his service and would come down to his shop the next evening. With a short greeting she turned away. The humiliated, depressed tone of the man remained in her ear and gave her something to think about.

Mylius went back into the house. Christine and Josephine had already withdrawn. Lothar was sitting in the kitchen where it was still moderately warm, working on a school exercise. In the big room Mylius walked up and down talking to himself: "What a person! Chases me out into the street! Speaks to me as if I were a bootblack! We are not accustomed to this, my lady. Collect yourself. Otherwise you may discover who H. O. Mylius is. Yes, you may. It is not impossible."

It was not unusual for him to talk aloud to himself, as he never would or could speak of his affairs to any one else. He distrusted every look turned toward him.

"Probably she thinks I am such a poor devil that I have only enough to eat for to-morrow," he went on, talking aloud to himself. "One of those hundred thousand little struggling rascals that swim along on the surface and tremble the first of every month with their knees knocking before the abyss which they have to hide from their families. It doesn't matter! Let her break her head over it. I have always managed best when I kept people guessing. That's the proof of the correctness of my principles, honoured lady. Silence! Hide behind the hill! Silence! Where men guess there is money, their imaginations break out like a conflagration. Every rascal has a claim when he thinks he sees money before his eyes. There isn't a fellow that doesn't feel his heart fail when one turns the key of one's cash box round in one's fingers. If I were to go to the market, as a man who had ample means behind him, deceit would tread upon my heels, and I should have to pay twice or three times the right value for everything. And if my own family were once to smell a rat, that would be the

end of all peace for me. One recognises this day by day; birds
of prey, all of them! Greed would eat them up and wishes
turn their heads. *Money, Money, Money,* their very eyes
would cry out! I should have to have a wild beast-tamer to
quiet them. I cannot even imagine how they would carry on
if they really knew, if they had even the faintest glimmer.
Yes, my dear young lady, I have to keep a sharp look-out."

For a time it seemed as if he were counting his steps up and
down and then he began to talk again. "Nevertheless there
ought to be one person, only one, well informed. Why should
one have gathered and saved otherwise? Why have denied
oneself all the enjoyment of life? Of course, enjoying life is
sheer nonsense. There is no enjoyment of life, which is not
in the nature of life itself, that one does not come at by forcing his own nature. Do you think I don't enjoy? Are the
fruits that I have picked imaginary? Isn't it all there, piled
up, palpable, valued, a witness to my caution and calculation
and all incontestably mine? Do I need anybody to confirm it,
to recognise it, to admire it, or to give me advice? Any one
to look on, to criticise, to denounce perhaps in the end? I
have been very comfortable with my secrets heretofore, why
should any one know now? He would have to be a damned
simpleton to keep it quiet. How would I meet his sophistries,
and erase the false pictures he would make at once? He
would see a capitalist in a tarn-cap; a tax-gatherer, a coupon-
cutter, watching over his treasure while his teeth chatter; one
whose whole goal in life is to deceive the State, his co-citizens,
his wife and children as to his real circumstances. It would
make life all too easy for you, young lady. For it is no literary miser you have here, no stage-struck actor with torn
slippers, no Uncle Clement with a spying Smirczinska hanging
round his neck. It is all very different; much more difficult,
complicated and inexpressible."

He nodded to himself, stared into the void, as if he were
following the thoughts that circled' before him like vultures.
"Nevertheless I must try her out first," he went on to himself;
"take the case of a sculptor who has made a beautiful statue;
a painter who has painted his masterpiece, thought and

drudged and worked, year by year, and yet no human eye
has ever seen his work;—is he a fool then, or a boaster, that
he would like to show it at last?   The question is whether
the one he has chosen is worthy of confidence; whether in the
end, horrible remorse may not follow.   It is a difficult question to answer; a dangerous thing to determine upon.   This
young person—let us look at her for a while.   Let us call her
before the judgment seat.   What kind of young person is she?
Why is it that from the very first moment she charmed me,
and that I chose her—her above all others—to open my
heart to?   A haphazard woman, probably an adventuress.
Family not so bad, and yet undoubtedly on the downward
grade.   Sly, too, devilish sly; a keen woman's mind; the
tough kind; determined to get there at any price; uncannily
resolute.   She knows what things are worth, and what people
are worth.   She calls things by their right names and looks
all danger fearlessly in the face.   It is a pleasant face; splendid
carriage; firm hand-shake; eyes such as the Lord God seldom
gives people, with which she can distinguish the useless from
the useful and worth-while in the world.   Good!   Now I have
it!   That is what it is that lures me!   I'd like to see those
eyes when they learn what H. O. Mylius's circumstances are.
It would be like lighting a torch in the night!   Then she
would stop looking down on me with those eyes.   'Why didn't
you put any gloves on?   Have you none?   Doesn't your business bring in enough?'   Pity!   It is enough to make a dog
laugh!   Only a word is needed and she would be silent, overwhelmed; she would tremble and drop that pretty head modestly enough.   An end to your irony and your sympathy!
Sympathy!—a dog laugh!   Then one would have her
down!   That would be a victory!   To live through that would
be worth the pains.   But not yet, not yet!   Caution, old
Mylius, caution!   Look to it first that you make no stupid,
false step!   Don't be led away!   Remain true to yourself!
Weigh every single word that you speak so that in the end
you can pretend it was a joke and take it back again.   Be
careful how you put yourself into the hands of a stranger."
    It was eleven o'clock, and after he had called Lothar in

his nagging voice to put out the lamp and go to bed, he turned himself to rest. But sleep fled from him. Those ironic pitying eyes held him and kept him awake for hours.

Meanwhile the source of all this unusual excitement had managed to carry out all her plans, and fulfill the wild expectations of her young charges; she found out what excitable blood flows in the veins of such sheltered creatures and what wild desires are nourished in dreams.

They were both hardly to be held in; they threw themselves thoughtlessly into that element whose breadth and depth seemed to them as great as their hunger. They talked wildly; they flew around intoxicated with excitement; they seized every hand that offered and were sorry to let it go when another was stretched out. Their glances wandered about with dazzling unrest; everything was so amazingly new, so full of promise of a happier life, excitement, danger and drama. Nevertheless they were a little frightened, especially Aimée, whose hidden longings were somewhat hemmed in by pride and reserve. But her eyes behind her mask glowed all the more longingly. Esther expressed herself quite openly: "The thought that one is only a guest in this world for a few poor hours is enough to drive one crazy. What sort of existence does one lead from day to day! Help me up out of the ditch, Ulrika, and I will be grateful to my life's end."

"What we haven't yet, we may still get," said Ulrika quietly and made her own silent comment upon this noticeable outbreak of temperament. To herself she thought cynically: "I could tie the two of them to the devil and they would think his tail was a rainbow."

As for herself she was bored. The tame merriment around her left her cold; such froth didn't deceive her; she saw only the empty dregs, the aimlessness and stupidity of it all; and the excited eagerness of her two companions, their youthful fever excited her secret scorn. But she remembered she was not there only to keep a pledge, she was there to teach. Once the earth is turned over, it must be enriched.

Something must grow and she had to look out for the future harvest.

Stormed at on the left and the right by both of them, with questions about people and what sort of relations existed between people, she held back none of her knowledge; and when she came to the end of her knowledge she invented bravely. She didn't have to be afraid that she would overstate matters; with what she knew of human society that would have been rather difficult. Women who were to be bought, men who were adventurers, gamblers, tempters, bankrupts, match-making matrons, bald-headed roués, decorated office-seekers, notorious spendthrifts in shining uniform, feminine aristocrats of questionable character, men and women of distinguished names who fetched and carried and of whom fame spoke little good—all received their stamp and passed in front of the astounded eyes of these novices—the intriguing comedy which is called the great world. In a short time she had unrolled before her two breathless hearers so monstrous a canvas of confusion, crime, baseness, lies, cruelty, private and public sins, that a clever writer of back-stair romances might have filled a dozen volumes from it, without appealing to his imagination at all; and as far as Esther and Aimée were concerned they felt the same voluptuous tickling which it is the ambition of just such an author to incite.

Ulrika was no moralist, and was not easily frightened off; she knew how, and she intended to make vice attractive and to paint ruin in its gayest colours. Everything that fluttered and waved, loved and hated, laughed and joked there was far distant from the worthy rule of average life; everything that happened, on and off the stage, ridiculed the bourgeois conception of moderation and correct conduct. Exemption from punishment was assured; yes, one even covered oneself with glory and enjoyed the admiration of the public when one pushed ahead of another in crime. Ulrika pointed this out to them and her pupils listened credulous and devout.

At first she left them to enjoy themselves in their

own way and during this time she crouched in a corner
of her box and slept. When she awoke it was already late
and she turned with motherly concern to look for them. She
found her young friends in a noisy crowd of young men, suspiciously gay, not altogether master of themselves—
warned them that it was time to break up, accompanied the
two happy creatures home, and accepted their overflowing
thanks with mild sarcasm.

The next morning Lothar came to fetch the promised forty-
eight gulden and an hour later he brought the snuff-box.
He crushed her hand in his thankfulness; in thankfulness
but something else, too. Then she caught a glimpse of a
personality, not unlike her own; a will that was akin to hers.
She had set a wheel turning, and it went quickly and surely
on its appointed way. She tripped up her thoughts as they
circled stealthily around the charming youth, but she shook
them off and the daily course made its usual claims.

She counted out her cash and saw that she would not be
able to keep up with the various demands of the Mylius
children much longer and that it would be necessary to tap
some source or else march straight to her goal. Events showed
her the way.

When she arrived late the next afternoon at the Mylius
house she found everything upset. Christine told her what
had happened.

The old Fräulein von Elmenreich had gone in a state of
great excitement to Mylius in his shop and told him that Lothar owed her nephew forty-eight gulden and fifty kreuzer and
all attempts to recover it had been in vain thus far. She had
noticed for some time Robert's depressed spirits and to-day
she had called him in and insisted upon a confession. She
was not rich enough to bear such a loss and therefore turned
to the father. Mylius, in uncontrolled horror, stared at her,
incapable of a word. (The fool, when it became clear to
her what she had done, rushed to Christine to inform her.)
Suddenly he had begun to scream; he would have nothing to
do with the matter; he denied his responsibility; at any rate
he must make a thorough investigation of the circumstances,

and she might come and see him some other day. Hardly had she gotten home, however, when Robert announced that in the meantime Lothar had brought him the money. Mylius however had reached home in an uncontrollable fury, had thrown himself upon Lothar, his stick in his hand, dragged him into his bedroom screaming, and demanding that he speak; awaited no answers, but beat the boy so fearfully that the stick broke in his hand and the boy lay apparently lifeless on the floor. The door was bolted; Christine, Esther, and Aimée shook the door and called, wept, begged; in vain; only when his fury was exhausted he reappeared with blood-shot eyes and dripping hair. The three women carried Lothar to his room, laid him on his bed, and bathed his face and head with cold water. Then Christine went to her husband who sat alone at the table, his features still distorted, swallowing the soup which Theresa had brought in to him; then, trembling from head to foot, but with quiet resolution she told him that such treatment of a child exceeded his rights—to say nothing of ordinary human feeling—and that she was determined never to bear such a thing again. Heretofore she had always recognised his authority over the children, whether she agreed with him or not, even when he had been too severe in his judgments and his principles had seemed too inexorable. But he had reached the limit; their ways were parted, and their partnership dissolved.

In all the twenty-three years of their marriage she had never before spoken in so determined a manner, and Mylius looked up at her astonished. He wrinkled his brows, looked about for a moment as if he were hunting for something and muttered through his teeth: "If that damned, mischief-making woman isn't behind all this then I'm a dolt. Talk no more nonsense, Frau Mylius. Rather take care that your son does not turn out a good-for-nothing."

Christine knew that Ulrika had been his helper in time of need, and her expression of thanks had not been free from shame. She knew also about the theft of the snuff-box. For beside himself with anger and pain over the cruel punishment, Lothar had told her; and told her to tell his father too; he was not afraid; any one who could beat him that way might as well kill him; the difference wasn't great. Ruminating sadly, Christine said: "He is a different being. He never would have dared before to speak that way to me. And the awful thing is that in my inmost heart I can't be as angry over the crime as I ought to be. For it is a crime. In such matters it is only the first step and then there is no holding back. I am half afraid that I am taking the crooked road myself. I don't know any longer when I am doing right."

"Don't be afraid for the boy," Ulrika consoled her somewhat coldly; "he is a good sort and easily led. I have often heard it said that the most honourable citizens pulled at the leash a bit in youth. Those are only moral slips. Just be glad that the treacherous rascal didn't tell about the snuff-box. Just imagine what would happen if Herr Mylius knew that. One shudders at the very thought."

"Certainly that is luck," replied Christine; "but now what shall we do with the fatal snuff-box?"

"For the present I'll keep it for security," said Ulrika laughing; "some opportunity will offer to slip it back to him without his noticing it. It does happen sometimes that the cave men sleep in their caves."

Christine stood at the window with Ulrika and with her face half turned away, said sadly, "How poorly you think of me! I ought to defend him. For twenty years I have defended him to myself and kept him on a pedestal. Now if I let you judge harshly of him it is just my momentary weakness and nothing else."

Ulrika suppressed a contented smile. "I don't think ill of him at all," she replied; "on the contrary I think very highly of him. I think him a powerful giant. He is so strong that he not only puts you and your four children but a couple of hundred other dwarfs into a bag and does not even quiver at your crying. It is not your weakness that prevents your breaking a lance for him, oh, no; it is a feeling of human dignity which I believe is awakening in you not altogether without my help. What is this all about then, really? Let's call things by their right names; what's all this trouble and worry for? For two gulden, for three gulden, for five gulden, for thirty gulden. Good heavens, you are not the woman to do that; you only do it because you once swore to; but your real inner consciousness has nothing to do with it."

Christine said: "That may be true or may be false; I will not look to see, I dare not look. Yes, I promised once. And what one has promised one must stand by once and for all."

Josephine heard these last words as she came in. She stood quietly in the doorway and the look that she turned upon her mother was so tender, so full of uplifting love, that Ulrika was dazzled by it, and involuntarily turned her eyes away.

She went into Lothar's room. He lay on his bed undressed and had not moved for hours. The white cloth around his forehead lent a new charm to his pale face and despite his condition he apparently knew it. Ulrika touched his hand; he opened his eyes and looked at her. The rigidity of his bitterness passed and his lips moved. Ulrika looked cautiously around. There was no one in the room. She bent down and kissed his lips and as a flaming red overspread his face, she whispered: "I will go to him. I will avenge you. Stand up. Be a man now." And she disappeared.

CHAPTER VII

ULRIKA DRAGS THE SECRET FROM
ITS KEEPER

IT was a quarter past six when Ulrika stepped into Mylius's
shop. The clerk, a bald-headed, sickly-looking creature with
blue glasses on, was getting ready to go. An old servant was
carrying out the blinds for the door and the show windows.
In the background of the long room, Mylius was peering out.
Most of the lights were out and an unpleasant, pale twilight
reigned over everything. But Mylius recognised her and
came forward with his wavering gait, his hands in his pockets and greeted her.

If it were all right with him she would be glad to write
the letters now, she said. She had had no time sooner; perhaps however, as she saw the shop was about to be closed,
it would not be possible?

Mylius took out his watch and considered. Ulrika recognised that he had been waiting for her and had already made
peace with himself. It was kind of her to have remembered,
he answered. For him it was not too late; he had no leisure
hours. Would she kindly come into his private office?

He pointed to the back of the shop and she followed him.
He ordered the servant to leave the lights on; he would
turn off the gas himself. Then he went out and gave
him an order in an undertone. Once more in his narrow
office, lighted only by two green shaded lamps, he took out
a couple of closely written sheets and handed them to Ulrika.
They were the German texts of the letters that she was to
translate. She sat down on one of the desk stools, evidently
the place of the man with blue glasses, for Mylius sat at the
opposite side of the desk and began to read. One letter concerned the sale of the entire furnishings of a ducal

72

palace; the other was about the buying of two pictures, a Watteau and a Turner. In both cases it was a matter of enormous sums. Mylius still had the stump of a Virginia cigar in his mouth; he smoked mostly unlighted cigars as it was more economical; he added up figures in an old account book and seemed entirely oblivious of Ulrika's presence. But the fact that from time to time he threw a penetrating glance at her did not escape her.

She laid the papers aside. It would take too long to do that to-night, she said; they were legal papers, and she was not prepared for that now.

"You might begin at least; to-morrow is a day too," said Mylius, discontented. "Or don't you want to do it any more? I might have known it. Young ladies have other matters in their heads."

"By chance, you have guessed right," said Ulrika, "but it is nothing very joyous. Will you let me speak openly to you? Will you listen or shall I wait until you have finished · your accounts?"

Mylius lifted his head. "Pray go on, gracious lady," he said with an unpleasant gleam in his eye. "I am entirely at your service."

"I wish I knew just how to begin," said Ulrika in a tone of almost soothing modesty. "I mean the tale about Lothar. Please don't interrupt me. It would never occur to me to meddle with your bringing-up of the children. It was a frivolous trick and the boy deserved the lesson he got. If one of my brothers had done such a thing my father would have beaten him to a pulp. A Belgian, Baron Saville, whom I knew, shut up his twenty-year old son in the dungeon of his castle for months with nothing but bread and water because he got mixed up with money-lenders. The police had to break in and set him free. And in London once I saw a butcher throw his hatchet at a hungry cur that had snatched a mutton chop from the block and break his skull open. The man was quite within his rights. Mutton chops are holy, especially in England and must be defended. Every man must defend himself as best he can. Here in Germany we are more sensitive than elsewhere. Here every mother screams murder if her little son is grabbed by the top of his head. But I feel sympathy for people like Saville, and curs that steal are hateful to me."

"Bravo, my Fräulein; you are not lacking in healthy human reason," said Mylius, unaware of the underlying tone of mockery in Ulrika's words. "It's experience. One can talk to people who have seen something of the world. I tell you that boy has the devil in him and what is to be done? The devil has always had to be driven out with a beating, even in old times. One has to stop up the hole if one wants to keep the ship from sinking."

"True," said Ulrika and her modest tone became positively servile. "One can learn from you. All the same the misfortune happened, and the debt has to be made good. The stick, useful as its services were, is no paymaster and the creditors wanted their money. Frau Christine did not have the money and I offered my services and advanced it. But be easy, I am not going to press you for it. I know how hard it is on you to take such a sum from your business. I know, for I too have been in poor cicumstances; one does not have money every day and what with debts here and there! and when one takes out one thaler, twenty more are likely to fly up the chimney! Accursed money! How noble one might be if it were not for money. You need not thank me. I ask no interest. You need only sign a little note, saying: 'I owe Ulrika Woytich forty-eight gulden and fifty kreuzer which I will pay to her or her heirs when I am able.' Or you can pay in instalments—just whichever is easier for you. Only I want to make you promise that you will say nothing at all at home of the matter. You are not annoyed to have me speak so openly to you?"

The question sounded very open and candid and Ulrika seized paper and pen to make out a note. She knew that she would never have to do it. Mylius shifted the cigar end from the left to the right corner of his mouth and bit with his little yellow teeth into the end. Ulrika acted as if she saw nothing. "It's hard on a man," she said pitifully, as if to herself: "Good Heavens—in these times! With a large family, shop rents, house rent, taxes, up-keep, the necessary appearances to keep up one's credit; and one does like to lay aside a couple of hundred for illnesses and extras; it's no small matter to manage all that. When one is young, all right; one can stand a set-back, one can pull through somehow or other, but as one grows older with such burdens and so many lives dependent on one—then it is bitter." She sighed. "If only I could help you!" She struck the desk. "Oh, if I weren't just a woman!"

Mylius got up. He walked up and down between the iron stove and his safe and Ulrika watched him curiously. Suddenly he stopped, turned to her and said curtly: "Such nonsense I have never heard in all my life." He giggled.

Ulrika looked up with a surprised and offended expression. "Come with me," he said, and beckoned her with his finger. "I want to show you something." He went on ahead and led her through the front room where the lights were still burning into a dark room that lay to one side. He lit two gas jets and said in an amused and humorous tone: "Now look, you innocent soul. Do you see that chest?" He pointed to a gigantic, worm-eaten piece of furniture that stood up black against the door.

"Yes; an old chest, certainly," answered Ulrika innocently; "in the market there are lots of that kind. What about it?"

Mylius laughed. "It's an old chest from Augsburg and dates from the middle of the fifteenth century, my dear. I bought it at an auction in Stuttgart for eighteen thousand marks. It is worth more than twice that. The carved angels on it alone are invaluable."

"Eighteen thousand marks?" said Ulrika with an expression of complete incredulity. "What is there about those old smoky boards to cost eighteen thousand marks? You are making fun of me. For that much money you could buy all the stuff that is standing round here at the Jews'."

Mylius only laughed. Then he began to be very busy. He dragged out a chair with a carved coat of arms on it and said that it came from the Strozzi palace in Florence and was a very desirable specimen for collectors. Were he offered five thousand gulden for it he would not part with it. He led her up to a saddle that had a shot-silk cover and ivory decorations that dated from the time of the Moors in Granada; for this he had been offered seven thousand gulden, cash down. He showed her a bronze figure by Riccio, a head with the snaky hair of envy, and said that if any one owned these they could laugh in their sleeves. He showed her a medallion by Pisanello and miniatures by Füger and Isabey, telling her that they represented, just as she saw them there, a stately fortune. While she still stood looking at them he came up with a goblet, at the sight of which she started, for it was of pure gold and Mylius said it was a vase by Jamnitzer, a celebrated master of the German Renaissance, and could not be had for fifty thousand gulden. Then he pulled her by the sleeve to a case. In this there was something really worth while, a miniature bed, with marvellously carved ivory angels and a baldachin. Mylius admitted that it was all made of real Genoese velvet, one of the rarest stuffs in the world; the whole had been the doll's bed of a Burgundian princess in the time of Charles the Bold; a museum piece of incalculable worth, that he had come by quite by chance.

Ulrika's eyes had a greedy gleam which she tried in vain to hide. By degrees her indifference had disappeared. The doll's bed of the Burgundian princess had pleased her. She could not turn her eyes away from it. She was learning every form and figure on it by heart. It awakened a new instinct in her heart, a mixed feeling of superstition, longing, shyness, respect for beautiful things, lifeless things, all heavily laden with the past, things bound up with the past, of which each one was unique of its kind; the expression of the desires of connoisseurs; each piece a kingdom in itself, and by this able to provide shelter and security from need and commonness. The doll's bed of the little Burgundian princess with its exquisite little columns and the velvet baldachin became for her a beckoning picture of an unknown world. She almost stretched out her hands to take it and to hold it, so compelling was the feeling: "This is made for me. It belongs to me."

She took care, however, that nothing of this sort should be noticed; also Mylius' conduct kept her attention fixed upon him. He rummaged around in desks, drawers, trunks, dragged dozens of objects out, explained, pointed out, admired, demanded that she admire, named prices, told where he discovered this, and what story lay behind, who had first discovered it, who had tried to get it, named the names of dukes and duchesses, princes and princesses, counts, barons, and great lords of all lands, quoted conversations with them, described the pains and the cunning it had taken to bring into his possession a certain shawl, a table service, an old desk, a bit of goldsmith's work, or a painting. He was a transformed, an entirely different man from the man they were accustomed to seeing; his whole bearing was that of a man in love, proud as a great champion. That alone would have given Ulrika an understanding of the value of the heaped-up antiques even if she had been less sophisticated and more unlearned than she was willing to appear. Mylius's smile was half good-humoured, half ironic, as if he wanted to say: "You were mistaken, poor dear; confess your sad ignorance." All his movements were caressing, stroking, smooth, his hands grasped each piece with proud care. This was a thing that a queen once owned; here was one on which the fate of a whole great race depended; there one that bore witness to the downfall of a once splendid house; and here one from an unknown source, important and valuable only to a connoisseur. Mylius touched them, caressed them, fairly clung to them with his looks, knew every hidden mark, every secret defect, knew whether they were single specimens or whether their worth was lessened by duplicates, copies, and imitations; he talked to them as if they were living or merely slumbering creatures, threw in an anecdote concerning this one, an historic event that added to the value of that one, a long lawsuit that had been conducted over another. Here was a chain of astonishing silver filagree work, set with diamonds; he weighed it, spread beautiful material beneath it de-

voutly; he said it had once been the property of the beautiful princess Sapieha, and his movements were as if he were
laying it about the neck of the princess—as if the princess
herself had become his with the chain and he still had power
over her departed soul and could make her rise again out
of her grave.

It was an expression of power. For the first time Ulrika
experienced in her innermost being and to the deepest depths,
what possession was. This man possessed! All these things
were his because he lived in them, ruled them, penetrated them,
worked with them, and his very blood flowed through them.
This old man was inaccessible, incomprehensible, by means of
possession, and through his possessions he grew in her eyes
to an immeasurable greatness.

But she never would have forgiven herself had she let him
see this. What she saw, what she had seen was nothing and
brought her to no decision. She wanted real insight, oversight, figures, certainty, measurements, and security. With
all her sharp senses she struggled keenly; everything that he
had brought out and shown her hid something else, something more important; this was only the foundation upon
which the great building was constructed, whose size and
height she wished to know, because like a magician he
had hidden it from the eyes of men; and she knew that the
blinder she appeared the more he would throw open to her
gaze.

Meanwhile it was eight o'clock, and Ulrika said she had
to go home and would not disturb him further. But Mylius
shook his head; he had sent a message to his wife by the
servant that he would either come late or not at all to his
supper; he had sent word that he had an important conference with a business friend who was leaving early in the
morning. But why? asked Ulrika surprised, for it was contrary to his most honoured customs. Every one knew that
for years he had not spent an evening away from his family;
what was it that prevented his going home? It just happened, he told her, suddenly sulky; he had planned it yesterday when she had announced her coming; and when she

stepped into the shop he had decided upon it. There was
something between them that must be settled. On her account? asked Ulrika surprised; naturally this flattered her
beyond measure; she couldn't imagine what it would be
about; was it about his shop, whose contents he had just
shown her, she asked in an intentionally derogatory tone. If
so, she must confess that it had interested her to look at
such things, but now that was over there was no reason why
he should not go home to supper. Mylius seemed vexed; he
replied that she needn't worry about his physical welfare. He
had slipped two rolls into his pocket and now with her permission he would eat them. He drew from his coat pocket
a not overclean package, unwrapped it and showed three
rolls with sausages in between; he offered her one on the
palm of his hand. She refused; for her part she must go
home she said, and got ready to pass through the front room
into the office to fetch her hat and coat.

This banal little dialogue was really a very ingenious
comedy of Ulrika's.

Mylius followed her slowly. He turned his eyes from her
face. His look was dark, gloomy, and restless. As she picked
up her coat he said: "You are mistaken. We are not nearly
finished."

"Why?" she asked, pretending to be frightened; "must I
stare at more frippery? This is enough for to-day."

Mylius turned the bite that he had in his mouth around
and said angrily: "Frippery? Frippery? The word seems
to amuse you. Have you then not guessed what this frippery is and what lies behind it? Is there so little room in
your charming little head? It cannot grasp that this frippery
points to a tremendous life work. Too bad! I really thought
the charming little head was cleverer."

"Kindly leave my charming little head alone," Ulrika replied crossly. Then, after a pause, she told him the place was
a regular mole's trap, that it was dusty, worm-eaten, ruinous,
with the leftovers from the whole world's household. She
wouldn't deny that there must be hundreds of thousands represented in the shop, but that was very much as if one wanted

to get gold coins out of a mountain. But who got anything out of the hundred thousands? He indeed got some pleasure out of it. But what a fool's paradise it was, for he hardly allowed himself butter on his bread. Moreover these were only imaginary values, entirely dependent on the whims of curio-seekers and the ridiculous moods of rich blockheads. To-day one fashion, to-morrow another. Some accident would drive the price up and another bring it down. Commerce was just so much borrowing; one thing pledged against another. There was nothing very fixed in that, nothing that could make one say: —this and this I have, no one can gainsay me, no one can take them away; I don't have to tremble in the night, I have no fear of thieves or fire; there stands my fortune like a tower. Nothing impressed her except security. She stood for the tower and not for frippery. If there were ten times as much of it there and it was a hundred times more costly it was no more to her than so many shimmering soap bubbles, blown from troubled waters. Perhaps he was cradling the illusion of riches, but she knew well that he himself had no real faith in it and in his inmost being knew it was all a vain illusion. If not, how did it come that he lived the life of a poverty-stricken cottager, and that he would beat his own son pitifully for a miserable sum of fifty gulden? He mustn't be angry with her, but she had to say that she had been thoroughly disgusted by the atmosphere of poverty about him. On the one side she was disgusted, on the other she was sorry for him, sorry for his wife, sorry for his children.

Mylius made no reply. He walked up and down, up and down, ceaselessly. That voice speaking to him gave him such pain as he had never felt before. It went through him. He felt as though she were literally tearing the skin from his body, and yet he could not remember ever having felt so singular a joy at the sound of a voice. She set him into a perfect fever of fury and hatred, and yet the fury and hatred ended in a kind of pleasure. He had sometimes felt something like this when, unknown, he had gone into some of his houses credited to a straw man, but in reality belonging to him,— his from attic to cellar, and yet no one greeted him, no one noticed him though every one would have dropped dead in devotion had they known who the unassuming stranger was. His whole existence was founded upon this—its enticements, its dangers, its Haroun-al-Raschid quality, its secret kingship, its fulness of power all pressed into an insignificant kernel, so that reality seemed almost a dream, and the hours of the days were transformed to a magic mirror which showed the world as a poor lie, but showed him the marvellous truth.

This voice was a poem sung by many voices along the three and a half decades of his weary way to his goal. He had never listened before; he had known how to stand fast and firm. One might say his heart had never been touched in thirty-five years and all his senses had been like a frozen lake. But this voice was different; he could not but listen to it. It promised everything; it sounded metallic like black iron. If it were only possible to silence it with astonishment, O glorious moment! He walked up and down, listening, fearful, undecided. Then Ulrika said: "Please don't forget to sign that note. You see, I must have some security."

His face was distorted with anger, and then he chuckled. He went to his safe, opened the heavy steel door, took out a green basket, full of silver coins, laid it on the desk and counted out with impatient, hasty fingers, forty-eight gulden and fifty kreuzer, chuckling to himself for he knew, and was glad that it would be awkward for Ulrika to carry away so much coin.

Ulrika counted it over, reached for her bag and calmly dropped the clanging money into it.

There was silence for a moment. Mylius sat down on his swivel-chair, gnashed his teeth, and then asked suddenly, as he stared at her, if she didn't think he was a very lonely man. She thought a minute and then said "yes," but quite as if she were thinking of something else. Had she the slightest idea of this loneliness? She wrinkled up her forehead and for a second seemed to question her hearing, but only for a second; a less sharp-witted person would have made a mistake, not easily corrected. She decided to reassume her modest, attentive attitude, and smiled. Mylius said that his loneliness came from fear; fear of people, fear of envy, curiosity, greed, claims.

He stopped then to watch the impression his words made. But Ulrika said nothing. The fingers of her right hand played with the little coral chain on her left wrist. Her eyes were dropped and her heart beat violently.

He did not know whether she was worthy of his confidence, he went on; but if he could be convinced that he could rely upon her silence, a silence as unbreakable as gold itself, he would tell her something that he had never told a human soul. But she must understand that it was a trust of highest importance, a confidence only to be given to one who had been tried and proved. However, although he took her for a very unusual woman, unusual through her experiences as well as through her inborn character, he still had doubts that made him hesitate.

"Shall I praise myself?" asked Ulrika; "have I any other witness than my face and eyes? And if I had would you believe them? For the world at large a man is what he seems, but for a keen eye that cannot be deceived he is what he is. I always see people better when they look at me; that gives me a certain advantage. Silence is a good thing at times and sometimes a bad thing. I can tell you a case where it was a bad thing. The first position I held was in Brussels, with a Baroness Desmarest; she was fighting a divorce suit with her husband and it was still quite uncertain to whom the children were to belong. Although the wife had the slenderer chance, the children, two angelic little creatures whom the Baron loved beyond all measure, were still with her. In her anxiety over losing them she seized upon the idea of sending them out of the house, which she did in the greatest secrecy. She took them to an old nurse in a village near Rouen, and I went with her on the journey and was the only human being who knew the children's hiding place. The Baroness was a very moody lady and the separation from the children and anxiety over the verdict, which really had been unfavourable to her, upset her and the kindly understanding between us ended in a quarrel, so that she went beyond the limits and grossly insulted me. She insisted that I leave the house at once and had really planned it, for since the divorce she was in poor circumstances and was ashamed to confess that she did not even have the money to pay my salary. I did not have five francs in my possession; I could not find another position and for weeks I dragged out a miserable existence until I did not have bread to eat for days at a time. It was naked hunger I was facing. Then one morning the Baron appeared at my place; heaven knows how he found out where I lived. He wanted to force me to betray where the children were, for since the verdict he had searched unceasingly but in vain. I refused. The first interview was short, but he came back again. He exhausted himself in begging and arguments, he offered money, a notable sum, he promised to make my future secure, he even wept and raged before me; but I would not let myself be moved and said that I could not betray the mother. How the story ended I do not know; but a few days after that I managed to get a place and I was doubly glad that I had not sold my honour. I would much rather have done it for kind words than money; I did not want to do it, perhaps from sheer stubbornness, perhaps from *esprit de corps*, for men are nearly always wrong in a contention with women, even when right seems to be on their side. So you see I can hold my tongue; but I would like to know what is at stake."

Mylius nodded, lost in gloomy thought. "Surely," he murmured, "an oath can't be sold for a trifle, nor am I going to exact an oath. A clasp of the hand is better and binds one more firmly. What is at stake? I don't know. I only know that the burden is beginning to weigh upon me. The net is too narrow; the threads too numerous. At times I fairly long for some human being to whom I can say:—'there is a hitch here, what shall I do? I am bothered about that; I am going to do so and so. Do you think well of it?' I don't even need an answer. All I need is some one to listen and understand. Did you notice out there in the front shop a marble pillar for a grave, with an inscription? According to the archæologists, it is that of the Roman Emperor,

Septimius Severus. I often stand in front of it and talk to him. I ask him for instance whether I shall buy the additions to the house on the Rossauer land; whether the saw mills by the Monks' Church might not deliver more product if one placed the dam higher up; is it advisable to cut down half the trees in the Duborczinschen forest; for if a war broke out the whole would be lost. When I wake up nights these thoughts prey upon me like ravening wolves. The manager of the Landskroner farm seems not to be an honest man; another under whose name the Gleichenberger manor was sold demands provisions, beyond bounds, and one must make one's position clear to him; perhaps it would be better to buy only ten thousand instead of fifteen thousand English consols and take the rest of the money in an African mine stock, which now promises so much; that sale of petroleum stock was too hasty; it will certainly rise in the course of time; and all this one does alone. Whom should one consult? My wife? She would hear with the ears of all her children and I am not yet quite a raven-father who lets his children starve because he has no feeling for them. It is they who have forced me to use my head. But I don't want them to know or they would devour it all. What I have built I have built for the future; it is mine; do you understand? Mine, exclusively. No bonds of blood, no fatherly weakness, no sentimental considerations can rob me; they have a livelihood, a roof over their heads and the rest is mine. But imagine a man grubbing in the dark, demanding treasure from the depths of the earth, conscious that it is there; despite his knowledge a certain faint-heartedness comes over him; he loses his sense of proportion, his insight, until a ray of light falls upon his work; he needs one whom he reveres, and who has not yet recognised him, to change her attitude toward the lonely groveller, gain an insight. After all, old Mylius is not just a scrap of dirt that one kicks out of the way with a dainty toe; you were mistaken; he is a rock, a hill, a mountain; look out or you will run your head against it. Well, see; that is my case; I have earned nine million gulden; earned, yes, that is what I have done; and here you come, my dear child, and take me for a beggar, to whom one must lend forty-eight gulden and fifty kreuzer."

He gave a mocking laugh and Ulrika, who was convinced that he had suddenly gone insane looked at him and laughed too.

"Now what do you say?" he asked, standing up, his arms propped on his hips, his head thrown back.

"I say that I think you are overexcited and that you ought to go to bed and take a quieting powder," answered Ulrika.

"I thought so," nodded Mylius, grinning. "Such figures were like a thunder clap to you. I thought you would think my works were out of order. It is quite natural, too; for it could hardly pass for the boasting of a braggart and a pretender. I kept on the inside of the limit. In your place I should perhaps have felt the same. But, thank God, there are proofs, irrefutable proofs. What sense would there have been in speaking if I could not have laid proofs before you, documents to show the truth of what seems so monstrous to you, my dear one."

He laughed his unbearable little laugh and went back to his safe. Out of an upper drawer he got a blue envelope and took out some papers and unfolded them with trembling fingers and held them before Ulrika's eyes. "What is that?" he asked in a hoarse, commanding tone. "What is that? A will; isn't it? Written out, signed by my own hand, authenticated by a notary and with an official seal. When? The second of January of this year. Good. Now what is written on the fifth page of this will, underlined in red ink; the total result of my labor? Read it, read it aloud!"

Ulrika obediently read aloud: "Statement of total amount of my fortune on this day; nine million, nine hundred and twenty thousand gulden."

Ulrika's face went as white as the sheet of paper before her. Her voice failed her and was lost in a hoarse gurgle. Her eyes were wet as they often were under stress of fear or tragic shock. She stared at Mylius with an empty look, dumb, motionless, breathless.

This was what Mylius had expected and what he wanted.

His face cleared up, an almost wild light of joy was in it, something like the happy content of a lover who has at last been accepted. He moved his chair nearer Ulrika, sat down and turned the pages, pointed with his bony forefinger to passages here and there, and his voice sounded almost tender as he spoke.

"You see, dear young lady and friend, how these not unimportant figures came about. One thing follows another and softly, softly, without any one noticing, it runs up into millions. Beautiful millions! brave millions! when year by year, by dint of industry, patience, watchfulness, economy, and instinct one has brought it up to a million, then the others follow, the second, the third, the fourth, and so on, as sheep the bellwether. Now you have definite information about the rummage shop as you were pleased to call it. Here: Division of moveables and immovable estate: one and three fourths millions: of course that is only a very general valuation, as it is a matter of changing values, but it is rather too low than too high. Then come houses: three houses in town, amongst them the house in which I live, and this one in which we are; and two in the suburbs. Standing under other names in the books to be sure, but secretly and by secure contracts belonging to me. They stand for one million, eight hundred thousand. The Galician forest, two millions. The farm, the manor, the castle of Gleichenstein, formerly owned by Count Weissenwolff, two million, two hundred thousand. And last, stocks, bonds, ground-rents, promissory notes, mortgages, money owing, bills of exchange, total sum,—one million, three hundred and seventy thousand. Well, Fräulein Ulrika Woytich?"

He looked at her surprised for the answer was no human sound, but a strange croak; and at once there broke from her wide-opened eyes a diabolic flame, devastating, yellow, like a jaguar's eyes, that suddenly dampened his tender, wordy eagerness. Still, in her look was unlimited astonishment, incredulous fright which flattered him; an utter inability to grasp and to think; a kind of numbness before a phenomenon that the imagination could not grasp and all this gathered together, without the slightest effort to disguise it, in one look from her innermost being. She got up. She said she was not well and that he must open the door and let her go; she needed air; she could listen no longer, talk no more; she must go away and think and get it straight in her mind. She threw her cloak around her, did not even take time to put on her hat, grabbed up her bag heavy with coin, and ran through the front shop. Mylius followed her but turned back to fetch his hat and coat, while she cried: "Open! open!" and fairly frightened, he obeyed.

And now she was out in the street. She ran a few steps; then she stood still and pressed her hands against her breast. Then she ran again. Carelessly she stepped into snow puddles. The water spurted up. She stood still again, drew her shoulders together, and whispered fervently, threateningly, with fleeting breath: "Nine million gulden."

A long time she stood dumb staring along the empty street, and then in a low, full voice she said: "Now, Ulrika, gather all your forces together. There is work and reward both for you."

A wild laugh escaped her lips, she went on a little quieter, devoured by stormy thoughts and deliberations.

A half hour later she rang the bell at the house of the Court Counsellor.

CHAPTER VIII

AND IT WAS NO DREAM

MEASURED by the habits of the old man it was late. The noisy ringing of the bell first dragged out Smirczinska. She appeared in a nightgown, rough and cross, and refused to let Ulrika in. The fuss almost resembled a fight, and the noise brought out the Counsellor, who stood like a ghost in his green dressing gown on the threshold. Ulrika pushed past into his room. He was sulky, but quieted Smirczinska.

"What is the matter with the old owl?" said Ulrika. "Has it come to the point of my letting myself be abused by that old skeleton? If you don't make peace between her and me, I'll take the very best chair and break her old Polish blockhead in two."

The Counsellor growled at her. He stalked around the table with his neck stretched out like a black stork. Time to lock up, bed-time, sleeping time; and nothing was worse to him than to be disturbed. Disgusting, upsetting frivolity; disturbance! A real Austrian idea, the repulsive mask of the official. What heresy is to the religious, a disturbance was to him; a thing one was not prepared for; anything that upset his habits and was not to a hair like yesterday; in a word, anything new or different. He had carried over all his official habits into his retired life; all the world-old habits of registrars and notaries that men recognise as easily as they do penitentiaries and cemeteries. When he sat at the window of his gloomy house and looked out into the street, at the stone Madonna in the niche of the wall opposite, at the baker's shop and shoemaker's, at the hats, caps, and umbrellas and tapping feet of the passers-by, he always had the feeling that all that existed because he allowed it, as if a formal vote, or marginal note would destroy it all. That he did not bring it about was entirely due to his wish to avoid disturbance.

He had already been in the official service in the time of Metternich. He had even seen the servile, sly, sweet-smiling, diplomat's face of the old Gentz.

He had been among the appointed guards when the revolutionist rovers of the year '30 cawed at the time-honoured structure of the monarchy, and thanks to the cautious provision of unaccomplished things had dropped back into the Gallic mud. In the year '48 he had helped to put down the highly dangerous mutinies and when the students had massed themselves on the glacis, he plead for them, urged them to send the penitent rowdies home with a whipping.

For what was it all? Disturbance. Under Alexander Bach he had been made public censor and had before his eyes daily the disaster that resulted from letting unchastened spirits spread themselves in ink and print unhindered; it had been rapture to him to break the nerve of the *literati* and newspaper smearers.

There was but one person in the world who could boast having gained some influence over him: Ulrika. How it had come about, he himself would not have been able to say, or he had perhaps forgotten, or did not want to admit it. When he heard her step he was intimidated and would gladly have hidden. Under her stern and penetrating glance he felt a weakness overcoming him which he could not master. Her appearance, her speech, her mischievous allusions, her cool, impudent criticism awakened a dumb, powerless anger in him. He might have lived out his days in quiet and peace if she had not come. Even when she was away the thought of her embittered him, her disrespectful interruption of his life, the possibility of her sudden reappearance, the whole disturbance that she had introduced into the evening of his days. "What's the matter now?" he grumbled as she sat there before him with her ridiculously impudent manner. "Why wake up an old man out of his necessary night's sleep? What are you running wild about Vienna for? Free me at last from your noisy fussing and fuming. Get out of my sight; you asked for four weeks' shelter under my roof and they are up now and the attic is to be rented on the first."

"I don't need your attic, uncle. I am taking other quarters," Ulrika answered indifferently.

"Where? What do you mean? Are you going to remain here? Not going to Paris?" She nodded pleasantly.

"That can't be done," he roared, "you've got to go away; tie up your bundle and see to it that you get out."

"Don't get excited; I am going to remain here," Ulrika answered coolly. "Right here in your neighborhood, uncle, under your protection. The Mylius family will apparently need me with them. You know my relation to those people; I told you about it. In the meantime a good many things have happened and especially to-day, something has turned up that in your own interests I should not like to withhold from you." She laughed suddenly to herself, seized her heavy, silver-filled bag and flung it against the door. A suppressed cry broke out. The Counsellor started. He wanted to be angry, but the clanging noise of the throw surprised him.

"Apparently you have a bag of gold there," he said and his yellow-parchment face showed both suspicion and astonishment.

Ulrika picked up the bag and emptied the forty-eight silver coins out on the table, arranged them in two piles, took out the snuff-box with the emerald in it, which was also in the bag, and laid it on top of the pile. "How much do you think that snuff-box is worth, uncle? You understand such things."

The Counsellor took up the snuff-box, looked it well over, smelt inside, weighed it, wrinkled up his forehead, and replied: "It is worth from two to three hundred; certainly as much as two hundred. Where did you get it? From old Mylius? Are you having an affair with old Mylius? That would not be so stupid." He laughed his toneless laugh, the muscles of his underjaw painfully distorted.

"Could you lay your hands on thirty thousand gulden, uncle?" asked Ulrika, paying no attention to the rude suggestion. "Would you like to pick up ten per cent without raising a finger; earn three thousand without any effort?"

The Counsellor opened his eyes. "I? Thirty thousand

gulden? Are you weak in the head? Thirty thousand gulden? I?"

"Now you listen before you begin to blaze out," said Ulrika, wrinkling her forehead. "It is only my family feeling that moves me to make you this offer and to let you first into the business. With so certain a return I can borrow money, as much as I please."

"What is she up to now, holy Mother of God," murmured the Counsellor in alarm.

"Now listen." She was almost whispering as she began to tell him. She leaned over one side of the table and the Counsellor leaned over the other. The hanging lamp lit up the brown and the grey partings. Now and then a piece of furniture cracked or a board under the carpet. It was a long story. The Counsellor listened in stony silence and with leaden eyes. But at the climax, and the mention of the will and the nine millions he jumped up from his chair. He turned round twice on his heels; it was laughable for the green silk dressing gown fluttered out round him and his slippers clattered till it looked like a ghost's dance. He broke out in inarticulate sounds and at last brought out the words: "Either she is lying like Satan himself or this is the maddest tale ever told since the world began."

"I don't mind your suspecting me; it doesn't hurt; I don't even bear any malice," said Ulrika. "It is a mad tale without a doubt. Now, I am going to tell his wife the facts. She will not hesitate a minute to rearrange her life to suit her circumstances, if only for the sake of the children. The old man will find himself up against it and I am going to play a trick on him, a sharp trick, from which he can't escape. He will have to give up and open the treasure box; but first we shall have to have some money—a good deal of money."

The Counsellor stared dumbly. He had hardly ever heard of such a fortune. It was improbable, ungraspable. He had heard of Rothschild; but then Rothschild was just a legend, something distant, imposing and ungraspable. The richest people he had ever known were worth about a quarter of a million. In his day a quarter of a million made a man a very

Crœsus. The figures that Ulrika quoted made him dizzy. He stared at the young girl and waited for her to break out into her sudden, ironic laughter. He would almost have been glad if she had. When it did not happen he began to groan softly. He said he had no money; how had she ever gotten hold of the monstrous idea that he had all that money; he, with his three thousand gulden pension and perquisites; it was not worth wasting words over. It was shameful of her to come around with such frivolous nonsense and disturb his peace.

Ulrika got up as if to leave the room and answered indifferently; as far as she was concerned he could send his money up the chimney if he wanted to. Then he waved his arms, walked around the table and asked her in a threatening voice if she were willing to swear that everything she told him was the pure truth; swear that she had seen the will and the actual figures with her own eyes. Ulrika raised her hand to swear. "Stop," he cried. "Swear upon the soul of your own mother; swear word for word what I say before you."

He pronounced the oath and she repeated it after him, looking up at the ceiling as if she were looking at a fly. Despite the oath the poor old Counsellor began to groan again, he had no money; where, where could he get hold of thirty thousand gulden? Could she tell him?

But Ulrika seemed to be disinclined for further discussion. She made a curtsey to the old man and left the room. She was quite satisfied with his despairing snatch at the hook; she knew she would catch her struggling fish. Money! Magic word! It needed only to be spoken and then, even the most high-principled, the most unapproachable went wild. No character was so armoured that it was proof against the poison-sweet intoxication. Miserable world! and all so transparent!

Hardly had she undressed in the narrow, cold, little attic room, when she was aware of the tread of slippers on the stone steps. She listened; laughed to herself, jumped swiftly into bed and drew the cover up to her chin. The Counsellor crept up to the door. He coughed, felt around with his fingers. "Who's there?" she asked gruffly. He put his lips to the keyhole and said he could not possibly manage thirty thousand with the best will in the world; if he were to gather together all he had on earth it would only be twelve thousand, but he thought he could promise twelve thousand free of all incumbrance. Perhaps that would do for a beginning and then perhaps later he could look about a bit. Ulrika answered that was too little and blew out her candle. She had better think it over, he groaned. Then she answered scornfully that she knew a perfectly simple means of getting the money; he could pawn the Guarneri violin; one thing with another, that would probably answer. He brought out a low oath and the slippers went slowly downstairs again. Ulrika had her own good reasons for trying to persuade the Counsellor to lend the money. In the first place there was his great age; should he die the money would fall to her and her brothers and sisters. Moreover she needed connections in the circles where such business was understood. If she turned direct to people of that kind she was afraid that their own eagerness and researches might interfere with her undertakings.

When she came down the next morning, Smirczinska complained to her that the Counsellor was ill and had staid in bed. "What's the matter with you, uncle," she asked as she approached the deep alcove where stood the old-fashioned bed with its canopy of yellow silk.

He was angry and silent. About four o'clock in the morning he had wakened and then the horrible thing had begun; it came over him every now and then—the fear of death,—like a clinging, purple frenzy. But it had never been so awful before. Death had appeared to him in its most horrible form,—bellowing. And as the twilight slowly dawned the more clearly he saw him,—a naked, hairy, fat, greasy, shiny, hideosity with chattering teeth.

What do you want with me, cried the Counsellor crouching; there are plenty of others; there is Mylius with his nine millions—a juicy morsel; what good am I compared with him? But the creature leaned over the foot of the bed and fixed him with a look. His proletarian manners waked the gall in the Counsellor. Why should such a thing be allowed?

Nine millions! You are leaving him untroubled the enjoyment of his nine millions, and you molest me who cannot afford to lose one single day of life. The hideous Thing shook
its skull. Overcome by fury and fright, the Counsellor began
to beg; just grant me a couple of years more and I will get
Mylius for you. Ulrika and I, we will bring him to terms,
and you shall lose nothing by it; I'll pay you in gold coin.
Moreover you must obey me; I am an official, an imperial
official; as long as I was in office I was always your secret
partisan; remember I brought you many unexpected sacrifices. This seemed to satisfy the creature. He gloated there
for a while and then faded away in the lead-grey February
morning.

Then the Counsellor realised that he was stronger than
Death, but the fright he had gone through kept him in bed.
He turned his watery eyes to Ulrika and admired and envied
this bit of stubborn, vital, inconsiderate youth. He was
afraid of her and envied her because of her free breathing,
her clear eyes and young voice. With shivering desire he
looked out into his own faded life. He had thought it all
out, he began, but he was not assured of the matter yet; it
was too risky; could she at least remember the name of the
notary who had sealed the document? Ulrika said, yes, she
had at once impressed the name on her memory; it was Helmbauer, who lived at the Tiefen Graben; but to try to get
information from him would be useless as he had to keep all
official secrets; and dangerous too, as he might suspect something and tell Mylius. Moreover she had sworn and was that
to stand for nothing? Nonsense, said the Counsellor; greater
folk than she had taken false oaths. Helmbauer, he said, as
he laid his finger on the side of his nose, he must know the
man, certainly he knew him, he was the notary who lived at
the Tiefen Graben; he had known him these forty years. He
would go to him and put it to him this way;—one of his friends
was about to go into a business transaction with Mylius, the
antique dealer, in the Himmelpfort street, and he would like
to know if said Mylius had credit for a hundred thousand
gulden. Ulrika was entirely satisfied with this idea. All of

a sudden the old man was well again. He made a hasty toilet, put on his long frock coat that reached to his shins and made him look like a telegraph pole blackened by the elements, and took his way to the notary.

Ulrika went all through the three rooms restlessly. Only once, six years ago, when she first came from home had she been left alone in the dwelling. Then too, she had spied about, looked in every corner, knocked on the tapestried walls, opened all the drawers; but in vain! And to-day again, her seeking was fruitless.

The Counsellor came back well satisfied. The strategy had worked. The notary recognised him and complimented him most respectfully. He laughed at his question, and putting his mouth close to his interlocutor's ear had whispered: "Good for many times that much, but I beg you not to ask me just how much; it is only out of old friendship that I tell you what I do and under strictest secrecy; but he is good for many, many times that much."

Still there was much to consider. Everything, for and against, was pedantically examined to the last point. Love of possession and fear of loss held the scales against each other. The most serious consideration was that of the amount of the sum. Ulrika refused to be satisfied with less than twenty thousand gulden. On the third evening the Counsellor gave in, groaning and cursing as if he had already been deceived about the money. His conditions were, first that he visit Frau Christine Mylius in her own home and that she sign a note in his presence; furthermore that the interest should be deducted from the capital when he lent it to her.

When they had gotten this far, Smirczinska appeared crying aloud. By dint of suspicion and bits that she had overheard, she had come to a fairly correct idea of what they were up to. She fell at the Counsellor's feet and begged him to withdraw from the disastrous undertaking. Indignant at the melodrama, Ulrika told her if she did not get out at once she would cool her blood with a bucket of cold water.

The Counsellor seemed touched. He said soothingly and with a real Jesuit's cunning: "Leave the good child alone.

She has her instincts. She has always prophesied wisely for me. In '65, when I wanted to send State-treasurer Gayling of Altheim—God be merciful to him—to Perchtoldsdorf, she tried to prevent me at the last minute. And what happened? On that day the State-treasurer had a stroke in his carriage, right in the middle of the day. See how easy it would have been for everything to have been swept away by that stroke! How easy! This woman should be honoured on account of her intuitions."

"I see, indeed," said Ulrika, in cool anger; "the State-treasurer was fetched by the same devil who will shortly fetch your Smirczinska and her apprehensions. And me too," she added as she saw the indignant and furious face of Smirczinska.

A shuddering smile passed over the face of the Counsellor. He was amused at the cut at Smirczinska. She bored him, as sooner or later, every one bored him whom he had to see daily. He suspected her of a sneaking interest in her legacy and he secretly hated her. He said grimly: "Tear each other's eyes out if you want, but I don't want to hear it. Only people who have neither faith nor religion carry on their rows before other people."

Smirczinska went out wringing her hands. When he began to talk of religion she lost all self-control. The Counsellor stretched his flat hand on the table and looking sternly at Ulrika said: "Done. The matter is settled. It is decided."

"Good," said Ulrika, "now you must wait till I bring you news that I have prepared everything. It may be a few days longer."

The Counsellor took up a piece of paper and a pencil, murmured a while to himself, wrote down some figures, and began to calculate, so absorbed that he completely forgot Ulrika's presence. After a while he got up, drew from under his flowered waistcoat, a nickle chain with keys attached, went into the third room where there was a glass cupboard that contained his collection of watches and sticks. But there must be something else there; probably the place where he kept his cash, since he never trusted a bank or a safe and therefore certainly must have the main part of his cash-holdings in the house. Perhaps here was the long-sought hiding place. Hot shivers ran down Ulrika's back. He seemed much absorbed. He left the door open and Ulrika, still as a shadow, saw that he went up to a corner and pushed the gold-framed wall mirror aside. The mirror moved like a door on hinges. Ulrika was triumphant, but the Counsellor stopped short, frightened, remembered her, came back and closed the door, not without throwing a distrustful glance at her, but she was looking innocently out of the window.

Before she went to bed that night, she tucked the house door-key into her gown. About two o'clock, she came down in her stockinged-feet, opened the door lightly and listened a long time. The roof opposite the window was flooded with silver moonlight. She sat down on the sofa without a sound and waited till she was sure that the breathing of the old man, heard through the half-open door was that of a sleeping man. Then she got up and went in. On the night-table in the alcove a small oil night-lamp was burning, and the light from it helped her to search his clothes which were laid over the back of a chair. When she came to the little key and loosed it from its chain, her hands trembled in their eagerness not to make a sound and she looked fearfully toward the sleeper. He lay on his back; his face was the colour of a lemon, his underlip hung down and he had an expression of hatred of the whole world.

Then she slipped back, but to reach the third room she had to open a door, and this required the greatest caution. She knew that the sleep of the old man was like the thinnest membrane that would snap at a sound. At last she stood before the mirror. The reflection of the moonlight from the opposite roof gave enough light and she had the kind of eyes that are sharper in the dark. She saw her own face in the mirror; it seemed strange to her and she almost drew back.

The mirror was movable as one pushed a lever underneath. This she discovered at once. There was a square cut in the tapestry beneath about fifty centimetres high and thirty broad. She raised it. In the depths of the walled-in cupboard, which she searched with her entire arm, in a leather case, was the violin. She took it out, opened the case and held the instrument in her hands.

She held it and looked at it a long time. It felt singularly warm, singularly smooth, and tender like a little human body. It seemed as if the wood vibrated under her fingers, and the two symmetrical openings by the bridge looked like two faded eyes. She felt an alien, endlessly sad emotion in her breast. She, who had never been touched by human suffering, or the breath of Fate, who strode through the world of men coldly and with fixed intentions, and had schooled herself to view the general human torment and need with cool calculations, needed the greatest self-restraint not to burst into tears at the sight of the violin. It was a strange, unfathomable power that moved her. She felt it as a kind of farewell. A farewell to memories, to the country of the soul, in which she once too, had a part, and that now sank forever; every man stands sometime at the cross-roads and must make an irrevocable decision. She wanted to hear the sound of the violin; just a single tone. She touched the G string. A fine, wailing, melodious, quickly expiring tone answered her and she listened, fascinated.

At that instant a heavy hand dropped on her shoulder. A mysterious, clucking noise sounded behind her. She turned around. There stood the Counsellor in his green dressing gown. He looked at her. His eyes seemed fathomless.

"Uncle Clement, you'll catch cold," Ulrika said.

Again the clucking sound as if it came from the neck of a bottle; it was half laughter, half angry astonishment. He took the violin gently from her hands, packed it back in the case, laid it in the wall cupboard, shut the trap-door, turned the key and said hastily, over his shoulder: "Can't you wait? So impatient? Too long till your times comes? Go away. I have seen nothing. I will forget. It shall be as if nothing had happened. But no more night-wanderings. Let us pretend we have dreamed this."

But Ulrika threw back her head and pointing to her breast

with her forefinger said: "Don't let us pretend anything. Here there is no dreaming." Then she went.

The Counsellor hobbled back to his alcove and, as he crept under the bed-clothes, he groaned: "Keep watch always and always keep watch. . . ."

CHAPTER IX

COUNSELLOR WOYTICH VISITS THE
MYLIUS'S HOUSE

DURING the three days that Ulrika had kept away from her friends, they had sent twice to ask if she were ill. The last day, Herr Mylius himself had sent the blue-spectacled Herr Schmidt to enquire. Ulrika saw that she had become a very important person and gave herself all the more leisure. Now nothing should be hurried.

But to smooth the way and to prepare the ground, she resolved first of all to initiate the two elder sisters and Lothar. Only in general outline to be sure. Complete illumination should follow later in as far as events themselves did not serve. Meanwhile, she had to build up her entire plan of action.

One thing she resolved upon. Josephine was to be kept out. She could not rely on Josephine. She would always have to fear encroachments from her that might endanger the whole proceedings. She would always have to be afraid of her conscientiousness. The best way would be to let her be gradually enlightened by Christine, but, of course, only after Christine herself had been entirely won over and there was no danger of the force of circumstances allowing her to turn back.

Sunday morning she invited Esther, Aimée and Lothar to the city park. It was beautiful weather and she took all four of them to an out-of-the-way bench where the brother and sisters, much intrigued by Ulrika's mysterious manner, waited to hear what was to come. Ulrika sat between the two sisters, holding a hand of each and Lothar she held with her eyes.

She said they must not be surprised if circumstances changed materially for them. Led by a long-nursed suspicion she had discovered that the financial circumstances of their father were much greater than those of the average citizen and that from now on they might live a very different life, much freer, happier, less careful. Lifted above all small considerations and narrowness, they might now look forward to the fulfilment of their desires, and things that yesterday seemed but an impractical dream, might become reality to-morrow or the day after. She did not feel that she could tell them any more at the moment, and even this they must keep absolutely silent about; a single indiscreet word and everything might go up in smoke. Step by step, with the utmost foresight, she, and she alone, would be able to reach the heights for them and she must meanwhile rely on their obedience, as the responsible leader of a difficult expedition.

The three listened with shining eyes, but Ulrika's revelation was too indefinite for them to make any picture of the future. It was a little too much like a fairy tale. Ulrika wanted to leave them somewhat in the air, anyway. All she wanted was aroused; hope and obedience. They promised everything and sealed it with a handclasp. She told them to tell their mother that she would be round about three o'clock for a conference and as it would doubtless be long, she should have nothing else ahead. Even this solemn message was carefully thought out. Also she knew how Mylius usually spent his Sunday afternoons; at three he started on a two-hour walk and then spent two hours in a coffee-house. So one had plenty of time without being disturbed.

"Where have you been this long time, dearest Ulrika?" Christine greeted her as she came into the room.

"Are we safe here?" asked Ulrika and locked both doors and without laying aside hat or coat, with her hands in her muff, which showed signs of moths, she walked up and down with long steps like a man. She had stage fright. At last she threw hat, coat and muff on a chair and sat down opposite Christine, and began in her low, cooing voice to tell, exactly, word for word, emphasising the important points, what had taken place between herself and Mylius.

The color left Christine's face. She sat by the window and never moved. Her pretty, little hands grasped the arms of the chair convulsively. She listened with round eyes, wherein horror, incredulity and childish astonishment were mirrored. When Ulrika finished she broke into uncontrollable sobs. She pressed her hands before her face and tried not to be heard outside.

Ulrika let her weep for a while.

"All right," she said. "That's enough of that. All that is behind us. All that hidden misery has come out into the air now. A new time is beginning. After the rain, the sunshine. An end of tears." She got up and as she marched through the room again she said: "Now you have complete insight. You have been mercilessly deceived. Deceived about everything that makes life pleasant and worth while, deceived about your security for the future; deprived of thousands and thousands of little pleasures that are perfectly harmless but keep the soul young and the spirit strong. Deprived of friendship with people, of society, of giving and receiving, of joy and laughter and warmth. You have been an abused and patient beast of burden, suspected over every little difference in the account book, obliged to deny your better education and upbringing—when a child was ill you had to beg before you dared call in a doctor, refusing yourself and your family every little cheap wish, because you believed you had to count the kreuzer; and you are broken and old before your time because of your household cares. So things are and it is enough to make one weep. A man who deceives his wife, with other women, is a scoundrel perhaps; I say perhaps, because one never knows whether the wife is not partly guilty herself and in the end, glad to be free of him. At any rate, it is a sin one can outlive, and a sorrow one gets over. But from my point of view, for the thing this man has done to you, there is no forgiving and no forgetting. It is a heap of small meannesses, harmful cruelties and unnecessary naggings; only a veritable devil could torment people unnecessarily. A thousandth, a ten thousandth part of his heaped-up fortune would have spared you all the daily worries and the feeling that here you stood, a woman of fifty years, with four children, a poor, plundered fool."

Christine had regained her self-control and sat motionless,

looking into vacancy. "These are frightful words you are speaking, Ulrika," she said, "and I fear, if everything is as you describe it, they are true words. Sometimes I had vague ideas about it, but even now it is hard for me to believe anything so monstrous. It is difficult to throw a whole lifetime behind one as if it were no more than a dirty rag. My eyes refuse to see it. I need not say that I do not question the truth of your information but the whole situation is so inconceivable that my reason refuses to grasp it."

"Yes; there it is!" cried Ulrika, and threw her arms up in despair. "It is inconceivable, it is impossible to believe it. I had made up my mind never to enter this house again, but to go away and leave a little note behind. For I could no longer stay and witness what was happening here; and yet I did not want to divide the family into two inimical parts. I spent three sleepless nights. For one voice that warned me not to burn my fingers there were ten to warn me of my duty. I did not dare leave you in such a fix. I kept seeing your dear, careworn, troubled face before me, and the girls, too, one by one, and the boy who has become like a brother to me. So I decided and I said to myself: 'Ulrika, no flowery speeches now, but go, do what your heart bids you.' So here I am."

Christine stretched out her hand to her silently.

"What is a person to think?" she murmured, half aloud. "How can one explain it and understand it?"

Ulrika sat down on the bench beside her and seized her hand, and as she tenderly stroked it, she said that when she first entered the house things did not satisfy her, here and there; she had been so sorry for the women and even more for the poor, suppressed, imprisoned boy; then she felt a deep suspicion of Mylius and deliberately watched him, and out of friendship she had become a spy to bring the man to confession. Now she knew everything, had seen it set down in black and white, and the only question now was, what Christine intended to do about it.

Christine wondered herself. What should she, what could she do? Very little, or perhaps nothing. So long as Mylius lived—and she could not wish him dead—there was nothing to be done. As Ulrika sat there with her head sunk down, and Christine really feared this silence, she added that no one on earth could give her the courage to go before him now and ask for money. Her pride forbade this. She was not capable of it. Moreover, upon what should she base such a demand? If she really had a right, she would scorn the use of it. What he had confessed to Ulrika, eye to eye, in some strange mood, he might deny outright to her. He would not mind doing that in his anger at Ulrika's betrayal. It was evident from his whole make-up, as well as from the tale, that he relied entirely upon her silence.

"No one would be stupid enough to advise that," said Ulrika, who could hardly control her anger at the heavy morality of her friend. "So pure a mind as yours thinks, of course, of only the directest method, where perhaps only the most devious will lead to the goal."

"What would lead to the goal?" asked Christine, with a troubled smile.

"First, I have to know whether you are determined to sacrifice five living beings on the altar of his miserliness. Whether you are going to continue to be his faithful, unpaid servant; if you are going on silently watching him as he robs your daughters of their happiness and holds your son on the pillory. Neither do I wish him dead—Heaven preserve me from such a sin—the more so since death in such cases is usually difficult and without results. I might sing you a little song about that. But if you think I am going to sit here doing nothing, while you fade away from sorrow and twiddle your thumbs, or weep with you, then you don't know Ulrika Woytich. No, I would rather get up and go."

"One never dies of sorrow; one just gets used to it like everything else," answered Christine resignedly. "What do you think ought to be done?"

"Well, I'll tell you," said Ulrika quietly. And she began to give Christine the results of her previous thought. She spoke to this woman, twice her age, as if she were talking to an inexperienced child. At first she was careful and did not even hint at her more wide-reaching plans. The bolder, more outstanding parts she suppressed. The impress of what she thought wise to impart was quite deep enough. The statement that money was always easy to get in any circle, at least when it was in proportion to one's circumstances, not only aroused doubt in Christine, but also her aversion to anything like debt. She was afraid of confusion, false sense of proportion, wrongdoing. That she had suffered was no reason for wrongdoing now.

Ulrika did not get very far with her, but she was prepared for that. It was the hardest part of her undertaking. The battle with Christine's sense of right needed all sorts of gifts and a cool head.

At half-past six as she got up to go, Christine was in a state of nervous irritability and helplessness as the result of all she had heard. Her look at Ulrika pleaded with her to stay and the request was on her lips. Ulrika saw it, hesitated and was doubtful. Then Christine gathered up her courage and asked if Ulrika would not stay that night in the house. "Why?" asked Ulrika, apparently surprised, though inwardly glad, for it was what she had striven for. She had reckoned upon it and planned it, though Christine did not notice it.

Christine felt almost ill at the thought of the first meeting with Mylius. She was afraid that her very face would cry out to him and she feared losing the self-control which had become a veritable second nature to her. She confessed it openly; she felt that at any price she must control herself, on the children's account, Ulrika's account and her own account.

"I know that if I gave way I should have to lose you, I don't want to lose you; anything, but not that," she said, and her restless hands reached out after various objects, a needle, a case, or a piece of paper, or she pressed her hands against her temples; "anything, only not that. Do what you think best, but stay here, stay near me, and then in case of need I can turn to you. If you are here, you will turn the attention of the children away from me; and I don't want them to know what is going on here."

Ulrika nodded. She would manage, she said, to remain in the house for the next few days; that seemed the best way to her, too; she would find room there. Christine breathed freely. With loving and true-hearted caresses, Ulrika told her that what they had before them required time, patience and a cool head. Nothing should be left undone and nothing hurried.

"Herr Mylius must never even guess what we are undertaking. We will only come to an explanation when we can place definite facts before him to which he must bow. There is not the slightest reason to offend, irritate, or wound him. But power must oppose power."

With every word that she spoke Christine yielded more and more. It was a pleasant feeling to give up one's will. A tormenting excitement calmed itself and at last it seemed that she might give in to a long-felt fatigue because a strong arm had arisen to protect her.

Nevertheless, she was much disturbed when Ulrika told her that Esther, Aimée, and Lothar were in the secret, and she had to begin all over again to soothe her and to justify an action which Christine thought inconsiderate and harmful. Ulrika questioned this. She said she knew what she was doing and would be responsible for it. Josephine, she had wisely not taken into her confidence, for with Josephine, things were different.

"Yes, with Josephine, it is quite different," repeated Christine and her head sank.

"She will never understand that sincerity is good for sincere people, but it is like dealing out trumps only to the sly," said Ulrika.

"You think then we cannot tell her?"

"It's the only way; we must avoid useless talk. Sometime, when there is an opportune moment, we will tell her, but then all our rough work must be behind us. We have no time now to plead with her."

Christine was not convinced. The necessity for secrecy oppressed her, for the relation between herself and Josephine was one of perfectly natural openness, as if they had been comrades of the same age. But it was as impossible for her to oppose Ulrika as to try and stop a moving railroad train.

Esther, Aimée and Lothar were standing outside full of expectation when Ulrika and Christine came out of the room arm in arm. Three pairs of eyes turned an excited and admiring look upon Ulrika and a questioning one upon their mother. Christine felt there was no turning back now; these hungry hearts dragged her toward the inevitable. There was great joy when Ulrika told them that she was going to stay with them for three or four days. Josephine joined them, heard it, and offered Ulrika her room, in which a second bed might easily be placed. "You are an angel, Josephine," said Ulrika, as she embraced her, "but angels are called 'thou' and hereafter we will say 'thou' to each other." [1]

Then laughing, she pointed to the envious looks of Esther and Aimée and Lothar's pouting underlip. Then a little ceremony was improvised in which they all decided to say "Du," which had Christine's complete approval and brought a lovely smile to Josephine's earnest face. In the cake box there was a flask of wine with a little bit of wine still in it; every one took a nip and Ulrika sealed the bonds of friendship with a kiss for each one.

When Mylius appeared for supper they were all at the table. A gay conversation was in progress and Ulrika managed, with the utmost skill, to keep the good humour from lapsing, with all sorts of little tales, witticisms, society gossip, and kept the attention fixed upon herself so that Mylius' presence seemed almost forgotten. She never addressed a word to him, her looks passed over him, or more cutting still, when she looked at him, it was as if he were not there. In fact, she never let him escape her glance for an instant and noticed, with some satisfaction, that he gave a contented grin when he came in and saw her in the room.

There was a questioning expression in his face; then the beginning of a friendly welcome; then he became highly incensed at the untrammelled gaiety, for he was accustomed to

[1] Translator's note.—In Germany the members of a family and all very familiar friends are called "thou" instead of "you." Duzen is the ceremony of changing the mode of speech from "you" to "thou" and is a much more formal and binding one than the English dropping of Mrs., Miss or Mr.

respectful silence. His face grew dark; he crumbled his bread between his fingers; and once when Lothar broke out into loud laughter he shot an angry glance at him from under his thin red lids. Then an unmistakable oppression came over him; he looked at his watch, pulled at his cravat, ceased to eat, lit a Virginia cigar, and got up, looking about the circle with aggrieved distrust. Then at last Ulrika turned to him.

"It seems that now I am about to begin a career, Herr Mylius," she said gaily; "I have had a row with Uncle Clement and Frau Christine has been kind enough to offer me shelter. I have the honour to commend myself to you as one of your household. I feel as if I had been born anew, and if we can only have your consent, and I don't doubt it, I shall have nothing further to wish for."

Mylius turned his head round in a circle in his stiff shirt collar, as he always did when he was embarrassed. "Well, well," he replied, with an attempt at being amiable, "that's what I call a surprise. A guest under my modest roof, and so rare a one, too. For, for some days you have made yourself very scarce, my Fräulein; or am I mistaken?"

"So good of you to have noticed it," replied Ulrika; "but I was ill for a couple of days, seriously ill. I have been through a great deal of excitement and had to come to some very serious conclusions. But now I am up and about again, and you have no objections to my resting awhile in your nest like a tired bird in flight?" She turned with a strange, long, sharp glance.

"None, none whatever," Mylius hastened to answer; "I hope you will be comfortable in the nest and will not rob it of its peace."

"Amen," said Ulrika, "be assured that I have not flown thither without an olive branch in my beak; I know what's proper. I have come, too, with the best of resolutions: 'Work for the day, the evenings for play, laborious weeks, and gay feasts!'"

"Now, now," Mylius defended himself, alarmed, "weeks and feasts is not a good rhyme nor is play advisable. I won't have any of that," but his look rested with pleasure upon Ulrika.

She bowed. "Just as you command," she said.

"And what have you ahead for the future?" asked Herr Mylius, with rather too pronounced an interest; "so practical and able a young lady as you are must be looking ahead to the future."

Ulrika laughed. "I can tell you a little verse about that," she rejoined; "I read it years ago." She stood up in a speaker's posture, her hands on her hips, her head on one side, and recited slowly, scanning the syllables:

> "Forgetting frogs and daily bread,
> The noble stork, with stately tread,
> Along the grey-green summer grass,
> Lifts each red leg from the morass,
> That all the world may, gaping, see
> How grand is idle propriety."

"But don't be afraid, Herr Mylius," she said, folding her hands in an attitude of prayer, "those are mere frivolous rhymes, but in reality I have plenty of plans, as I shall soon show you."

This equivocal and ambiguous conversation made a painful impression upon every one, but Ulrika's wit and quick retorts enraptured them, though they did not dare show this before Mylius. Christine smiled like a person watching a tight-rope dancer and little drops of perspiration stood on her forehead.

At ten o'clock Mylius went to bed. Christine sent the children off and Ulrika sat for an hour or more, whispering with her by the lamp. The next morning they went to market together, and in the evening again they sat late over the lamp; and conference followed conference, discussion upon discussion.

Ulrika played all the registers. If she fanned the slumbering indignation and angry complaints against Mylius into fresh flames, she also painted the future in enticing colours; called duty, what Christine believed to be betrayal; she preached cunning and deception; plead with her to consider the fate of her children; mixed up her affections and sense of justice, showed herself sharp and impatient, caressing and uncertain, until she had aroused a complete confusion in Christine's mind. As she built up her strategy and wove an ever more complicated web, and step by step became bolder and more domineering, more certain of victory, she overthrew Christine's last objection and brought her to the point of declaring that she was ready to receive the Counsellor Woytich and to give him a note for the payment of eighteen thousand gulden, a sum that seemed to her dangerously large.

"You are not risking anything," her friend soothed her; "first it is your natural right and the law stands on your side; moreover, I will become your advocate and stand up for you."

This labor is harder than carrying stones, she said to herself, as she hastened back to Dorothea Street, to set the Counsellor in motion. Then she went up in the attic and packed her belongings into the little wooden trunk that had followed her on all her travels, and sent it by a servant to the Mylius house. She had a violent quarrel with him first about the eighty kreuzer that he demanded; then she went to Christine, told her that the Counsellor was coming at five o'clock and instructed her in the most didactic way just how she was to behave. As she knew exactly what he would say and how he would behave she was able to tell Christine exactly how to answer and in what way. Ulrika developed all the gifts and scenic imagination of a practised stage director, and Christine, although she was embarrassed, had to laugh.

At noon Ulrika was not at home and when she came back, she learned that Mylius had gone to Geneva to be present at an important auction. His absence would probably last a whole week. She showed the greatest delight at the news. Now things could move on with more dispatch. She could go forward quite a bit in that period.

On the stroke of five the Counsellor arrived. Frock coat, brocaded waist-coat, buckled shoes, top hat, cane with an ivory crook handle; a picture out of a past era.

He was frosty, gallant, and formal. He studied the house

and he studied the woman. He looked at the rooms with the eyes of an appraiser. What he saw satisfied him. There followed a conference, at which Ulrika was the prompter, standing behind his back and helping with frowns, nods and shakes of head. When it came to the formality of signing names he became a veritable pedant. Two fingers' breadth, not more, not less, the space had to be between the text and the signature; one finger's breadth between the date and the left border. When Christine put down the pen he stopped her and demanded her certificates of baptism and marriage as proofs. Christine was indignant; Ulrika boiled.

Finally he counted out the money on the table; ten thousand gulden in bank notes, five thousand gulden in Lombards, three thousand gulden in gold. He started and drew his brows together when Christine, trembling like an aspen leaf, made no effort to count it over. Ulrika murmured something and did it for her, with due earnestness; note by note, and the gold pieces five by five. It was as much a token of respect, in the mind of the Counsellor, who stood by, stern and motionless, as any other formality in closing a business transaction.

So all went well and Ulrika could begin her activities. No time must be lost now.

CHAPTER X

THE CONQUEROR AT THE FEET OF
THE CONQUERED

THERESA was dismissed and received wages for the remainder of her term, a magnanimity that Ulrika reckoned very highly, as according to her they might have found plenty of excuses for escaping this duty.

"Don't bother," she said to the inconsolable old woman, "everything in the world has an end and even a position in the Mylius family can't last forever."

The same morning a perfect cook, who had held high positions, came in. There could be no question of this lofty person taking care of the rooms, making beds or washing; on the contrary, she demanded a scullery-maid to help her. Until now the daughters had always taken a part in the housework; but Ulrika forbade this now; also Christine was no longer to meddle with the housekeeping; she was to spare herself and be looked after. That afternoon there appeared a smart looking chamber-maid, named Nanette; she looked as if she had missed her vocation and should have been a soubrette.

To provide room for these three people was not so easy. The cook and the housemaid had to share a room, and the scullery-maid had to sleep in the kitchen. Ulrika said to Christine: "We certainly will have to look around for a more decent home. Here we tread on each other's heels, and there isn't a ray of sun the year round; our bodies and our spirits will decline. We need," she counted on her fingers, "nine, ten, eleven, twelve rooms, not counting our company rooms."

"Twelve rooms? Company rooms?" stammered Christine; "you are wild, my good Ulrika. How will you ever bring Mylius round to that? I am already mortally afraid of what he will say, increasing the servants and everything else we have done behind his back. Don't you know what fear is?"

"Not in the least," said Ulrika; "all tyrants turn as cowardly as pug dogs if you growl at them and show your teeth. I would deserve to be whipped if I did not know what I was about, because then what I am doing might make your position worse instead of better. Everything will be as smooth as silk, and I am counting on a little luck myself."

Her courage overcame reason, and she rushed headlong into the danger. As a child she had sometimes put her head into the oven to hear the flames nearer; and when her mother once caught her she bit her hand. She had an impertinent trust in luck at the last minute; her favorite fable was the one of the man in the well, hanging between destruction below and destruction above and consoling himself with sweet berries.

The household machine ceased to creak. All the friction that had come from lack of service and help disappeared. Bad humours gave way to comfort. The rooms were warmed throughout. When they wanted things, they were bought. The food became richer and tastier. The storeroom was filled day by day with dainties; southern fruits, preserves, chocolate, pastries, game, poultry, fresh vegetables and boxes of caviar. When they were hungry they ordered and had things served.

Materials and costumes were brought to the house for the girls and for Christine. Cloaks, wrappers, hats, silk stockings, embroidered nightgowns, shoes and gloves of all sorts and for every cccasion. They looked at them and did not know what to do. Lothar got an entirely new outfit, the dearest and most elegant that could be bought in the fashionable shops. Words failed him when Ulrika told him that he should have ten gulden a week pocket money and he did an impromptu Indian dance. He ran around saying: "What's up then? Has Ulrika laid down a law that it shall be Christmas the year round? Or is it all just a magic play?"

"I don't understand myself," Esther whispered. "Do you understand, Aimée?"

"It may be that we are all dreaming," she answered.

Although Ulrika had tried to prepare them, reality formed so striking a contrast that their astonishment was beyond measure. They were just beginning to believe in it.

Ulrika said to Christine: "You see what these children have had to go without. Isn't their joy more than the whole rubbish heap?"

And she hunted for new wishes, urged them on to new desires, promised them greater fulfilment and was almost angry at every sign of contentment. "You have starved and done without long enough," she said; "this is not the time to be modest; drink the cup to the dregs." It was not a doctrine that had to be preached very often.

Josephine was silent and wondered. Too silent and unsympathetic, Ulrika thought her; "I'll have to keep my eye on her; not only that, but I will have to keep her busy, interest her, and chain her attention down to some fixed point." And she thought and thought, until at last she came to a shining trail.

But first everything hastened toward the most important resolution. It was a Tuesday evening when Mylius returned. He saw at a first glance that the house had changed since he left it. Even its outer order had undergone a complete transformation; he was given a bedroom all to himself; Christine's bed had been put over into the living room.

"Just provisionally," Ulrika said laughing. He stared at her.

"How so, provisionally?" he stammered.

"Provision signifies that one applies a sufficient means to a difficulty until a better one offers," Ulrika declared with amiable eagerness. He stared at her.

Nanette, curtseying daintily, brought him hot water in a beautiful new crock. He stared at this strange person.

"Pretty child, isn't she?" Ulrika asked gaily; "but you will want to get ready for supper. Good-bye until I see you at the table."

She smiled at him and disappeared.

He stared after her with his mouth open. He took off his coat and waistcoat, rubbed his forehead with his hand, lost

in thought. He forgot that he was standing there in his shirt
sleeves, left the room and went into the living room, but finding no one there, went through the corridor to the kitchen. He
noticed that new copper utensils hung over the stove and that
a new bright-burning modern lamp, with a round wick, stood
on the shelf. The cook and the scullery-maid greeted him
humbly, according to the custom of the land. He stared at
them and went on.

When he opened the door of the former salon, Ulrika came
out. She turned a surprised look upon him; the woolen shirt
he was wearing was not particularly clean, and his suspenders
were old and spotted. "You can't see your wife just now,"
said Ulrika with a pitying shake of the head, "she isn't well."
He stared at her and turned around without a word. A few
steps and he stood by Josephine's door; he hesitated, turned
the door-knob and stood there on the threshold. Josephine
sat between the stove and the wardrobe, apparently lost in
thought. She started up. "What do you want, father?" she
asked pleasantly. He wanted to ask a question, but gave it up
as Ulrika was in the hall, shook his head, and went back to
the living room. Esther, Aimée and Lothar were having a
lively conversation by the window. Lothar looked at his
father shyly. Mylius was startled. He saw that both the
young girls and the boy had new clothes on, clothes that
fairly sang out their newness. Aimée's feet were in patent-
leather slippers with shining buckles; Esther had thrown a
rose-coloured gauze scarf over her shoulders; the boy looked
like a dandy, ready for the races. "What's all this?" said
Mylius, "have you all gone crazy? And what gay faces you
have; red cheeks and shining eyes; and what is the best china
doing on the table? Cut glass tumblers? Wine? Mineral
water? Flowers? Am I at home or where am I?"

A gong sounded in the corridor. Nanette, like a little rococo
fairy, brought in the soup tureen. "We are all waiting for you,
Herr Mylius," he heard Ulrika's warning voice.

He staggered back into his room. "Provisionally," he
thought, wrinkling his forehead; has she lost her head? A
gong, a parlour-maid, wine, mineral water, flowers . . . again

he stroked his forehead with his hand. He poured the can of hot water into the basin and began to wash mechanically. Suddenly he stopped rubbing his face with his soapy hands, his eyes opened wide, his look was wild and wandering, he picked up the crock and threw it on the floor and it broke into innumerable pieces. Then he gave a hideous shriek like an animal that has been stung.

Outside was a tumult, voices were loud and steps hurried by. But Ulrika's voice dominated all the others. "May I come in?" she asked. He didn't answer; he was tearing up and down like a caged animal. Ulrika stepped in, having first looked around with a warning and motioned the others to go away. Mylius looked at her with a fiery, angry glance, seized his towel, dipped it in the water, wiped the soapsuds from his face, dried it with the dry end of the towel, slipped hastily into his coat, and stood close to Ulrika, boring her through and through with his troubled blood-shot eyes and called out in the voice of an animal, angry to the point of madness: "Explain! Give an account! At once! Explain! Account to me!" and he beat his right hand with his left fist.

"Perhaps it would be better to eat first," Ulrika said quietly; it would be easy to talk it all over afterwards. No, he raged, he would not eat; before he sat down to any table with wine, mineral water, and flowers he demanded an explanation and an accounting. He needn't come to the table, Ulrika said softly; she would bring him everything; and when he felt stronger and had satisfied his hunger he would listen more calmly. Under the influence of her innocent, clear glance, he was silent. She went out and came back in a few moments with a service tray, a plate of soup and a plate of meat and vegetables. Mylius had not moved from the place where he stood. She placed the tray on a round table, moved up an arm chair and with a gesture invited him to sit down. He was overcome by her complete calm; those innocent, clear eyes looking like brown enamel, struck him down. He sank into the chair and began to eat his soup. Ulrika took another chair, sat down opposite him and looked at him with an expression of benevolent interest that struck him as the very limit of impudence. The meat he left on the plate. He turned his black look questioningly upon her.

Without raising her voice at all Ulrika said: "In her great need Frau Christine found a way out that seemed permissible to her. She has taken out a mortgage upon a portion of your fortune. She knew no other way to manage."

"That's a lie," Mylius shrieked, "a twofold lie; Christine would not know how to do that by herself, and who on earth would give a mortgage without security and pledges?"

"In this case the very name of Mylius was adequate security," Ulrika answered coldly.

"So it's an affair with usurers," Mylius raged; "usurers and unlawful interest."

"We dealt with a perfectly honourable man," said Ulrika; "you mustn't always think the worst."

Mylius's face was distorted. He gnashed his teeth: "I recognise no claims from whomsoever they may be. I did not give my consent and I will not pay a heller."

"You are mistaken," Ulrika said affectionately; "you are bound by the law and you will have to pay. Moreover it's the matter of a sum so small you will hardly notice it."

"Oh! Oh! Oh!" said Mylius and rubbed his hands like an insane man. "So the lady betrayed me. She listened to me like a low eavesdropper and then hung up my secret in the highest town bell. Of course, of course; and the higher the church tower the finer the sound. The lady thought she could overthrow me, drag my secrets out of me and then have her fun with me. But the lady was deceived. Oh, yes, the noble lady was sadly deceived. I am going into the courts. I will prove that I have been made the sacrifice of an unexampled deception. I will insist that this false transaction shall be annulled. I will bring a lawsuit. I will go through every precedent. It shall come to an open scandal. I'll have you put in prison. Yes, the purse shall be taken away from the noble lady with abuse and shame. Yes; that is what will happen, just that—" He stopped, he panted, he almost strangled.

"If you were only capable of reasonable thinking you would

see what nonsense you are talking," Ulrika said scornfully. "You know very well that there is no question of deception here. There is no judge who wouldn't send you home with your plea and say, 'That man is not right in the upper story.' Moreover you know very well that you are responsible for all the debts of your wedded wife. At most you can prevent her from making new debts, and to do that you must first prove her irresponsible. To prove her irresponsible you will have to show either that she is mentally unbalanced or that according to the judgment of appraisers, who have full knowledge of your fortune, she is making an extravagant expenditure of it. You try that; I'd like to see what doctors and what appraisers would help you out. And as to your daughters and your son, when they reach their majority, I would like to see if you can keep their share away from them as you seem to imagine that you can. It would be an undertaking. In this noble land people daren't take off their baby shoes until they are twenty-four years old, a principle that apparently helps to uphold the state; everybody must remain a fool until he is ready to have gout; nevertheless Esther and Aimée are slowly reaching their majority. I tell you that Frau Christine will no longer scramble to fill your bursting bags while she lets them appear as Cinderellas; she is going to bring them up properly and get her own hard-earned rest; she is going to find a healthy, roomy dwelling, in which she can live comfortably and play the hostess and entertain people when she wants to. Yes, and you are going to help her do it though you strive against it with hands and feet and though you would like to throw me out of the window into street. But you will never be free from me now. You may try to put heaven and earth in motion but I will follow you like your shadow. I am the ghost that your conscience has created, and I will present my bill until it is paid down to the last heller and farthing. Dare to show me the door! Just dare it! Bring a suit against your wife, against your own flesh and blood, against right and reason, against the whole world, dare it! We will see how far you go and who is the first to yield. Go on! We are not afraid. We are ready for anything."

She had gotten up and her eyes shone at him laughing, with a real gipsy wildness in them. All the colour left his face. His glance turned unsteadily from one object to another. He seized his knife and fork mechanically and cut off a bite of meat, and let it fall again and sank over so that his back was perfectly round. He swallowed violently. He reached for a glass of water and emptied it.

"Now the simplest thing for you is to resolve upon a really big-hearted action," Ulrika went on in a gentle, harmless tone; "the crowned heads have to do the same thing. When a rebellion of this kind has won, so that they know their crowns have begun to tremble, they declare a general truce, and the next day the people are crying hurrah. Now you save what is left to be saved, and the hurrah will not be lacking. But what do you get from the hurrah? There are really great practical advantages. You will see how a man feels who is petted and spoiled in a beautiful, orderly, happy household. You will breathe as if you were free from a nightmare; you will really live, after having vegetated for thirty years; every one will love and respect you; every one will read your eyes to guess your wishes. You will really possess, where heretofore you have only grabbed in fear and trembling as in an evil dream, and I," and with these words she went up to him and laid both hands upon his shoulders and her voice was actually caressing, "I will be your servant, your protector, your friend. Is that nothing? Is that too little?"

"The devil! The accursed, false, double-tongued devil!" shouted Mylius. "What is he doing to me, the perfidious, dishonourable devil in a woman's shape. Now he will torture me day and night, talk me out of my property and my goods day by day and then throw me into a burning hell." He buried his head in his hands and rocked from right to left like a pendulum. It was an expression of weakness, discouragement, breakdown, and Ulrika recognised it as such, for she stood behind him smiling sympathetically. In his whole bearing and the murmured complaints and curses there lay a bizarre, pathetic tragedy, which Ulrika really enjoyed, in full consciousness of her power. "What absurd, unjust speeches," she said in a gentle reproachful tone; "you ought to be ashamed of yourself."

Mylius turned upon her and stretched out his arm. "Get out of my house, you miserable creature!" he screamed. "Get out of my house this instant! Don't dare speak another syllable to me! Get out of my house!"

Ulrika shrugged her shoulders and replied scornfully, "Are we giving a tragic drama in the theatre, Herr Mylius? Don't make yourself ridiculous. I am not your paid servant whom you can send away, nor your apprentice whom you can punish. Of my own free will and desire I have put myself at the service of your family who needed me, and human obligation keeps me at my post. You think over quietly everything I have said to you and then if you want to deal with me seriously, you have only to send for me. I hope you will sleep well."

Mylius's eyes glowed green as he watched her. When she got outside he rose, hastened to the door, turned the key. His hands behind his back he wandered up and down for hours in the little triangle round the bed. "You wait, you devil, I'll have you on your knees," was the only thought that sounded monotonously in his brain like a hot searing blast. This thought became a disease, an overpowering desire, a formless, gaping insanity. He saw her humiliated before him, begging for mercy; he heard her soft, cooing voice, broken, and only using its caressing tones, while he made her drink her stored-up penitence and frightful destruction drop by drop.

All night long he wandered up and down and in the morning his tired feet were still involuntarily following the triangle. He went to his shop, the effect of many years of regular habit, and wandered there from room to room. He let the blue-spectacled clerk attend to the customers and he took no thought for his books or his mail. At noon he came back to the house, the effect of many years of regular habit, but did not go into the room where they were eating, but waited until the parlour-maid—distasteful figure—brought him his meal upon a tray. Shy as a thief, he crept around, went back to his shop, wandered again from room to room, and at seven o'clock went to the little coffee house, waiting in black impatience on his chair until it struck eight o'clock, and then went home. Again he saw the distasteful figure, like a miniature of the immeasurably hated one, and he would not eat a bite. This Judas feast I can't eat, he said to himself. The next evening he brought home a package with his food in it; sausage, cheese, dried fish and bread. He emptied a compartment in his bureau drawer and put the food in it. Then standing before his wardrobe he took a frugal meal. Some one knocked on the door. He didn't answer. After the second knock Ulrika came in.

"I wanted to ask," she said in a modest tone without leaving the doorway, "if your anger isn't somewhat appeased?"

He did not answer.

"It is about time that you had a little talk with your wife," Ulrika continued; "the present position is not exactly pleasant for Frau Christine and the children."

There was no answer.

Ulrika waited for a minute or two before she gave the fearful blow which was the real reason of her visit. "Also I feel obliged to tell you that we have rented the palace of the late Duke of Chamfort," she said with complete composure; "we shall move into the house on the first of May. It is not dear, if you take into consideration the situation and the circumstances. Coach houses and stables, ample servants' quarters, tiled kitchens, five or six bathrooms, marble salon and an acre and a half of park."

No answer, dumb rigidity. The horrified little man standing by the wardrobe might have been made out of wax. His eyes stared glassily at his little box of food. Monstrous, this that he heard! His brain turned round and round.

The voice went on speaking. It mentioned several details of the new dwelling. But in Mylius only formless shards of thought arose. Rented the Chamfort palace; he knew what that was; a great lord's estate suited to the most elaborate style of living. He wanted to scream. His throat burned as if from alcohol.

Perhaps one would have to ally oneself with her he thought; speak to her conscience, and try to prevent this monstrous thing; perhaps he could bring her around. He breathed heavily. Must he bow before her then? She would understand, but the wickedness, the wickedness of her; that was stronger than anything else.

In case of need one might grasp the most unheard of means. This was the next thought; I'll go to the chief of police, give him a large sum for the poor, say a thousand gulden and beg his help in getting her out of the country. If it doesn't work? People are so cowardly and they hate scandal. She is the niece of a Counsellor. I might get hold of the radical element. And yet all these debts stand that she has made in my name. And they are growing from day to day, growing now, merciful God! How would it be if I took the whole family away into another city or if I offered a bribe to the woman herself and bought myself free of her? She must give in to some pressure.

But just this thought which promised relief brought the most crippling fear.

During this time Ulrika, still in the same modest posture, spoke in a heartily concerned voice and told him that he really must change his life in order to preserve his health. He needed to see people, he needed diversion. She could easily get him more amusing society than hers later on. Pretty women, temptingly pretty women. Young society. For example they had made the acquaintance of a young Count Lex; he had called at the house twice; a jolly fellow, full of fun and gaiety; the girls were much taken by him. Moreover there was a young friend of hers, Edward Melander, whom she would like to introduce, a first-class fellow; profoundly clever, handsome as a picture, of blameless manners, professor of economics and *persona grata* with the bank president von Wallersheim. And there was some one else whom she had in mind first of all, her brother Franz. He was giving up his post in Madrid and she had written him to hurry home. He was the most entertaining man that she knew; beloved in the highest circles of society and a real master at the pianoforte. She told a little anecdote to illustrate this. In Paris, Anton Rubenstein and he had each played the Berceuse of Chopin behind a Spanish screen and none of the hearers had been able to tell which one was playing.

Mylius thought to himself: suppose I went to a lawyer; he would say you have so and so many millions and wish to cut your family off from enjoying the interest; what is your idea then? I add them to my capital, I would reply. Five per cent of three times a hundred thousand gulden are fifteen thousand gulden, and so the guldens heap up without my putting a finger to it, ever new gulden. Don't you see? The whole upkeep of the house, the education of the children, everything together heretofore has cost me about four thousand gulden a year; and the rest have heaped up. Don't you understand that? Perhaps he won't even understand that. Perhaps he will turn against me and betray me in the end. The whole world is against me. Everything is lost.

"The children have gone to the theatre this evening," Ulrika went on; "I took a box for them. Only Josephine is at home. It is hard to do anything with Josephine; she cares nothing for pleasure. Frau Christine has gone to bed. She complains of headache all the time. In June she will have to go away, to Nauheim or Aix-les-Bains, and later to the Engadine. She has to make up for lost time."

At nearly every word Mylius shuddered as if a needle had been stuck into him.

"It is cold in here," Ulrika went on, "I am freezing. Come over into the living room where it is more comfortable and we can chat just as well. Do you know how to play piquet? We will make up a hand. In London I used to play every evening with Sir Edward Craffts; he called me his little care-dispeller; it is really child's play; in a quarter of an hour you will learn if you don't know how."

She went up to him and offered him her arm, laughing. He did not move. She fixed him with her eyes, bent over a little and looked attentively into his red lashless eyes. Her face took on an expression of anxiety.

"That is not good," she said, shaking her head; "your eyes don't look right. If I am not mistaken something is the matter with your liver. Now let me see; keep still a moment; the iris is quite yellow; and you look so strained and so uncertain. Those are sure signs. But do not be afraid; it is a trifle hardly worth talking about; if you take a little care, we won't even need to call in the doctor. To-morrow a glass of Carlsbad water, then a little exercise and strict diet. I understand it down to the ground. For five months I took care of a lady who had liver complaint. The good Lady Pomfret of Tettenham. But above all things you must avoid excitement. Excitement is a poison. No outbreaks of wrath, no little scenes, no sudden rages."

Up to this moment Mylius had never once thought of his health. He had never thought of his body or its functions and never felt the slightest discomfort. This discovery of Ulrika's startled him, principally because it was so unexpected and Ulrika showed so much concern. It seemed to him now that he had overlooked certain symptoms, suppressed certain warnings, and he turned pale at the thought that some ill had befallen his organs which might be incurable. Like all sound men he had believed himself immune from sicknesses and the more he thought of Ulrika's words the more they frightened him.

As he did not move, she took hold of his damp cold hand and dragged him with encouraging sounds out of his rigidity. He went with her, and his face was the very picture of inner storm and downfall, coupled with shame and discouragement. She led him into the living room, made him sit down in an armchair and then as she saw that his feet were still in his heavy dirty boots, she went back to his room and brought his slippers. She knelt down, untied the strings and drew off his boots. He was wearing rags that were not very clean; but she showed no trace of disgust. He looked with grim wonder as she kneeled there before him. She smiled. He turned his eyes away frightened.

Then Ulrika became suddenly aware that Josephine stood in the doorway. She had stepped in quietly and was looking earnestly at Ulrika as she knelt before her father.

"Do you want anything, Josephine?" Ulrika asked, wrinkling her forehead. Josephine shook her head and went out.

CHAPTER XI

JOSEPHINE

THE room which Josephine and Ulrika had in common brought them closer together in every way. Heretofore, Josephine had been in the habit of going to her mother with everything that she thought and did; she gave her an account of all the books she read, of everything that happened to her, resolutions she formed, and events she heard of. In all this she showed an innocent, natural confidence and what she told was direct, as if it welled up from a spring before it had a chance to spread itself over the surface. Conception and words were twins; her feelings came out to the light and then took shape and form.

Since she no longer found her mother ready to give her all the spare time which they formerly shared, because Ulrika always came in between, she felt as if she were living in a colder climate, and the most joyous of her outlets was closed to her. Before Ulrika came to live in the house, it often happened that when the activities of the day had kept them apart, Christine would go to Josephine's bed late in the evening, and midnight would still find them deep in conversation. Now Josephine missed this.

It was important to Ulrika to break down the relation between the two, in order to manage both of them. She recognised that her influence over Christine was not lasting when Josephine stood against her, and that she must get control of Josephine if she wanted to manage Christine. It was a difficult undertaking, especially in view of Josephine's reserved character. Where should she take hold of this wise and prudent girl? With coarse flattery—even with delicate flattery—with the honey one used to catch the others one didn't get anywhere.

There was something baffling to Ulrika in Josephine's love for her mother. It made her uncomfortable, like a confirmed sceptic who is forced to go to mass daily and assume a reverent mien. The mythical-religious element in the relation, particularly noticeable in Josephine, awakened her aversion, especially after she learned how deep the roots of the feeling were and how far back it reached.

One night they talked a long time. The lights were out and each lay in her bed and Josephine, who became lighter hearted and more communicative as the hour advanced, could not come to an end of memories. Ulrika turned them in the direction she desired and finally Josephine told her the following tale.

When she was a little eight-year-old girl she had had diphtheria very severely. Her two-year-old brother, the mother's spoiled darling, had died of the disease the day before. She knew it in that dim way in which a half-conscious mind knows such things. She had heard the uncontrolled weeping of her mother; she had been faintly aware of strange people in the house and a vague impression reached her of mourning, darkness, and farewells. She lay there alone in the room. In a corner there was a dim oil light. Then the door opened, it seemed, and with a ghostly step, all white, with a white face, weighed down with the heavy crown of blond hair, her mother entered and came up to the bed, in her arms the newly dead child, this darling of her later years, and strangely enough she was nursing him at her breast. Although there was no life left in the little body, his lips still clung to the mother's breast and it seemed to Josephine that he was drinking in some higher life, something incomparably more joyous, that had nothing in common with his existence and his love here on earth. She had stretched out her arms to take the little brother; her mother gave her the child and said: "Take him into yourself and hide him safely there." She understood the words and then suddenly she had a powerful impression of her mother; there was something noble and solemn in the very word "Mother"; something so deserving of thanks and so indescribably her own that her whole being was filled with new life, new confidence and resolution. She knew then that she would get well, and wanted to, also, and what she had seen that night remained an indestructible image in her heart.

In the dark Ulrika made a grimace. That was all too high-strung for her, like the eccentricities and illusions of the North where she had once lived. But how was it that Josephine generally made the impression of a very sober and reasonable person; it seemed that at some particular point her sobriety broke; with these Mylius people one never knew where one stood anyhow; her imagination, which was of extraordinary activity, seemed to lie in a hard shell, only broken open by some passion. However, that might be turned to use too.

And again Josephine told her that in her twelfth year she had been at home alone once and had heard frightful screams from the maid's room. She had hastened to her and had witnessed a birth. In the dark room a candle was burning and its light shone upon the arrival of a new life. She had understood it all without fright, almost without sympathy. She kept the secret, but it had impressed her inmost being. She now looked at her mother with new eyes as if she were a painfully broken-off twig and her mother the stem; as if her very existence were a kind of robbery, a robbery of body and soul; as if her ego and her separate existence were an unpaid debt and the divinely mysterious wonder of motherhood demanded the highest respect and reverence.

"Really one should not spy into such things," said Ulrika with a peculiar sensation of prudishness. "In such matters a woman is no different from a cow in its stall and the Lord God has wisely arranged things so that we cannot look into His apothecary shop. If He puts up the window blinds and bolts the door, He must have His own reasons."

"God is not an apothecary," Josephine answered and by her voice one could tell that she was smiling. "I think perhaps he is a watchmaker."

"A watchmaker? Why that?"

"I don't know exactly. I always think of Him so. For the dearest man on earth to me is the watchmaker. He sits so earnestly and patiently there and looks so carefully through his magnifying glass at the little wheels."

"Patiently, yes, quite right," Ulrika said. "One has to be patient with people in this world."

During other nightly conversations, it was Josephine's restless demand for truth, for information about men and human things that embarrassed Ulrika. In former times she would have turned with all this to her mother, but now her full heart flowed out to Ulrika. And what would she not ask about; the futile chatter of some social superior which she had taken seriously; brutality toward a servant which no one had blamed; the consideration offered the rich and the hardness and humiliation given the poor; the whole question of double measures and weights; the deceitful solidarity of class interests; the comments in which she saw ill will and meanness; the impudently defended privileges of the malignant; the bold overthrow of right, permitted whenever it was might also; the shamelessness with which people sacrificed their ideals to advantage; the way people were flattered to their faces and scorned behind their backs. Why were these things so? Josephine wanted to know and urged her questions as she pointed to examples. Everything that people did and said awakened her burning interest and the slightest gestures, the most trivial motions remained in her memory.

Ulrika, unwilling to answer, turned to mere forms of speech. She excused this and that because it was customary, a necessity of the general order, the insufficiency of institutions, or else because it was decreed by Fate. But Josephine would not let that pass; custom could not excuse lies and hypocrisy; the social order could not excuse servility; nor could the force of circumstances be the excuse for allowing the powerful to oppress the poor. Her replies and statements had all the settled logic of a perfect inward incorruptibility. There were moments when she fairly clamoured at Ulrika her experiences and her convictions; she demanded light, answers, reassurance. She turned to religion, and, true Protestant that she was, the doctrines which had died down in the world around her to the mere letter lived as a fiery flame in her breast.

By means of her conversations with Christine, Ulrika had learned that it was just this restless questioning, this devout spirituality that had kept Christine both tender and melancholy. It refreshed her, it gave her youth and courage, endurance and resolution. But these she only had under Josephine's direct influence, the magic of her presence, her touch, her glance, her tender and tireless attention.

To Ulrika, however, all this questioning, explaining, digging and investigating of Josephine were in the highest degree unpleasant. The whole attitude toward life of the young girl was objectionable to her nature, and it was with only the greatest self-control that she could force herself to attentive listening and sensible replies. It became harder and harder for her. Troublesome little meddler, she thought, why is she always stirring up the cooked food, putting words on the scales and weighing them, martyrising her brain to find out why the grass is green, and the snow white, why Herr Meier has a crooked mouth, and his wife freckles on her face? Futile effort! One should leave things alone and not stick one's nose into everything.

And it was not only because it would advance her confirmed aims, but out of a slowly growing hatred of Josephine, that she directed her plans and activities against her. Josephine was her born opposer. The thought that Ulrika was working to keep her away from her mother never entered Josephine's mind. Had it occurred to her she would have found no reason for Ulrika's destroying the greatest pleasure of both their lives. What she did think about was that Ulrika seemed to have gained suddenly such a dominant position in the house, that her power seemed to be widening from day to day and that she brought unheard of innovations into the management of the house. She wondered what had happened between her father and Ulrika and how she had gained such power that she would stand before him as equal to equal and was not afraid of him whose word used to intimidate all of them.

Whenever she asked Ulrika and tried to get her to explain, Ulrika evaded her. Even in the confidential nightly talks she was evasive. "Some other time," she would say; or, "That's not a thing that you can understand; it is a merely practical matter," and then she would be silent.

The quarrel between Ulrika and her father could not be hidden from her. That it was about money there was no doubt, nor yet the relation of this money to her mother, to her brother and sisters, and to herself. It seemed that Ulrika was fighting for them all against their father. But how had she gotten the right to do this? Why was it that she could put their father into such rages?

It would be useless to turn to her sisters, they would not even answer. Moreover they were constantly with Ulrika and never finished telling their secrets. Lothar did not count. He was always busy; he had a crowd of new acquaintances whom he met in luxurious places. So there was only her mother left. But Ulrika prevented this, talking a great deal about the nervous shock that Christine had suffered and insisting that she be most carefully spared. Out of thankfulness to this faithful friend Josephine gave in to her orders, and in obedience to Ulrika only spent those hours with her mother when Ulrika was there. The excitable and vacillating spirit of her mother was not calculated to quiet her fears.

The evening when her sisters had gone to the theatre she heard the voice of Ulrika talking uninterruptedly in her father's room. It did not sound like a quarrel to her, but as if it were borne on the air to her, she had a vivid impression of what was happening to her father, saw his face distorted by ineffectual wrath. Then when everything was still again, restlessness drew her from her room and she was astounded to see Ulrika and her father, peaceful, in the sitting room, Ulrika sitting at his feet in the act of drawing off his boots. She had been prepared for anything, but not for this, and the sight did not in the least serve to calm her, but moved her with a sense of something secretive and fearful, not only the rigid position of her father, his drawn features and helpless blinking eyes, but Ulrika's servile attitude which did not seem to suit her character. After Ulrika's unfriendly question she left the room and went back to her own, got up again and decided to go to her mother. She could reach her through the corridor and her sisters' room.

Christine lay upon a sofa, cowering in a corner like a little bird that has fallen from its nest. Her look was one of listening and anxiety.

"Mother, what's happening to us exactly?" asked Josephine with hard-won calm.

"What ought to have happened long ago, my child," Christine answered, looking out into vacancy, "but we have been too weak and too cowardly."

"I don't understand what you mean," Josephine said, shaking her head. "It seems as if you had some misunderstanding with father. Why don't you talk it over with him? Why is it that only Ulrika speaks to him?"

"You have already heard," Christine said abstractedly; "I am too weak and too cowardly, moreover I hardly know what I should have to say to your father."

"To my father? To your husband?" whispered Josephine timidly. "It is not you who say that, mother?"

"Yes, Josephine, it is I, I and none other," Christine replied; "my husband, yes, if you will; but also my jailor. Your father, yes; in as far as he got you into the world. But that is all he did do for you. He did not treat me as a friend, that has only just been discovered, and so he has no further claim upon my friendship. Pardon my bitterness, Josephine; this is not for your ears; you are a child still and ought not to judge such tragic circumstances."

Josephine looked at her a minute steadily. "I am no child," she said then, "and if I were, childhood is only a burden."

Overcome by this utterance, Christine stretched out both arms and Josephine bent down and drew her mother's hands to her lips. "You speak of sad circumstances, mother," she said surprised; "what sort of circumstances? Why do I know nothing of them? Am I no longer worthy of your confidence?"

"No, no," said Christine confused; "Ulrika and I thought we would not trouble you and drag you into the cleft which had suddenly opened in our family. We wanted to spare you as long as we could. But I really can't do it any longer, and Ulrika will hardly object now if I tell you about it."

Hastily and in outline she told Josephine as she sat

quietly listening, how Ulrika had succeeded in finding out about the tremendous wealth of her father. Such a
discovery naturally must change their whole lives; apart from
the fact that new moral rights had been given her by the
prolonged secrecy and hateful material deprivations that she
had suffered, her whole position as a wife and mother would
be placed upon a surer foundation. "What that means, you
can guess," she ended; "we all feel as if we had been buried
alive and were now stepping out of the tomb."

Josephine, her head bent down, answered nothing for a
long time, then she began faltering; "I don't understand you,
mother. Everything that you say is a puzzle to me. You
say that father is tremendously rich, and that he kept his
riches a secret. Had he no right to do that? After all, it
seems to me, that he can do what he wants with what he
has earned by his own work, his knowledge, and his industry.
Perhaps he had adequate reasons for keeping quiet about his
possessions. Have you asked him about it? You ought at
least to listen to him. Has one any right to take out of his
hand what is so exclusively and unquestionably his own? You
speak of material deprivations. But did we suffer any deprivations, mother? Were we hungry? Were we cold? I
mean cold as the poor are cold. Did we have no shelter, no
clothes and no shoes? How can you talk of deprivations;
you know well how many people fight in despair for bread,
you know how many people out there in the whirl of life go
down, and their lives are just as precious as our lives. Of
course, it wasn't easy for you. You have never been free
of care and you have had to humble yourself on account of the
miserable money; but after all weren't they little cares and
little humiliations, and isn't it really sinful to complain of
them seriously? It is your opinion that a man, a father, must
give and portion out just what he earns and possesses; that
those who belong to him should know of his possessions in
order that they should never deny themselves a wish. But I
don't think so, mother. I think that we have no rights except
those he gives us. Teach me, if you believe otherwise."

Christine looked at her daughter surprised. She pressed her

clasped hands under her chin and shut her eyes. "How self-righteous you are, Josephine," she said suddenly, "how self-righteous you are!"

"Really, mother," said Josephine frightened; "how? Teach me then."

"Think then," Christine went on with more self-control, "what would you think of a person who had bound you to comradeship, for better or worse, for a whole lifetime and who rewarded your share of the trouble, your little contribution toward existence with distrust and secrecy? Take it for granted you had lived at his side, looked after his possessions and got indeed your living but all the time you had longed, longed your very heart out of your body—say, for a bit of bright-coloured stuff. Say, that you lived in solitude with him, that he did everything to cut you off from people, that no temptations might come near you, that your life might be narrowed down to just his home, and that you submitted without murmuring; but still you yearned for that bit of bright-coloured stuff. He knew you yearned for it but said it was impossible to give it to you. You suffer: it may be a foolish suffering but still you suffer; for there is such a thing as the hunger of the eye, of the soul, of the imagination and that is sometimes as hard to bear as suffering of the body. But finally with time you give up, convinced that it is necessity; and then fate leads you to find, in some hiding-place that he has made, whole mountains of your bright-coloured stuff; a little would have been enough for you, would have made you happy, and he, your life-companion, had hidden it away only that he might keep it; do you understand? Just to have it, not to give it up, not to let you be happy; what would you do? What would you think? What would happen in your heart?"

"I don't know, mother," Josephine murmured so she could hardly be heard. "There is something wrong about your simile, but I can't tell what." She felt all the time something strange in her mother's manner and voice—something that did not harmonise with her whom she knew and loved and she had not the strength to reply.

"Deceit?" asked Christine hurt. "What is deceitful about it? You can't fathom it because it is unfathomable. The truth lies on the palm of my hand. I have been the battering-ram long enough and the means of his savings. My life has been drained to the dregs. I am a wife and yet no wife; do you understand? I have borne five children and that is all I have done as a wife. Warmth, protection, shelter, love—as a wife I have had none of these. Don't be so puritanical, Josephine; you know me better than the others; I am fifty-one years old and look," she drew the hairpins out of her hair with painful, hasty movements and let it fall over her shoulders, "my hair isn't even grey yet. That means that my inward emotions are not grey yet. But everything else is old about me, Josephine. Old, yes, and tired. But my piece of bright-coloured stuff I will not forego, not now. I am going to have a little sunshine; I yearn for it, I am going to have gay faces about me and lights shining and a little beauty and freedom blooming. In my youth that was all a dream; to have holidays and to spend money joyously, and to have guests not only when it was gross necessity. My forefathers had such things but I came too late. Everything about me was small and covetous and niggardly and frosty. Without you I should have broken under it and now you, you blame me, Josephine?"

She sank back on the cushion and turned her face to the wall. Josephine bent over and breathed a kiss on her mother's temple. "I will try to understand, mother," she said tenderly. "Don't be angry with me; it is all so new and so strange." Looking up she shuddered, for there stood Ulrika in the doorway. She looked at the mother and daughter irritated. "Any one dead?" she asked harshly. "One might imagine there was some one dead in the house." She knew at once what had happened. Josephine looked at her with wide-open eyes. She sat down on a chair and folded her hands. "Mother has told me everything, Ulrika. It was time to do it. Why should I alone not know?"

"Well, and how did the Fräulein Josephine take it?" asked Ulrika sharply, with displeasure. "It seems she does not look with favourable eyes upon our great changes. Perhaps she takes no pleasure in being rich. Or does she?"

"Being rich?" Josephine said to herself. "Does that really mean so much, Ulrika? Does it mean so much to you? What difference does it make anyway?"

"And she asks that!" cried Ulrika and pressed her hands against her cheeks. "She asks that! Suppose you lay under an apricot tree and the sweet sap dripped into your mouth. And yet you need not stretch out a finger to pick what dripped and dripped and your mouth was full of the sweetness and freshness. Or imagine you are surrounded by a hundred thousand little brownies to fulfil your wishes before you speak them, swifter even than the spirits of Aladdin's lamp; think of that and you need not ask."

"A real fool's paradise," interrupted Josephine. "But then I don't want a fool's paradise."

"Call it a fool's paradise if you like," said Ulrika, speaking ever more vehemently; "at any rate you have the key that opens all doors, and the magic formula that bends all backs. The whole world will drape itself in flags for you; and every one will strew roses in the path before you. Wherever you go there will be music and joy and laughter; you will be recognised everywhere and paid court to, and the completest kill-joy and misanthropist will try to please you. Do you despise that, perhaps? Do you find humanity so kindly and serviceable? Is it pleasanter to wander through a vale of woe, with sighing spirits than through a paradise? Even if the paradise may fade in the wash? But your fate, what could be more splendid than that, what could you dream better? It is the promised land where milk and honey flow, and it is I who have brought you there, I, Ulrika, who have taken you by the hand and said: 'Now breathe out, freely, now enjoy.' "

"Enjoy, that is a strange word," said Josephine, who was less and less happy as Ulrika became more and more enthusiastic. "It is like the sweet apricot sap, I fancy; it does not last long; it cloys you and you long for something bitter and tonic."

"How clever, how Methuselah-clever!" mocked Ulrika. "Tell her, Frau Christine, that you have drunken your bitterness to the very dregs. But no one will prevent you from taking your heart to the waters where you may sit down and weep. But never forget that riches make freedom, and that idiots who dream of sufficiency and potato soup cannot satisfy a single starving person that way, nor give a single free outlook or lift any one out of the mire. Have you thought of that, you newly born wise man?"

Again Josephine looked at her, but this time her look cleared up.

"It is half-past ten o'clock and your mother ought to be in bed." Ulrika rose, and putting her arm around Josephine she led her away.

Josephine was weaponless. There was a conquering power in Ulrika that she could not withstand. Unalarmed, she tore down whatever stood in her way; even the clouds in another's mind she blew away with her powerful breath; the obstacles that her foot found as she walked she threw aside. Her laugh was contagious, her words were living, her suppleness and caressing ways strengthened and enticed; her abrupt, fearless candour scattered doubt; and Josephine felt a sort of shame when they reached her room and she offered her hand, for Ulrika did not want to come in with her.

"Yet you must know, Ulrika, that though father has all of you against him, I am on his side."

Ulrika's look darkened, but she said nothing. When she got outside she murmured: "We'll see, my dear. We'll find out what has to be done to you." In Christine's room she found little things to do, pulled the curtains, gathered up covers and put them on the chair, placed the night light on its table, filled a carafe of water, lingering, as she said mockingly, "to put things to rights." Then she stood before the mirror, pulled at her hair and said with a deep, short laugh: "Now we've got him."

As Christine looked up interested, she added hastily: "It's not as if he had promised anything or come to an explanation. We haven't got that far yet. But he has begun to feel our resolute will and to creep into his last entrenchments. And we'll have to drive him out of those."

"If it might only be done by kindness and persuasion, Ulrika," said Christine. "Nothing is worse than this feeling of catastrophe in the house. It wears on me."

"Certainly with kindness and persuasion," said Ulrika, ill-humoured. "I am kind from morning to evening and do nothing but persuade. I am tired to death of my own voice. But you are quite right, the more so as now we can see that he will soon yield. We can't do very much with our eighteen thousand gulden and we'll have to set the play going. But good night, my dearest, sleep well."

Christine held her hand. "I hope you won't leave us in the lurch," she said; "even if it were only that thereby you would rob me of my right to pay off the debt of gratitude that began when I first saw you; that would be bad enough."

"Don't talk to me about gratitude," said Ulrika impatiently. "Thanks are payments and Ulrika does not allow herself to be paid. From head to foot she is priceless."

Christine laughed and Ulrika joined in.

A few minutes later she stood shading the candle by the bed of the sleeping Josephine. She breathed deep, threw out her chest and smiled like one who has done a good day's work. While she slowly undressed she threw a glance into the mirror, nodded to herself appreciatively, but a little condescendingly, lay down and folded her hands over her beautifully formed breast and yawned comfortably. Outside in the corridor the sisters and Lothar were coming in from the theatre. And as the yawn disappeared, she said: "This mattress is no good. To-morrow I must look around for a comfortable bed."

She could not sleep. It was not only the uncomfortable mattress that kept her awake. She was thinking of Josephine and she was afraid that Josephine might interrupt the work that was going on with so much promise. For a long time she stared with drawn brows into the darkness; but at last she was clear about the way she must go about it.

Josephine came halfway to her. The next day she asked

Ulrika just what she had meant with her hints at the help which riches might offer. Ulrika at first talked in general terms, but let her see that she had something particular in mind. There were so many miserable people in the world she said, and the worst cases were to be found just where one's conscience would not allow one to feel down in one's pocket and get out a few thalers to throw on the table. Such people could not be helped with money but only with work to which one was willing to sacrifice one's days and one's time. But who could give time to it except the rich? The poor had not time enough for themselves.

As Josephine begged for clearer explanation, Ulrika told her that when she sat, idle and full of care, in her attic room in the Dorothea Street, she had often looked across at the opposite houses and what she had seen there had made so deep an impression that the tears rose in her eyes. There were blind people; blind men, blind women, blind youths and hoary old men, blind maidens and matrons, about twenty people. They moved like shadow-figures, as if they were not made of flesh and blood at all, strangely quiet most of the time, but sometimes they shouted shrill words at each other or broke out into harsh laughter. Sometimes she had heard weeping, screaming, scolding and it sounded as if it came from the underworld, the kingdom of the damned. But the most frightful thing of all was their eyes, this colourless gelatine, the lids shut from lack of functioning and with that expression of extinction in all the features, the groping of their hands and the seeking of their feet. She had enquired about it and had been told that it was a private institution, founded by a rich man, a certain Doctor Ritter who had lost his wife and six children with cholera in one week. She used to go again and again to the window, but because looking on as an outsider at a circus seemed to her ugly and unworthy, she had resolved one day to go over, driven by the dumb longing to do something, to help in some way, for amongst these creatures without any light—and there were thousands like them—one person who could see was like an all-powerful God. But in her own uncertain and limited circumstances, which kept her constantly anxious for bread and the barest needs of the body, what could she do?

Any one, however, relieved from such cares, might be a messenger from Heaven; from the simple taking them out and guiding them to the difficult and most needed work of all, that of preparing them reading matter, here was a real field for charitable help.

"Reading? Can they read?" said Josephine surprised.

Then Ulrika explained the Braille system of writing for the blind; how by a system of raised letters everything printed and visible was translated into something tangible; the blind touched it and the ends of the fingers were turned into eyes.

Josephine considered and it was not difficult to notice that what she had heard was fermenting in her. The next morning Josephine asked her to go with her to the Institute. Ulrika had expected this and was at once prepared. And as she had hoped, this little world of the blind made a powerful impression on Josephine's inexperienced spirit. Without further consideration she offered her services, and went back again the same afternoon and remained until evening. That night she discussed for hours with Ulrika the tasks that had grown up about her and declared with eagerness her conviction that what she was about to do was useful and right and would put an end to the contemptible condition of laziness and ignorance in which she had lived. She expressed new thankfulness and admiration for Ulrika also, who knew so well how to lighten the dark and confused paths of her life.

It was easy to foresee that she would at once busy herself with the writing for the blind, as this task demanded the highest measure of patience, exactitude, and industry. Every institute of this kind demanded chiefly help for the library of their inmates and the head of the Ritter Institute immediately secured Josephine for this task. After a few hours of instruction she was able to begin independent work; and one day the metal tablets and all the tools were brought over to the house. Josephine moved the table up to the window, spread out her apparatus, and from that moment was lost to the world.

She had no other interest than this; no other goal; she did not hear what they were saying about her; seven, eight, yes, even nine hours a day, and often in the evenings she would sit with a stylus in her hand and bore into the little grating of the tablet, forming the letters. She had chosen Schiller's *Don Carlos* and at first she was glad when she had accomplished fifty stanzas a day, but little by little they grew to a hundred and a hundred and twenty. But her cheeks lost all colour, and her fingers became callous and the rims of her eyes red.

In vain Ulrika warned and scolded. But to herself she said contentedly, "She is busy and out of the way." The scruples and anxieties that she expressed to Christine were pure comedy. If at first Christine did not refuse her consent to Josephine's activities she was now fairly frightened by her absorption. Ulrika upheld her in her fears and pointed out to her that only a stern motherly command could turn aside the danger. But Christine could not bring herself to this point; she was not capable of a decisive word with Josephine's eyes resting upon her with so earnest and penetrating a look. She tried begging, in the end, even with tears; but as soon as Josephine showed herself wavering and inclined to yield, Ulrika would shake her head when they were alone and make ironic mocking remarks about sheltered young ladies, who began their tasks with great resolution and exaggerated earnestness but gave up at the first obstacle. Josephine replied: "You must not say that, Ulrika, it is unjust," and she doubled her exertions.

"It is foolish of you to work here in the house where so much is going on," said Ulrika. "Why don't you arrange a little work place in the Institute? There is surely a quiet corner to be found there. And there nobody will control you or disturb you, and moreover they won't let you sit all day at that nerve-racking machine. There are plenty of other things to do; you can read to the blind, take them out on walks, and live with them as a human being. I don't think your mother would have anything against it."

Josephine followed her advice. She left the house early in

the morning and often would not come back until late in the evening. When Christine asked after her or expressed anxiety over her absence, Ulrika said: "Don't bother about her. It is better to let her work it out herself. Some day the whole business will be a bore to her, and she will come back home and be the same little gentle daughter of the house as formerly."

But from time to time, when in despite of what she had said no change came, she shot little poisoned arrows into Christine's innocent heart, spoke casually of Josephine's desire for independence, her lack of family feeling, and her false ideas of freedom which had done her harm as it had many others.

Christine was very sad; she had a feeling of loss. She had a great deal of leisure, for Ulrika would not allow her the slightest care in the house and she became a prey to her own thoughts. Ulrika seeing that this was not desirable found an unfailing and simple means to hinder it. She had noticed that the new won freedom and leisure had awakened in Christine the desire for mental activity and she used this desire to fill up Christine's lonely hours. She bought books upon books; every day she brought in a new package of them and Christine seized eagerly upon the nourishment which she had had to forego since her youth. She began to read and would not stop. She read the long evenings through and sometimes half the night or all night, and then sank into a narcotic dream that gradually veiled from her the whole of reality.

CHAPTER XII

"MON HÉROS QUOIQUE PETIT . . ."

THE seed planted by the well-known hand, falling into fertile soil, sent up shoots on all sides. There was no lack of results; the luxurious growth rewarded the gardener. Whatever came into the circle of her influence was changed as by the touch of a magic staff. People were changed, things were changed; the old became new, the crooked straight, the broken made room for the unused, and the faded became shining. The well-appointed servants obeyed a gesture; serving arms without number and in eager haste stretched themselves out, and to the fulness of demand came the fulness of supply. She remembered that as a child when she stood upon the highway tired from a long walk she had uttered an Abracadabra and a great golden coach with liveried lackeys had rolled up and she had sat down in it and, to the astonishment of all the people, rolled away. Then the golden coach was a fancy of the imagination but now the Abracadabra had brought tangible results.

Even the astonishment of the people was not all imagination. The striking change in the once modest household was the talk of the town and spread from circle to circle until curiosity and notice were aroused everywhere. The news that the family was to move into the Chamfort palace made a real sensation and quick-footed gossip exaggerated at once the riches of the antique dealer. People talked about it in the streets and in the coffee-houses. Some said they had always known it or at least guessed it; some shrugged their shoulders as if everything was not all right; and some flattered themselves with groundless hopes—for instance, various young people of the better social class who heard that there were three marriageable daughters; others burst with envy and ill-will.

142

When Mylius found himself the central point of public interest he lost his head entirely. That was just what he had feared, the menace of his dreams. He did not know where to hide. He looked like an escaped convict. Any one who did not know him would think, upon seeing him, that he was marked with a brand of indelible shame. His manners were crabbed, his looks grim and shy. In his shop he refused to see any one and locked himself up in his office. On his way to and from home he chose the out-of-the-way side streets and slunk along the walls of the houses. He no longer went to the coffee-house in Baker Street. If people greeted him he turned away; and if an acquaintance spoke to him he growled like an ill-tempered dog and passed on. When he reached home he slammed the front door, hastened into his own room, turned the key, and standing before his cupboard he swallowed quickly the cold meal which he kept in his drawer for provisions. If one of the children met him, he never looked up; he did not bother about Christine; and since the last meeting he had shunned Ulrika with fury, contempt, vengeance, and secret longing in his heart.

Ulrika was waiting her time for she realised that he did not admit himself conquered.

One day shortly after dinner he stood on the threshold of the kitchen and to the fright of the three kitchen maids, he said suddenly: "You were employed without my consent, I herewith give you notice to leave. In three days I don't want to see any of you here."

They looked at each other in amazement and then at him, but in the meantime Ulrika had come. As usual, when he was in the house, she was spying about, in wait for some unpleasant accident. She stood behind Mylius and made three signs, waved her hand before her face and then touched her forehead with her finger. Then she stepped forward and asked, "What are you doing in the kitchen, Herr Mylius?"

"I have allowed myself to use my rights as master," he answered sullenly. "I have given these women notice."

"Given notice?" said Ulrika, pretending to be greatly surprised. "Why? Have you any reason for dissatisfaction or any complaint to make? We, Frau Christine and I, are quite contented and I think that is sufficient. But if you have complaints to make, you must be so good as to make them to me. It was all a misunderstanding, girls." She turned to the three amazed, staring servants, "You need think of it no more."

She took Mylius by the arm and left the kitchen with him.

At the door of the living room Mylius stopped short and choked out with difficulty: "So I am no longer master in this house? You are determined to seize my authority from me and to rule yourself? I only want to know. Yes or no?"

"Let's be calm, Herr Mylius," Ulrika replied with complete indifference. "Don't eat me up. I have told you often enough that you get nothing out of me by using that tone. Your whole method is a mistaken one. As far as authority goes, I don't want to interfere with anybody. But I have never heard that the authority of the father of a family could be shown by dismissing, without reason, the servants whom his wife has engaged. Such a foolish action does not show authority, it destroys it. I beg you now, for the last time, not to interfere with the arrangements I make and also to let my authority stand."

Mylius stood before her like a chidden school boy. He gnashed his teeth. "Ah, the method is false you think," he murmured after a while and drew his brows together. "All right; you come into my room a minute, please."

She followed him this time in unassumed amazement. He sat down on a chair, folded his arms and looked at her with a penetrating distrustful look. "Let's get down to business," he said. "We will make a bargain in the right way. I am ready. How much do you want?"

Ulrika's eyes narrowed for a moment. "I don't understand a word," she said. "A bargain about what? How much do I want for what?"

Mylius shrugged his shoulders impatiently. "But, honoured lady," he croaked, "don't try to pretend you can't count three. We are here alone to make a bargain. You know very well what I want. Since it pleases you to play that you are shame-faced, I must take the initiative and ask without any beating

about the bush: How much do you want to get out of this
house within twenty-four hours, to leave the town and never
come back again? You may think it over or answer at once,
but name an adequate sum."

A hateful gleam shone from Ulrika's face. But she gathered
herself together and smiled pleasantly. "What would it be
worth to you?" she asked cautiously.

Mylius smacked his lips. "It's hard on me," he answered
thoughtfully. "I am making a colossal sacrifice and really
for nothing. But I am willing to go very far to do you a
favour; shall we say three thousand gulden?"

A little cooing laugh, like a pigeon's call, sputtered out of
Ulrika's throat. "You miser!" she teased.

"Too little?" Mylius asked restlessly. "And yet, think, that
is quite a considerable sum for you. With that your future
would be fairly well secured. It would really be culpable to
turn aside such an offer."

Again the half-stifled cooing laugh. "You miser!" was all
that Ulrika answered.

"All right, I'll go the limit and say five thousand. But I
advise you to accept it before I repent."

Ulrika put her hands on her hips and broke out: "Will you
look at the man! A curiosity such as there is none to match
him in his whole shop! He wants to buy me! He wants to
buy me for money! And I am to be cheap, too! He wants to
buy me cheap! Three thousand, five thousand, as if I were
up at auction; now one, two, three! Zip, zip, little hen, come,
eat the little worm! This is the place to make studies in manners and customs! Open your safe and let me hear the
money! Coins in a bag, aha! But you have unfortunately
forgotten that I am not a smoky chest or a worn-out grave
monument but something quite different, a thing for which
the gentleman has very little power of appraisement. I am,
sir, obediently yours."

And therewith she whizzed out of the room and left Mylius
sitting there annihilated.

He did not even guess now how irrevocably he had put himself in Ulrika's power by this hasty step. Now he really had

a guilty conscience in her presence and in his speech she had
a hold upon him and a powerful one, too.

The mistake that he had made began to writhe in him. He
could not forget the indignant, flaming face. It struck him
as singularly attractive—that face; it had features of fine
nobility. And as his bribe had failed, he had the further vexation of anger against himself.

Now his whole effort was to conciliate her. It was possible
that one could reach an agreement in some kindly way. He
overcame his aversion toward the family, an aversion that had
consumed him ever since the great rebellion and he appeared
sometimes unexpectedly in the living room. He would look
at Ulrika in embarrassment, with his red, lashless eyes, or try
to catch her glance, and assume an aggrieved manner. Ulrika
appeared never to see him. When he came near her she threw
up her head and looked in the other direction.

His mouth got dry. She rose constantly in his estimation.
Either she was an infernally cunning creature, he reasoned, or
she really didn't care anything about money. But was such
a thing possible? Was there a human being in the whole world
deaf to such an enticement? Was she a virtuous heroine,
proud and unheedful of her own interest? Was that probable?
Did not the whole of experience reject the thought? Everything had its price, some price. And was she serving like
Jacob without reward? he brooded; but for whom? Why?
There must at least be a Rachel somewhere; who was the
Rachel for whom she served?

There came a day in which Ulrika seemed to view his sins
more gently. To get into her good graces, he had asked
her to play piquet, remembering that she had asked him some
weeks back if he knew the game. After some hesitation she
consented. Her whole manner seemed to say: "I am a good
fellow and bear no grudges." He played very badly. After
he had lost the first rubber and paid up twenty-six kreuzer, he
began to complain of his nerves and that his head hurt. Ulrika
at once showed kindly interest and asked him to describe his
symptoms. When he had finished she said that it all showed
how correct her first diagnosis was. She brought in a medical

treatise, which she owned and opened it at the article headed
LIVER. When he saw that her opinion and warning were actually confirmed in print, he became really frightened and
anxious. She gave him certain rules to live by and he promised to follow them.

The next morning he had to drink a curative water and lie
down an hour and a half after dinner. His diet was very strict.
If he failed to follow the prescription, she became really angry
and he had to beg her forgiveness.

During the prescribed rest-hour she sat by him to entertain
him. His condition furnished the material for it. She strenu-
ously discouraged sending for the doctor. She had had the
worst of experiences with doctors. She told all the experiences. It was a frightful picture. Doctors always cured what
they undertook to cure. They took a disease for granted and
the patient had to have it. And no matter how completely
they had deceived themselves they would never recognise their
error but go right on stupidly, since medical etiquette did not
allow them to admit an error to the laity; better that the laity
should give up the ghost. His colleagues would naturally stand
solidly behind him, and so people were heartlessly sacrificed,
who had nothing serious the matter with them, rather than
let the officially sealed science be suspect. She had known
one fellow who would look at the patient and enunciate some
deep-sounding phrases and then run home to look up the symptoms in a book. Another had cured a riding master of cancer
but it turned out to be tape-worm and another had treated a
farmer's wife for dropsy and it turned out in a few months
that she was pregnant. The really great doctors knew it but
there were very few really great in any profession; if it were
not for a few really great the whole science of medicine would
break like a bubble. But why throw money out of the
window?

That was water to Mylius's mill; first, because he hated to
spend money and second, because he too distrusted men down
to the ground and in all their activities. The related string
trembled sympathetically. He could not get away from the
admiration he felt for Ulrika's self-government, the wisdom

of her judgment, her penetrating mind. What a woman, he thought; how good it would be to own her.

In a short time he began to feel all the ills that she had told him about. She knew how to bring up a hypochondriac, for she had a wide knowledge of what fear is in others and a perfidious system of questioning, by which she attached every single organ of the body to a bad conscience. And so the symptoms grew: a dislike for eating and drinking alternating with a devouring hunger and perishing thirst; a feeling of dizziness when one made quick movements; restless sleep and nagging dreams; a dull pressure in the right side; a fluttering pulse; a tendency to excitement and outbreaks of rage.

Ulrika studied it all lovingly and when she gathered all her conclusions together it didn't sound very comforting. But she also knew how to divert and amuse and when she was tired of hearing of the dreadful apprehensions and inner upsets she took shelter in piquet where her merriment and ambition amused him and brought a grin to his face. And so at last she caught him entirely and those evenings when she had no time for him he seemed lost and forsaken.

He shut his eyes completely to what was going on in the house. The ant-like activity, the coming and going of delivery wagons, letter carriers, messengers, invitations, and visitors he wiped from the tablets of his perception. Sometimes there was such a racket that he could not find a quiet corner. In the corridor the servants would be chattering; in the kitchen some one was hammering; chests were being packed and taken away; curtains were being taken down from the windows; Christine was running to the left and Ulrika to the right; a dressmaker was asking for Fräulein Esther and a tailor for Herr Lothar; a jeweller brought an inexplicable message; a furniture dealer came to ask for time before he made his delivery; a decorator wanted to know about the plans for lighting the grand staircase; a carriage dealer was making a very convincing offer in the hurly-burly; Aimée came in with a young Russian greyhound which she had just bought; the whole place was like a railroad station. A hundred times one heard the name, "Ulrika"; everything depended upon her;

her word went; she had to decide, to advise, to meditate, to soothe and to inspire.

Mylius pressed his hands over his ears and when the noise got too wild he shortened his siesta and went down to his shop. But he took no more pleasure in his business. The beautiful, old, costly things had lost their hidden life. The battle for them enticed him no more. That deceptive, exciting increase in their worth as time went on, the cunning depression of prices when he bought, which brought all his mental powers into play, had no charm for him now. He left the business to the blue-spectacled Herr Schmidt and even made no objection to his proposal that he have an assistant. Heretofore he had spent hours daily in the care of his gigantic fortune, the ordering of his papers, his bank certificates, his tax assessments, the keeping of his books, his public and his secret accounts; now all that tired and bored him. "I am not able to do it any longer," he complained. He looked around for a trustworthy man upon whom he could throw the burden of the work and the responsibility. He thought of retiring from business with his present fortune.

Herr Schmidt, who had served him silently and faithfully for twenty years and knew many of his secrets, could not conceal his horror at the changed conditions.

"Did you ever hear of the Danaides, my dear Schmidt?" Mylius asked in a resigned tone. "These Danaides were people who were supposed to use sieves to fill up a barrel; but everything ran out of the bottom which they carefully put in at the top. Pitiful, isn't it? Now you see that is what has happened to me. Since everything runs out at the bottom, I can take no more pleasure in creating."

And moreover, he went on to himself, there is damned little sense in gathering together and increasing one's possessions when death has already made its nest in me. Let them inherit; inherit and laugh. But one thing I will not do for them, in my lifetime, they sha'n't spend it all as they please. What can be saved must be saved. Old Mylius will not turn into a thief and robber of himself.

And so his inborn nature remained unbroken and unbreak-

able despite all attempts to bend it and Ulrika found it out.
She had calculated that Christine would have to have the sum
of a hundred thousand gulden at her disposal for the current
expenses of the year, the cost of moving, the furnishings, repairs, rent, and the new mode of living. After a closer calculation she said that this sum would do for a beginning, but
was not enough to go on with full freedom from care, and
one would be forced to deal with Mylius again, and as she
had foreseen, fight down his despairing opposition. Therefore
she resolved upon an important step and a consultation to
which she solemnly invited Mylius; and she demanded for
Christine, and in Christine's name, credit at the bank for three
hundred thousand gulden.

Mylius broke out into neurasthenic laughter. The sweat
stood out upon his forehead.

She began to persuade him. She talked for an hour and a
half. She brought all her psychology, imagination, cunning,
and patience into play. She appealed to his feeling as a father
and a husband; she pointed to the wasted fleeting existence and
the rightful demands of youth; she painted the beneficent
results of his generosity; the high respect of his fellow citizens; the love of his family, his old age surrounded by honour
and reverence; and with the same breath she drew horrible
pictures of his loneliness and invalidism; she overwhelmed him
with threats, pleas, sarcasms, accusations, contempt, and assurances of her devotion. She seized his ice-cold hands and
stroked them and as he still sat dumb and stiff and rigid on
his chair she called to him, trembling with anger, that he
might stay there with his miserliness and his filth—she was
going, she had had enough of it all; why should she eat up
her heart for others and talk her tongue sore? She was going
and would leave him alone in his tragic misery.

Then he roused himself. He tried to bargain with her.
"Nothing doing," said Ulrika, interrupting him. "Not a tenth
of a heller less will I take." Then he made the condition that
each quarter she should give him an exact accounting of how
the money was going, so that in case the expenditure should

exceed his means, he could recall his acquiescence. To this
Ulrika consented.

"Ugh!" she said to herself when she had gotten him to that
point and he had signed the order to the bank before her eyes.

Mylius dropped his head upon his hands with the gesture
of a broken man. He began to whimper low to himself that
he was a ruined man. "Why should all this be? Why?" he
cried in pain. "Only to eat and to drink and to dress. Can
any human being be so low that they ask me to sit here and
watch while my own flesh and blood flings itself into orgies,
rushes into the arms of vice, and gives itself up to debauchery?
And with my money, my hard-earned money! Don't let it
go on, my good Ulrika." He seized her hands and shook them.
"Stop this crime. Let me take it all back and I will be grateful to you to the end of my days." And the old man broke
into sobs that sounded like the creaking of rusty door-hinges.

Ulrika assured herself first that she had the signed order
and then she said severely: "If you excite yourself in this
way all my beautiful care of you will go for nothing. After
supper you must go to bed with a dose of bromide and a hot
bag on your stomach. That is soothing. And think a little.
What is it we are taking from you? Just your income. Nobody wants to touch your capital. Capital is holy—that I
understand. But your income? An income is like the tender
leaves of cabbage that are to be torn off and eaten. The roots
remain the same. Who would howl and wring their hands over
such a thing as that? You ought to be ashamed of yourself."

Mylius looked up at her in agony. "Promise me, swear to
me, my dear friend, that no abuse will be made. I see that I
carried my anxiety and economy too far and that your intentions are entirely noble. I put the knife to my own throat,
I know it, with my own hand. But stop extravagance, useless
expenditure, the love of display, and gluttony. I could not
live through it. I never had extravagant tastes, you know it.
I never drank wine; always travelled third-class and never
hired a carriage. I possess just two pairs of boots, one for
Sundays and one for week-days, and only one everyday suit,

and whenever I wanted to go to a place that cost an entrance ticket I denied myself. I always said: 'You can wait; the time will come when you can go in for nothing.' And it turned out true or if it did not, then I gave it up. All that is illusion: a moment's enjoyment and then it is past. It's only a crumb, after all, that each one gets, and though he may think he has something very glittering in his hand, when he looks at it, there is nothing there. The desire that I know may be fulfilled stays warm in my breast but the already fulfilled desire is dust and ashes. There's but little time between the getting drunk and the next day's headache and man ends in nothing after all. It is the man who can renounce who wins the crown. My children have no idea of the value of wealth, except, perhaps, Josephine. Christine is a weak reed; I have to turn to you. Watch over my property, Ulrika; swear that you will use it rationally and carefully."

Ulrika was amused at this continual swearing to old men, and she saw into the dark comedy of this clinging to her person. She said: "Don't bother! I know my duty. There is no need for an oath. And now you draw a heavy line through the past and begin a new life with us to-day."

He shook his head in deep melancholy. Ulrika hurried off and carried the signed order triumphantly to Christine and held it up before her eyes. Christine stammered: "I did not believe it was possible," and fell on the neck of her brave friend. Esther, Aimée, and Lothar were near-by and the moving scene brought them in; Esther saw the paper that painted her whole future gold and gave a cry of rapture; Lothar seized his sisters by the hands and all three of them danced around Ulrika, who, much moved, sniffed into her handkerchief. Josephine had just come home and saw the joyous scene from the threshold. The evening was well along and she was tired; even her surprise had something tired about it but that was not the only reason that her presence was chilling. Her sisters and brother already thought of her as a stranger; an embarrassed silence fell upon them and even Christine did not know just what to say.

In fact Josephine had closed accounts with such happenings.

So much took place that she did not quite understand that she had almost forgotten to be surprised.

She knew the goal of the happenings but the single steps of the changes were too confusing for her to be able to judge where they stood, even with her quiet attentiveness.

To-day, for example, most of the rooms were empty. The next morning a moving wagon was there and instead of the accustomed things one saw the naked walls. This was despite the fact that the actual move was to take place only in a fortnight, the middle of May; for Ulrika had decided that their new world should be ready to the last hammer blow and brush stroke before they left the old house.

"The dear rooms," Josephine thought, as she went thoughtfully from door to door; "here I was born, here I babbled my first syllables and fell with unsteady steps into my mother's arms, and she was everything, heaven, earth, light and sound. And now we are going away from it as if it were a ruin and others will come here and build an unknown life."

In every corner there lay some little child's dream carved in stone, and the vacant windows stared at her like dead eyes. This is not right, Josephine thought, and she shook her shoulders as though she were cold; it can't be right. She remembered that Ulrika had once said: "City children have no homes." The words ate into her heart now.

The next evening when she came home there were guests in the dining room. She was quite used to this; for weeks there had been constant, gay company, and as soon as she opened the house door she heard the joyous chatter of many voices. She did not know the people and had not the slightest desire to know them; she was always much too tired for that. But when she went into the kitchen to get her dinner, Nanette would tell her the names sometimes in a reverent tone, sometimes indifferently. Count Lex was mentioned oftenest and a Herr von Pillersdorf; and then a Baron Althann. "Why don't you go in too?" asked the friendly Nanette. "They are all so jolly." But Josephine answered: "I am too tired."

In the vestibule there were coats and stiff black hats and inimical looking canes and umbrellas. Her father walked through the corridor in his felt shoes, peeling an apple as he went. This depressed Josephine unspeakably though she did not know why. "Good evening, father," she whispered. He nodded to her without answering. She was holding a plate of asparagus in her hand and music sounded from the inner room, the piano played by a master, unmistakably. "That's Fräulein Ulrika's brother," Nanette told Josephine, slipping up to her side to listen, too.

When the piece was ended Josephine sat down on the bench in the hall, like a beggar, and bit off the heads of the asparagus. She heard four people saying "Good night" and wanted to escape but she noticed then that it was her mother who was going to her own room; almost immediately she rang for Nanette. Josephine sat still, her head against the wall and listened to the chattering voices. It did not last very long and then the tones of the piano began again, this time playing a prelude, and after a few bars a voice began to sing. It was Ulrika's voice, deep, not quite clear, but yet a well-sounding alto. She was singing a French comic song; Josephine understood the words, and could easily tell that the song was being accompanied by the acting and gestures of a soubrette. Suddenly she remembered how Ulrika had recited the little poem of the stork to her father and how, despite the innocent content of it she had been offended by Ulrika's posture and exaggerated gestures.

Ulrika sang:

> "Mon héros quoique petit
> est mutin comme un grand diable;
> sa bravoure et son esprit
> l'ont rendu considérable.
> Mais à table, mais à table
> il vaut encore mieux qu'au lit."

Josephine would have found nothing surprising in the text had it not been for the laughter that followed it; but then she blushed. She went to her room, went to bed and brooded long over Ulrika. When she saw Ulrika in imagination, she had a warm trustful feeling; but when she put this and that together and drew conclusions, she could get no concord out of

them, and the more she thought about it the stranger did the
picture become, and the more frightened she was.

It became an absolute torment until in the middle of her
thinking and doubting she fell asleep. She must have slept
heavily for two or three hours and then she awoke and faced
the torment again. She was accustomed when she awoke in
the night to hear Ulrika breathing from the other side of the
room, and she believed now that she heard the steady rhythm
of her breath, but when she listened more carefully it seemed
to her that the sleeper over there must be awake, for she heard
no sound.

"Ulrika!" she said hoarsely.

No answer came.

Then she struck a match and made a light. Ulrika was
not in the bed and the bed had been untouched. She looked
at her watch. It was half-past three. Through the windows
she could see the dawn breaking. The guests could no longer
be there, she said to herself; perhaps something had happened.
She saw now that Ulrika's clothes and stockings lay on the
chair by the bed, in a disorderly heap as usual. She was
seized by anxiety: perhaps something had happened to her
mother; perhaps she was ill and had called Ulrika. Fear
drove her; she slipped into her dressing gown and went out
to listen at her mother's door. She had hardly taken two steps
on tiptoe when the door of Lothar's bedroom opened, and
Ulrika appeared on the threshold in her nightdress. Her head
was thrown back; the candle light fell upon her gazelle-like,
slender figure; her hands were held up jestingly, and she
whispered, just hinting at the melody: "Mon héros quoique
petit . . ." With a light laugh she shut the door carefully;
and Josephine stood before her.

With a spring like a panther she seized the girl's shoulder.
"What are you spying round about for, girl?" she hissed.

But when she saw Josephine's pale, astonished face, with
its childish uncomprehending, brooding expression, in the twilight of the corridor she was angry at her own anger and self-
betrayal. She shook her thick, unbound, tousled hair and with
a nod toward Lothar's room she said in her usual chipper

voice: "He has a sore throat and a little fever; I made him some camomile tea."

Josephine knew that she lied. And she felt, although she looked down at the ground, the look of unending hatred in Ulrika's eyes. She wanted to do or say something to soften this incomprehensible hatred, but her whole being seemed dumb and fettered.

CHAPTER XIII

A CHAPTER WITH NO SPECIAL INCIDENTS

On the twentieth of May, a housewarming took place in the Mylius's palace, as it was now called, with a dinner of fifty people, a gipsy band, a dance, the garden illuminated, and every possible luxury.

"The beginning is the important thing," said Ulrika. "If a comedian has a successful début he can then allow himself to act badly from time to time. The public is clapping not so much what he does as his reputation."

The roomy house had big, middle-sized and small company rooms for which they had taken over a large part of the beautiful old Chamfort furniture. Every evening the marble salon, a widely famed show place, was thrown open to visitors.

Considering the shortness of the time and the fact that the Mylius family had no social connections, it was a noteworthy achievement of Ulrika's, that she had gathered together so many people of rank and social standing; and not only that but had managed it so that they fairly manœuvred for invitations. Still, it was not the very first entertainment she had given, though she tried to make herself and others believe it was. Ulrika understood baiting down to the ground. She had three baits for her hook: one for the curious, one for the ambitious, and one for the bored. Ulrika showed her sophisticated knowledge of the world when she said: "If I tell Frau von Berber that Frau von Gerber is coming, then Frau von Scherber gets jealous and Frau von Sperber begs to be allowed to come. When they are all four there they know what they can find at our house, and they come again because they have been there once. That's the way it is done, and that is the way society is founded."

She had managed the great undertaking with the help of

Count Lex and his friends, Pillersdorf and Althann. At pic-
nics, on excursions, jaunts, and at the theatres, they had learned
to know all the mothers, aunts, sisters, and cousins; people
were asked to call; and the calls were returned; no prejudice
could stand against the magic of millions. Aristocrats blessed
with ancestors condescended to the obscurely born, and those
whose caste was slowly sinking downwards, could only follow
the magnanimous example. "Not surprising in the least," said
Ulrika. "We have plenty of bacon and can catch mice."

By degrees it became known that one always got one's
money's worth at Mylius's. Everything there was costly, gen-
uine, abundant, the last especially in the matter of culinary
enjoyment. The lady of the house was quite a personality,
they said; one could see she was well brought up and of good
family; the older daughters (the youngest and the master of
the house were usually invisible) were interesting and charming creatures, more than could really be expected in heiresses
of such wealth. It should be mentioned that Ulrika let nothing go undone that could prepare her young friends and pupils
beforehand; they had been drilled by a dancing-master for
weeks; she taught them posture, the art of standing and walking, of dressing and carrying their heads and how in many
words to say nothing, and with few words to tell everything.
It seemed that she had in such matters extraordinary insight
and wisdom, and even better instinct.

She said: "The main thing is that you should learn words.
Believe me that all in all there are only about five hundred that
one needs to know. In this matter sophisticated people of
the world are no different from postmen and market-women.
They are just other words, and nothing else. But one must
learn to know them."

Or: "Two things you must understand and control; your
smile and your eyes. A married woman must not smile like
a girl and one looks at a General differently from the way one
looks at a Lieutenant. If you stretch your mouth and blow
out your nostrils at every witticism, as if it were irresistible,
people won't think much of your mind. A lady, even if she
has not a trace of mind, must know how to behave so that

the dullest bookworm shall not for a moment doubt her profound culture.   If you don't know anything, keep quiet, and
if you are afraid of saying something silly, hum the multiplication table to yourself softly and call your eyes into play,
that is what they are for.   I have known silly geese who could
look as if they had taken in the whole history of philosophy
with their mother's milk."

Esther and Aimée were apt pupils and followed her advice,
each in· her own way.   But a day came when they resolved
to be free of their guardian.   To obey the centrifugal instead
of the centripetal power, to break away from their solar system and wander through empty space.

One of the main attractions in the Mylius's salon was Vice-
Consul Woytich, whose brilliant playing upon the piano was
the admiration of all hearers.   Moreover his gift of conversation and inexhaustible fund of anecdote brought him an ever-
increasing popularity.   He knew all the celebrated and important people in Europe, or he said he knew them, for one
could not help suspecting sometimes that he was exaggerating
a little.   Still it was amusing.   For the name of a great man
rarely passed his lips without his appearing somewhat ridiculous; yes, Franz Woytich believed that all great men were
really ridiculous if you only looked at them from the right
point of view so that they became comprehensible and the excited reverence of the masses was alleviated.   That really was
amusing.   Everybody breathed more freely when a colossus
began to waver on his pedestal.   If any one were present, by
chance, who did not like this, one could always shut his mouth
with music, a tested means.   What cannot a virtuoso's hands
whitewash!

Often the question arose: who are these Woytichs?   And
information about the family, the property, the military grade
of the father did not satisfy, not even the familiar fact that
there was a Counsellor of the same name who lived upon the
echoes of his former fame.   But who was this Fräulein Woytich, who filled so important a place in the Mylius's house,
overseer, friend, guardian, or secret agent?   Neither very striking as to beauty or elegance, she somehow managed to draw

attention to herself. Candid to the point of curtness, bizarre to the point of repulsion, she yet had a swarm of young and old admirers around her, who idolised her, listened to her with rapturous attention and spared no pains to catch a glance from her shining oriental eyes. Wherein lay her charm? What was her attraction?

So the gossip went and naturally the voice finally reached Ulrika. She laughed. "The good people really don't know what to make of me," she said; "I cannot really take it amiss, for looked at by clear daylight, I am really the fox in the hen coop and I cannot complain of the disturbed cackle and frightened fluttering. If I only had time, I would explain myself to them, but fortunately for them, I have something better to do."

In fact her duties filled up the eighteen-hour day to the rim. She had two footmen, three housemaids, a parlor-maid, a chef, a cook, two scullery-maids, a watchman, a gardener, and two gardener's assistants to manage and overlook. As she was no longer able to do it entirely alone she got Christine's permission to send for her sister Anastasia, who held a poorly paid post as governess in the provinces. Anastasia Woytich was a silent, polite, moderately pretty, but rather sour-tempered young woman, with the empty look of a bird, who always jumped when she was spoken to as if she had been caught doing something wrong. Whether she loved her sister, feared or envied her could not be found out, but she took the chief burden of the management from her and Ulrika could dedicate herself with more freedom to representative duties.

She was bargaining for the purchase of a country house and brought it to a conclusion. She wrote all the invitations to the evening parties and discussed the visits to be paid with Esther and Aimée. She kept the accounts, all the household books, overlooked all major expenditure and attended to all correspondence. Here and there furniture was lacking in the house; a Chippendale desk for the library; all the furniture for the pavilion in the park; plants for the winter garden. She bought everything. Some of the things she brought right out of the Mylius shop, which Herr Schmidt for the present

was managing; for example, a costly Leroy clock and a wonderful English doll, one metre high which she placed in Esther's
room, not without silent plans for the future; for this strange
work excited in her a violent desire for possession.

Moreover she had to take care of Mylius, who lived in the
farthest wing of the house in stubborn loneliness and who
would allow no one else to come near him.

The day of the move he had suddenly disappeared. He did
not come home in the middle of the day and in the afternoon
he was nowhere to be found and he stayed away all evening.
The next morning Ulrika enquired for him at the shop,
although she was overwhelmed with work. Herr Schmidt
was embarrassed and pretended to know nothing. But Ulrika
could see that he knew where his chief was and in a quarter
of an hour she had found out where the poor old man had
hidden himself, namely, in Herr Schmidt's own house. Ulrika
took a carriage and went to the house in the suburbs. She
went up two or three flights of dark stairs, rang at the door,
waited, drew the rusty bell handle again, then heard steps
inside, the door was opened a crack, and Mylius's distrustful,
peering face showed itself. He was frightened when he saw
Ulrika, but allowed her to come in. She asked him harshly
what he was doing there. He replied that that was nobody's
business. It was her business she insisted, for his intention
to bring shame upon her and his family was perfectly clear
and she refused to leave the spot until he came with her.

With ironic satisfaction she saw that his resistance was
already partially broken down by her mere appearance. And
she felt too that the very sound of her voice worked like
magic upon him. He was uncomfortable and at odds with
himself. He was glad that she had come and although he put
on an air of silent and angry stubbornness he could not quite
hide the secret, shivering rapture that the sight of her gave
him. And so he let himself be taken home like a little boy
who has run away and is brought home again by his governess.

And so his dependence upon her was sealed, and the relation between them settled once and for all. An old man's
suffering and an old man's shame; he knew now what it was

that he could not resist; it was the voice—the voice; he could stand at a door, his ear pressed against the wood and with beating pulse listen to hear whether that voice was distinguishable anywhere. He had taken shelter under the roof of the gigantic palace and he trembled with happiness whenever that voice scolded him and mocked his hiding away. Oh, that irony, how it hit and tore wounds and yet was the oil that healed them up! Was there such a thing as irrevocable loss? The years, like milestones, lay along the vale of battle and had crushed something blooming and beautiful beneath them. And now he could only stand at the door, his ear pressed against the wood and listen, and listen—

He allowed no one to come to him and no one to speak to him. He would answer Ulrika only when he was questioned and when it happened that sometimes for a day or two she could not find time for the accustomed game of cards and did not appear at all, he would come down in the evening, appear suddenly to the painful surprise of his family and his guests, in the smoking room, creeping over the waxed floors in his felt slippers, staring with his red, lashless eyes disapprovingly, almost angrily at the strange people and going away again only when Ulrika accompanied him and patiently listened upstairs to the tale of his infirmities. He never asked after Christine; it was exactly as if she had died and he had no memory of her left.

On her side Christine gave herself no concern for him and had cut him off entirely from her life. She too demanded Ulrika's society and was put out when she had to do without it. Surrounded by her guests she laughed and chatted gaily, showed all the delicate traits of a refined roguishness, a thirst for knowledge, and real gratitude when others revealed their personality to her; she was enthusiastic over capacity, culture, and power. But as soon as she was alone, she withdrew at once from reality and shut herself up with her continual reading. Great packages of books were piled about her, lay on the chairs, sofas, floor, and tables. The novels of all nations, Balzac and Dickens, Daudet and Spielhagen, Edgren-Leffler and Tourgeniev, Boccaccio and Andersen; philosophic and popular science works, drama and poetry. Late in the night she cowered over her lamp and read, wallowed in the imaginative life, hastened from book to book, from figure to figure, from phantom to phantom. Morning found her yellow and faded; by degrees her body was coarsening. But when she had wandered until she was tired in the phantom world and no guests were on hand, she demanded that Ulrika be with her. Ulrika's presence was compensation for everything, for children and husband, books and the world. If only Ulrika were there, there was no need of opera and theatre, excursions and daily entertainments; Ulrika solved all problems, settled all counts, untied all knots, softened all hardship, explained all signs; she could induce sleep when the nerves were excited, and made the tired heart beat strong again. Ulrika was the impetus of all things, the very elixir and soul of things. Christine idolised her. She had no thought that did not cling to her or a breath that she did not share with her.

She had so much to do that Ulrika found it hard to be just to every one. She needed fine scales and well-prepared chess moves to save the necessary and worth-while from being swamped and darkened in the rush. On the one side she had plans to marry Esther to Count Lex; this project she never let out of sight, and it required all her skill and art of handling men; on the other hand she was troubled about Lothar, whose madness she was hardly able to rein in any more. On his own initiative he had given up the last class of the Gymnasium and led the life of an aristocratic do-nothing. His time was filled with costly love affairs, and not less costly comrades, and he often spent half the night away from home. Ulrika understood the depravity that burned his flesh; it burst out from the healthy bourgeoisie; the unfathomable stigma and vengeance of the ageing century.

She had foreseen degeneration; it was too, a part of her plan, but this was going faster than she approved. When she gave herself to the boy, she hoped to tie him to her and to still his burning desires and hold him a little longer. Her plans hung upon him; she needed him. Under no circumstances could she allow him to be alienated. She had taken it all lightly, had given herself lightly, for Nature had so created her. It was the passion of the senses—of the hour. A worthwhile man goes through such things, she had taught him, as if it were a blooming bower; worth only a longing sigh and a pleasant remembrance. "Two kinds of men," she said, "I hate as I do spiders and toads, the love-sick and the lustful. Everything beautiful and joyous goes under with such people."

But her calculations ran over. What she had not taken into consideration was that straw catches fire quicker than coal and burns out quicker too. She had to reproach herself with unwisdom, for having unbarred all doors to the desires of this weak, wild youth who was suffering from the curse of generations of desire. The clever magnanimous friend did not satisfy him long and he hungered for new sensations. Still Ulrika was the only one to whom he actually submitted and who had a controlling influence over him, until Edward Melander came into his life. He respected Ulrika; through her he had grown up, gained knowledge. He felt toward her a sort of animal gratitude. As she could no longer look out for him, or follow his wild courses, she begged Ferdinand Lex to watch him and keep him from bad comrades. Lex promised but he had not the endowment of a guard and much less that of the leader.

Ferry Lex, as he was called, was without fortune and up to his neck in debt. Around him and behind him everything lay in ruins. Some years ago he had been talked about more than was good for him. He had had a love affair with a beautiful, young actress and had run away with her to his mother's palace while she was absent. There the beautiful, youthful girl had shot herself in her bed at night. The circumstance threw a bad light on the young count, and the honourable, middle-class family of the young girl had spread the story that he himself had incited her to suicide because she was pregnant and he did not wish to be burdened with cares. At this point his private affairs underwent most unpleasant criticism. It was said that his mother, who was of questionable birth, had, as the mistress of a nobleman, merely bought a sham marriage and this gave cause for a lawsuit with his cousin for his inheritance. As far as Ulrika could see, he had not much chance to win. But Esther ought to be married as soon as possible. "Once she is Countess Lex, no cock will crow," Ulrika said, "and as for purity of blood, I'd like to know how many family trees could stand an investigation. Not a dozen in the whole court register of Gotha. At any rate, once at the altar the rest can be managed."

So she drove Lex about his business. The lawyer who was working for him seemed to Ulrika lukewarm. She went to another who was sly and ambitious and spurred on by Ulrika, promised to make the impossible possible. She advised Lex to get his creditors together and make an agreement privately. For if the hyenas scented the Mylius millions, he could not get away without paying a hundred per cent too much.

However when she returned in October with Christine from a trip, everything stood as before, and the lawsuit was dragging along hopelessly. Ulrika lost patience. She asserted that Esther was already compromised, and had a little quarrel with her as they drove in with Aimée and Anastasia to the city from the country villa where they had spent the summer. The truth was that Esther could not make up her mind to accept Ferdinand Lex. She and Aimée laughed a great deal at him secretly, at his red cheeks, his hastiness, his absentmindedness, the mediocre verses that he made, and the sentimental feelings that he liked to give way to. But the uncertainty of the situation only assumed a dangerous aspect when Edward Melander came to the house.

Ulrika had become acquainted with this young man a few weeks before she came into the Mylius's household, through an odd occurrence.

One late autumn afternoon, as she was walking in a hilly suburb west of the city, she had stopped at a peasant's house and bought a handful of grapes, and sat down with them in a picturesque spot on the banks of a brook. The sun had sunk below the horizon, the sky was flooded with carmine and gold, and Ulrika eating her grapes said aloud to herself: "What a wonderful evening." A voice answered behind her, "Especially for one who knows where he is going to spend the night."

She turned around surprised and saw a man with dirty boots and crumpled clothes lying in the grass, to whom she would have paid no attention, despite his touchingly discouraging remark, had she not noticed the almost maidenly beauty of his face. She let herself be drawn into a conversation; he told her that for three days he had been without a roof over his head and for two he had eaten nothing; his landlady had turned him out into the street, his possessions were all pawned, he had no relatives, no friends, in short he had come to the end of everything.

Ulrika, questioning him further, found that he was a student, that he had come from Schlesien to Vienna with a hundred gulden in April, and with the hundred gulden which he had earned as a tutor he had held out for a half year, sleeping by day and working by night; for night, he added bitterly, is always cheaper than day and spares one time-consuming acquaintances.

Ulrika acted like the resolute person she was. She went back to town with him and that evening he was already in lodgings for which he had paid in advance. Then he became ill from his privations and she nursed him. She brought him food and wine, she cleaned his room and made his bed, and was convinced by his conversation, during the progressive recovery, that she had not wasted time, money, and pains on an unworthy person.

He was a man after her own heart. Brains, a clear head, cool blood, and iron resolution. This was the more surprising as he had a body so delicate that every rough wind threatened it, and a gentleness and amiability that seemed almost Eastern and allowed no one to believe that this twenty-three-year-old youth had poverty and deprivation behind him.

He had tightly clenched teeth that one never saw. Ulrika taught him to reach the good that he wanted, however false the means. He had imagined that he could stand alone, full of knowledge, laden with energy, that he could, by dint of his genius, force people to put him in the situations that he thought belonged to him. That was naïve, though it did prove great self-confidence. Ulrika repudiated his pride entirely.

She showed him that in his position he needed people and that it was much more praiseworthy to accept servility and humiliation than to pass the best years of his life and best powers of his youth in an attic room in quixotic loneliness. In London she had made the acquaintance of a capitalist, who, when she had left England, had offered her his help and service whenever she might need them; it was a relationship which she only mentioned very casually.   She wrote to him, and asked a recommendation for a friend whose culture, inclinations, and gifts she would vouch for.   In five days she received an answer with a recommendation to President von Wallersheim, one of the most powerful and influential capitalists of the day.   She took him two works of Melander's, one, *Causes of Mortality and Their Relation to Civilisation*, and one, *On the Fixed Value of European Currency*.   The President read them and immediately felt a profound interest in the writer, sent for him to come, was not less interested in his personality, and Melander had a smooth road in front of him. Herr von Wallersheim gave him a salary, handed him over some difficult tasks, which Melander handled to his satisfaction, and which really did him honour; kept him, enchanted as he was by the qualities of the young man, near him; opened his house to him, prophesied a great future for him, and spoke of him as a veritable wonder.

And all this had happened within a year.   Besides being always at the command of his patron, Melander had gone to lectures, written a doctor's thesis, taken a degree, tried his examinations for the bar and was admitted, gave two or three evenings a week to his social engagements, was a man of the world, a noticeable figure, the cynosure of many eyes, and when Ulrika thought of him or heard of him she felt the satisfaction that an artist feels for a successful work, all the more because of its secrecy.   Although both of them were enmeshed in an existence that for months at a time kept them apart, they still found the way to each other now and then from their separate circles.   It was a confirmation of the likeness of their two natures that the ascent of the one destiny kept step with the other.   For days they would only see each other for a breathless quarter of an hour, but there existed between them a silent bond of comradeship that had grown up in the days of hardship.

But we must stop here an instant to make clear one of Ulrika's noticeable characteristics. Not only did she retain the unconditional devotion of her victims but she knew how to grapple to herself with iron fetters those whom she had helped, and their fidelity was the greater the more they recognised her superiority in good or in evil. She gathered up life. She collected all the loose ends. Nothing must be lost. Everything must be made to pay.

CHAPTER XIV

ULRIKA BALANCES ACCOUNTS

ULRIKA prepared for the introduction of Edward Melander into the Mylius house as if it were a matter of receiving a prince of the royal blood.

She had told a great deal about him, true and untrue, and knew how to make every one curious. She herself was not free of stage fright, and when he was announced, she blushed and went to meet him with a beating heart.

He was quite sure of his effect. He needed only to smile for every one around him to smile likewise. The way he monopolised everything, his merry superiority, and then his roguishly modest way of depreciating himself in a conversation showed both brains and tact. And with all this he had a charming manner, and the long oval of his beardless face, the shimmering tone of his ivory pale complexion, the dreamy look that alternated with the shining, ironic glance—all this was striking. He seemed to want to turn away the sympathy that rushed out to meet him, and he had a manner that seemed to say: I am unworthy of your approval; really, good people, I am not conscious of any superiority. All this gave him a sort of noble shyness by which he won over even the distrustful.

He was a born fascinator and did not have to study human weaknesses carefully.

Esther had not been five minutes in the same room with him when she was a changed being. She kept her eyes fixed upon him in a striking almost reprehensible way; she jumped and turned pale when he spoke to her, and when he left she rushed into her own room and burst into tears. Ulrika followed her and saw it. She said nothing but shrugged her shoulders. She confessed to herself that she had not thought her capable of such passion.

At first he came seldom, then oftener, and then finally with Ulrika's consent every second or third day. It was soon evident that not only Esther, but also Aimée, had fallen under his spell and Lothar especially was attached to him with a glowing emotion which was really disturbing.

I can make it all right, Ulrika thought, for it was not her intention to favour any such confusion now, when she was planning to put everything into legitimate order. She had several consultations with Melander but they ended every time in mutual laughter. The world was so mad, they were at one upon that point, that there was nothing to do but be merry over it. This they did as well as they could and poured out their hearts over the stage where fools played and other fools watched. As the delight in Melander was also felt by all the friends of the house, Ulrika smothered her anxiety, and contented herself with warning him; warnings which he pretended to take seriously and to follow.

For a while Pillersdorf and Althann were inseparable from him. Lothar was fourth in the group, and if at first they were unwilling to have him in their midst and his youth seemed to them a nuisance, he yet managed by the unbroken stubbornness with which he clung to Melander to make good with them. As Melander was too busy during the day to give them even an hour they spent the nights with him, and Melander, who was no kill-sport and, moreover, had a burning ambition to know all the nobler as well as the lower delights of life, managed to get only a short nap in the morning. This did not seem to hinder either his capacity or his endurance; he was made of steel. But Pillersdorf, a simple country youth, who had married young, could not stand the strain; he fell off noticeably and had to endure terrible pangs of conscience, while the forty-year-old Althann, a ruined man like Ferry Lex, with health destroyed, finally gave up the pace as a necessity, since he had official duties to fulfil. He had hopes of Aimée, which, nourished by Ulrika, were ironically destroyed by Melander. Did Melander want to keep the way open for himself? Probably not, for he loved his freedom and thought very little of marriage. Or was he like the greedy man who stretches out his hand for every dish and refuses to let his moderate neighbour even look at the menu? It was difficult to judge him. In his whole relation to people there lay a candid, if impudent, egoism; he looked upon them as the spokes of his mill wheel which he had set together to grind his corn. With the best of good will he could say to a cripple: "My good fellow, I have dropped my bread and butter out of the window; run and fetch it for me," and then he both surprised and touched when the poor fellow pointed to his lame feet.

He never noticed when people had crutches. He never noticed if they were not quite prepared to run and fetch his bread and butter. He believed so devoutly in himself that he believed that the bread and butter that he dropped was worthy to hold the interest of humanity at large and he was indignant when others felt differently about it. And yet he was so dependent upon the world's opinion that it would upset him if he heard that any one had spoken unkindly or even doubtfully about him. He had to have everything; everything was created for him; it was worth his while to win over the biggest idiot, and blame from the lowest clerk in the bank would make him cowardly and unhappy.

Lothar looked up to him as if he were a god. When Melander spoke the world was dumb for him. A gesture of Melander's and everything in him listened and waited. He gave the "go by" to all his friends and acquaintances and nothing and no one existed for him except this man who was his first thought and his every word. Without actually knowing it he imitated his walk, his attitudes, his idioms, his laughter, and his smile, and yet he was no monkey but a worshipping youth as soft as wax. If Melander's name was mentioned in his presence, he caught his breath. When a day passed that he did not see him he sent his servant to him, or went himself to his out-of-the-way dwelling to wait for him there if he were not at home. Once when Melander had gone to a party given by the Minister of Instruction, such a longing fell upon Lothar that he went at eleven o'clock at night to the Minister's palace and, despite storm and rain, he waited until three o'clock in the morning among the coachmen and lackeys who stood about the door, only to get a glimpse of him as he came out. Like a child he confessed to him later that he had been happy just to look at him so from afar and to think what life would have been had he not known him.

He bought the most expensive flowers and sent them to him. He chose books, rare editions, illustrated works, etchings, and engravings with most noticeable taste. This embarrassed Melander and he begged him to stop; but when he was seriously angry with him, the alarming wildness of Lothar's nature broke out; he raged like a madman and overwhelmed his older friend with reproaches and complaints.

When he perceived with the quick keenness of sense which was native to him that both his sisters were interested in Melander, as so far they had not been in any man, and that Melander was not entirely indifferent to them, especially not to Aimée, he was seized with tormenting jealousy. During a conversation in which he tried to draw Ulrika out on the subject, he suddenly seized her arm and said threateningly: "That shall not be, do you hear?" Ulrika shook him off and asked: "What, what shall not be?" He stamped his foot and stammered in a hoarse voice: "That, do you hear, that!" Ulrika looked anxious and said: "I believe cold baths are good for this condition."

Perhaps she would have been more surprised by his outbreak had she not just had to set Ferry Lex to rights when he complained of Esther's behaviour and blamed Edward Melander for her turning away from him. Ulrika denied everything and promised to patch up the misunderstanding. She had it in mind to speak a few determined words to Esther but forgot it as Pillersdorf, who had also made her his confidant, came to tell her every phase of his difficulties with his young wife. She listened to him and decided that on most points he was in the right. Pleasant as Ulrika found it to make matches, she was just as competent when it came to breaking even the closest bonds.

Lothar was driven by his strange jealousy to turn to Melander himself and to question him without reserve. It suited Edward Melander to appear surprised. At the moment, it did not suit him to still the wave he had raised. His only reply was a few uncertain words and a little fault-finding that seemed to be fault-finding on the outside, but was really at bottom self-conscious, flattered pride. After all, power over the boy meant power over worshipping youth—the beginning of the path of glory—such as demagogues dream of. If one won over youth, one won the world. The question never arose in his mind as to whether he might turn this enthusiasm into human achievement and worth-while strength; whether instead he was driving an impulsive nature into chaos to sink in the mud there. But that was because the paper flowers with which his triumphal arch was crowned were too like real ones to him, and they had hung there too long. He ran his hands through the embarrassed young man's hair, thrust back his head, looked laughingly into his eyes and said: "No nonsense, friend."

It happened that the next afternoon, Lothar, as he often did, went to Melander's room to wait for him. Absent-minded and dull, he looked over newspapers and books, and then went to the writing table and looked no less dully, at the perfect desert of papers and letters. Melander was careless and often left letters of even important content about. So Lothar barely glanced at them. Then his eye fell on an envelope and in an instant the expression of his face changed. He knew the writing; it was Esther's. He tore the letter out and read it. It was rather a puzzling missive; it might mean nothing or it might mean everything; it might convey all, or it might be just a conventional communication. There was not even a form of address at the beginning. But for Lothar it was the much-feared discovery. He crumpled up the letter and stuck it in his pocket. Muttering foolish words to himself, he rushed away.

At about the same time, Ulrika was having a consultation with Aimée about Althann. She asked her with no circumlocutions if she would have Althann for her husband. He, on his side, showed the most serious intentions. He had given her to understand, several times, first how entirely attractive Aimée was to him and second that he was tired of his lonely, homeless life. Moreover his old father wanted him to marry. How did Aimée feel, Ulrika asked with a heavy frown on her face.

Aimée looked at the floor. "Why not?" she said. "Why not Bodo Althann as well as another?" She stroked her little white dog tenderly and said: "All the same, isn't it, Flock? One is as good as another."

"I must say you have turned into great ladies very quickly," said Ulrika angrily. "What does that mean—one is as good as another?"

They were interrupted here by a servant who announced the vice-consul; he had to speak to his sister at once. Ulrika went into the drawing room where Nanette was laying the tea-table. Franz Woytich had occupied the time joking with her. He told Ulrika that he had just left the Counsellor and that the old man had said he would look up Ulrika in the course of the afternoon; after a moment's hesitation he added that he had felt obliged to forewarn Ulrika, as nothing very pleasant could be expected from that quarter.

Ulrika clasped her hands over her forehead. "Good heavens!" she cried. "The appointed time! The time is up; and we had clean forgotten. He wants his money. He advanced a couple of thousand gulden while we were still living on bread and water," she added by way of explanation. "I wonder why he waited this long. There's something behind that."

"And nothing good either," laughed the vice-consul. "Still while you are speaking of money, Ulrika," he turned confidentially to his sister, "could you oblige me with four hundred gulden? I have had losses at cards and for the moment I am bankrupt."

"Four hundred gulden?" said Ulrika astonished. "My dear fellow, do you take me for a Mexican planter? I have no plantation. Don't you earn anything? I don't even know how you live. What do you live on anyway?"

"Oh, I manage somehow," the vice-consul answered calmly; "one can always pick up something. My position brings in a little; enough for tips."

"You ought to marry," said Ulrika, thoughtfully. "Marry a good income. A dowry would not last long with you. I will attend to it; in fact, I am already arranging it."

"Not for anything on earth," exclaimed the vice-consul. "We Woytichs were not made for marriage. Would you go off with a strange person to live in a rented house? I can lay no claims to the grand style and the lesser I decline with thanks. Three rooms and a kitchen; bawling infants; Sunday afternoon walks, arm-in-arm, with best coat and high hat on; smell of onions and carpet beating. No, thank you very much. I'd rather go to Cayenne."

Ulrika laughed. "Quite true, we Woytichs have no taste for poverty. And yet we are poor people. We want to stand high up and we have a taste for luxury. But one must do something to get it. For my part, I plough my field. There's no prize without work."

"Certainly, my clever Ulrika. We used to call you that even as a child. The clever Ulrika. You were always our Providence. Without work, no prize, certainly. And the honest man waits longest; and busy hands make a golden floor; and morning red and evening grey, etc. All excellent maxims for the people. But how about that loan?"

"I'll have to think it over. Come to-morrow," said Ulrika. "I think I can let you have two hundred."

The Counsellor sent in his card and appeared immediately, somewhat bent and very thin, on the threshold. Ulrika greeted him pleasantly and had the tea served. When Franz Woytich had taken his leave with respectful haste, the old man explained to Ulrika that for the coming half year he would have to demand ten per cent interest. In the note nothing was stated about a yearly interest of ten per cent! On the contrary it was there, clear and easy to read; Herr Counsellor Woytich was to receive ten per cent for the money overdue for six months.

He took the document from his pocket and held it up before Ulrika's eyes that she might read it, taking the utmost care that she should not touch it or take it from his hand.

Ulrika was furious. She struck the table with her hand.

"You should have forewarned us before the time was up, Uncle Clement," she said. "We forgot it, for we have a great many cares, and now you are profiting by it. We have not needed your money for a long time past."

"That seems to be so," the Counsellor replied and his watery eyes wandered devoutly about the room. "This is really princely splendour, a worth-while sight. Still that does not prevent me demanding my rights. Every six months an increase of interest. Why should that vex my niece who is so clever about money matters?"

"Because it is such ungodly usury, Uncle Clement," Ulrika stormed. "Twenty per cent. No Jew would demand that. It is against the law and I won't do it. No, there I stand firm."

The Counsellor put his teacup to his thin lips, took a piece of pastry and broke it, smacking his lips, fixing a malicious look upon Ulrika from time to time. "Against the law," he murmured sulkily, wiped his mouth and folded his hands. "Who would talk of legal punishment between blood relations. In those days you whined and wanted to promise me the blue out of the sky, and to-day you resist and talk about legal punishment. Your employers here will hesitate, I guess, to let loose a scandal for the sake of a miserable two thousand gulden."

"I have no employers, Uncle Clement, and I want you to know it," Ulrika set him right.

"Ah? So. Then you are the boss here? Well, you have brought things along very well. I always prophesied: Ulrika will go far. You ought to be all the more charitable toward an old uncle, who stands with one foot in the grave, about the two thousand gulden. But that is the way of the world. No one can count upon thanks."

Ulrika got up and went to the window, in a bad temper, to think over the case, and meanwhile the Counsellor took a handful of pastry and stuck it quickly into the back pocket of his coat. He wanted to carry Smirczinska some of these costly pastries and have a few left over for his little night table.

"I'll make you a proposition, Uncle Clement," said Ulrika and turned round. "Give me a fifth part of the two thousand gulden. I have honestly earned that much as a go-between. If you refuse we will see what will happen. If you consent I will bring you to-morrow morning the sixteen hundred gulden and we will say nothing further about it."

The Counsellor took out his shell snuff-box and snuffed. "This is a new law that you have brought into parliament," he whispered. "Revolting, nothing but revolting. A Richelieu is needed—or an idiot. The thumbscrews are lacking, my good girl. We lack a Spielberg. I have always told you, how can we govern without a Spielberg? But no, they splutter and shake as soon as one of the rebellious heretics looks into his inkwell. The freedom of the press! That is what has ruined us. Konigsgrätz was not enough, they needed another Austerlitz and another war of communists, after the famous French pattern. It will come to a horrible end, I tell you, a horrible end."

"Well, Uncle Clement?" said Ulrika, who stood with folded arms before him.

"First the government gets the people under, and then the people the government. That is the way of the world. And youth has no religion any more and the clergy no power." He sighed. "A fifth part?" he said in the same sulky tone. "That is a much greater usury than the one you reproached me with. But we will see, we will see. And no more vexations? All right, all right. You have cunning wits! We will see how long it will be before you come slinking up to my bedside, stealing my keys, and starting new tricks. How did you feel then?" He had gotten up and with a low groan he scratched his chin with his hard forefinger. "What did you say then? We are not dreaming— What? That was fine, Ulrika, fine. Just remember it. We are not dreaming. Our eyes are wide open. We are both on the *qui vive*. Ten per cent for me and twenty per cent for you—after all I don't call that dreaming."

He is getting a little weak-minded, the good Uncle Clement, thought Ulrika as she accompanied him out. When she came back she heard a horrible shriek from the other wing of the house. The door of Esther's room was open. Aimée rushed toward her and called: "Quick, Ulrika, quick, for Heaven's sake!"

In the middle of the room stood Lothar bending over Esther whom he had thrown on the ground. His hands were buried in her hair and he was spouting half-wild words. Ulrika seized him. "Will you let go at once, you madman!" she demanded.

He fell back against the wall. "Ulrika," he stammered; "Ulrika."

It was the call of all these weak-willed, desire-ridden, confused souls: "Ulrika." "Now what is the matter? What are you doing to your sister?" Ulrika scolded. "Aren't you ashamed? Are we to put you into a strait-jacket like a madman?"

Lothar stretched out his arms to the girl lying on the floor, the whole upper part of her body buried in her yellow hair. "Just let her not show her face," he hissed, "she knows why. Let her look no one in the eyes. Every one shall know why. There!" He thrust his hand into his pocket and drew out a crumpled letter and threw it at her. "She is writing to Edward. She is writing him letters. She is offering herself to him. You may all know it. Apparently she is his mistress. You may all know it. The whole world may know it. I'll see that it does."

Esther sat up with a jerk and said low and threateningly: "Take that common animal out of here, that thief who steals his friend's letters." She was pale as a corpse.

Aimée stepped up to her, looked at her with cold scorn, and said: "You had better justify yourself. Is what he says true? Answer, your dishonourable creature!" Then she broke out bitterly, "Answer or I will spit in your face in disgust."

"She daren't deny it," Lothar screamed and laughed out shrilly. "You can read it here in black and white. Read it!"

Aimée bent over to get the letter but Esther seized it first and threw it in the open fire. With a scream Aimée bent over the hearth and tried to pull the paper out of the flames. Esther stood up, looked at her brother, then at her sister, and said: "What kind of people are you? What are you saying? What are you doing?"

"It is very easy to play offended innocence, when you can't deny a charge," said Aimée bitterly, and Lothar broke out into hideous laughter again.

"Leave this room immediately," said Ulrika to him with her head held high. "I don't want any answer or you will have to deal with me. And you are not to go one step out of this house, but wait upstairs for me. And you, Aimée, march, get out of here at once. I am going to talk to Esther and to no one else. Look," she broke in ironically, "your sister, Josephine, is staring her eyes out."

Josephine had come up to the threshold and was a silent witness to the whole scene. She understood nothing; what was happening was like an evil dream. She looked at Ulrika, a deep, long look, amazed and sad. Then she went quietly away.

When Ulrika was left alone with Esther, she closed the door, went up to her and laid her left hand heavily upon her shoulder. "Listen to me, dear child," she said quietly and coldly. "You will live with Ferry Lex. You need have no grey hairs about the necessary ceremonies before hand. But don't turn your beautiful eyes elsewhere for," she pointed with her thumb over her right shoulder significantly, "he belongs to me for the present. Do you understand?"

Esther looked at her silently and trembled. Then she dropped her head and covered her face with her hands.

"We can still be the best of friends," said Ulrika. "But everything must be perfectly clear between us."

She went to Aimée. The conversation with her lasted hardly longer and had the same overwhelming effect. Ulrika's real power lay in being laconic; she only used a superfluity of words when she wanted to hide herself. With Lothar she was more indulgent. When she sat down by him and began to talk reasonably to him he began to sob. He said that he did not know what had happened to him and that he wished he could go away to some country where nobody knew him. But when he thought he would see Edward Melander no more, life seemed perfectly empty to him. Could Ulrika explain this to him?

Was it anything wrong in him? Was it rottenness? Did she scorn him or could she help him?

Ulrika answered that she would try. That above all things he must not let himself go. That matter of going to a strange country was not a bad idea, and they would talk it over again. In the meantime he must see that he conquered his rebellious spirit and she would ask Melander to help him too. She quieted him and comforted him. This she called leading people by the nose.

Then she was tired. It had been a very exciting day. Fortunately no guests were expected that evening. After dinner she went to Christine to give her the usual account; at ten o'clock she withdrew and sent up word to Mylius, who had asked for her, that she could not come.

In her beautiful and spacious room she sat down in an armchair breathing heavily, pushed the little Japanese embroidered screen against the lamp, shut her eyes, and gave herself up to thought. From time to time she threw a log onto the fire for it was cold outside, and the fire heightened her sense of security.

Once the two villains are married there will be peace in the house, she reflected; nor can the boy loaf around here forever, he feels it himself, and I shall have to find a suitable match for Josephine. We must not wait too long with that; she will soon be seventeen, and the sooner we get rid of that virtuous saint the better. The good Mylius will at last have to go the way of all flesh even if he lives to be a hundred years old, but he is visibly failing. Then I will have to deal with Christine alone and then . . . she smiled.

The look that she threw into the past prepared her for more pleasure in the future. I have set the old man along the right way. I have Anastasia and she has enough to eat and to live on; I have attached Franz to the house and when I send for Severin from Bosnia, he will find room at the table too. I have accomplished something, achieved something, and there is an end to all things.

She wanted to strengthen the image in her mind by actual evidence. She got up, took the key from the leather pocket that hung at her girdle and opened the door of the wardrobe, then the bureau, then the painted chest that stood at the foot of her bed. In the wardrobe were the dresses that Christine had given her; a black silk evening dress with a real lace fichu; a costly white evening dress, pleated and spangled; two street costumes, an English costume, an astrachan fur, two winter coats, and a spring suit; then there were hats, umbrellas, shoes, everything new and everything of the finest kind. In the drawers of her bureau was the linen; lace nightgowns with the name "Ulrika" embroidered on them, colored ribbons, lace stockings, blouses, handkerchiefs, stockings of every colour, an Indian shawl which Aimée had bought her for her birthday; seven yards of satin and nineteen yards of batiste; Brussels lace and Valenciennes, the latter four yards long.

Then she took out of her chest a fan of brown tortoise-shell with white ostrich feathers, a present from Lothar; another fan of ivory inlaid with gold with old Viennese painting on it, a present from Mylius for her self-sacrificing care of him; then a ring, a big square diamond surrounded by pearls and a gold bracelet, representing a much wounded snake whose eyes were two sapphires, a present from Ferry Lex; a little, but beautifully made tiara, a birthday present from Esther, and last came her savings book. She opened it. She had on hand the sum of thirteen thousand, eight hundred gulden. Thereby stood an accounting of how she had managed to save this sum, witness to her exactitude and conscientiousness. For instance: remuneration from the furniture factory and furniture dealers. Commissions from the market; commission received from the Duke of Chamfort for managing the deal; requisitions from Christine; pocket-money; and so on indefinitely.

People wished her well. People knew how to value her services. People saw her usefulness and held her blameless. She was invaluable. She gave herself no rest. She was on her feet from morning to evening. Without her the whole work would drop into ruins. She served people with her eyes, mouth and hands, with her heart and with her feet, with her understanding as well as with her body. She had a right to demand recognition, and if the reward seemed not too little for so short a time, still she hoped that it might be much greater.

She locked up everything again, fetched out a bottle of Chauteau Lafitte and a glass from the mahogany chest, uncorked it, filled the glass, and sipped it with the deliberation of a connoisseur. Then she leaned back again in the armchair, lit a cigarette, and gazed with contented restfulness at the little clouds of smoke.

CHAPTER XV

JOSEPHINE'S FLIGHT

THE next morning was Sunday, and when Ulrika arrived in the Dorothea Street to bring the Counsellor the money she had promised, she stood on the threshold listening. From indoors she heard the sound of a violin, and it was the Guarneri violin, she knew the tone. It was as if she was hearing the voice of a long estranged, long missed friend. She listened for a while and then knocked gently on the door; she did not wish to knock louder because she did not want the unknown player to stop. Who might it be? Was there some secret to be discovered?

Smirczinska peered out distrustfully and after some hesitation decided to let Ulrika in. Her position showed that she too had been listening; Ulrika made her understand by a gesture that she was not going into the room and was not going to let her go. Her whole manner had something depressed and sad about it and Ulrika felt that the situation in which she found the old servant was not an unaccustomed one. This soon proved true; when the playing ended suddenly with a crescendo cadenza Ulrika pushed Smirczinska into the kitchen and questioned her hastily. Smirczinska shrugged her shoulders, unwilling to do a favour for the hated niece of her master. Finally Ulrika pressed a silver gulden into her hand and that brought results.

In her soft Polish idiom she related monotonously that it was a thirteen-year-old boy, who for the past year had come every Sunday to play to the master. His name was Tino Waldbauer, and he was the son of a poor maker of feather trimmings, an illegitimate child. Whether this feather trimmer had stood in some other relation to the Counsellor in former years, as the old woman believed, or whether, as seemed more likely, it was her mother who had had something to do with him, was uncertain. Certain it was that this Tino was his god-child, that

183

they had discovered his musical gift when he was seven years old, and that the Counsellor had had him taught by a well-known violin teacher. He was already earning money; he was a member of a suburban orchestra and the Counsellor paid him every Sunday thirty kreuzer for playing for him. He seemed to know what to do with the violin, that was not to be denied, but in all other matters he was an idiot.

Inside the playing began again. Ulrika said: "I must get a look at him. Then I will go straight away for I have no time. Tell the Counsellor that I will come again to-morrow. Don't be afraid, I will see that he notices nothing." She slipped to the door of the room, opened it softly and peered in. The Counsellor and the boy had gone into the bedroom and so Ulrika dared to step into the room; as she peeped into the bedroom she saw a picture. In the middle of the room stood the boy, his back toward her, in a calm, well-poised position, and it seemed as if the rising and falling bow was moved by magic; not only did the indwelling voice of the instrument come out with a most wonderful tone but there was a powerful increase of tone, such as one could hardly believe possible for the frail boy and weak arm. Opposite the boy sat the Counsellor in his century-old chair. He sat so motionless, so abstracted and lost in thought that one might have believed him a corpse. His chin rested upon his breast, his eyes were shut, his face rigid and waxy, his mouth tightly closed, his nose was like the beak of a vulture.

Ulrika's amazement stopped her. She did not know what to think. She could hardly believe that this was the same Counsellor whom she had known for so long. She slipped quietly away; on the stairs she stood and thought. A sharp fright awoke in her. Then she decided not to let the thing weigh upon her.

The occurrence occupied her to such an extent that at home they noticed the change in her manner at the supper table and plied her with questions. She told the whole thing from beginning to end. With her gift for describing what she had seen and for making an impression nothing was lost in the telling. Christine, who had already acquired the art of rich women of making a claim upon anything distinguished in the world and acquiring it for themselves, told Ulrika that she must bring the little virtuoso to the house and that perhaps they could do something for him. At first Ulrika would hear nothing of the matter, but when Josephine also begged for it she promised, for Josephine to-day had forsaken her usual habit of eating in her room and at Christine's urgent request had joined the family after a long absence. Besides the brother and sisters Lex was there, Althann, Melander, and a young attaché of the German Embassy. Melander praised Ulrika's resolve and exchanged a quick glance with her which Josephine noticed.

"It's a shame that he can't play upon Uncle Clement's Guarneri," said Ulrika; "we will have to get hold of an instrument, and I will bring him straight from the Dorothea Street here. He seems to be a very shy youth and we will have to deal carefully with him. But you will all see that I have not said too much about him. Franz will be amazed at his performance."

After they had gotten up from the table Edward Melander went with her into the billiard room, nominally to play a game of patience, but they sat down in a half-darkened corner. "Of course, you understand what disturbs me about the whole thing?" she began.

"I understand entirely," was the answer; "you fear for the inheritance."

"Afraid for the inheritance, but above all for the violin. That has been once and for all promised me. I have promised it to myself too. If that were to escape me, I feel as if I should never have any luck in the world again."

"You overvalue the magic of the thing," said Melander, smiling. "Don't give way to that thought. In every superstition there is room left for free will. You are too clever for that."

"There is a certain point where cleverness ends and the supernatural begins," Ulrika replied, looking down at her folded hands. "How would the matter stand legally?" she enquired, turning quickly away from the superstitious element. "He promised me the instrument in writing, as you know . . ."

Melander smiled again. "Such a paper has little weight before the law," he said; "any will made later may overthrow it. The old man knew this all too well."

"But if there is no will, will this Tino inherit in despite of that?"

"If it is an illegitimate relation, no. We will have to investigate whether the mother can make any legitimate claims. That is improbable however. People like the Counsellor do not bind themselves and they rarely have secret connections that cost money."

"That is quite true, but I will have to have certainty. Do you think I will let them snap away from under my nose what I have fought for with tooth and nail? Was it only fun to spend my days and nights and spill my heart's blood to bring that old fool to reason? Who am I, that he dare grin in my face pleasantly and play me a trick behind my back. Not a single leg of a chair of his shall go to any one but me and my father's children, not a button off his coat, not a scrap of paper. It would never suit me to have a beggar woman and her offspring, knee-high to a grasshopper, come and fetch the wages of their sin and decrease the share of his blood connections. None of that, my friend." She laughed and struck her breast. It was an elemental outbreak.

Melander remained quiet. The swift process of refinement that he had gone through in the last few months had brought him to a point where Ulrika's occasional outbreaks of commonness, the lack of discipline of a peasant under the thin veneer of culture both frightened and revolted him. But since in a decisive moment of his life she had drawn him back from the abyss, with a bold and resolute hand, he tried to be faithful to her, a fidelity which was not native to him, and which had nothing whatever to do with any sensuous attractions which she exercised over him, face to face. But he knew that there were women that one could not forsake because they are too strong and because they have outposts on every path that a man might go. He who cared so little for people that he played with the most important relationships and threw away friendships without consideration that might really serve his ambition, found himself bound here by chains which he had no power to break. He hated the secrecy of their relationship, hated the memory of their common past, hated the matter-of-fact way in which she took possession of him; but he had not the courage to break loose. He was simply afraid of her.

In order not to let her see what he thought, he tried to turn everything into a joke, and when Ulrika curtly declared that she saw nothing to laugh at, he replied that if the little violinist were such a danger to the inheritance as she suspected, one might with money and kind words remove him out of reach of the Counsellor; at any rate it would not be difficult to make the boy harmless in this respect.

Ulrika had folded her arms and was looking at the ground. She was about to answer when Josephine entered and said she had been searching through all the rooms for her, as her father had sent an urgent message that he wanted her at once. Ulrika arose with an unwilling sigh. She asked Melander if he could wait until she returned, but Melander said the minister was awaiting him at half past eleven; he smiled uncertainly at Josephine, for he remembered that just before supper he had made an appointment with Althann, which proved that he was lying to Ulrika and he feared that Josephine had overheard him. Josephine was quite unsuspecting, yet something in his voice surprised her and she threw a swift glance in his direction. When she looked into his beautiful face, it seemed to her that a curtain was torn aside and she saw a quite different face there. It was only for a moment but enough to make her heart ache.

As she was leaving the room she dropped her handkerchief; she stooped down for it and he bent over at the same moment and they bumped heads and Josephine gave a cry of pain; Melander seemed overcome; she quieted him, blushing, and he laughingly begged pardon for his awkwardness and they went in laughing, both of them, to the others; Christine, delighted to see Josephine gay, went to her and embraced her.

But just this gesture immersed Josephine in sadness again. It was no longer the mother she used to know, neither her face nor her gesture. The whole relation between them, which had once been so free and unrestrained, was reserved and constrained now. Josephine knew it and felt it; Christine knew it but felt it no longer. That was the difference and that was the cause of Josephine's sorrow. Her eyes could no longer penetrate the high walls, her call no longer reached her mother; the walls had been too firmly built, the work too ably done. The watchman could afford to go away and her captive would not stir. And Josephine asked herself in despair why it was so. How could it be? Why would not God enlighten her that she might understand?

Her work with the blind had helped her along for months to bear her pain. But she had made too severe demands upon herself. Her body was not able to stand the strain indefinitely. It was all the worse because she had lost her chief source of joy; for not only did the constant intercourse with the blind depress her spirits but she began to see that just the misfortune of their blindness made them distrustful, peevish, and inclined to untruthfulness. She had seen things that she wished never to have seen or heard, examples of low greed and meanness in these pitiable people. Or was their world like the rest? And with all this she had to protect herself from an importunate young blind man, who almost lost his mind when he heard her step, and became only the wilder when she tried to quiet him and teach him moderation so that she had to complain to get any peace at all. It was a disappointment not easily overcome, but it healed her of her general desire to make every one happy.

She was waiting for something that did not come and perhaps never would come. In her, form and will developed with a devout slowness and she was as composed as a root in the earth. She watched things and people; her heart was a clear tablet upon which life wrote an impressive text, letter by letter. And she stood there and read it: attentive, conscientious, letter by letter, until she got the meaning.

Ulrika no longer felt it necessary to win her over and to spin a special deception for her eyes and ears. She gave herself no more pains with her; everything was going smoothly now and no serious hindrance was to be expected. Josephine was puzzled sometimes, startled by a word, an ironic remark, or an outburst of vexation, but that was all; she never bore Ulrika any grudge and in her intercourse with others she kept the distance that they set for her.

The next Sunday evening, Ulrika, as she had promised, brought the little violinist. But even without her promise, she would have gotten hold of him; for she wanted to know where she stood and to penetrate the secret. The information that she had managed to get during the course of a week had been fairly unimportant; she had learned nothing more than what Smirczinska had already told her. To visit Tino's mother might be too harmful to her plan, and certainly it would be wild and foolish to speak of it to the Counsellor. So she turned to Smirczinska again and bribed her. She was to prepare the boy before he left the house and influence him favourably. Ulrika would then wait for him on the steps. Smirczinska, who saw her future no less threatened than Ulrika's, was not unwilling to let herself into the scheme, of whose outlines indeed, she knew nothing, but from which she hoped to get something advantageous, knowing the character of her rival, Ulrika.

Everything happened as planned. Smirczinska accompanied Tino right into Ulrika's arms. He was extraordinarily shy and Ulrika had to coax him a long time before he even understood what she wanted. She flattered him every possible way. She told him that rich, aristocratic people were dying to hear him play; that they would give him money and delicious things to eat and anything else that he might want. At the door stood the Mylius carriage with the coachman in livery; she led the boy to the coach door and indicated that he could drive to the wonderful house where they were awaiting him. That overcame his shyness; he was weaponless against a coach, a coachman, and two horses; his eyes shone and he stepped in.

In his poor little blue linen suit, a quite insufficient protection against the November weather, he stepped into the drawing room with Ulrika. Everything confused him, the brilliant lights, the coloured decorations, the dressed-up women, the solemn, high room. At the table he sat between Ulrika and

Josephine and both of them had to encourage him to eat what was set before him. It was a strange sight to see this little child of poverty, this little unknown creature of the streets, in his beggar's rags, in this setting of luxury, and among the careless, laughing, shining faces. To Josephine it seemed outrageous and heartless insolence. She tried to make the boy forget; for he certainly suffered in the same way as she did, though more frightfully and less consciously. She asked him about his teacher, his mother, what he did all day, where he lived and all in the tenderest, most loving and patient way, but Tino gave only the curtest answers and withdrew more and more into himself.

Then they went into the music room and they begged him to play. The Vice-Consul had brought a violin and Tino took it and tried it, plucked the strings, raised his bow, let his deep melancholy eyes wander around the circle and seemed to sink into a sleep. Then a loud laugh sounded through the expectant stillness. It was Lothar; the dreamy look of the boy, the expectant look of the people sitting round had suddenly seemed comic to him; perhaps he was upset about something else and simply awaiting an opportunity; enough, he let himself go and the shocked, partly dumb but partly reproachful sounds from all sides came too late. Tino laid down the bow and the violin and said he could not play. All urging was vain, Christine's promises vain, Esther's and Josephine's coaxing vain; in vain did Lothar go up to him, offer his hand and beg his pardon; he simply shook his head with the long black curls and seemed to shut himself up in himself. Ulrika was furious and said that one could really not beg such a child on one's knees; it was all so futile that the Vice-Consul sat down at the grand piano and began to improvise to try to lure back the frightened spirit of music.

In the meantime Edward Melander put his arm around Tino's shoulder, led him aside, and talked softly and confidentially to him. And marvel of marvels, he managed to break down his resistance. The boy looked on the ground, raised his eyes slowly to Melander, whose voice undoubtedly had a certain power over him, smiled a little, and when

Melander turned back to the others with him he announced with conscious composure: "Tino is reconciled and he will play."

And Tino played indeed; a song of Schubert's, then some variations; then an air by Bach.

His listeners were much moved. If it was not mature artistry, it was a soulful stream, a song released from muteness through the magic of destiny. Only Ulrika missed anything because the sole instrument to which her ear was open was not sounding.

Josephine could not enjoy it, because what had happened beforehand made too deep an impression upon her. She kept still too when all the approval burst forth. It seemed to her as if she were praising one who was fighting in the waves for his very life, because of his good swimming. All the faces around frightened her. All their words pained her. She instinctively felt so much that was low, evil, and hateful in these faces around her. As she moved about she felt every instant that something frightful might happen, the walls might fall down or the earth break open.

The guests began to leave. Christine gave Tino a leather purse with some gold pieces in it. This too pained Josephine, this open payment; she could hardly see why they did not all blush for shame. Tino was too embarrassed to say thank you. "Say something," said Ulrika and shook his elbow. He stood dumb and Ulrika grumbled: "Smirczinska is right, he is just a little idiot able to do nothing but fiddle."

Melander offered to take Tino home and explain to his mother where he had been. Christine wished him to do so as she suspected the boy was afraid of getting a scolding. Again it seemed to Josephine as if Melander and Ulrika exchanged a quick look. Lothar greedily seized the chance to be with his friend and left the house with Melander and Tino.

Now it happened in the same night that Josephine had a dream, in which as it often happens with sensitive natures, she saw, pressed together into one endlessly tormenting picture, a number of presentiments and half-ripened fears, though she was, however, entirely uncertain of the cause of her distress.

She dreamed that she was in a sort of twilight landscape, a bare hilly land covered with wet snow, and was walking toward a person whose face she could not recognise. But on this person perched hundreds of black crows, and also with a kind of wicked gravity they perched on all the green emerging from the snow; and as the figure came nearer they began with a sort of malicious slowness to rise up and flutter round it like a black moving cloud. Then the person, whom Josephine now recognised as Ulrika, laid a wooden doll in a blue dress down on the snow; the crows pounced upon the doll with hideous screechings, and thus the person—really Ulrika—escaped the danger of being torn to pieces by the birds. Josephine awoke with a scream: Ulrika! but the thing she really feared for bore another name which came at once to her lips, the name of the little violinist.

When she left in the morning she heard that Lothar had not come home that night, and was still not there. She paid little attention to that, but instead of going to the Institute as she had intended, she took the horse car to Mariahilf, and looked for the little Kasern alley where Tino lived. He had told her the number but Josephine could not remember it exactly; and it was only after a good deal of questioning that she found the lodging of the feather-trimmer in the cellar of a big tenement, with old stone steps, floors, and court-yards. She stepped into a clean room and met a neat looking woman of about thirty-five years old who asked her what she wanted. "Are you Frau Waldbauer, the mother of Tino?" asked Josephine. "I am Lena Waldbauer, certainly," was the answer, and the emphasis on the first name evidently signified that she felt she had no right to the title Frau. "Are you bringing me news? The boy went yesterday afternoon, as he does every Sunday, to his godfather and has never come back." The face of the woman, a strong, firm, pleasant face showed deep anxiety.

"Never come home?" stammered Josephine. "Did not come home yesterday?" All her blood streamed to her heart. They hastily exchanged information. Lena Waldbauer said that late in the evening she had gone to the Dorothea Street; the housekeeper of the Counsellor said she knew nothing at all and abused her for disturbing them at night; then she had gone to the police station and in the end had walked the streets, back and forth without plan. The next morning she had gone again to the police station, then it occurred to her that he might have gone to some of his comrades in the orchestra, but it had been impossible to find and to ask all of them.

"It is unpardonable of us not to have let you know," said Josephine, and told where Tino had been, who had brought him to her parents' house, and that her brother and his friend at half-past eleven had undertaken to see him home. "It will all be cleared up," she concluded and squeezed the hand of the somewhat quieted woman; she would go at once and tell her people and bring back the boy that afternoon and, if she could, bring news of him earlier. When she got home it was noon. Ulrika knew nothing. Lothar had not gotten in yet. They had sent to Melander's, but he had not been at home since yesterday afternoon. Then Josephine told of the disappearance of Tino. Ulrika collapsed. She began questioning Josephine about her reasons for making the visit to Lena Waldbauer. Josephine could give no reason and that did not lessen the suspicion in Ulrika's eyes. Esther and Ulrika consulted; Esther thought they should give notice to the police, but Ulrika refused, frightened; under no circumstances should they raise an alarm; they must wait. Pillersdorf came in for the after-dinner coffee. Christine had a headache and had remained in bed. Ulrika went with Pillersdorf into the smoking room and they whispered in great excitement. Esther and Aimée foresaw something dreadful and looked questioningly at Josephine.

Josephine went into her room and forced herself to go to work. From time to time she rose up and pressed her hand to her breast. Everything was so frightfully still in the house she was seized by anxiety. She laid her watch upon the table and followed the moving minute-hand. She had never felt so lonely in all her life. Every human bond seemed broken; there remained to her only her reliance upon that Divine

Being, whose sacrificial death and shining resurrection pointed her way through the human desert and made her feel that her heart had a band of gold that held it firm. She did not think, there was no definite image before her, but she rested in the grace that flowed from Him.

As the twilight broke she slipped on her cloak and hat and went out. As she went down the big staircase she looked out into the garden, and there she saw Lothar. He was leaning, in the rain, against a statue, a Hercules armed with a club. His coat was spattered with mud, all his clothes crumpled and dirty. He had no hat on, his brown curls hung uncombed over his forehead, his face was ash grey with red spots and swollen lids. In five steps Josephine was with him. "Man, what do you look like!" she whispered horror stricken, but as he neither moved nor answered she looked at him again, shook him by the arm and asked trembling: "What is the matter with you? Where have you come from? Where is Tino?"

At this name he opened his eyes, looked at Josephine, and then turned his glance away again. "Where is Tino?" Josephine repeated her question like a command.

"He is . . . I don't know . . . They have taken him to his mother."

"When?"

"I don't know. Leave me alone."

Without another word Josephine rushed away. She flew through the streets. Her breath failed her, the rain beat into her face. Half fainting she stood at last at the doorway of the alley and had to lean against the wall to rest before she went in. First, one entered the kitchen and the door on opening sounded a little bell. In the room her searching look fell upon Tino; he lay in bed, covered up with a red covering to his chin. His little shrunken face was as white as paper, his eyes were without any expression and fixed upon a point upon the wall, his mouth gasped after regular pauses, like a fish that one has landed. A second was enough for Josephine to see that he was in a dangerous condition.

"Yes, there he is," said Lena Waldbauer grimly.

After a long silence she said that some one had knocked rapidly and twice on the door at about half-past three o'clock; when she went out and opened it she found Tino lying on the threshold apparently dead; there was no one else there. Later a janitor across the way told her that a cab had stopped at the door; a man stepped out with the boy in his arms, carried him into the house, and then came out again in the greatest haste and drove away. The janitor had fetched the doctor, who examined the boy carefully and shook his head. His breath smelled of wine he said; he appeared to be drunk; then again, he said that was not all; and he examined him again; he could find no injury on his body, he affirmed, but he must have had a great mental shock; he would come again the next day and then perhaps the boy would be able to give some information.

"But I don't believe it," said Lena Waldbauer, walking up and down restlessly. "He sees nothing, he hears nothing, he will not speak. They must have done something frightful to him. But what? And who? And why?"

Josephine stood with her head down and thought.

"He is not like other children of his age," Lena went on; "in some ways he is developed far beyond his years, and in others he is like a six-year-old child. Nobody knows how sensitive he is. He would break under things that others hardly feel. What am I to do!"

"Hasn't he spoken at all?" asked Josephine.

"Yes, once. He said he wanted the beautiful ring, the ring with the green stone. He felt all round for it, and asked for his clothes and felt through the pockets. There was no ring there. What could they have told him!"

Josephine remembered suddenly that she had seen a ring with an emerald in it on Edward Melander's hand.

"We will have to find out," Lena said resolutely; "but I am alone. I can't leave him here and go out and no time must be lost. Who will help?"

"I," answered Josephine, "if you will only trust me; I."

The woman looked at her, a searching look. "What interest have you in it?" she asked with the distrust of the lower classes. "I do not even know who you are. I have never even understood why the boy was taken to your people. Of course he was to play, you told me that, and in my excitement I hardly listened. You spoke also of Ulrika Woytich; that name I know indeed; she is the niece of the Counsellor and I have often heard about her. But all that is unimportant now. I must know where my boy has been. And the doctor must know it. And the guilty must be held responsible. Will you really help?"

"Yes," said Josephine.

"How are you going to begin?"

"I don't know exactly. Just trust me and believe in me, I need nothing more. And as soon as I know anything definite I will come here and tell you."

"That may take a long time."

"I hope it will be to-day."

"Very well, then I will wait for you."

Once again Josephine submitted to the searching glance. From moment to moment the face of the young woman seemed more attractive to her; it was beautified by its expression, an expression that was new to Josephine, the straightforward expression of a human being who lives and works openly and aboveboard. Also her speech was not that of a common woman of the people; despite her bright colouring she had the look of one of whom they say that she had seen better days. These impressions passed quickly and after Josephine had looked once more at Tino, who gave no sign of life, she hurried away.

A half hour later she rang the bell of Melander's apartment in the Reissner Street. Of a sudden an endless fund of courage had arisen in her which threw all conventional considerations aside. A servant came; it was quite a fine apartment that Melander had established there in his youthful pride in his social position. Josephine asked if Doctor Melander was at home. The servant said no; before she could ask any more questions Pillersdorf appeared at the open door and looked utterly astounded when he saw her. She, however, lost none of her composure. "It is well that I find you here, Herr von Pillersdorf," she said. "Can you give me a few moments? I must speak to you."

He bowed but seemed embarrassed, and openly did not know whether he should go with her or invite her into the room. To enter was forbidden by convention, and to leave, by the bad weather outside. Josephine scratched the stone tiles with her umbrella impatiently and made the decision herself as she stepped into the corridor. "As Doctor Melander is not here, you must spare me a few moments in his room," she said, and dried her wet gloves with her handkerchief. Pillersdorf followed her in growing embarrassment. Inside she turned a straightforward look upon him and asked, without preliminaries: "Do you know where Doctor Melander and Lothar spent last night?"

He jumped as if he had been struck with an axe and turned perfectly white. "You? You ask that, gracious Fräulein?" he stammered.

"Certainly, you hear that I ask it," she replied firmly. "And your conduct shows me that I have come to the correct address. Evidently you know. Did you learn it from Lothar or Doctor Melander?"

"From Lothar," Pillersdorf answered, hesitating; "he came home in an indescribable condition; Fräulein Ulrika and I put him to bed. It needed but little urging. He was so broken down that he confessed everything at the first question. Melander has never been found up to the present moment. He has not been at the Ministry nor the University nor at home. So I resolved to wait here for him. It is inexplicable where he is. It seems that—but forgive my curiosity, gracious lady, my anxious curiosity . . . I must say, what have you to do with this—this unfortunate incident?"

Josephine shook her head, as if this information had nothing to do with the matter. "So Lothar confessed," she said; "and did he also confess what happened to Tino Waldbauer and why he now lies in a condition between life and death, which is nearer death than life; why two hours ago he was thrown in front of his mother's door like a bag of potatoes? Did he confess that?"

Pillersdorf nodded; his face became gloomier.

"And will you tell me?" asked Josephine.

"No," was the quick and decisive answer.

"Why not?"

"Because it concerns things that are not suitable for your ears, gracious lady."

"But if I still insist?"

"No matter how you insist it is impossible."

"Nevertheless I will find ways and means to find out, you may be sure of that."

"I doubt it, my gracious lady," said Pillersdorf, with offended coldness.

"Will you be so kind, Herr von Pillersdorf," said Josephine angrily, "for the remainder of this quarter of an hour that I have to stand here, as to drop the 'gracious lady,' I am unaccustomed to it. I was not brought up to it. I was not born a 'gracious lady.' Although it is only a social title it does not belong to me. And because it does not belong to me, you see, for that reason and for that reason only I am here, and I throw myself upon your honour as a man and your conscience as a human being, and beg you to hide nothing from me. And however horrible it is I must hear it, for it would be much more horrible to leave the poor mother, who is watching in terror by her child, in ignorance. Perhaps you will say that it is not necessary for her to hear it through me; that I will not accept. If there are actions so bad that they must be hushed up at any cost, then they are so much the worse for those to whom they happen. And if they happen so close to me that I might almost touch them and yet cannot name them, then I have a right to know them, and it is no more than cowardice and hypocrisy and actual participation in crime to behave as if I did not dare to concern myself about it. No, I am very much concerned about it."

Pillersdorf's eyes were opened wide. Such eloquence upon such a subject from a young girl of seventeen years was new to him, and he had not had the faintest idea that the quiet Josephine, the Cinderella of the Mylius's house, and butt of all Ulrika's jests, should one day unveil herself so before him.

He had little mind and his education was very mediocre, but he was honest and good tempered and his natural modesty made it possible for him to recognise superior character and bow before it. He was silent a while, then he said with a forced smile and an embarrassed gesture: "Shall we sit down?"

Josephine sat down. He rubbed his big hands over his knees, swallowed once or twice and began: "Beside my painful position in regard to you, this story has another special difficulty for me in that Edward Melander must be protected. First I have solemnly promised some one, have promised to do whatever lay in my power to get him out of this hideous affair . . ."

"I can imagine whom you have promised," said Josephine, looking down.

"Moreover I am bound by a feeling of friendship. Too much depends upon it for him, who is at the beginning of a splendid career, and his friends must try to save him from the consequences of a frivolous deed. His position, his fame, his honour, all that weighs something. Could you give me your promise that you will not use my information to injure him in any way? I can only speak if you do, and even then it is very hard for me."

Josephine considered. "I think I can," she said. "If I cannot hear otherwise, I must do so, for it is not a matter of punishment either for me or for Lena Waldbauer; it is a matter of responsibility. And that lies between those two. And it is also that one would like to protect the people one loves from breathing the same air with such people. I cannot give up my own brother to justice and Tino's mother will understand what considerations hold me back. I think you need fear nothing."

"I am really not of the slightest use in the matter," sighed Pillersdorf. "As you sit there before me and I listen to you, Fräulein Josephine, I realise for the first time what a world it is. It's purest accident that I am not caught in the net too. I have plenty of such things on my conscience. A man such as I am goes his way so thoughtlessly, here, there, and everywhere, and hardly notices what he is doing or where it may end. Everybody wants to get the first crop of hay, and grind the corn on the ear; and he goes with the others and does what they do though he has learned and ought to know that they are impossible things. It is robbery; robbery of one's strength, one's time, and God's grace. And all the rest that follows; the distrust of those that love us and the misery of one's own heart. Don't be impatient with me over this litany, for it seems to me suddenly that scales have dropped from my eyes and I am grateful to you for it."

He paused, cleared his throat, and then began to tell with much consideration and sensitive circumlocutions what had happened to Melander, Lothar, and Tino. They went to an all-night show, of low variety, where there was dancing and singing and drank a lot of champagne. Tino had rebelled at first, but finally given in to the friendliness and persuasion of Melander, also Melander had given him a ring and this worked upon the imagination of the boy as if it were a magic treasure. During the entire time that they were in the night show he held the ring tight in his hand and looked at it with shining eyes. Melander now told him that he had a number of young women friends and that he must go with him and play to them and they would give him something much more beautiful. The boy was already half out of his mind, not only on account of the champagne he had drunk but because of the hideous noise around him and not least of all because of the emerald ring. So they went to the house where the beautiful young friends were.

What happened there, Pillersdorf could hardly even hint at. It seemed that a regular orgy had been planned. That the presence of the shy, strange, innocent, dreamy boy had made Melander quite wild. Only a person out of his senses, or moved by secret desire of vengeance or for some such reason, could have acted as he did, determined to ruin a little creature of whose tender and sensitive organism there could be no mistake. There had been other people there, the night-birds of a big city, a sham-elegant rabble; they brought Tino forward as a wonder child; a violin had been brought in;

they had stripped him stark naked, tied a blood red rag around him, stood him upon a table and with threats forced him to play. And then they did other things to him.

Great drops of sweat stood out on Pillersdorf's forehead. He could not go on with his story. Toward five o'clock in the morning they had thrown the little boy on a straw sack out in a wooden shed. He was unconscious, or rather in a sort of cataleptic rigidity. Nobody paid any sort of attention to him, and as no one wanted to concern themselves with him any more they got rid of him and left him to himself. A couple of hours later Lothar and Melander were called from the rest which they were sharing with two of their young friends. They went into the shed where Tino lay. It was a fearful sight. He had lain there already for half an hour, and now convulsions had set in. He screamed for his mother and hit about himself wildly while a white froth came from his mouth. They didn't dare call in a doctor as the whole thing might come out. Melander, pale to his very lips, tried every way to quiet the boy; he laid hot cloths upon his heart, he had hot tea made and tried to comfort him with urgent words but only about two o'clock of the next day the fury of the attack calmed down and Tino fell into a deep sleep. What the woman did who owned the house was not mentioned. The incident had overwhelmed Lothar and brought him somewhat to his senses; but he was quite differently struck by Melander's unexpected declaration that hereafter they would have nothing more to do with each other and that everything was over between them. Melander had sent for a carriage and carried Tino out in his arms.

Pillersdorf hesitated often. Opposite this stern, clear, girlish face, even the most veiled allusions struck him as crude and rough. The utter unworthiness of these things became clear to him, for the first time, as he touched upon them in her presence. To Josephine it was a general, troubled, detached continent of life that would hereafter weigh upon her imagination as an immovable burden. She did not take in the details, but she felt the dirt and slime of the story through and through. A deep sadness showed in all her features.

When Pillersdorf finished, she rose and offered him her hand. He did not dare address another word to her and she left.

Slowly she took the short route home. In the corridor Anastasia came forward to help her off with her hat and coat; she did not notice it, and asked where Ulrika was. Just then she emerged from the store-room and stood there.

"I have to speak to you, Ulrika," said Josephine.

Ulrika led her into her room. "Why don't you take your coat off?" she asked angrily. "You are wetting the carpet; you are dripping."

"I must demand something of you," said Josephine, standing stiff and still.

"And that is—"

"I demand that Doctor Melander never again enter this house."

For a moment Ulrika was speechless. "You are not in your right mind!" she cried, pale with anger.

"You can't well misunderstand me, Ulrika. I demand that this man never again step over this threshold." Her tone had something so cold and firm in it that Ulrika stared guiltily.

"And who gave you police power in the house?" she called out in derision. "What has happened to you that you are mixing yourself up in things? Please don't get beyond yourself. Stop and think what is fitting for you and what is not. You Pharisee, do you want to set up as judge of Edward Melander? Who allows you that? What do you know about him?"

"Enough," answered Josephine, coldly. "Do you hesitate to do what I demand?"

"Spare yourself the question; of course I refuse."

"And that in despite of the fact that you know why I ask it?"

"I do not think you are able to judge in such a matter," said Ulrika angrily, shutting her mouth tight.

"Very well," answered Josephine, "then you and I can no longer remain under the same roof." She turned around and left the room. With a firm step she hastened through the corridors, the music room, and the library till she came to the door of her mother's room. She knocked on the door and a soft "Come in" answered her.

Christine was cuddled up on the sofa in a gold-silk dressing gown and was reading *Le Cœur Humain Dévoilé*. Without raising her eyes from the book she stretched out her hand to Josephine.

Josephine sat down by her and said tenderly: "Mother, can you listen to me for a moment?"

"A moment?" Christine repeated reproachfully and turned toward her daughter a face that was becoming ever heavier and sleepier. "When have I ever been too busy to listen to my Josephine?"

Josephine suppressed a little sigh. "Really, I have only a word to say, mother," she began. "You must choose between me and Ulrika."

Christine started up with a jump.

"Only one of us two can remain near you, Ulrika or I," she went on quietly. "But you must not ask the reason, for I cannot tell you. You must just give me so much trust and faith that you believe it is the most important of reasons. I am quite clear about it; I know the choice is painful for you, for I know just what you have in Ulrika, and just what you imagine you have. And if your choice falls upon her, I shall not complain, I shall make no claims and no efforts to change your mind and I shall never love you less, but you must choose."

"For Heaven's sake, child, what's all this about?" Christine cried, springing up. "Why all this solemnity? Why are you sitting there in your coat and hat? Where have you come from? Where are you going? I must choose between you and Ulrika, right now, a half hour before supper, and without knowing what is the matter between you? Josephine, I beg you to be more reasonable. What am I to do without Ulrika? How can I get on without her or without you? How can I choose?"

"When necessity demands, we must choose," said Josephine.

"But explain the necessity."

"I have already told you, I cannot do that."

"Then your demand is straightout foolishness and I must really doubt your sense."

Josephine bit her lip till it bled. She had not yet learned that a person, when he undertakes to act as his conscience dictates, often falls against words as obstacles and that it is the chief end of these words to make his actions seem foolish and his resolves useless. But she was firm. She would not answer any more. The decision was taken from her and the blow had fallen. When the door opened and Ulrika stepped in she remained only out of a kind of sad curiosity. She thought that Ulrika would suspect that she was with her mother and would think up a pretext for coming in. But Ulrika scorned all pretexts. She gripped the subject without any preliminaries and the very way she did it showed her perfected mastery of every register of human weakness and its possibility of being deceived.

"The fool," she said in the tone of a rough, good-hearted person who has been hurt but is ready to forgive, "she has a grudge against me, because I attract people to the house who do not rise to her moral standards. But it would mean cutting ourselves off from all society if we demanded that people show their certificates of character at the front 'door. They don't throw bombs in here, and they don't steal our winter coats, and it is not our business to enquire how they amuse themselves when they are not here. You know Dr. Melander somewhat, do you not, Frau Christine? What do you think of him?"

"I think he is a gentleman through and through and very congenial to me," said Christine convinced.

"There," triumphed Ulrika and then played indignation which controls itself; "Josephine thinks, however, that we should forbid the man the house. Slanderous and harmful, but entirely unproven rumours, are going around about the man; he feels that it is entirely beneath his dignity to defend himself; but Fräulein Josephine, from the height of her moral conscience, orders us to boycott him, to mark him with a brand and avoid him. Say nothing, Josephine," she turned to her although Josephine had not made the slightest sign of speaking, but stood there with a pale, drawn, astonished smile at so much deception and lying, "say nothing, for you can't make the matter any better. Your mother is so boundlessly good to me, to you, to friend and foe, that she cannot understand these outbreaks of exalted pride. You see it. It torments her. Yes, I must call it pride. Everything that you do and think is pride. And it troubles me, that I can tell you honestly; for every man, if he is not a downright murderer, is worthy of love and honour to me. Learn to know something of life, my dear Josephine, before you take the judgment seat."

Christine went up to Josephine, who stood motionless, and said: "Ulrika really means all right, my child. I will forget your ruthlessness. Go now. Later or sometime to-morrow we can talk it all over. To-morrow will be better, when your anger is quieted down, will it not?"

"Yes, mother," Josephine whispered, and bent down her head to take the customary kiss on her forehead.

On the staircase, between the two floors, she met her father. Every time she saw him he seemed to have aged years. With a dead cigar stump in his mouth, his Scotch shawl around his shoulders, with an old jacket that lacked several of its buttons, and ragged house shoes, he slunk still and shy through the house at certain hours of the day. He wanted to see what was going on and how long it would go on; his mind was always busy with the coming collapse; he waited for it; he reckoned on it; he hoped that they would tear each other to pieces, and that this sinful palace, founded upon cunning, deceit and robbery, would become a waste place like that of Belshazzar. Then he would be avenged.

In her own room Josephine packed up some underwear, a dress, a few books, and things that she needed for her daily use, in a leather bag, wrote a few lines, put them in an envelope, and laid the letter on her table, waited then until she heard the signal for supper, and then slipped quickly down the servants' stairway at the back and out onto the street.

For the third time that day she took her way to Lena Waldbauer's.

CHAPTER XVI

CRYING OVER SPILT MILK

"I DIDN'T believe you were coming," said Lena and looked with astonishment at the travelling bag.

"Yes, it is late and I am very tired," said Josephine, "I have come to beg you to let me stay. Things have happened that have forced me to leave my parents' house. Whether for a few days, or weeks, or longer I don't know. I will tell you everything. Can you give me shelter until I find quarters? If necessary I can lodge in the Institute, but I don't want to do that."

"You can stay here quite well," said Lena after thinking a minute; "but you must understand that it is a dark room on a court, that I used to rent. Now no one will take it. A spoiled young lady like you will hardly be able to live there."

"I am not spoiled," Josephine answered, smiling.

She was in no condition to talk this evening, and she fell into bed and slept eleven hours. The next morning she sat down by Lena at her work-table, and watched with interest the skill with which she curled the white feathers that covered the table and cut off the quills. Tino lay with the same expressionless look, staring at the same point on the wall. Josephine told what Pillersdorf had confided to her, to her horrified listener, who never stopped work for a moment, because it helped her to control her face and her feelings.

All that had been carefully softened in Pillersdorf's account was now made even more mild, for Josephine wanted to be careful and because, too, the horror of the thing had a sort of helpless naïveté in the mouth of this innocent, which roused the experienced Lena to fury.

She stopped work and leaned her head on her hand. After long silence she opened the drawer, drew out a letter and gave

206

it to Josephine to read. It was from Melander; a messenger had brought it in an hour before.

The writing ran: "It would not occur to me to try to escape the guilt which I confess in full. If, however, you ask for the reason and ground of my actions, I am unable to give any account of them. I cannot but believe—and I offer it as a very poor excuse—that a demon lives in my breast, awaking from time to time to rush out and destroy my world. The object of these lines is to beg you to forego any public action in the matter, but principally I want to tell you that it is my inmost desire and resolution to try and make good all the harm I have done and I ask your permission to take upon myself hereafter the material care of your son's future. In order to wipe away my guilt from his imagination, I am resolved to spend some months abroad. Before I go I should like a short interview with you to arrange what can be arranged in these unhappy circumstances."

Still holding the letter in her hand, Josephine told of her interview with Ulrika and her mother.

Lena Waldbauer said, "That explains a good deal. They will know at your house where you are and the letter is written much more to you than to me. How can he fancy that a poor feather trimmer should understand such words as demon. Fräulein Ulrika, of course, told him that you were in the game and his friend will also have told him the same thing and now he is building upon it. He is going abroad and so you have managed to put it through that he shall not enter your house. A clever man."

"Yes, certainly a clever man," Josephine muttered, "but it is all too late now."

"However it may be, my hands are doubly bound," Lena went on; "he has bound me by his confession, and you have bound me by your break with your mother. Now what more can I ask? Shall I run into court? What for? Our kind know what is likely to happen then. It would just be mud-slinging. The poor are always down-trodden even when apparently they do them justice. He talks of the demon in his breast; but I can only think of the sorrow in mine. What has that to do with right and justice, I'd like to know? It is life and we are used to it."

The next day a university professor came around, sent by Melander. The investigation was thorough and lasted a long time. He said that it was an extraordinarily heavy psychical disturbance. Complete cure in a short time he could hardly promise, but it was a possibility. In a few days he would come back with the physician in charge of the case and consult with him.

Toward evening when Josephine was still at the Institute Melander appeared at Lena Waldbauer's. He remained about half an hour, convinced her of his repentance and, despite her resistance, forced her to accept a considerable sum of money which he said was mere advance payment. Lena told Josephine that he had been there and that at his request she had given his letter back to him; but she was silent about the money and was depressed the whole evening. She really suffered that she had allowed herself to be paid instead of showing the criminal the door with scorn and loathing. "One isn't really a human being," she said to herself; "only a rotten, cowardly animal."

The next morning Ulrika sent the pretty Nanette to Josephine to demand that she come directly home. For Ulrika had guessed immediately where Josephine, with her "leaning toward common people," would go; and Edward Melander had confirmed her suspicion after his visit to Lena. Josephine wanted to know how her mother was; and Nanette quieted her on that score, then she dismissed the astonished girl without even answering Ulrika's categorical command.

Ulrika was really in a dilemma. Christine was so hedged round by her that she learned of Josephine's departure only what Ulrika thought advisable to tell her. The letter that Josephine had written her mother, she intercepted. She said Josephine had gone for a few days to the blind Institution just to give vent to her wicked stubbornness. When Christine became anxious, Ulrika scolded her and said the traveller would come back quick enough when things became too uncomfortable for her, when she found that the bread basket hung too high.

Christine shook her head and replied that the last thing in the world that would have any influence upon Josephine would be a bread-basket. She wanted to go out and fetch Josephine and ordered the carriage. There was no way to prevent this except to tell her that Josephine was not in the Institution, but had gone to stay with a friend; and Ulrika added she had done this for the very purpose of frightening her mother and injuring Ulrika. It was a complicated story, she said, but she would sometime tell Christine how things were; but everything depended on their not being weak and yielding to Josephine and if Christine could not restrain her impatience and upheld Josephine in her stubbornness she, Ulrika, would know what to do.

She knew how to intimidate Christine, scattered the seed of misunderstanding, slowly and carefully estranged the mother from Josephine and daily sent short, sharp messages to Josephine that disturbed her and gave her no peace.

Josephine and Lena took care of the boy. Some one had to sit by him, feed him, move him in the bed, wash him and do all the little personal services. In the evenings Josephine read or studied and her conversations with Lena lasted often deep into the night. Josephine began to see the life of the people; she got an insight into their work, their needs, and their joys. She was interested in the manifold life of the tenement. There was a comb maker who lived over the entrance; next door to him a button turner, above, a fan painter, a cobbler, a book-binder, a glass blower, an engraver, a tin founder, a stocking weaver, a sewing woman, people who worked at home, independent producers, prostitutes, male and female, casuals and permanent people; they buzzed up stairs, down stairs, in doors, out of doors and laughed and chattered and worked, and loved and hated and hoped and despaired, day in and day out. It seemed to Josephine that she was listening to a never-ending melody, sometimes sad, sometimes joyous, sometimes loud, sometimes low.

On Friday Lena wrote to the Counsellor that Tino, on account of his illness, would be prevented from coming, and indeed it was uncertain whether he would be able to play for

him again. She showed the letter to Josephine; it was strangely
stiff and reserved and when Josephine looked at her questioningly she said, pointing to Tino: "He is not only his god-
child, he is his grand-child."

That evening she told her story. "In the fifties my mother
was a famous soubrette. She had a great many suitors, for she
was buoyant and jolly and a woman just after the heart of men.
For a certain time there was a regular cult for her, which is
not unusual here. I do not know how it came about, but despite all the casual connections that she had which suited her
nature, she entered into a really serious affair with Counsellor
Woytich, who at that time was a great man and possessed
power and influence. I say I don't know how it came about,
for the Counsellor was famous for his miserliness and my
mother was a spendthrift; so they must have suited each other
ill. It is idle to think about it now, but at any rate I thank
that connection for my existence, if one can speak of thanks
in such a connection. My father never bothered about me in
the least, and I repaid him in kind. If I were to say there
was the slightest feeling for him in my heart I should be lying.
I was well enough brought up until I was fifteen years old,
then my mother lost her voice and things went down rapidly.'
She lived to be very old, dying only six years ago, but she
never could overcome poverty. There is not much to tell
about myself; I have always managed to pull through, but it
was a close shave; I have had my share of love, my share of
care, and out of the share of love came that child. One day
my mother had the idea of taking the child to his grandfather,
who had never done a thing for him since he saw him christ-
ened; it was hard enough for him to give the godfather's
present. We had discovered Tino's musical endowment by
chance, and my mother mentioned it to the Counsellor who,
to our astonishment, declared himself ready to educate him.
From time to time he sent for him, always with the greatest
secrecy; at last he arranged that he should play to him every
Sunday afternoon. My mother made me promise her a few
days before her death that I would not prevent the boy from
going, as some real blessing might come to him from it. I

have never believed that and don't believe it to-day, but it was wonderful to hear these Sunday concerts on the beautiful old violin. The one or two times that I listened at the door, when Fräulein Smirczinska happened to be in a good humour, tears burst from my eyes. Now that is all over."

Josephine sat by Tino's bed and thoughtfully stroked the boy's hand, a fine, narrow hand, a real musician's hand.

Sunday afternoon at five o'clock Smirczinska arrived in the greatest excitement. Tino was to come at once to the Counsellor, she said; he had waited an hour for him, had laid out the violin on the table and insisted that he must be played to.

Lena shrugged her shoulders and nodded toward the boy's bed.

Smirczinska continued: he was going around and screaming, his little cap on his snow-white hair and his fashionable cul-de-Paris under his crumpled coat made him look perfectly ridiculous; he cried out that he did not want to have spent all that money for nothing; he would accept no excuses and evasions; he would not forego his Sundays; he had too few Sundays ahead of him anyway and if the boy were unwilling to come of his own accord he would have him brought by force.

"Did he never get my letter?" asked Lena calmly.

Certainly, Smirczinska replied, but he declared that he would take no notice of it; he would not accept it; he would read no letters from strange women.

"Just listen!" said Lena, turning with a smile to Josephine.

But he did read the letter, said the old woman, and fell into a violent rage, hunted round amongst his papers, took things out of drawers and off shelves and fussed and fumed half the night interruptedly. To-day he refused to eat his dinner, and ever since three o'clock he had watched the clock every instant. Could not the boy come? Not for just a quarter of an hour? The Counsellor depended so upon it. God knew why; she had never seen him as he was to-day and she was literally afraid to go home alone to him.

Lena said: "Go across to Doctor Reitlinger; he lives quite near, 15 Neubau street, and it is his consulting hour now. Explain that you have come from Tino's grandfather. Yes, that frightens you; but his grandfather he is. Tell him to write you a certificate that my child is ill, very ill. There can be no question of his playing the violin. That may pacify the Counsellor."

Smirczinska stood still a moment with her mouth open. "All right, that is what I will do," she said then.

"But tell him to leave me in peace," Lena added bitterly; "I have had enough of it."

Smirczinska looked without a word at Tino's white face, sighed, and went out.

"Suspicious," Lena murmured between her teeth. "After a lifetime of heartless scorn and humiliation, he adds this. He won't accept it! I believe that. He has never accepted anything that was uncomfortable for him. He would like to paint the sun with soot when he wants a cloudy day. Darkness, yes, that is what he likes. Why should wickedness ever live to grow so old!" She sobbed, controlled herself quickly and drew the curtains over the window.

Josephine felt that not only anger and grief burnt up again in Lena, but that besides that she was uneasy and she did not know what it was that made her so. She brooded for a moment and then said: "Lena, if you wish and I think you do, I will go to the old man and make him understand why Tino cannot come. Smirczinska will not know how to tell him and the doctor's certificate may have just the wrong effect. When I think it over, it seems to me that he really loves the child; there is no doubt that in his own way he really does love him, and you, Lena, know it. All this about the violin is only an excuse that his hard old heart uses to protect or deceive himself. I will go to him, don't you think I had better? I will talk to him. Who knows but it will do good?"

Instead of answering Lena took Josephine's hand and pressed it in hers.

When Josephine had climbed the four steps in the Dorothea Street, she found Smirczinska standing at the house door showing every sign of excitement. She rushed to Josephine and burst out: "Where is she? Is she coming soon? Is she on the way? Was she not home?" Apparently she did not even know who Josephine was and remembered only vaguely that she had seen her earlier in the day.

"Who? Who do you mean?" asked Josephine.

"Ulrika. I sent the girl from the third floor to get her. What else could I do? Somebody must go for the doctor. Perhaps it would have been better to send directly for the doctor. But he always bound me upon my honour not to get a doctor; never a doctor. Oh, the poor Counsellor! He has lost his mind."

And she told how the Counsellor, when he saw the doctor's certificate in which Tino's illness was described in short, harsh words, had begun to jabber in anxiety and excitement, had driven her out of the room with frightful curses, rushed into the kitchen, taken an axe and, swearing frightfully, he had chopped the costly old violin to which he had clung, and always defended as if it were a beloved child, into bits. Now he was sitting before it and would neither speak nor move.

During her last words Josephine heard quick steps coming. Ulrika came in. Smirczinska gesticulated. "What are you doing here?" said Ulrika, breathless from running up the stairs as she became aware of Josephine, but Smirczinska gave her no time to hear the answer, and drew her into the house. Ulrika disappeared through the door and Josephine heard a hoarse, wild scream. She did not dare to follow them in, but went into another room, waiting on the threshold of the second room to see and hear.

Ulrika knelt before the chopped-up instrument; her slender back trembled convulsively. The Counsellor sat in his old armchair, just as he sat when Tino was playing to him, motionless and dazed; his chin lay upon his breast; his eyes were shut; his face was set and waxen, his mouth one thin line, his nose was like a hawk's beak.

Last night the awful vision had appeared to him again, groaning horribly. As the dawn came on, the figure was easier to discern, naked, hairy, a greasy horror. This time no begging or excuses had served; it would not hear of a substitute; he had knocked with the bones of his fist on the bed post and insisted that his demand be made good. "Only a little while," the Counsellor whined, "only a couple of weeks; only that I may get used to the thought; only let me prepare myself to give up all the sweetness of life." And then the hideous vision had made a hideous grimace and faded away.

Ulrika rose, went to the Counsellor and screamed at him in her shrill voice: "You horrible, envious old dog, you, what have you done! Give me back what is mine! Give me back what you have stolen! Will you or won't you? It is like you, you sly thief, you housebreaker, that even in your grave you should grudge one what you have stolen. Give it back, I say, or I will tear out your rascally eyes, before you die, you old cat!"

She seized his shoulder and shook him like an old scare-crow.

Josephine shuddered at the hideous words.

The Counsellor did not notice it, or perhaps he really understood the mad woman, for he pushed out his evil underlip so that it looked like a scornful smile and half opened his eyes. But his eyes were terrified when he noticed that a paper had fallen from the pocket of his dressing-gown. Before Smirczinska had returned he had taken out of the secret drawer a five hundred gulden note which he meant for Tino when he came. He was trying to flatter fate. Ulrika picked up the paper and stuck it hastily in her pocket, paying no attention to the despairing, feeble gestures of the old man.

"He is still alive," she said to Smirczinska, "he will live a long time. Such old criminals are hard to bring down. I will make an inventory of everything in the house, everything, furniture, clothes, and money, nothing shall escape me. When I go I will send Anastasia here to watch, and she will see that the things don't take wings unto themselves."

Paying no attention to Josephine, she passed by her, blind with anger and pain. She wanted to go into the third room, where the secret wall cupboard was, but dropped suddenly upon a chair and buried her face in her hands. Josephine thought: "Crying about a *thing!* crying about a dead *thing!*" and she seemed to see the whole life of this woman, the part that she knew and the other part that she barely conceived. She whispered sympathetically: "Ulrika."

Ulrika looked up. "What are you doing here, Josephine, tell me that?" She spoke harshly. "Were you sent for to be a comforter? Must you spy around everywhere at my heels? Get out of this accursed house. Here wickedness and commonness colour everything as chalk does a blackboard. He has chopped up my violin, the wretched fool, and you see, that is the same as if he had chopped up the soul in my body. All right; I will go on living without a soul in my body."

Josephine was horrified and silent.

"Go away, Josephine," Ulrika went on. "While your mother is grieving for you, you wander around the world where it is saddest, and meddle in every one else's affairs. Go back home; I am giving you good advice."

Josephine wandered back to the suburb with conflicting feelings. She told Lena all she had seen in the Dorothea Street. Lena listened and shrugged her shoulders as if she wanted to say: What happens there does not concern me. Josephine told her about Ulrika's warning and Lena guessed her inner uncertainty.

Later in the evening she said to Josephine: "In your place, I would take her advice. A mother is a mother. With one's mother one is never in the right; with a father it is different. And then, as far as I can see, you are the only one who might keep the danger from her that this Ulrika may cause. You daren't give up your mother altogether. I shall lose a great deal when you leave me, lose it even if you come to see me every day. It will no longer be the same thing. It was so lovely—our doors side by side. But that must not count. You are not weak if you go home, only clever. To run your head against a stone wall, that is weakness. And believe me, Josephine, the guilty are never quite so guilty as we think, and the innocent never quite so innocent as they feel. Everything is interwoven. And everything goes its own predestined way laughing at the pains we take. It is time that plays tricks with us. When I was a child there was a little running brook beside our house. And twenty years later when I came back there I was frightened and thought:—good Heavens, is the same water here still? As if it could be the same water! Stupid, wasn't it?"

The next day Josephine went home.

CHAPTER XVII

MARRIAGES AND LEGACIES

THE Counsellor could not die. His strong will to live fought bitterly against the hairy horror. He lay rigid with fixed eyes, in which from time to time a gleam of fury and hatred appeared, when they were speaking near his alcove, a place that they anxiously avoided in the days of his health.

He could not even take up his soup spoon. Smirczinska attended to all his personal service. But Anastasia was there, from early morning till late evening, watching. Ulrika had appointed her to this task, while she undertook the general oversight and control of things.

She came every day for a half hour or longer, to see how things stood and if the life-clock of the seventy-eight-year-old man still ran. She went up to his bed, looked down upon him and nodded as if to say:—now, old fellow, still crawling? how long will you keep us from more useful duties?

Every day she counted the chairs, examined the curtains and hangings, assured herself that the secret cupboard was still closed, the key to which she had long since taken, and went over each piece in the collection with the help of an inventory she had made.

Anastasia followed her with peering eyes. Smirczinska, who believed that she was in the will, dared not peep.

In the Mylius house, at this time, the fate of Lothar was the object of much discussion. He was confirmed in his plan to travel in foreign countries; since the break with Edward Melander and his departure, life in his parents' house was unbearable to Lothar. He was in a constant quarrel with Ferry Lex, who was now Esther's declared fiancé. They had had the official celebration on New Year's day, and a few days later, the day of the Three Kings, Aimée's engagement to Althann had been announced. Lothar had a great deal of fun over the two couples; he was vexed at their turtledove ways, as he called them, and the sisters had a great deal to bear from his quarrelling and derision. Althann, who was a quiet man, did not notice it or put him off good humouredly, but Lex grew seriously angry with him. He agreed with Ulrika that he ought to be sent away soon. Althann, however, opposed this. He said so rich a fellow might just as well be idle; why should he snatch bread away from others or add a new Mammon to the old one? If he was bored and annoyed people with his tricks he might go to Africa and hunt elephants. "And lead astray the daughters of the Zulu Kaffirs," Ulrika said dryly.

"You must learn to bring some sense and reason into your life now," she said to Lothar; "you have lost your first horns, now see to it that you get a regular pair, and don't show your cards to every donkey that comes along. In a few years you will be your own master, and then no one will be able to interfere with you. Then you can throw your trumps on the table."

Various investigations were made, and he entered as a volunteer into a celebrated Amsterdam firm of art dealers who had long had relations with H. O. Mylius. Reasonable and sensible he was not yet. Depravity still clung to him. But he was now at a good distance and Ulrika felt easier about him.

She and the betrothed couples had taken him to the station. Christine, who was troubled with headache, had said good-bye to him at the house. He had only casually pressed Josephine's hand. That same afternoon Lex had a conference with Ulrika about the dowry. He demanded some binding arrangement. Heretofore Ulrika had kept him in uncertainty. Althann was easy to manage; he did not worry about it much and placed his confidence in Ulrika's foresight and capacity. Lex, however, was hard pressed by his creditors and could not arrange with them although the engagement was now known.

Ulrika was worried; she was afraid of a decisive explanation with Mylius, and put it off from day to day. Now that circumstances forced her to act she decided quickly, and after supper she went up to him.

He sat by the lamp at the table with a mountain of old letters and papers piled up before him, which he was handling with trembling fingers. He was only the shadow of his old self. His face was yellow. His eyes had no shine to them. His threadbare old clothes hung loose on his body. On his head he wore an embroidered cap and his iron-grey hair hung uncombed over his forehead.

He hardly looked up when Ulrika entered, but rose and went to another table, where the piquet cards lay. He picked up a scrap of paper on which figures stood, the winnings and losings of their last game, coughed, and began to add.

"Leave that alone," said Ulrika; "we have something more important to do this evening."

"What is it, my child, what is it?" he babbled, out of humour. "I don't like important things. Especially those that concern down-stairs. What sort of important things can they be? I know. I don't want to know any more of your important things."

Ulrika sat down and folded her arms. He knew that this attitude meant battle and was disquieted. "Well, what is it then, what is it?" he groaned and shrugged his shoulders, "What sort of important things?"

"Esther and Aimée are to be married in three weeks."

"What of that? It doesn't concern me. Let them get married. I don't care."

"You want to send your daughters into marriage, as a man sends cattle to slaughter? With nothing? Naked? I think you will have to care. If not you, who will? To beget children and then when it is a question of looking out for them to stick one's head into the sand and say: 'I am not here, do as you please,' that is all too easy. Anybody can do that. But we have not planned for this. Quite the contrary. You will have to give each one of them six hundred thousand gulden as dowry. Do you understand?"

Mylius's face seemed to shrink suddenly. He stared in front of himself for a while, stood up, put his right hand into the left arm of his coat, his left hand into the right, as if he were cold, went around the room, and began a very singular little

singsong. This was to signify that he had heard nothing and
was determined to hear nothing. It was a monotonous little
song, half idiotic, half insane, an endless, sleepy, tra la la. It
was his last weapon, the end of his tether.

Ulrika's words fell powerless before this singing. All arguments and representations disappeared in thin air. She recognised the futility of her attempt, and, laughing angrily, she
went out of the door, slamming it behind her. After an hour
she came back again. He was still wandering up and down,
hands in his coat sleeves and as soon as she entered the room
he began the sick, insane singsong again. Ulrika hit the
table with her fist in vain. She screamed at him and made
him stand still by planting herself in front of him. In vain.
She sat down by the window and waited. It struck ten o'clock,
half-past ten, eleven, and the singing still went on. Then she
went into the next room, fetched a mattress and cushions and
arranged a bed on the floor for herself. Then she ran down
to her own room, fetched her dressing gown, comb and brush,
reappeared in a few moments again, put the white gown over
her shoulders, sat down beside the improvised bed, let down
her hair and began to comb and brush it.

Suddenly Mylius was still. Overcome he stared at the long,
rich, brown hair, and the glowing young face framed in by it
seemed to him more beautiful than ever. He sank down into
his armchair and gazed: astonished, curious, anxious. From
time to time Ulrika sent him an ironic, enticing glance, and her
mouth smiled.

"Have you thought it over?" she asked him.

"Ulrika, my good child, have mercy on me."

She answered that it was no question of that, but a mere
matter of right and duty.

He replied that he had remembered her in his will, had
written a codicil that would take care of her; he would have to
cancel it if she made this demand for his daughters.

Ulrika listened. She told him she did not believe him; he
would have to show it to her or she would believe that he
was trying to escape. He insisted; she demanded that she
see the will. At last he admitted that he had lied, but swore

that the codicil should be drawn up in her presence the next day, and that she could send for the Notary Helmbauer. How much? she asked, not without greed. Twenty thousand gulden, he told her. She said that he owed her that before God and men. Hadn't she given half her life to him? Who would have taken care of him, if not she? Who else had ever loved him or taken care of him? But all this had nothing to do with the claim made by Count Lex and Baron Althann for a suitable dowry for their wives.

He whined: "Come here, my good Ulrika, come here; feel how cold my hands are. There is no blood left in my veins. You have pumped all the blood out of me."

She went up to him and took his hands and rubbed them between hers. It was a sin, she told him, to talk about money as if it were his heart's blood. He put his arm around her and laid his head on her shoulder. Now he felt better, he stammered, better than he had ever felt in his whole life. His distorted face peered through Ulrika's veil of heavy hair like a rotten fruit. He had had a wife, Ulrika said, a wife high above him and had tasted love. No, he replied, he had never reached it, he had been too much worried. He had loved his money too much, Ulrika said, and that had been his heaven, wife, and world all in one. He clung to her like a child and asked if she did not love money, too. Oh, yes, she loved it, too, she admitted, all at once strangely thoughtful and silent. Then he exulted, in a hectic shrill voice; he had always felt that in her, and it was because of that he had loved her and given her his confidence. She answered cruelly that his life's course was run, he really could not line his grave with ducats, and if the warning of death did not make him gentle he really did not deserve having his eyes closed for the last sleep.

Mylius shuddered. He said: "Mine, mine, mine!" and after a pause: "My money. Oh, my money!"

It was more like the outbreak of a witch's dream than like human speech between the four walls of a house.

It was not difficult for Ulrika to overthrow him in his present weakness. Suddenly he became obedient. She put him to bed and covered him up. In a corner on a shelf stood a Bible; she took it up, opened at a page in Corinthians and read with a stern expression:—

"Did I make a gain of you by any of them whom I sent unto you?

"I desired Titus, and with him I sent a brother. Did Titus make a gain of you? walked we· not in the same steps?

"Again, think ye that we excuse ourselves unto you? we speak before God in Christ: but we do all things, dearly beloved, for your edifying."

"For I fear, lest, when I come, I shall not find you such as I would, and that I shall be found unto you such as ye would not: lest there be debates, envyings, wraths, strifes, backbitings, whisperings, swellings, tumults."

At two o'clock that morning she got his signature for liquidating the dowries.

The next morning the Notary Helmbauer came and the codicil was made.

The preparations for the double wedding filled the days and demanded every one's help. Again Ulrika was manager and moving spirit. Again calls came from every door, "Ulrika"; from every staircase, from morning till evening. Ulrika bargained, paid, scolded, praised, was in three places at once, arranged with the dressmakers, the decorator, the pastor and the caterer, gave the brides rules of conduct and the future bridegrooms good advice and made rain and sun in the house.

Esther and Aimée couldn't get enough of buying and making. Their insatiability, their extravagance astonished even Ulrika. They were showing the results of their bringing up in all its glory and the master was outmastered. What they chiefly wanted was jewelry; every way in the town lead to the jeweller's. Aimée had a restless desire for pearls, Esther preferred diamonds. The most costly Parisian toilets were ordered by the half-dozen, the very finest furs found grace in their eyes, hats and shoes were ordered in ridiculous quantities. There was no holding them in now; they threw money away as if they hated it, as if they were trying to avenge the privations of their youth.

"It is beginning in a very promising way," thought Ulrika, and grinned.

The wedding and wedding dinner went off with the greatest brilliancy. The great spaces of the palace could hardly hold the number of illustrious and less illustrious guests. On the streets the carriages crowded and the people stood devoutly before the door and the wrought-iron fence. The drinking of toasts and rhymed and unrhymed congratulations at the table lasted for an hour and a half. Christine was radiant; and old Mylius lay up stairs ill.

The Lex couple were going to travel in the South and later spend a time in London; the Althanns were going to Paris where they would remain for the next few years. Before they left, both sisters fell upon Ulrika's neck and kissed her with tears. Ulrika shed tears, too. The farewell to their mother and Josephine passed off much more quietly. They stood silently at their father's bedside and Mylius looked at them silently, too, and hesitatingly offered his icy hand.

He was near his end and Ulrika knew it. In order that the wedding might not be disturbed or postponed she had kept the seriousness of his illness a secret. The day after the wedding the doctor had sent for her. He shook his head thoughtfully; why had he not been sent for sooner; a week ago something might have been done perhaps; but now it was too late. Ulrika seemed quite broken. She said that she had had trouble enough to persuade him, as he had been unwilling to believe that he needed a doctor's aid. The doctor gave him no hope, and Ulrika went to Christine to forewarn her.

It was only fright that Christine felt, but when they announced his death the fright took on the colour of mourning. When they went to wash the dead they found under Mylius's pillow a purse with seventy-five gold pieces in it.

Strangely enough Counsellor Woytich died the same night as Mylius. They were buried on the same day, one in the Catholic, the other in the Protestant, cemetery, one at four o'clock, the other at five o'clock, and Ulrika had to rush to be able to pay the last honours to both of them. She was lovely in her black dress. Of all Mylius's children, Josephine only

followed his body to his grave. Lothar had been sent a telegram; the young married couples were only notified by letter
that they might not turn so swiftly from the wedding altar
to the grave.

A stubborn fight now began between the Woytich brothers
and sisters about the inheritance. At the very worst Ulrika
and Anastasia got to pulling each other's hair. One accused
the other of an underhanded hiding of important papers and
valuable things. There was no will to be found. As Anastasia had nursed the Counsellor to the end, and been with him
day and night, it seemed that Ulrika's accusations might be
just, and Anastasia could only meet them with counter-
accusations and oaths of innocence. Smirczinska, in a condition
of complete disappointment, took the side of first one and
then the other as the hazard of war went. One day
Anastasia voiced the suspicion that Ulrika, who swore by
all that was good and holy that she had seen the will during
the Counsellor's life, had purposely let it be lost. Anastasia
reproached Ulrika with this deed as if it had been proven,
and there was a fearful fight, in the course of which Smirczinska left the house in which she had lived almost as mistress for forty-seven years howling with rage. The Vice-
Consul stood heartily on Ulrika's side, though his convictions
were on Anastasia's, but he sought to bring about peace.
Severin, who was an opportunist, said both were right and
declared that he was injured by all. At any rate, after the
end of the fight and after all the moveables of the Counsellor
had been sold Ulrika had brought away into safety about
twenty-three thousand gulden for herself, which with her
legacy from Mylius, made about forty-three thousand
gulden. Also as her efforts for the happiness of Esther
and Aimée were gladly admitted by the parties interested,
the payment of the dowries was not without adequate reward,
which she reckoned up and demanded according to customary
per cents, in full consciousness of her efforts and in consideration of the magnitude of the sums for which she had
fought; and, as, moreover, her perquisites, fees, indemnifica-
tions, commissions, tips, and other casual rake-offs that came

with the enlargement of the house, with the ordering of a number of festivities, kept even step with them, her cash fortune in the middle of this year ran up to more than a hundred and sixty thousand gulden which in consideration of the modest demands of the time might be called a dignified fortune. She carefully avoided touching it at all. Adding interest to interest she had learned from the unforgettable example of Mylius whose picture, with an evergreen wreath around it hung always by her bed.

Now she was living in the spacious palace with only Christine and Josephine. But the life that began there was anything but cloister-like. Twice in the week Christine held her big reception days which it was the fashion to attend. Everybody praised her intellectuality, her culture and her hospitality. She always knew how to say to each one the thing that would give him pleasure, and then when she had surprised him with her friendly words, she flattered him by a thorough knowledge of his personal circumstances, which, although they rested on the wide reaching news-service of Ulrika, seemed as if they came from heartfelt sympathy. But more than this, there was hardly a meal, midday or evenings, at which a half dozen friends and acquaintances did not appear, and after the meal there was music or literary discussion. There was no lack of talent and celebrity there, and Christine took pride in making her house a home of the arts.

By degrees Ulrika had gained complete power over her. Opinion, judgment, mentality, moods, expression, and form— it was all Ulrika. Ulrika's will ruled her nerves even to the exciting of her taste and casual desires; it would have been so foolish and senseless to try and contradict this will, that she might as well have tried to contradict the weight of the atmosphere. She was bound, and she smiled at command, was angry at command, saved or spent at command. Ulrika watched her every step and her bedside, and lent her eyes, tongue, and thought. Christine no longer felt the telepathic power of this personality, of which she was only the obedient and expressive organ and she leaned as if asleep on this strong element.

One day she was wandering arm and arm with Ulrika through the upper reception rooms. Ulrika expressed her pleasure in the rooms, how beautiful every piece of furniture was and how it looked as if it were just in the right place here and could not be placed anywhere else. Then Christine leaned tenderly on her shoulder and told her that she liked to hear this, and that whatever she liked in the house she must look upon as her own. "So? I would like to have that in writing," said Ulrika, laughing; "one never knows where life may bring one." Christine, laughing also, said: "Very well, you shall have it in writing. How shall we do it? I will write on a sheet of paper twenty times or fifty times or as often as you wish the sentence: 'This belongs to my beloved Ulrika Woytich.' It will be a twenty- or fifty-fold blank check for all needs. Is that right, Ulrika?"

Was it right for Ulrika! They sat down side by side at the writing desk in the library and, still laughing, Christine did as she had promised.

To have Josephine, who was now maturing and becoming a woman, as a constant presence and house-mate was a thorn in the flesh of Ulrika. She never hesitated to speak slightingly of her to anyone who would listen and said quite openly that she would make a red mark on the calendar on the day she was free from the sight of this nun. "A healthy person can bear a great deal," she jested, "but when one must be ready all the time to have the virtue thermometer stuck under the moral bed-covering, one's patience gives out. I like to eat my beefsteak without conscientious qualms and *Memento Mori.*"

And then a new plan, the most insolent of all, occurred to her fertile brain.

In the early autumn Edward Melander had come back from foreign lands. His powerful protector had given him important and most responsible business to attend to which had great significance for political affairs. It was a matter of great risk and capitalistic aspirations and his activities were not only informative but also executive and constructive. He had justified the confidence placed in him in every detail.

He had hardly returned when he was made special professor of economics and at the same time became director of the First National Bank. Such astonishing success for so young a man, he was just twenty-six, attracted general attention, and Christine, who learned of it, was surprised that he remained away from her house. Ulrika quieted all his fears of Josephine and persuaded him to come again to the Mylius house. He wore a moustache and goatee like Louis Napoleon, whom he resembled, and his hair instead of standing on end was parted and smooth. His carriage was firmer and he rarely smiled. They all become stern men in time and drive the wild youths from the circle of their acquaintance.

The relationship between himself and Ulrika, carefully hidden from the eyes of the world, was still undissolved. He had written her conscientiously every week and she was as precisely informed of his activities as of his thoughts and opinions. But she was not so inclined to play the rôle of sisterly friend as he imagined; despite all comradeship and a feeling, which he thought was quieted and finished, although they had both tackled life together like the two prongs of a pair of tongs, he had no real comprehension of her feelings, and was not a little surprised when they suddenly came to light.

In Petersburg he had an affair with a dancer of the Imperial Ballet, and in Berlin various adventures of a slight and casual order. All this Ulrika knew. But soon after his return he had a violent passion for the beautiful and much-courted wife of a diplomat. The *liaison* was very dangerous; it went to inconsiderate lengths and gossip was already busy with both of them. For the first time Ulrika knew nothing about it; she learned of the relation to the beautiful Italian through the Vice-Consul, who was a living newspaper and brought her all the news and gossip of the big and little world in first editions.

One hour later she was with Melander. She had heard so and so; was it true? He could not deny it. She laid both hands upon his shoulders, looked at him with gleaming eyes, and said: "All right; you are to break off this relationship, and do it at once."

He laughed, surprised, but turned pale and replied that no one could force him to do this.

"Except me!" said Ulrika. "Never forget that."

He said grimly that he did not understand; what did she mean?

"Everything," she answered and shook her head wildly, "everything. I will not bear it, and if you hesitate to do as I say I will ruin you. You know me; act accordingly."

He looked at her speechless. She threw her arms around him and pressed him to her so that he almost lost his breath and then she flung him from her and broke out into half ironic, half bitter laughter. "You don't take me for such a goose as to be jealous, because we lived together for a year and a day," she said. "The pillows are cold but what I took away, no one can steal from me." She walked up and down, her eyes glittering. "What are you staring at me so for?" she called out suddenly. "Oh, you men! What fools you are!" and she laughed again.

"Evidently it is fun for you to set riddles for me," Melander murmured.

She became quiet, smoothed her hair, stretched her elastic body, thought for a second or two and then said: "What you need is security. A man like you needs a firm frame for his life. The frame makes the picture, and the picture needs a definite and recognised place on the wall of the bourgeois world. Thereby you will stand or fall. If there were no such thing as marriage it would have to be invented for you. Old Voltaire said something like that."

Melander answered by shrugging his shoulders: "You are speculative as usual. It takes two to make a marriage. I know no woman suitable for me. I have never yet met one."

"But I know one," said Ulrika.

"Namely?"

"Josephine. Josephine Mylius."

He started; he turned pale; he smiled, but gave no answer. And this was the first stitch sewn in the web of destiny.

CHAPTER XVIII

YES

THE advantages for Melander were manifest and Ulrika never tired of singing them; princely wealth; and with such wealth secure independence forever and a straight road to social prominence.

Josephine could thank her lucky stars if she could get Edward for her husband. It was a great stroke of luck for her, most unexpected, a great destiny. And then Ulrika would rid herself of her guard, of that constant, quiet inquisition.

Melander remained thoughtful, although in the end nothing was less desired by him than such a marriage. Of course, it would take him to the top of the ladder. It would give him power such as the wildest of his dreams had never imagined.

His objections did not arise from the feeling of responsibility; he had long since gotten rid of any such considerations; and when apparently he was forced by an inward sense of duty, brought to light, it was invariably a method of self-protection; nor did his objections arise from the shyness that he felt toward Josephine and which he had never been able to overcome. They had their roots in fear of Ulrika. He could not make clear to himself why she wanted to marry him to Josephine; and he was the more uncomfortable about it, as he really knew how much she cared for him and what he meant to her. The silent bond between them for the practical use of all opportunities in life was not sufficient to clear it up; Ulrika was not the woman to forego anything herself in order to give happiness to others; her instincts were very primitive, very earthly, and very direct.

They consulted like two managers of a political movement, and as each knew every corner and reservation of the other

229

before they admitted or spoke them, they pretended to be very open and confidential, though they were watching each other sharply. Sometimes in the midst of the dryest discussions Ulrika's brutal passion would burst forth and in a second the schemer was a mere animal who did not want to let her prey out of her claws. This frightened Melander but he played with it lightly; either he could protect himself or buy himself off by giving himself up for a stormy hour to the elements. "She thinks that I am her chattel," he said to himself angrily; "and Josephine is so little of a woman in her eyes that she sees no danger in chaining me to her and destroying my freedom; at the same time she wants to humiliate Josephine, and make her harmless as an inimical principal. Humiliated and made servile by me?" he stammered. "Am I to be used as a punishment for others? Ulrika seems to think so."

Disturbed by such considerations, who knows what Melander would have given if he could have looked into a sort of psychic mirror and tested things. For men like him, who are weighed down by ambition and blind to reality, really know nothing of themselves and are surprised when through others they recognise themselves. He shuddered but sought Josephine out; then he realised that Josephine avoided him. That excited him. He wanted to justify himself to her. But every effort built a new obstacle. The resistance aroused his stubbornness. Ulrika fanned the flame. Her tenderness all turned to spurring him on to the goal. But he really did not need that. The one question with him was: Which is the quickest and the surest way to win over Josephine?

Ulrika's next task was to make Christine look favourably upon the plan. She began cautiously drawing circle after circle until one day she came out definitely with the plan. Christine was horrified and wanted to hear nothing of it. The thought that she was to lose Josephine was unbearable, for her feeling over the loss of close relationships was not superficial. As to Melander himself, she felt strangely about him; she thought him too sceptical, too worldly, too frivolous for the serious Josephine, and also too young.

"There are reasons enough against it even if the matter were to be considered at all," she said.

Ulrika told Melander: "It's no good, you will have to take more trouble with the old lady. You will have to convince her. If you can't bring her over to our side we will never get a step further."

Melander himself saw the necessity. He began by bringing flowers to Christine and dedicating his political writings to her. He consulted her about his life plans and described his painful and poverty-stricken youth. He had tones and words for her which were more than the finest form of flattery; it was an inborn trait of his to conquer; to make himself a place in the heart of his opponent and never to leave it except as victor. He did not have to be a hypocrite, for the means were right at his hand; he had no consideration for people and was pleased even when he was unfolding himself to the most unworthy. "He has intellect," said Christine delighted; "he has real intellect." Intellect was the great word of that day. But even this kind of admiration had not succeeded in changing her mind; she felt by degrees deeply moved by her intercourse with him, more deeply than by any one else heretofore, and something came into existence which she tried with all her power to suppress, because it seemed to her unsuitable and despicable.

Ought her heart to stop when she looked into his young and beautiful face? Ought she to tremble when she heard his voice upon the step? The pallor of her cheeks when he came in, the constrained smile when he kissed her hand, her happy yet fearful willingness to listen to him, her yielding of herself at a word, this faith, this epitomising of a whole human existence in one person, this return of a long-dead dream, this spiritual awakening of a never-used youth—were these only ghosts and sins, to be suppressed because of their absurdity?

Having reached this stage, Melander decided that he would speaks of his love for Josephine. Christine felt that she could listen to this. It was an escape, a release from shame. Josephine was beloved and she, Christine, received the confession. It was a sweet deception of the imagination enmeshing her in an exciting double rôle. She could imagine that she was smoothing the way of Josephine's happiness, that she was taking motherly care of Josephine's future, and she was intoxicated by the illusion which drove a pathetic longing to its late blossoming; fooled by a feeling that she had never really experienced and that became known to her now in this painful form.

A tormenting helplessness overpowered her, and she could no more bear to be alone. She envied Josephine and while inwardly she beheld her in all the glory of her virtue and blessedness, she was afraid to see her actually before her eyes. She wished that she could prolong this time of uncertainty, and she hated herself, her age, her foolish hallucinations, her empty life. One day it happened that Melander was developing to her his theories of marriage and Josephine's suitableness to such an eternally holy bond, and he described Josephine's personality with such eloquence and tenderness that Christine was touched and overwhelmed; she took his head between her two hands and kissed him upon the forehead. She had given in completely; there was nothing more to be said.

Ulrika took care that the fire should not go out. In the long nights' discussions she brought Christine to a definite decision, although she still fought against it for reasons difficult to explain. The first argument, that Josephine could not choose better than to take this man of practical deeds, a bold pioneer of future ideas, had become a matter of course, for Christine saw much more in him and secretly laughed at Ulrika's stupid valuation. She liked to hear Ulrika speak of him. Ulrika told all sorts of things and Christine drank them in thirstily; some rash deed showing his nobility, some manifestation of his strange strength of character, to-day an instance of proud deliberation, the next day an example of self-forgetfulness and heroism. Just to hear his name was a tonic to Christine. Her trust and affection had already decorated him with all these advantages.

Josephine was quite unconscious of all this. She went her

quiet way, avoiding people and avoiding the noisy activities of the house. Ever more devoutly she turned in upon herself and became more and more indifferent to what happened about her. The most incomprehensible thing of all was her mother. Buoyantly gay amidst her guests, but alone, uncertain, subdued, complaining of bad nights and insufficient sleep, most careful about everything that she called politeness and convention, and above all completely lost in a passion for reading.

Josephine brooded over it for hours. What could it be, she thought, and took up this or that book to read. She found nothing in them; or only deceptive things; or else something that she could not believe would hold one's thoughts or feelings; or else she found a world of characters and pictures, which lost all nobility if it was not set apart and kept as an example.

When she wanted to go to her mother it seemed as if she had to wade through poison to get there. When she got into her room, however, her mother seemed deaf and she herself dumb. Either they did not speak or when they did neither heard the other.

Sometimes she looked at her mother with frightened astonishment; as if she were not real; as if an artistically imitated Christine Mylius had taken her place, a soulless double. And in her mind she had an image of a grim fairy tale; at the bedside of the sleeping one there appeared a little kobold, visible and yet invisible, sucking up the warm real blood which always re-makes itself during sleep, so that life may not quite disappear, and fills the veins with the cold, false blood of the kobold. Who this vampire was and what name it bore, Josephine desired to suppress, as one is silent about a severe illness, but truth has a shameless mouth; and it shrieked it at her at every hour. These were fairy tale thoughts; how was she to break the enchantment? And her heart answered: through patient, firm, unfailing love.

When she heard that Melander was in the city again, and she saw that he was coming to the house it made no special impression upon her. So many came and amongst them many of whom one could not hope the best; why should she especially object to this one? She had learned to think more mildly of his crime; life and knowledge had taught her to think more gently. Also the fact that he was faithful in the duty he had undertaken to fulfil toward Tino Waldbauer who was beginning to get well, helped to reconcile her.

As her mother desired it she appeared sometimes at the evening parties. Melander cautiously lured her into· conversation. He sought to win ground and felt his way carefully. She listened to his words attentively, but remained reserved and restrained. When he was talking to others she watched, for watching had become a second nature to her. With the merciless keenness hidden behind her soft and gentle nature she observed three outstanding qualities in him: a vanity that could bear no slightest contradiction; a falsity that wore the garment of gentle irony; and complete coldness of heart.

Ulrika knew how to bring about conditions in which he could shine and stand as the central point of observation; little readings and debates upon scientific subjects but while all the others were astounded and overflowed with praise and approval Josephine remained cold.

Ulrika showed the greatest eagerness in reassuring her and giving her examples of how complete a transformation had taken place in him in the last few months. Josephine would gladly have believed and looked for the signs of it, but only with the result that her dislike grew. Ulrika began to bring about little unexpected meetings between them but Josephine always withdrew shyly. She was afraid of him. When he offered his hand she had to overcome a singular feeling of repulsion. His smile was such that she dropped her eyes before it in a sort of inexplicable shame.

He complained to Ulrika of her frosty behaviour. Ulrika answered grimly: "Patience. She will be warm enough. She is one of these shut-up natures like an oyster. You will have to hammer her open."

They took counsel together, discussed the for and against, and one day just before Whitsuntide Melander asked Christine in all formality for the hand of Josephine. Christine burst into tears, then she embraced him and said that she did not doubt destiny had chosen to make her most beloved child happy. Shortly after that she sent for Josephine and told her that Professor Melander wanted her for his wife. What answer should she give him? Josephine's eyes became round and she laughed: "Mother!" she said, and then began to talk of something else.

Still a shiver went down her back. How strange, thought Christine, she doesn't seem to grasp it; and disappointed, she told Ulrika how little affected she had been.

Ulrika said: "If you think that that will turn it aside, then the good Josephine is not mistaken when she believes that she can scatter her mother's wishes to the wind."

"What am I to do?" said Christine. "I can't force her. In these days no girl is forced into a marriage. Moreover you know that there is no such thing as forcing Josephine. She is hard-headed and knows what she wants."

"Then it is when Greek meets Greek," said Ulrika gaily. "You must have a will too, and having one you must put it through. Force her to marry; good heavens, these are very modern pretenses; a well-built, respected, cultivated man woos a moderately pretty, moderately clever girl—begging your pardon—who brings him a big fortune. He idolises her and promises her the life of a princess. But she puts on airs and withdraws, why? Because she doesn't understand the honour that is done her. Because she is still lacking in comprehension of how she has been preferred among thousands. So you should say to her: 'My dear daughter, I cannot throw aside my responsibility and let you tread your happiness under foot; if you are blind, it is my duty to see for you, and I wish and demand that you submit yourself to my finer insight. Heretofore you have never done so, but now it is too important a matter for me to let it pass without further insistence.' Do you call that forcing? Where is the force?"

"Certainly I hope that she will come to reason," Christine said gently.

"Otherwise we are to wait," Ulrika closed her philippic; "Edward will write to her. We may be sure that as he knows how to write it will make an impression upon her. Let us wait."

Melander's letter was indeed a model of style. Without letting himself be led into exaggeration which he realised would awaken Josephine's suspicions, he wrote of his deep feeling and admiring submission. He pointed out to her the battles, mental, spiritual and physical that he had been through, and also the high tasks that stood before him, and said that he was conscious of the holy duty that he was taking upon himself, when he begged her to become the companion of his life. But he said he was drawn to her by a transcendent faith; he needed her as the lost in a desert needed a guardian angel, and though he might not yet have won her heart, he trusted in her noble instincts and in Time which cleared up all things. At any rate, he laid his fate, for good and evil trustfully in her hands and knew of no better protector.

In her first excitement, Josephine tore up the letter, as if it were burning her hands and threw it into the waste-paper basket. After a while she calmed herself and answered Melander, thanking him for his offer but explaining that any such decisions about her life lay very far away. She felt herself in no way adapted to marriage, and desired to remain free as her freedom seemed to her the best of her life. She begged him not to feel hurt by her refusal but after careful consideration of all the circumstances, she could not decide otherwise.

Melander brought the letter to Ulrika that night and said: "Read it!"

Ulrika read it, shrugged her shoulders, and asked: "Well, what next?"

"According to this we will have to lay this incident away with past records," he replied.

Ulrika threw up her chin. "I am not in the habit of laying a case away among records, as long as there are precedents that show it may be won," she said grimly. "And it will be won. I will vouch for it."

"I am curious about that," he said.

She said, "Give me the paper. I will show it to Christine."

Christine knew about the letter Melander had written, for he had read it to her to get her approval before he sent it, and she had been much touched by its contents. She felt that a heart of stone would be softened by it; she thought of all the celebrated lovers and all the romantic tales in literature. Secret envy made her blind. When Ulrika showed her the answer, the first thing she felt was a throb of joy of which she was inwardly ashamed. Then followed surprise, discomfort, disappointment, pity, and a feeling of being in some way injured, but she remained mute.

Ulrika raged. She picked the letter to pieces syllable by syllable and declared it was the outcome of arrogance and conceit. "Conceit," that word was repeated emphatically and passionately. "A person eaten up by conceit must be brought to her senses by force," she cried; "such creatures are lost, who think only of their own opinions and wishes. If they are allowed to go on, they will build misery upon misery and land one more useless member on the shoulders of society."

She folded her arms and laughed indignantly. "So much is always said of Josephine's candour and trust and single-hearted love of her mother, and how different she is from other people. But I see none of it. Do *you* see it? The very first opportunity she has to give a proof of it, it disappears in thin air. Beautiful words, and nothing more."

Christine sat, her elbows on her knees, her chin in her hands, looking straight before her.

"Does she know that *I* wish this marriage?" she asked.

"Does she?" answered Ulrika. She had made her understand it, plainly enough. She had made it clear that her mother's deepest interest lay in seeing her married to Melander; that she was devoted to him; loved him as her own son and had promised to do everything to persuade Josephine to be his wife. But that meant no more to her than if a soap bubble had burst. The girl's stubbornness had embittered her and she had given it up.

"How did Edward take her letter?" Christine asked, depressed.

"That is just the trouble; he is wild," Ulrika lied freely.

"I never believed anything could make such an impression upon him. It has floored him. He is ill. He had to go home and to bed."

Christine turned pale. "Call Josephine to me," she said.

Ulrika left the room and came back with Josephine. "Shall I go?" she asked with hypocritical tact.

"No, Ulrika, stay," Christine answered.

That she should begin to persuade her in the presence of Ulrika, and should definitely demand this of her, opened Josephine's eyes painfully to what lay before her. It was a blow to her heart. Every word of Christine's was a blow. She had never believed she could hear such cold, harsh words from these lips, so lacking in all justice, so foolishly destructive of what was once the very germ of her being. And her undoer, her enemy, the vampire standing by with folded arms, looking harshly at her—it was like a dream of hell.

Christine asked if she persisted in her refusal to marry Edward Melander.

Josephine's answer could hardly be heard: "Is not that at least my right, Mother? Does it not concern me, and me alone, and my future?"

That could hardly be denied, said Christine, with a strange intonation in her voice. But what reasons had she? What were her reasons?

Did one have to give reasons for such a personal decision, a decision that concerned one's whole destiny, stammered Josephine who became so pale that it seemed as if a pump were drawing all the blood out of her body. The most important reason she had written, but there were others; amongst them, a difference of religion and lack of sympathy.

Ulrika uttered a suppressed laugh.

Josephine designated it as lack of sympathy because she wished to spare her mother, whose preference for Melander she now began to feel, but what she really felt since she had read his letter, was an icy terror. She did not know how to explain it to herself, or whence her horror-struck resistance came. What she had learned of him was insufficient to justify, to her usual friendly way of thinking, her fright and horror. It was something hidden, something only vaguely felt; and to give her life over to him, to be bound over to him till death, and separated from other people, was already a foretaste of death.

Christine said quietly (and Josephine would rather have had bodily punishment than this quietude) that difference of religion, that one was a Catholic and the other a Protestant by upbringing, was no longer a gulf to educated people; to hear such a thing from Josephine really hurt her; we lived in more enlightened times. The God of the good was the same God for all; could he condemn a creature, because it chose to recognise him under a given form, which seemed to the arrogance of another creature, error? Would it not be wiser and more pious to serve God with deeds, obedience to example, than through a commanded confession? All that was popish play and she hated popishness.

It was a banal sermon, the outcome of the middle-class views of the time, and in this special case, embarrassment and escape from truth.

Josephine turned bright red, a flame over all her pallor. She stretched out her hands, her fingers pressed together, and said pleadingly: "Mother, you misunderstand me. Perhaps I expressed myself badly. It is not just a matter of difference of religion, a difference of faith, it is a matter of believing or not believing, of faith and unfaith. You know this, you must know it."

That was really no excuse, said Christine; the chief beauty of cultured people was tolerance. "As to the lack of sympathy, my child," she went on, "ask yourself if there isn't a lack of good will, a lack of readiness and of modesty on your side. When one honours a man, and there is certainly reason enough for honour here, one can at least meet him in a friendly spirit. You need nothing more and you need demand nothing more. I asked for no more in my youth, and received no more, rather less. Think this over. Edward is so wonderful, so extraordinary a man."

Ulrika nodded at every word as though it were spoken from her own soul.

A deep pallor had again spread over Josephine's face. She spoke tremulously to herself: "I don't understand it—I don't understand it—"

"What is it you don't understand, my child?" said Christine softly.

Josephine said: "Suppose I am not willing to content myself with respect and friendliness? Let us take it for granted it is that. Perhaps I am unable to give him even respect and friendliness. Perhaps others can and I can't. Let us take it for granted it is that."

"But why not then, why not?" Christine went on restlessly, and now she wished that she could talk to Josephine without Ulrika's being present.

Josephine in agony searched for words. "I don't love him," she burst out; "I shall never love him, never! Does that mean nothing? What, then, would mean anything in this world?"

Christine, who was hanging upon Ulrika's looks as the hypnotised hangs upon the hypnotiser, wanted to answer, but Ulrika interrupted her. "Love! Rubbish, love!" she began cuttingly and full of scorn, shaking her head like a lioness. "I was just waiting for that. How have you ever earned it? What have you to earn it with? You demand love? Love at once? First earn it! Whoever gets it as cheaply as that, by just saying: I want—? Should I have had love, if I had not dragged it lump by lump out of the fiery stove? Or any one else? Love is a word to conjure with, my good Josephine. They don't skim the milk and give the cream to us women. We have to do the milking and make the butter and then the one who puts her mouth to the crock gets a swallow. We are not talking about love here, we are talking about marriage. The one has nothing to do with the other. Marriage is a contract between two parties with mutual guarantees. The pleasure in it is always doubtful. If you must have pleasure get it as and where you can; that is your own private affair and you pay for it with your life. My father used to say, he who goes hunting in the mud must wear high boots. There, I just wanted to mention that, because you are talking of love again." She paced angrily up and down, muttering to herself: "Love—love."

Josephine, leaning upon the arm of the chair, looked down at the ground, then her eyes gleamed and turning to Ulrika she said with immeasurable disdain: "Oh, that I had nothing to thank you for! Oh, that I had never seen you! I would rather have been burned to a coal than that you should have saved me!"

"Josephine!" Christine cried out, overwhelmed.

"May God forgive me my sin," said Josephine.

"You are always talking about God and warming your wickedness under your pillow," Ulrika put in poisonously. "I don't care. I am used to trouble."

There was a pause. At last Ulrika, raging in the middle of the room like a fiendish power who is dictating conditions, said: "What is submission? What can be done for the poor creature eaten up by impatience? For the love-hungry Josephine does not seem to know that out there," and she pointed with her forefinger pathetically to the door, "that out there is love, more than enough for the household. Out there waits an honourable fellow, a man in the truest sense of the word, to whom one can only give silly phrases. Speak, Frau Christine; what is to be done?"

Christine shuddered; avoiding Josephine's eyes, she said to her: "Think this over, Josephine. I cannot believe and I will not believe that you will resist the wishes of your mother so stubbornly. I have given Edward Melander consent in my name and in yours. Perhaps I was mistaken, but after conscientious thought I could find nothing that would prevent your giving him a joyous 'yes.' I feel bound to him. Of course that does not bind you. You must decide your own fate. I wanted to make you happy and Edward, I must admit it, has become my friend and I have boundless confidence in him. I would gladly trust you to him. Of course that does not bind you, as I said. But this much you must know: if your hard and unreasonable refusal stands we can no longer be what we have been to each other. We can have nothing more to do with each other until the wound is healed.

That may last a long time. Think it over. You will have twenty-four hours' time, then send or bring me your answer."

There was a roaring like a waterfall in Josephine's ears. She rushed into her own room and fell tearless on her knees and prayed. Then she got up and walked up and down. Then after a long time she sat down by the open window and looked into the garden, her hands in her lap.

Everything was in full bloom. Silver clouds floated around the moon and far away a nightingale sobbed.

Yet it was all empty and all inimical.

Mother! my Mother! and again: My Mother! Where is my Mother? She cared nothing for her own life; the sacrifice that was demanded of her seemed nothing to her. She could voice but this one thought: where has my Mother gone?

There was one thing that might be tried. One might go in the silence and quiet of the night to her bedside and try to awake the sleeping one to the truth. One might say to her: wake up, you prisoner, wake up, you bewitched one! Horror clings to my tongue against this man that you want to throw me to; his breath is poison, his glance terror, the pressure of his hand winter and frost, his voice lying and deception. You know him no more than you do your own keeper. Tear the bandage from your eyes, listen to me, look at me, see how I shudder at the future and how I foresee what it must bring. Wake up, lost soul, wake from your unholy sleep!

But a word had fallen that broke down the last bridge between them. What good could speech and reasons do? It was a case for God to decide and destiny to judge.

Her resolve was taken. As one who leaves a grave behind her, faint and despairing, she wrote upon a piece of paper the word "yes," and sent it to her mother.

CHAPTER XIX

DEPARTURE WITH BAG AND BAGGAGE

AFTERWARDS, when Christine came to embrace her weeping, Josephine had made two conditions: that the wedding should take place as quickly as possible and all festivities should be avoided. Christine consulted with Ulrika, who wrinkled up her nose. "Caprice," she said vexed, "I suppose she wants to make her wedding into a funeral pomp. That would be like her. But Edward certainly will be ambitious to ride in a coach and four to the church."

"I wonder what her hurry is?" said Christine. "Why does she want the wedding as soon as possible?"

"Good Heavens, plenty of people who are afraid of the water go in with a dash. They hang around and then at last take the plunge from the top of the spring board. Perhaps she thought differently about it; you can never tell what to expect from such moody people; perhaps she can't wait now to rush into her husband's arms."

"I hope you may be right," sighed Christine, "but it does not look that way to me."

In the next few days Christine showed a buoyant activity and sympathy. But in the depths of her consciousness there was a heavy weight that she tried to overlook and ignore. She showed Melander a gentle, almost depressed, tenderness. When he spoke she hung upon his lips; if he expressed a wish she hastened to fulfil it. She loaded him down with presents and was rewarded by the slightest smile of thanks. When she was with both of them, Josephine and Edward, her eyes turned unceasingly from one to the other, testing, questioning, and she was touched by Melander's gentle manner, by every one of his clear-cut words, every attention that he showed Josephine, his constant, patient, pleading wooing of the serious, silent girl, and it seemed to give Christine painful pleasure and a care-laden excitement.

Josephine concerned herself in no wise with her trousseau or her residence. She sat by her mother and talked to her; she sat by her fiancé and listened to him. Except that her face was pale and her eyes heavy nothing was changed about her. Her whole manner toward Melander was that of a person making a difficult study with utmost stubborn effort; she often watched him, her eyebrows drawn together and then was frightened when he, unpleasantly affected by the piercing look, asked her with gentle surprise if anything weighed on her heart.

No, she had nothing on her heart, nothing at all. It certainly demanded a certain amount of courage to ask her such a question, for she looked as if that organ, her heart, had been lost and as if she were wandering around in the world restless and broken, trying to find it and put it back in its place. She did show a certain interest, yes, even curiosity and excitement, when Melander talked about other people with whom he worked in his office and calling, when he talked freely, with his dry sarcasm and quick wit, and explained the difficult relationships. He reminded her then, somewhat of Franz Woytich; just as Franz had a masterly fluency on the piano so Melander mastered the instrument of life's realities and characters. Sometimes Josephine contradicted him, asked questions with a touch of irony, a shy stubbornness, a childish resentment, and then when she was conquered, which usually happened, she looked up astonished at him or dropped her eyes in embarrassment.

It was the day before the wedding. The weather had been most unfriendly; the evening was humid although the sky had begun to clear. Josephine withdrew early in the evening; she shook her head at her mother's plea that she remain with her a little while. However, as she went along the dimly lit corridor to her room, she saw Anastasia standing motionless by her door, with a strangely evil look on her face. Josephine started, and Anastasia said: "May I have a few words with you, Fräulein Josephine?"

Josephine was surprised for her relationship to Anastasia had been most superficial. However, she opened the door and invited her to come in, and when they were in the room, to sit down. Anastasia remained standing by the door.

"Something oppresses me, Fräulein Josephine, and I must let it out," she began in her saccharine voice; "even though you may think ill of me, I must tell you. I don't like to denounce and there is nothing I can gain by being the betrayer of my sister, but I can no longer watch the thing going on. My chances in life are not so good that I can risk them, especially risk offending Ulrika, who makes the rain and the sun in this house and who will punish me severely if she finds out that I tell you her secrets—"

"What is the matter? Why all these words? What do you want?" Josephine broke into the unpleasant sounding speeches with an unusual sharpness.

"I thought," said Anastasia, offended, "I would be doing only my duty if I told the Fräulein, before she takes so serious a step as that of to-morrow—"

"No, no, no," Josephine interrupted her for the second time with a commanding gesture; "tell me nothing. I don't want to hear it. Nothing. Nothing."

"Oh, so you know already?" Anastasia asked stubbornly. "You know it already? I need not have taken all this trouble? There is nothing left for me to do but wonder. And that surely is allowed me? I only felt that since the period of the engagement-time itself is not respected and they have not shied at having secret relationships—"

"That is enough!" Josephine said, threatening her. "Not another syllable or you shall repent it."

"I beg pardon," Anastasia murmured, suddenly humble and bowed.

Josephine's mouth quivered scornfully. "I thank you for your friendly intentions," she said, cold and trembling. "I would like to be alone now. Good-night, Anastasia."

Anastasia pressed her lips together, threw a pious look toward the ceiling and went out in her noiseless way.

Josephine sat a long time without moving. She had known

and had not known. Was there any difference between the one and the other? Knowing and not knowing were all the same and nothing was changed. She sat as if listening to the past and the future. Sadness streamed in upon her on every side. Where can I find shelter and where can I hide myself? That was the question that she continually asked herself and that reminded her of the terrible word of her mother in her childhood's dream.

She had yielded but was not broken. Her very soul was rigid. For a soul, to remain in the current of the earthly and the divine, must learn to bend. While she lay there in bed, hour after hour, and brooded over herself and other people, and what was happening to them all, she lost her humility and plunged into a loveless, icy loneliness.

She looked out into the darkness and thought and thought. By degrees the circle of her thoughts grew narrower and contracted into a sort of smoke that took upon itself the form of Ulrika. Ulrika filled all space, Ulrika was the world. Ulrika was the wall against which her longing heart broke; Ulrika was known and unknown humanity. Ulrika was the voice outside her and below her that silenced the one from above; Ulrika was law and fate.

Dawn turned grey at the window and the morning came. They called her, came into her room, brought garments, dressed her. She went down to a carriage; she drove; she stood beside a gentleman in church and the people were like snow-flakes. She was back again at home, people were congratulating her, she sat down at a table, she got up to go, she said good-bye. Christine embraced her. She smiled emptily. She stood in front of Ulrika for an instant, white as chalk; Ulrika pressed her stormily to herself and wiped away a tear with her forefinger.

The wedding trip to Constantinople and Greece was an official one for Melander. He had business with the Governments there and was provided with plenipotentiary powers. Christine received her first news from Athens, a greeting on a card. Three weeks later came another card; they were on the return trip from Naples. Then one from Quarnero, where they were staying for a week.

Christine held this card for a long time in her hand and looked at the two empty words on it. Her eyes had that strange piercing expression of people who are trying to remember something and cannot.

"See, Ulrika," she said; "Josephine has a quite different handwriting."

Ulrika bent over her shoulder. "Why? I don't see it," she answered. "Perhaps it is a little bit more pointed and a little stiffer; that often happens when girls get married without the proper imagination and impulse; they often get stiff and pointed and not only upon paper."

Christine said nothing but she went on studying the handwriting.

That evening as she went to bed she said: "I don't know what has happened to me to-day; I feel very strangely. I wish you would stay near me, Ulrika. Your room is so far away that I feel forsaken."

Ulrika laughed. "You are not going to become a hypochondriac, are you?" she answered. "Sleep well and tomorrow we will talk over our summer plans."

In the night at three o'clock Christine awoke with a terrible shriek. She felt as if her heart had broken open. She sounded the alarm. Nanette appeared and right after her Anastasia who ran to fetch Ulrika.

When Ulrika entered Christine sat upright, one hand pressed against her left breast, her corpse-like face covered with sweat. "The doctor," Ulrika cried out shrilly. She poured water into a basin, wet a cloth and wanted to lay it upon Christine's heart. Then Christine looked at her with an indescribable expression of terror that grew from moment to moment. She stretched out her right arm and stammered: "Don't touch me. Go. For Heaven's sake, go. I can't bear it. Go way from here!"

"What is the matter? What has come over you!" Ulrika asked.

"For Heaven's sake, get out of here!" groaned Christine.

"But it is I, I, Ulrika," said Ulrika, greatly disturbed.

In despairing torment Christine turned to Nanette: "Tell her she must go, Nanette. If she does not go at once, I shall die."

Nanette, herself frightened and surprised, persuaded Ulrika, who believed it was only a passing illusion, and shaking her head and muttering she left the room.

Panting, with short indrawn breath, Christine demanded a piece of paper and pencil and scribbled in the greatest haste a dispatch to Josephine and made Nanette swear to give it to the servant to carry to the post.

It was done.

Meanwhile the doctor came. Ulrika walked up and down outside waiting for news. His manner betrayed nothing good when he came to her. He told her the aorta was injured and that death might occur at any moment, though it was not impossible that life might linger a few more days. It was important that her children should be notified.

Ulrika was very sleepy; she said to herself:—it is probably not as bad as that quack imagines and she went back to bed. When she woke rather late in the morning she sent telegrams to Esther, Aimée, and Lothar. Then she went cautiously to Christine, thinking that the strange mood of the morning would be passed and forgotten.

Hardly had she stepped over the threshold when Christine started up as if struck by lightning, and stretching out both arms in wildest horror she cried: "Oh, Heavens, she is here again! What does she want of me now? Why is she here? Take her away, away, away!"

Ulrika turned pale to the very roots of her hair. She turned round quickly, closed the door and stood outside fighting down her feelings and then looked up toward heaven and said bitterly: "That's the thanks I get."

Somewhat later Nanette, prompted by Ulrika, bent over the invalid and said gently: "What is it you have against Fräulein Ulrika, gracious lady? She used to be the apple of your eye, your one and all. What is it all of a sudden?"

Grasping the arm of the girl with both hands and looking close into her face, Christine whispered shyly: "Don't say a word. She hears everything. I beg you be silent. She has taken out my heart, bit by bit, and eaten it. I daren't look behind or before, and when I see her I am afraid of myself. But keep quiet I beg you."

Ulrika went into the kitchen and gave her orders, sent some of the younger servants out on errands, then she went into her own room, lit a cigarette and took from the top drawer of her bureau the carefully preserved paper upon which Christine's hand had written, and signed with her full name, the sentence: "This belongs to my beloved Ulrika Woytich."

Ulrika cut the paper carefully and evenly into as many parts as there were sentences, and when she had done that fetched a little bottle of glue and a brush, and so provided with the proper utensils she went through the upper floor.

She began in the upper rooms and salons, alcoves. and corridors, and pasted the little labels on all the things that she had had her eyes upon and chosen for herself.

She took plenty of time. Humming a little waltz to herself, she walked from piece to piece like a dealer. Her clear glance chose with a connoisseur's severity: tables, chests, chairs, sofas, beds, consols, bureaus, divans, stools, mirrors, pictures, vases, marble and bronze statues, carpets and candelabra. Whenever an especially fine piece came under her eye her humming changed to a light and joyous whistling and she stopped to calculate whether she dared demand it. She went about her choosing so that not too many noticeable gaps should be made when her things were carried out. She mustn't leave a void; she respected the void. As she was despoiling sixteen rooms in which she had brought together with the utmost forethought her favourite ornaments, her chosen pieces were hardly missed from the luxurious abundance.

While she was doing this, midday had come. The Vice-Consul came, as usual, to the table; she had notified the other guests not to come. Ulrika told her brother how

Christine was and above all how Christine felt toward her.
She told him that he must go out to-day and at any cost rent
a house for her as she would leave this one early the next
morning, having no desire to see the family return.   She
would probably not occupy the house for another half-
year, but would go off for six months or so on a journey
and see the world and look around to see where she would
be most useful.   Yet she must know that in case of need
she had a home to turn to, and also she needed a secure
place to put her chests, her trunks and her furniture.

Franz Woytich understood and nodded.   He asked what
she was going to do with Anastasia.

"I will put her into the house, give her an allowance and
make her look after my things," Ulrika answered, arranging
the fate of her sister in her usual prompt manner.

"Come this evening," she said at the end, "and wear your
dress suit.   I will have a few friends in for a farewell party.
I will write the invitations right now and send them by
messengers.   I hope it is not too late."

"Who are the chosen ones?" said the Vice-Consul,
chuckling.

"Let us have a little council of war," said Ulrika good-
humoredly, "just a little council of war with our intimates."
They sat down side by side at the table and Ulrika, taking
the gold pencil in her hand, drew up the protocol.   Captain
Kroner; Secretary von Phillippsborn; Baron Hartwich; Lord
von Cocheran; the painter Ittstein; the actor Merz.   "There,
that is enough; it is just a pleasant number, and if any one
fails or is prevented from coming it doesn't matter."

"Now I have something to do," said Ulrika, and dismissed
her obedient and useful brother.

Long before dinner she had ordered chests and boxes in
sufficient number.   Her factotum, the old servant Nicholas,
had taken over the task and done it to Ulrika's satisfaction.
The actual packing she attended to herself.   She did not
want any witnesses.   It lasted the whole afternoon.

Everything that she had gathered together in the way of
gifts and presents, everything that she looked upon as her

own and the hard-won result of her labor, was packed into the roomy boxes: clothes, materials, rolls of linen and chiffon, curtains of satin and curtains of damask, table cloths, table covers, woven pieces, laces, a silver table service, a Delft service, flat silver enough for twenty people, embroidered cushions, statuettes, endless bibelots and costly wall decorations, books, curtains, miniatures, ivory boxes, watches, snuff-boxes, carvings, engravings, antique coins and last but not least, the wonderful old doll from Mylius's shop.

When at last everything was properly and securely fastened up she nailed up the chests with the help of two servants and with her own hand painted the initials U. W. on the covers.

Then she dressed for the evening.

The Vice-Consul came first. He told her that he had carried out her orders; the apartment he had rented was in a quiet, aristocratic vacant house; and she could move in at once.

"You did that well," said Ulrika; "to-morrow morning the express-man will come, and to-morrow evening, à la fortune du pot, you will be my guest, naturally. Then we will discuss the future."

She had made a point of receiving her friends in state. The hair-dresser had made an imposing crown of her luxuriant hair. Her dove-grey costume of heavy satin was trimmed with lace and cut very low. Around her throat she wore a gold chain with a gold medallion and in her hair a diadem. The corals which she had worn in early youth as ear-rings were dispensed with and two lovely pearls had taken their place.

She had an incomparably beautiful bust; strong, supple, glowing with sensuous life. Her skin had the bloom of an apricot. Her gleaming face, free from all care with the dark, laughing eyes and sensuous mouth, ready to devour everything sweet and tasty that life offered, worked upon her guests like an elixir. No one was surprised that the lady of the house was not present, no one thought it singular that this splendid supper should take place in the rooms of Frau Christine Mylius. Ulrika was giving a banquet; she had no doubt about what she was doing; every one could depend upon Ulrika. "The gracious lady isn't well," was what she said, "and perhaps she won't appear." Ulrika winked her eyes and shook her head.

She chatted, joked, teased, mocked, blew away the heavy moods of those who came depressed, brightened up the melancholy, urged everybody right and left to help themselves, for the table fairly groaned under its burden of dishes, roast meats, vegetables, salads, shell-fish, fish, fruits, sweets, wines, and champagne. Franz Woytich played like a virtuoso potpourris from the operas; the actor told anecdotes and offcolour stories, and laughter flowed like a cataract.

At midnight old Nicholas appeared and whispered something in Ulrika's ear. She smiled and shrugged her shoulders and went on with the sentence she had begun.

He had told her that Josephine had arrived.

Upstairs, far upstairs, many rooms away from this gaiety, as if in another country Christine lay and waited in frightful torment. The servants went in and out quietly; sometimes the young doctor entered who had taken on the night-watch, bent over the bed and changed the ice bags or gave her her medicine. She lay with her eyes shut and now and then she heaved a sigh. Sometimes she opened her eyes, looked longingly toward the door, and whispered the name of Josephine.

Then at last, at last! The rustle of a skirt; hasty steps; a sad little call; the slender childish figure: she was there at last.

"Come to me," stammered Christine weeping, and clung to her closer and closer; "stay with me, quite, quite near me!" And Josephine said: "Are you yourself again? Have I found you again? My mother? My own mother again?"

And Christine: "Can you ever forgive? Tell me that one thing: Can you ever forgive?"

And Josephine said: "Be still. Oh, be still."

Ulrika and her guests were in high feather. Ulrika had a notebook in her hand and was writing, interrupted by protests, demands, laughter, and applause, the names of those who in the next few years would change their way of life. First of all: the Captain would go to Italy; Phillippsborn to France; Hartwich, up North; Herr von Cocheran to Tunis and Egypt; Ittstein to Switzerland and other mountainous regions; only the actor, fat and comfortable, wished to remain at home and localise his vocation.

A merry quarrel was started; every one pretended that some one else had snapped away the best bits and the best plans. Every one called the other one's post a sinecure. At last Ulrika got up, looked at the joyous faces around the table, knocked on her glass and said:

"The migratory birds have always seemed to me the most mysterious animals upon earth. Perhaps they don't belong to this earth alone but have their nests in other stars too. If I disappear now for a time, my dear friends, don't bother about me, but take care that your memory of me does not die. Remember one thing: nothing final can ever be said of Ulrika Woytich. She is not what she seems, and yet she often does more than she promises. I may be beautiful, or I may be ugly; I may be good, or I may be bad; I may be Cleopatra, Messalina, or Lucretia, but in the hearts of friends I shall always be what I was from the beginning. And when critics and back-biters shake their white heads, and when all those who are our comrades sing their death-bed proverbs, and when old ladies raise an outcry, and cousins carry on the legend, don't be disturbed, for truly I can say to you, with Sganarelle: 'Throw fullest light upon this image, and when you have seen everything believe nothing, believe nothing.'"

Then with a joyous gesture she seized her glass of wine and they all gathered round her. The Vice-Consul played the Coronation March from "The Prophet."

At six o'clock the next morning a big furniture wagon drove up to the door. Ulrika, gay as a cricket, watched the transport of her costly pieces down the stairs and through the corridors. Her warning voice called out continually through

the morning quiet of the house: "Don't knock that mahogany chest against the wall! For mercy's sake, take care
of the Renaissance mirror! That table top is malachite;
God be merciful to you if you drop it." Above all she cau-
tioned the people a dozen times to be careful of the glued-on
labels and abused them like a truck driver when her orders
were not well carried out. The boxes and trunks came last.

For an hour there was noisy running to and fro, hasty
chatter, questions, curses, noise, then quiet spread again over
the forsaken rooms.

With a leather satchel in her hand, Ulrika stood in front
of the house, looked happily on, while the doors of the giant
wagon were closed, put up her umbrella as it was beginning
to rain, and when the heavy wagon started, she followed on
the other side of the street.

After a few steps, she turned round and looked at the
front of the splendid palace. Her eye travelled from window
to window until it finally stopped at that pair where, as she
perhaps dimly realised, Christine, her mistress and her friend,
breathed out her soul in the arms of Josephine.

PART TWO

CHAPTER XX

ACCUSING GOD

ONE evening at the end of February, 1921, the Honourable Mrs. von Melander received a sealed letter, in her city palace where she always resided at this time of year. Its contents threw her into the liveliest state of excitement and tore open again an unhealed wound, which had never ceased for a single hour to burn.

The letter ran as follows:

"DEAR MOTHER:—

"You will be not a little surprised to receive a communication from my hand, and I suppose your surprise will not be a very agreeable one; but that can't be helped; what has to be done, has to be done, and I am under pressure. For five years you have heard nothing from me, a fact that you must recognise. The last news that I sent you was, if I remember rightly, from Geneva. At that time I asked you for money. We had been burnt out; but you were not in the habit of fulfilling my wishes. You contented yourself with not answering. Anna never forgave me the futile demand; she raged when I confessed it and said things about you that made me crimson with shame. But I had to keep silent. I had resolved rather to beg upon street corners than to call again upon your motherly consideration. And if now I am untrue to that principle, it is not for my own sake but for my child's, that I appeal to your perhaps not entirely frozen heart. To be comprehensible, I must go back further.

"I will not try to hide from you that things have been desperate with us since the days in Geneva. The papers upon which I had been reporter for more than half a year broke connection with me; either they were not satisfied with my work (which would not have been surprising, for there

257

is nothing more horrible in the whole wide world than earning your bread with a pen, quite apart from the poisonous people it brings you in touch with); or else something leaked through from my past—since there are always rascals about who are not satisfied to let the fallen get up and try to walk again. At any rate, things went downhill with us. Anna tried to do some of her old soubrette stunts; and I knocked around on the exchange, as a soap agent, and did little jobs at the Embassy. The war brought one sometimes into odious situations but in the end a man must eat and take care of his wife and child. I don't want to bore you with the various stages of my suffering and degradation; you will doubtless say that I deserved it and to that there is no answer. Deserved it, yes; but remember this, that when a man comes from his mother's womb, he has already received the law and limitation of his life.

"Sometimes I turned for help to Uncle Lothar in Berlin. Would you like to know what he wrote me after my third letter? He would keep my conduct under observation and not answer until after a year; then if he heard no complaints of me at all, and if I was willing to forsake Anna, he would give me a trial in his Dresden office. I never laughed more heartily in my life. Who is there, between the North Sea and the Alps, who when he hears the name of Lothar Mylius is in any doubt as to what sort of viciousness is hidden behind him and his riches:—the lowest business tricks, profiteering and usury. But they are all like that. Swelled up with morality till they are ready to burst, but if one stuck a needle point into them, the pus would burst out. Any such society as this is bound to go under.

"But to the matter in hand. Five months ago we resolved to return to Vienna. It was not so difficult. Under the name which I had assumed ever since the change in my circumstances, Anna's maiden name as you will remember, I have lived here unrecognised up to the present day, when the hospitable walls of my native town are to be forsaken again. If you will go to the place, which it is the object of these lines to beg you to go to, at 158 Fünfhauser Street, on the

fifth floor, you must ask for Stephen Heinroth, or rather for
his little daughter, Fanny. I can picture your horror, when
you hear that after all that happened eight years ago I have
lived for months in this town. But what happened then
doesn't matter now, I am not the same man. I am Stephen
Heinroth. I have even shaved off my moustache, whereby you
can see how seriously I take my incognito. Trouble and pri-
vation have drawn deep lines in the once smooth Melander
face. There was no risk at all. Home called to me and as
usual I was too weak to resist. And I will be frank; something else called too; the transformed world, the new possibilities, of which one formerly would not have dared to dream,
but which are now so common to all poor-house inmates that
at the mere mention of them one's mouth waters. What a
changed world! What a seething existence! What a county
fair for trickery and bargaining—truly it is a joy to be
alive. My good compatriots have not passed over the time
blindly either; one has to grant them that. They have
profiteered. The old coquette Vienna has put all fear and
shame aside and has been the most insolent, adulterous, undisciplined Messalina that Europe ever saw. Why should I
not take my fill too? Why should my father's son hesitate and
be dainty? Why should I not drag my net too and fleece
the generous 'daughters of joy' of some of their unlawful
treasure? So I too put my little dry prongs into the food
trough. People do not overrate me when they grant me a
little wit and cunning. With these and a new frock coat,
the adventure might begin again. I became pianoforte player
in a bar. That was really my greatest talent when I was
a well-protected little Baron. Anna found work as a mani-
curist. How civilisation has advanced! There isn't a single
dirty butcher's wife or unappetising Polish girl in the whole
metropolis who isn't careful to have polished fingernails. I
used my time well and made worthwhile acquaintances and
earned all sorts of patrons and now and then I ate from a
full plate and I peered round and looked into the mechanism
of manipulations, and now I have the honour to announce
that the *coup* was successful. I am going to be a gentleman

again. But the ground under my feet is rather hot, and circumstances demand that I and my faithful spouse should seek out a new hunting ground. We are used to wandering. I need give you no further explanation for it would not interest you anyway. But you have no grounds for fear. This time, at any rate, I have not disturbed the slumber of your lordly laws. And should any one desire to do it for me, they will soon think better of it. For they have burned their own fingers. We are going into a new world; Brazil is said to be a beautiful country and I hear one can be inoculated against yellow fever. You will hardly reproach me that I did not pay you a visit since you have determined to be unreconciled unto the very grave. When you receive this we shall have already crossed the mountains. But the child we left behind. It hampered our movements and anyway, the uncertainty of our circumstances would have been harmful to a nine-year-old girl. It was a difficult resolution to make and I do not deny that I counted upon your help. Protect the child. Let it not forego what its parents have trusted you to supply. I dare even to assert that you will have joy in the child. Otherwise, I will not praise it; for the word of its father will only awaken your distrust. Fanny knows nothing about you. She doesn't know her relation to the nobility. She lived for four long years with strangers in Yverdon on the lake of Neufchatel, so she has had little opportunity to hear the name Melander, which you forced me to give up. If it was not easy to persuade Anna to forego the explanation, she did it to please me and to satisfy my pride, for though you may smile scornfully at this idea, I did not want to play the rôle of the prodigal son to my own child. Tear me entirely from your heart, if you will, I will make no complaint, I will not beg for mercy, but be merciful to Fanny. God alone knows when I shall see her again. Protect her. And doing this you may skip the generation, the person and the name,—Stephen."

The sheets fell from the Baroness's hand. She sat in her chair as pale as death, and her usual quiet face was frozen stiff.

It woke up again the whole sad past; all the frightful, miserable, unworthy things that lay enfolded in that name.

The early struggles, the fight against frivolity and laziness, the playful stubbornness, the unconquerable tendency toward lying—and she alone struggling with him in every undertaking, in every disappointment, alone. The father in his princely indifference, was blind, deaf and unaware of the growing danger. At that time his amazing success had begun; the title of nobility had been conferred upon him; orders and honorary degrees rained upon this favourite whom every one idolised. Too great, too proud, too busy to bother himself about his child, too spoiled by fate to fear any evil, he turned every warning aside, and was angry at the mother's anxieties and protected the evil disposition of his son against his wife.

Then came his unexpected, universally-mourned death; Josephine's first release. It was bitter that she had to say it, on this day, after nineteen years. But now her responsibility could no longer be turned aside. The fourteen-year-old boy became alarmingly wild. Although any real authority had failed before this, yet the iron hand of the father, his cold looks, and silent power had been a restraint.

Of a sudden all his bad qualities became immeasurably worse. Words were perfectly futile. The adolescent youth spent thousands and thousands. If they refused him money he borrowed from servants, stole jewels and gold, and other precious things. He laughed at severity; to him there was no such thing as dignity; he mocked his teachers; he had neither timidity nor faith; he did not know what love was, nor a single tender emotion; what he looked for was enjoyment, extravagance, amusement to the point of madness and self-destruction. Josephine remembered her brother Lothar and what he had been like as a boy; had the taint in the blood passed, secretly avenging itself, on to the later generation and must he fearfully finish what had remained unfulfilled by dint of knowledge and discipline? Sometimes the likeness between them comforted her and then that hope would disappear, for she knew that the Melander blood was the stronger. Me-

lander blood!   An element that she alone knew, she of all the
people on earth.

And it became worse.   It became so much worse that she
believed that she would have to put an end to her life.   Scenes,
day after day; demands of insolent extravagance; bills enough
to paper the walls with; social sensations; and finally police
investigations and warnings.   By the time he was twenty years
old he had thrown away four hundred thousand crowns and
the complaints from the Court of Chancery were numbered
by the dozen.   There was no help on any side.   Where were
her sisters and what were they doing?   Mere legendary figures
in foreign lands; and the brother egotistically avoiding every
common interest with her; in years she had not had a single
confidential friend.

She sent the culprit off to travel.   But he spent ten times
what she allowed him.   Then he went into the army and for a
while it seemed to be a little better and she breathed more
freely.   Then came the connection with Anna Heinroth, a girl
of questionable reputation, lurid past, and moreover, five
years older than he was.   She had gained a positively uncanny
influence over him; and every one was dazed by the riddle, for
she was neither beautiful, nor attractive, nor gifted.   Now his
extravagance became positive insanity.   In a few weeks he
had thrown away his entire inheritance.   The influence of his
wife showed in every word he said, and his conduct to his
mother was that of a drunken stable-boy.   Suspicions, reproaches, outbreaks of temper, threats, quarrels every hour of
the day and night; and then suddenly, like a thunder clap,
came the news that he had married this person.   Josephine
refused to receive her.   On this point she was adamant.
Everything pointed to a crisis.   Of course, as soon as he was
married there was an end to his career as an officer.   Scandals
began to be whispered about various irregularities; for the
sake of his name and his father, whose high services still remained in the memory of the ruling classes, they had avoided
holding him to account.   He made debts upon debts.   Josephine could no longer keep count of them.   Stormed at by his
creditors she announced her irresponsibility for him and re-

nounced her guardianship. He came into the house one evening with a revolver and threatened to shoot her, but she remained adamant, then finally with a great burst of hypocritical tears he extracted a large sum from her. Shortly afterwards he began forging checks. An hour before he was arrested Josephine and her lawyer managed to stay the arm of the law after giving him a severe warning and bringing him before the justice, who was an old friend of Edward's. He seemed crushed and stubborn, dazed and frightened. The justice dictated conditions while Josephine sat, half swooning, beside him. A last arrangement was made. He was exiled and any return to his native land would bring upon him the fulfilment of the law. He had to submit. Then there was peace. For years nothing had been heard of him.

At that time Josephine no longer knew what sleep meant. In the following years she slept only under the influence of drugs, or occasionally by chance or grace. No footstep and no voice were allowed to be heard in the house.

At the birth of this only child her life had hung upon a thread. But the skill of celebrated doctors had saved her. As she recovered she dared not touch the child. When little by little she became aware of him as a living creature and belonging to her, she did not dare to love him. She did not dare to love him, and that expresses all that her nature had undergone. After five years of married life the child had come. At the end of these five years she wondered if she were really living still. It was as if her soul had been hacked to pieces with an axe.

Things happened; she felt them vaguely and had somehow filled in the days, hour by hour. She had been silent, and was still silent and would remain silent into all eternity. There were pictures hanging there, and furniture standing there that had seen it all. Words had eaten themselves into the draperies; her memory reaching back found only the debris; and between her and the outside world there was loneliness as impassable as ice a yard thick.

Crumpling up the letter convulsively in her hands she rose and walked up and down. She would not read it a second time. Its cynicism, roughness and scorn made her miserable. She thrust aside the thought of this child which he had tried to awaken in her again. She shuddered. He was the outcome of the curse of her existence, the embodied vengeance for her sinful weakness, the most sinful a woman could be guilty of; to take him back, to care for him again, would only be a new link in the chain of her suffering. What could come of this but misfortune and wickedness? Melander blood, mixed with the scum of the gutter.

On the gold tapestry above her desk hung her portrait, a young woman of twenty-eight years, painted by a master hand. A Norn. No one, at twenty-eight years, who had fought and lifted themselves above a tragic fate, should have looked that way, faded and joyless.

Directly underneath on an ebony pedestal was Edward Melander's bust modelled by a master hand, still youthfully beautiful at forty years, with a winning smile around his charming lips and his fine forehead like a guarantee of trust, crowning the face. What can one tell from human faces, she asked herself bitterly, if even the artist cannot see what lives behind them? He and she, of one name, bound together by the holiest of bonds—God should never have let it be. For thirty-six years she had held it against God.

She opened the door and went into the next room, where it was dark and cold, walked through three more rooms, all dark, cold rooms of the old Mylius palace, and brooded, and tried to excuse herself from the responsibility that the letter laid upon her, seeking a shelter where she would not hear its call.

CHAPTER XXI

A WONDERFUL TRIAL

WHEN she came back into her workroom, she had made up her mind. She touched the electric bell and stood waiting motionless until Fräulein Schönpflug, her companion and factotum in all her outside work, appeared.

She wrote the address on a bit of paper and said, in a weak voice, with her helplessly wandering glance, "I am told that there is a child here whose parents have forsaken it. It must be fetched away to-day. It is a nine-year-old girl. Please drive over there at once, Elizabeth, and bring it with you. It can be left with the janitor for the present. But to-morrow morning call up early at the Dornbacher home and ask if they have a vacancy for her."

The Dornbacher home was one of three important foundations that Josephine had endowed, an asylum for the daughters of former officers; it was very richly endowed and gave regular high school training. She had also founded a hospital and an orphan asylum and kept both of these institutes going by unusual sacrifices in money. As a result of the rising prices, however, her former payments were too slight and this was giving her constant trouble.

As Fräulein Schönpflug hesitated and looked stealthily at her watch; it was already very late; Josephine added: "Good. That is all. Inform me just how you find the child. I will wait up."

Fräulein Elizabeth did not dare to object. If she had not had to spend the greater part of the past night reading aloud to her mistress she would have obeyed more willingly. But such errands, late at night, were not unusual and the Baroness frequently put heavy demands upon all who served her. It was often a matter of children who were in danger and need.

The town was full of lost and forsaken children. As a ship throws its debris upon the coast so these unsettled times threw young souls upon the street from its stormy current.

When Elizabeth read the name Heinroth, she was startled. True, she knew nothing definite; she had only lived four years in the house and absolute silence reigned about her mistress's past. But still some echo had reached her. She determined to ask old Casimir, who, for the past twenty-five years, had been more of a major-domo than servant and had held his post throughout the lifetime of the Baron. It was to him also that she was to bring the child.

The restless and excited look of her mistress lead Fräulein Schönpflug to say gently: "The Frau Baroness should go to bed. She is overtired. I will attend to everything as well as possible."

"Ah, sleep," said Josephine in a hollow voice; "it would be good indeed to sleep, but how is it possible? How can any one sleep in such a world?"

Inwardly dazed she waited for the return of her companion, while hour after hour passed, and it was almost midnight when a knock came upon the door and Elizabeth came in, timidly eager. Her unlovely face was freshened up and there was a merry gleam in her expressionless eyes. She looked as if she had been taking part in an eager and interesting conversation, as if she had had an unusually refreshing experience. Josephine turned her searching glance aside, for she feared every word that might be spoken. She was distrustful of any joyous impulse; she did not believe in joy and in this evening's happening there lay for her nothing but threats and sorrow.

Elizabeth announced that she had found the child and as ordered, had taken her to Casimir's wife, whom she had notified beforehand. The Frau Baroness wanted to know how she had found the little Fanny. Not at all as one might expect, an unhappy child grieving over its parents' flight. Josephine tried to stop her with a gesture, as if she were no longer interested to hear anything, but Elizabeth overlooked it and laughed a little infectious laugh. It did not appear, she continued, as if the relation of father and mother had been a

particularly tender one; quite the contrary; the child seemed
not to have received tenderness and care or to have given trust
and love.

"I do not understand your gay mood," Josephine said,
frowning, "really, I don't understand it."

"It was all so odd, Frau Baroness," her companion excused
herself and tried to subdue her spirits; "it was all so surprising; I wasn't prepared for it. A strange child, really, a wonderful child, if I dare trust my judgment. Frau Baroness really
ought to see the child. I am not saying too much."

Josephine replied coldly: "No. I don't want to see it.
There would be no object. And now get to bed, Elizabeth.
You can tell me to-morrow whatever else there is to tell. By
daylight things take on their soberer colours." And she thought
disdainfully: I have to endure around me people without tact,
mind or nerves; what agony! Yet she was fond of this faithful and modest servant.

What could have happened to have caused this outbreak of
admiration and buoyancy in the sour Fräulein Schönpflug? It
came to light only bit by bit when on the following day she
drove with her mistress to the Institute. Josephine appeared
indifferent and managed to hide the interest which rose in
her against her will. Now and then she turned the subject
aside as if she were bored but when Elizabeth began again with
the same smile of amusement to tell about it, she consented to
listen though not a feature of her stern face changed.

It was half-past ten when Elizabeth reached the house.
She told the woman who opened the door what she wanted
and asked her to go up-stairs with her as she supposed the child
would already be asleep. But when she reached the door of the
room she heard shrill laughter. The families to the right and
the left had gathered there, a postman with his wife and two
daughters and a typesetter with his wife and three children.
Fanny had spent the evening with them alternately and had
been very merry and lively. Her parents had left that morning
and in order to conceal their preparations from the child they
had sent her over to a neighbour, a washwoman, who lived near
them. When Fanny returned at midday she found a letter

from her father with some money in it, telling her not to be afraid, that she would soon be taken to live in a beautiful house. She had cried a little, but quieted herself almost immediately. This was what Elizabeth had been told.

When she stepped into the room, Fanny was sitting on the edge of a table with her feet on a chair, over her shoulders she had thrown a torn green shawl which her mother had left behind and over this fell a flood of beautiful blonde hair, like a cataract. The sight, in these surroundings, was most surprising. She had a finely-cut oval face, rosily tinted, and here in the impoverished looking room, with its naked walls and lack of furniture and its circle of listening, laughing people sat Fanny. Instead of going to bed as they had begged her to do, she was telling them what her plans were now; she thought she would go to the island of Sweden where she heard the sun never went down and children got their every wish as soon as they expressed them. There were lots of princes there whom one could marry, and the bakers baked buns every day, and there was plenty of meat and nobody wore torn shoes.

She knew a place where one could get an airship; but to reach it you had to wander for ten days and ten nights and the air pilot, who was also a Swede, would take any passenger who could answer three questions. The questions were: How does our dear God look? Where is the end of the world? And how does a tree grow?

She accompanied all this with the most excited gestures, her fresh little mouth laughed, showing her little white teeth, her dark grey eyes gleamed with fire, and as Elizabeth stood surprised on the threshold, little Fanny stood up on the chair and asked her mockingly: "Can you answer? Do you know those three things? Just see how uneducated you are. You will never get to the island of Sweden."

It was easy to see why the two men and their wives and their five children were all in fits of laughter; perhaps they thought they were really in the theatre; it was all so amusing and strange in its naïveté; the words, gestures, meaning, the actual magic that streamed from this little person; at any

rate, they were overcome with merriment. The women fairly
shrieked. But Elizabeth made a quick end of it all when
she told the object of her coming. Fanny did not in the
least resist going with her, she took it all in the day's work, laid
aside her poor little decorations, and standing in front of Elizabeth, looked sharply into her face and slipped into her thin
coat which the typesetter's daughter handed her. The people
became suddenly silent as if ashamed; the sudden farewell
touched them. Fanny waved to all of them, promised to visit
them shortly and tripped joyously down the stairs with Elizabeth. It happened that the street car was no longer running and
they had to walk all the way back. Then Fanny began to
talk and chatter untiringly, full of confidences, mixing up the
cleverest and the quaintest things. As it was a clear night she
tried to count the stars that she could see between the houses,
told the names of all the people and places that she had
known; enquired whether everybody would die if they did
not eat for three days; whether there were any pretty picture
books where she was going, then seemed tired and said, half
laughing, half sighing, as they turned down a narrow street:
"Is it not funny, the ground wants me to go quickly, but my
feet want to go slowly."

The next morning the house-keeper said to Elizabeth, throwing up her hands: "What sort of wild little witch is this that
you have brought?" Fanny had been lively until two o'clock,
had asked a thousand questions, enquired most curiously
about the Frau Baroness to whom the house belonged, how
she looked, what she did and how old she was. When the
child had at last gone to sleep she had called her husband in
to look at her, for she was like an angel among her pillows.
As the matron of the home had announced that she was quite
able to take in Josephine's protegée, Elizabeth had to arrange
everything for her at once. She could hardly talk enough
about the bath and the changing of her clothes; it was such a
wonderful, splendid little body; shoulders, hands and feet,
like those of a miniature Venus; and the chattering and the
laughing and the twittering that went on; the splendour of her
pale gold hair as she washed and dried it with care; the joy

over the new linen, the new dress, a happiness which for a moment made her still and devout. Elizabeth recommended her particularly to the kindness of the matron and hoped she had not gone beyond the wishes of her mistress. She said it was hard for her to leave Fanny and showed a feeling in saying this that Josephine thought exaggerated; she even begged to be allowed to visit the child from time to time. Josephine could hardly refuse the wish, but remained very reserved about it, thinking "a fire of straw does not last long," but she only said that they must wait and see how the child behaved in the Institute and what reports they got about her. Moreover, they had a great many other things to attend to and there was no lack of business. Elizabeth shook her head; she thought her mistress was too harsh.

But in reality it was only natural. Josephine's whole mood was oppressed. Her general grief over the condition of things, of which she knew more than most women of her class, was increased by something special of whose influence over her life she could give no account but which troubled her conscience. The picture of the past seemed to threaten her power of self-preservation and she stood alone in the world with a heart torn by anxiety and loathing.

It was a mistake both of seeing and feeling, but her nature had been overburdened by its experience of human tragedy, into which indeed she tried to reach daily, though daily, too, she saw how little impression she could make. In her whole life she had had only sorrow, indeed, the very deepest; now she added to that physical weakness and she shut it all up in her own heart. She could no longer distinguish and discriminate and the breaking down of existence, the constant seeing of despair and destruction in these last years put her body on the rack so that she no longer breathed freely and never had a happy thought or inner refreshment, except music, which she loved with the whole power of her hopeless loneliness.

The people around her began to feel it, and especially her destructive doubts. She followed each one of them around and gave them a hundred orders that were superfluous. She wanted to keep them always busy, always at their duties, and always ready at her command. At the same time she often forgot their faces, their qualities, their obligations and their names; she would contradict her own orders and then order again what she had contradicted, complain of how badly she was served while everybody waited at her heels, and she was both feared and honoured by all, pitied and execrated.

Fräulein Schönpflug let no day. pass without asking after Fanny's conduct and welfare, and whenever she had a couple of hours free she made an excuse to go there and visit the home. Josephine saw through all her little efforts, but took care never to speak of Fanny. She relied upon Elizabeth's telling her everything but Elizabeth, after a while, became absolutely silent; either because she was angry with the Baroness's lack of enthusiasm and sympathy or else she feared in her modesty to overreach her mistress's wishes. She watched, but she was not very clever and drew false conclusions; Casimir had not satisfied her curiosity, diplomat that he was, and kept her in complete ignorance of what the name Heinroth meant.

One day it happened that Josephine, in a casual tone, asked if Fanny had any relatives in the town, or if she knew anything about them or had heard anything about them. Elizabeth denied it so quickly and candidly that Josephine now had no more doubt that the child had been left entirely in the dark as to her family. That lightened her heart considerably.

After a while she asked how Fanny was getting on. Oh, very well, was Elizabeth's hasty answer. Did she like being in the home? Very well indeed, as far as one could judge. What did the matron, and the teacher, and the little comrades say of her? Oh, all sorts of different things, utterly different things, one could not imagine more widely differing opinions. How was that, asked Josephine, surprised. Had she then not all the fine qualities that Elizabeth had at first believed in? Was she already disappointed? Oh, certainly not, the Frau Baroness was greatly mistaken; but Fanny was an untamed creature; it was hard for her to wear chains; and when any one expressed their authority or claims too strongly she was apt to take refuge in disrespectful mockery; but she learned well of her own free will; she was willing to obey but only out of affection; she loved everybody, but sometimes upset the whole Institution and had to have serious punishments which made her suffer.

That was the end of the conversation; and Josephine stared in front of her with a nervous twitching of her eyelids, from which Elizabeth knew she was thinking hard. She had enough womanly intuition to feel hidden torment. She wondered and wondered and thought and thought, but the right track which she sometimes almost found, she never followed, perhaps out of consideration. She was afraid to lift the curtain which Josephine, for her own reasons, had dropped around her life. In her simple soul she fairly idolised her mistress.

Another evening as they were drinking tea, Josephine began to question her again quite unexpectedly. They had both gone over the accounts of the three Institutes and at the end Josephine had said, much moved, that if things went on this way, prices and rents increasing all the time, she would have to close up in a few months. Elizabeth replied discouraged, that the Frau Baroness had been corresponding with Herr Valerian de Groot and he had promised to give a concert for the benefit of her Institute; one could hardly doubt that so famous an artist would add a considerable sum to her benevolent undertakings. Josephine shrugged her shoulders; it would be too little; if it were enough for to-day, it would be too little for to-morrow; she felt like some one who was drowning in a swamp and the more effort she made to get out the deeper she sank in it. Then she had been silent for a while and then suddenly began again her singular, stubborn, piercing questions about Fanny.

Elizabeth had now had time and opportunity really to form a judgment about Fanny (Elizabeth had noticed that Josephine never used the name Heinroth); could she now tell her something definite about the child's character, something final from which she could really get an idea of her?

Elizabeth reflected. She thought that the simplest way would be for her to go herself and see the child and get the information there; why did not she do that? What should prevent her? She hung her head and answered reluctantly. It was not easy to do what the Frau Baroness desired; she did not know enough about human beings to express her impressions correctly.

"Well, then, I'll help you," said Josephine. "Do you think she is frivolous?"—Elizabeth pressed her silver teaspoon to her cheek and stammered—"or vain or trifling?" Elizabeth's eyebrows went up, uncertain. "Does she tell lies?" asked Josephine, suddenly impatient and domineering. Elizabeth blushed and said alarmed: "No, I don't think she does, I think she is too proud." Josephine leaned back in her arm chair, looked at the ceiling and continued the investigation. "Is she capable of taking an education?" Elizabeth replied uncertainly: "Do you mean does she study well, Frau Baroness? Yes, she is very diligent, though she sometimes lets her hair loose and climbs trees and behaves naughtily and is hard to discipline, so the matron says; she has been sternly forbidden to let her hair down her back and she disobeys every day unfortunately." Elizabeth, for some unknown reason, was almost ready to cry. Josephine paid no attention to it; she leaned over and took Elizabeth's left hand by the wrist, pressed it violently and asked earnestly: "Has she a heart? Everything that you tell is only an amusing little comedy, you know, for children play comedies, but has she a heart?"

Elizabeth looked at the restless shining eyes as if she was hypnotised and answered anxiously: "I don't know, Frau Baroness. I would rather jump out of the window than knowingly tell you anything that was untrue. I don't know. I only know that she is a lively, blooming, sincere little human being, who makes you feel that you have a heart yourself."

Josephine got up and went to the window. The answer had pleased her. She stood quiet a long time, then turned back to the table and said: "Good. We will go and see. I will drive out there and get acquainted with her, but not at once" —she smiled gently at Elizabeth's joyous gesture—"not tomorrow or next day. The de Groot concert comes off the end of next week and we have a great many preparations to make;

when that is over I will make up my mind." She paused for a moment and then added with a strange coldness: "Perhaps, my dear Elizabeth, it is superfluous to explain to you why this is all so difficult and unnatural. A little keenness and a word from you and the whole thing would be open to the public. I cannot talk about it. And don't look at me as you are looking at me now, it is too much for me. One has to hide the more painful things one knows about others." Elizabeth dropped her eyes.

CHAPTER XXII

UNEXPECTED RESULTS OF A PEDAGOGICAL UNDERTAKING

As Valerian de Groot had not played for eight years on the continent, the hall in which he gave his concert was full to bursting, despite the enormous price of tickets. In that audience there were but a few who had heard the world-famous violinist in that time when one listened to music with another mind and other expectations. To the naturally sensitive there was the difference that there is between the vivid and excited description of a dangerous sea voyage and that sea voyage itself.

Perhaps just for this reason, the really critical listeners felt a certain twinge of disappointment. It was not just the distrust that is felt of an unproven fame or of the always harmful disproportion between a noisy *réclame* and the most significant performance; all the circumstances here were favourable, an enthusiastic audience grateful for the readiness with which de Groot had lent himself to an act of social service. But the change in de Groot's playing could not be overlooked, and deep as the impression his personality made, his mere presence, his noble bearing, touchingly as he played this and that piece, a *cantilena*, a melodic figure, the schooled ear could not fail to know that there was some break between the man and his work, as if fatigue or indifference or secret revulsion prevented his throwing himself into it. However, the mass of the people were wild with delight.

As he had only arrived the morning of the concert from London, Josephine had not yet had time to speak to him and had to satisfy herself with a mere greeting as she stood at the head of her committee. She had not seen him for ten years and was fairly frightened at the appearance of age which the man, hardly fifty-three years old, offered. When he stepped onto the stage, approval thundering about him, it still filled her mind and her questioning looks were fixed almost reproachfully upon the slender figure, the silver grey hair over the powerful brow, the feminine, sternly-closed mouth, the tired little eyes under their heavy, bushy brows. She was so preoccupied with tormenting thoughts that it was almost impossible for her to fix her mind upon the music as she wished to do.

The years rose before her, and in the dreamy distance she saw the picture of the boy Tino, stretched upon a bed looking like a body without any soul. For eighteen months this had lasted before the results of that unholy night were overcome, that night which drew Josephine into the circle of his existence. Then there came a time when his broken spirit arose again marvellously and seemed to have gained ten times what he had been robbed of by the criminal deed. Josephine went to him nearly every day, and with his mother she sheltered that valuable life so that the boy was bound to her by an almost passionate tenderness. It became evident that his mother would have to take him into the country. The small allowance which Edward Melander had allowed him until his recovery was continued for three years longer through Josephine's intercession. The boy, showing now both his will and his ambition, wished to go to Italy to study, for he needed light and sun in every way, and he went to the conservatory at Bologna. There his mother died after one year. At one of his first little-noticed public recitals in Milan he made the acquaintance of a Hollander named de Groot, an odd man and a great enthusiast for music. He became the young artist's friend and impresario and spent freely enormous amounts on the boy who loved him and owed no little to his thorough, though somewhat one-sided taste. De Groot surrounded him with luxury, smoothed his way, and finally adopted him, for it was his happiest dream that this rising star upon the sky of art should bear his name, Valerian de Groot. It was easy for the boy to submit to his will, for he felt no obligation to cling to the name to which his tragic childhood bound him. For three

years de Groot enjoyed the fame of his adopted son; the fortune that he left him was fought for by the brothers; they
threatened a law-suit and the adopted brother threw the inheritance at them with a grand gesture and contented himself with the old house in Bruges, in which he still had the
valuable library of his dead patron.

Then began the restless wandering of a virtuoso, year in
and year out. At the time of the changing of his name he had
written to Josephine and they kept up a lasting correspondence,
which on Josephine's side was restrained, although full of sympathy, and on his was full of unchangeable fidelity and gratitude. In every decisive moment of his life he turned to her
in whom he saw a motherly friend, despite the slight difference of their ages, and the tone of his letters was always full
of submission and reverence. He told her everything, he complained to her, he told her his sorrows, he announced his
triumphs and was never surprised that she did not answer
with the same openness and confided only the most superficial things about her own life. In the course of the years
they saw each other, in Paris, in London, in Berlin, in Rome,
in Vienna; and he always brought the same beneficent, knightly
friendship. His natural strength and elasticity seemed to
serve him against all the blows of an exciting life; but Josephine remembered at the very height of his accomplishments
he had spoken with impatience and revulsion of the hollow-
ness of such a gipsy life; how it tired him to see the same
excited, thirsty, listening faces below him; to make the same
bows, and the same grimaces, and to play the same programs
and to hear the same praise, to read the same chatter in the
newspapers, to sit at the same dinners and suppers and carry
on the same annoying bargains with agents and managers,
winter after winter, year after year. Nights were spent on
railroads and in hotels, weeks upon ships, months in strange
lands, over and over again, without let-up. And the knowledge that this must be his life, this and nothing else, and his
disgust at it did not prevent him from living eagerly with
every nerve and breath of his body, eager to such a degree
that he could no longer have gone without the excitement than

a toper could have gone without his daily quantity of alcohol.

Twenty-three years ago he had married in Baltimore and withdrawn to his house in Bruges and become a Belgian citizen, in a mood of disgust at his vagabond life and out of longing for a home. But soon living with this spoiled and vain woman proved impossible and each went a separate way, though he was left with two sons, whom he idolised, the fruit of this marriage. He sent them to Cambridge to be educated and they developed into splendid men; he often wrote Josephine that they were his pride and his happiness. He lost them both at the same time in the war. Then in one night his hair turned perfectly white and from that time on Josephine had heard nothing from him.

The next day as he sat before her, his thin legs crossed over each other, his slender white hands lightly folded, he said in the respectful tone which he had always used toward Josephine, and which ill-suited his usual dominant manner: "I want to thank you, Baroness, for having spared me an official breakfast. It means a great deal to me to see you alone."

Josephine, somewhat embarrassed, expressed her delight over the concert. He turned it aside with a disdainful gesture. He spoke of her sister, Lady Esther Wincherly, whom he had seen in London, and who still had a great house there and still made all tongues wag despite her advanced years by her adventurous ways. Also the other sister, widow of Von Althann, or Madame Aimée de Althann, as she now called herself, he had also seen and he had to admit, that she was an old woman destroyed by morphine, who had been the scorn of two decades for her silly love of dogs, which really took a most questionable form.

"Yes, she has spent most of her fortune on dogs," said Josephine, with a bitter smile. "People seem hardly to matter to her. She has never seemed to have any feeling for man or woman. Her dog-cult is insane. But it has gone on for years and years. Ten of her favourite dogs live in a palace in the Faubourg, and each one has his own separate lackey to wait on him and a gold kennel. On the day of the outbreak of the war she bought a little fancy dog for a hundred and sixty thousand francs. Yes, that is what has become of Aimée."

Valerian's head dropped. "Yes, that is what has become of Aimée," he repeated, laughing hoarsely, "and that is what has become of the beautiful Esther, too. And what has become of us, dear Baroness? What has become of our world?" He looked angrily from under his bushy brows, put both hands upon his temples and burst into hard, dry sobbing.

Josephine did not move, but she trembled up and down her spine.

Throwing back his head of floating hair, he said with the same angry glance: "Who is Aimée d'Althann? And who is Lady Esther Wincherly? Why should we trouble ourselves about them? And who am I? Look at me! What has become of me! I am a tragic ruin—a caricature of my own self."

Josephine stretched out her hand shyly to comfort him. I, too, have lived through the impossible, she wanted to say, but her lips brought out no word.

He guessed her intention. "Not that, Baroness," he went on in a troubled voice, "not that. You are thinking of the losses I have sustained. But it isn't that. To sorrow over that now would be childish. Two fine men; my only two. Perhaps there exists somewhere a being, who with not less right may say: my two million men. But it isn't even that. Six years have passed and the rest are passing. Still one is here. Each day is a sovereign lord and commands us to give a report. You feel that as I do, you faithful soldier. Be ready, is the command and one is. No one can deny that I am ready."

He arose then and walked through the room and then threw himself again into his chair. "Ten years ago, dear Baroness," he scolded in his deep voice that had no more humility in it now, "ten years ago, I could still believe that I had a mission to fulfill. I could deceive myself, 'You have an ideal, you are working for Art, you are giving men food for their souls, you are building upon an invisible temple.' It was possible though one knew by heart all the cheating and swindling that goes on. But to-day the ship that stood then with swelling sails lies a pitiable wreck on the shore. There is no hope that it will ever be seaworthy again. What the storm left the worms have finished. There is no hope that we shall ever see the beloved shores of Ithaca. The helmsmen are drowned, the Captain has no more authority, the seamen are raging and tearing each other to pieces. Dear friend, do you expect me to make music to all that? Nothing but a dance of death ought to be played." Scornfully he hummed the opening bars of Saint-Saëns' "Danse Macabre" and laughed threateningly as he threw himself back into his chair.

Discouraged, Josephine said that he must have seen yesterday evening how he melted all hearts and how impulsive was the demonstration of thanks to him for releasing them even for a moment from the dark monotony of their daily lives.

"Oh, don't tell me that," Valerian growled; "don't tell me that; I hear it on the right hand and on the left, but you can't catch an old fox like me with such platitudes. Do you know what it is? I will tell you what it is: it is the hysteria of relief and remission. In their need and anxiety they slipped down there, where no man needs to justify himself or tell what kind of a mind he has, where each one can be paid with the native false coin of feeling for his sins and negligence. Who will ask or report? Who will demand it of them? Their consciences are lulled to sleep and they dream blissfully even though the hour before they may have cut their own brother's throat. How it tortures me to look down into a hall stuffed full of human faces; you can't even conceive it. It seems as if out of all the houses in the town the gathered-up rubbish heaps of dusty opinion and outlived judgments and impudent desires and lying culture and cowardly foresight have been gathered there in front of me and I, as a spider draws threads out of his own body, I draw out tones with my bow and ask myself as I do it: for what object is all this foolish weaving? They say: thanks so much for the pretty magic; and go on doing just what they have always done. Exalted? Made better? Cleansed? If any one were to affirm that, my answer

would be: 'Man, you are either a fool or a rascal or both.'
And then perhaps he will say cynically to me, 'Spider-webs are
not cables with which one can save stranded ships.' And he
would be quite right."

He rose then and went up and down with big strides, his
hands in his coat pockets and talked with a grimness that had
something majestic about it: "I wish I could disappear entirely from this hideous unnatural stage. Even if it were
only for a year. I wish I could go somewhere and bury myself with my books, any place where the odour of this pestifer-
ous world would not reach me. In my own house everything
reminds me of something I don't want to think about. Where
is the shelter in all the walled-up lands? Look at the piteous-
ness and ridiculousness of my plight: I was born in Austria,
brought up in Italy, married in America, found my home in
Belgium, gave my two sons to England, and for thirty-six
years I have wandered in homeless freedom from one end of
the planet to the other without finding a door closed to me.
Now whenever I step over a threshold I have to submit to a
cross-examination by rascally custom officials, dirty fingers
meddle with my wash and I am worried by officials and my
time is stolen and I am deceived about the distance that I
wish to keep from these noxious human insects. Why should
I respect everything that calls itself a nation? One is treated
like a truant school-boy if one does not keep a continual boast
in one's mouth as formerly the hireling did the name of his
superior. Shall I, who have wrestled with the enlightened
thought of mankind, be condemned to go back to the most
infantile conditions of primitive peoples? Bastards boast of
their descent, and the Wahiti stand armed to the teeth at the
border of their pile-villages. They have destroyed the earth
and are fighting over the ruins. What shall I do? Risk my
head for the sake of going between Scylla and Charybdis?
No. A man of any dignity will not put up with that."

Josephine sat silent, smiling strangely, for his flaming excitement released her for a while from the dull pressure on her
heart, which time had heaped up there, the constant endurance of force and injustice. He is the same as ever, she

thought with a sort of relief, a noble rebel who cannot understand why there should be villainy in the world, and who does not yet quite know that the whole world consists of villainy. The gentle smile remained about her lips after Valerian had gone, and after, with his usual respectful voice, he had begged pardon for his vehemence.

His despairing demand for a place of shelter remained in her mind. She talked about it that evening with Elizabeth; she, knowing the secret thoughts of her mistress, usually knew what Josephine was thinking of but did not wish to be the first to speak, in her fear at the utterance of any wish. For she never believed that any wish that she cherished could be fulfilled.

Elizabeth suggested boldly that they might offer him Eckern! There he could be at peace; a more undisturbed island could not be found for him. Josephine nodded happily.

Eckern was a beautiful estate and country house that belonged to her, six hours by express from the Capital, among wooded hills, near a well-known summer resort, whose guests, however, rarely reached this hidden place. She loved this property very much, but had not been there for many years, and when, with the shyness of a beggar, she offered the retreat in Eckern, he asked her after a few moments' thought why she herself did not spend her summers there; she dropped her eyes to the ground and did not answer. He thanked her heartily, kissed her hand, and said he could not make up his mind at once; at any rate he would have to go home first and look after some business and pack up a part of his library to send. Then he became more interested, asked about the lay of the land, the climate, the people, talked until he became quite enthusiastic about it, mentioned his astronomical studies which he might carry on undisturbed there and finally decided on the last day of May as the latest day on which he would come. Josephine was jubilant.

The next day, however, he was moody again and wanted to hear nothing of the plan. Agents had been after him and though he had given the sternest orders that they should not see him they had finally gotten hold of him. His refusals had been very gruff and now he was sorry for it and regretted the haughtiness which he felt was rooted in his feeling about the weakness of his position. Josephine shook her head and the gentle blame that it expressed touched him; he made her a half jesting, half sincere declaration of love and said that he felt now for the first time how he had missed her in all these years, her goodness, her patience, her silent understanding. She was the physician whom he needed. Josephine blushed like a young girl and laughed embarrassed.

He said he would be glad to go to Eckern, but only on condition that she went too and stayed until Autumn. He was afraid, he said, to be entirely alone in a country to which no past experience bound him.

"In former years I used to spend spring, summer and autumn there," said Josephine, in her plaintive voice, "and when I came back I was always made over, with new plans and new hopes. But it is all different since—" She stopped again; she looked down at her hands. Then at Valerian's surprised glance she mentioned the name of Ulrika Woytich.

He shrugged his shoulders, not understanding.

Ten years ago, she told him, Ulrika Woytich had built herself a little villa in the same neighbourhood, a comfortable well-arranged house; not exactly in the immediate neighbourhood of Eckern, but about twenty-five minutes away on the other side of the valley. In Ried, as it was called. But since then Eckern had been completely spoiled for her and she could never make up her mind to go back there.

Valerian's surprise grew. "Woytich—" he murmured, "Ulrika Woytich? What is it I remember about her? Where have I heard of her?"

But he needed only to look at Josephine's stern face for the connection to come back to him. Long ago with anxiously shy restraint Josephine had spoken of her. It was in Rome, where they had spent a few days together. There she had met him one morning in the midst of an excited crowd of Italian nobles in the Borghese gardens, after he had disappeared from the circle of her acquaintance for a long time. Her limbs had trembled as she told him; a deadly horror had overpowered her and she had neither rest nor peace afterwards until she left Rome. Valerian had noticed this at the time; and she had reminded him also of the double-faced and hideous rôle that Ulrika Woytich had played in the tragic incident of his boyhood. But now that was all so far away, the Roman days and all the rest of it, so buried in the dust of the things that he had lived through since, so entirely a shadow and a past, that no picture or image could bring it back to him. Less than ever he understood Josephine's objection to Eckern and he said that a reason that was no better than a fear of ghosts was not worthy of her.

No, she answered, it was not a fear of ghosts. It was a real physical fear. A terror of a repetition of the past. She knew that in many people there was real longing for a repetition of the past and that the whole tendency of their disposition was a longing to bring back some part of their past; but as to her, her whole feeling was horror and terror.

He looked at her thoughtfully, for her face was as if veiled by destiny and he wondered what were the secrets of her past. Involuntarily he bowed before her. But now he was more than ever incited to overcome her shyness of Eckern and to make her look forward to their common visit there. She could avoid any one she wished to avoid. Who would dare to break down her barriers if she placed them? Why be cowardly and take to flight when circumstances demanded only that she have the pride to ignore? Why shudder before a phantom, which if she looked at it coolly was no more than a ridiculous, poor human being. "To tremble at a bugbear is allowed," he called out, "but to tremble at a human being? Then really we ought to have refused to come into the world for fear we should have nothing else to do but tremble. Shall one go on carrying the memory of disgrace when it is already only a legend? That is to be more refinedly cruel than our misfortune."

He saw that Josephine was yielding. He described the coming months .in such enticing images, and was so determined, so joyous, so heartily persuasive that she could no longer refuse. She admitted that life in the city had become a hell to her. A vapour rose from the city streets that seemed to devastate the whole earth.

Moreover, the Government threatened to commandeer a portion of the property which she had thought safe, a threat that she turned aside only after quite a sacrifice of money; this gave her the necessary impulse and she withstood Valerian's persuasion no longer. Elizabeth's whole face lighted up and she almost fell on the baroness's neck.

Although the removal was not to take place for three weeks, the preparations, according to the careful methods of these women, were begun at once. Elizabeth was up at daybreak and with memoranda and written directions she wandered from room to room, up and down stairs humming lightly to herself. She knew Eckern and adored the place; once she had stayed there several weeks while recovering from an illness. She would have been endlessly delighted at the Baroness's decision if the thought of Fanny had not disturbed her. The child seemed to her forsaken if she went away. It had become a precious habit with her to visit her and she was troubled as to how she would get on.

One morning she was called to Josephine, who handed her a letter which she read silently. It came from the matron of the Dornbacher Institute, in which moderately, but quite candidly, she gave an account of Fanny's conduct. Although she had unmistakable gifts, really surprising quickness of understanding and a certain liveliness of disposition, she had shown a constantly increasing self-will and revolt against the discipline of the house, that had now become a definite disobedience and breaking of the rules which could not be put up with. The matter was the worse that she had qualities of fascination for the other children, charm and amiability, which led them to imitate her. Warnings and punishments had been fruitless; she therefore respectfully begged her to speak to her protegée herself, since if her disobedience continued, the unavoidable result would be to turn the child out of the Institution.

"Now, what do you say?" asked Josephine grimly; in her heart she heard a scornful voice saying: "Melander blood."

Elizabeth shrugged her shoulders. Hiding her discomfort, she said gently: "I think the Frau Baroness should follow the wishes of the matron and speak to Fanny; I think you would see that it is not so bad as is made out."

"Good, we will go there this afternoon," came tonelessly from Josephine's lips. "I will not fall short of my duty; I will do it to the end." And she turned quickly to her worktable and Elizabeth went away full of thoughts and trouble.

As Josephine for some time had not used her automobile and never missed an opportunity of economising for herself, they made the long trip in the crowded tramway, standing. She was much exhausted when she reached her destination. Elizabeth, without Josephine's knowledge, had telephoned of their intended visit and asked that Fanny be notified, that her appearance before the baroness might be unhindered. Josephine was received by the matron most graciously and taken into her private office. One of the younger teachers was sent to find Fanny. After a while she returned; Fanny was nowhere to be found. The matron was pale with anger. Only a quarter of an hour ago the girl had been in the class room; but the teacher replied that they had searched everywhere in vain and called for her all through the garden. The matron turned a significant look upon Josephine; Elizabeth was sitting on needles. "I told her most emphatically to hold herself ready," scolded the matron, "and she promised in her most angelic manner. Now we have proof." Josephine looked reproachfully at Elizabeth, who realised that by forewarning them, she had brought about this painful situation. "Why did you have to warn her, is she so shy or is she afraid of me?"

The matron replied, "Oh, no, Frau Baroness; she does not know what it means to be afraid of any one. But when she is expected to do any particular thing she is immediately bent on escaping it. She is a difficult child, I may say, an impossible child. The child has been sinned against and now, as I said the other day to Fräulein Schönpflug, it is almost impossible to eradicate the weeds from her nature."

To lighten the general embarrassment and bad humour

Josephine suggested that they all go into the garden and Fanny would doubtless appear soon. She hardly knew what she was saying. Her heart beat in her very throat and she was almost glad that the child had disappeared. As they went down to the garden, Josephine and the matron in front, Elizabeth following, and a few teachers and pupils with eager and interested faces behind, they heard the chatter of gay young voices under the apple trees which were just putting out their young leaves. Immediately afterwards they saw a group of a dozen girls of from eight to fifteen years old, all surrounding one in their midst, laughing, scolding, coaxing; in their light dresses they made a lovely picture.

These were the pupils who had been sent out to call Fanny. They had found her behind the gooseberry hedge of a near-by vineyard, hidden under the bushes. They had half pulled and half coaxed her and now she was coming along, looking with mocking composure upon the companions gaily surrounding her; tall and large for her age, her hair, shining gold, crowned with leaves. It was like a swarm of bright coloured birds startled by a strange intruder who drove them on.

Then Josephine saw that the child was beautiful. And a sharp, long-silenced emotion of joy swept over her, and she felt sure that this beauty was not only external. It was fresh as happiness itself and old as a dream; something hard and heavy was lifted from her heart; she went forward as if moved by an inner power, smiling anxiously. Elizabeth followed, eager and expectant, and the group of girls stood still; some of them giggled.

"Make your curtsey, Fanny, as you have been taught," came the cutting voice of the matron. Fanny did not move. She was fingering a little branch she carried, and she looked steadily at Josephine. The matron, angry, wished to go up to her, but Elizabeth held her back. "There you see again the child's perverse stubbornness," she whispered in Elizabeth's ear. "And I can only wonder if she will follow her usual habit of addressing every one with the familiar 'thou,' instead of the respectful 'you.'"

Josephine did not weigh her words because they sprang impulsively to her lips: "Would you like to come with me, Fanny, and live in my house?"

A searching look of Fanny's rested on the Baroness's face and then she answered frankly: "Oh, yes; I would like to be with you (she used the familiar address) very much indeed." The matron listened with open mouth and Elizabeth nodded like a Chinese idol.

CHAPTER XXIII

A RUSTIC IDYLL

THE old post-chaise drawn by a weary nag rattled through Ried. It was usually used to carry only mail and packages; for passengers there were but two seats, namely, on the box with the driver Sauerbrand, who was now serving his twenty-eighth year on the venerable vehicle, as he assured his two lady passengers with variations from time to time. They knew it anyhow for they had gone the same way with him often enough; at any rate one of them knew him to the point of intimacy; but it was not necessary to talk to prove oneself an accessible human being and the two women seemed not inclined for conversation for it was raining in streams and the coachman had no roof to his seat.

From time to time the nag stood still as if he had something important to think over, snuffed up a little of the pine odour along the way, turned his streaming head away again and resolved upon further exertions. Each time, Sauerbrand nodded approvingly; the moral victory that the animal won over his sleepy nature roused his respect. The older of the two women could not restrain a little abuse in her rough, deep voice—she would rather be carried in a hearse outright than be bumped black and blue in such a bouncing old basket. The horse was no use any more and ought to be used for carrion. It was easy to see how the blessed State put upon its patient subjects; it was a wonder to her that they did not have to drive with square wheels. Sauerbrand, half offended and half subdued, kept silence, and philosophically concluded that the gracious Fräulein Woytich was in a bad humour again, and it was better to avoid differences of opinion.

The discontented lady on the seat wore a headdress that looked like a pancake, entirely indistinguishable as to material

and colour, from which a hen's feather stuck straight up in
the air. About her throat she wore a woollen scarf of likewise indistinguishable color to shelter her from the weather.
Her gaunt figure was covered above with a garment that reminded one of a hunter's jacket from which most of the
buttons were lacking and which was far from clean. Below
she had on a shiny skirt, drenched to the knees. One would
have hardly supposed that this costly costume would have
required an umbrella; but she had put one up apparently
merely out of abstraction as it was full of holes and rips, one
hole big enough to give a fine view of the surrounding
country and the cloudy sky. While one hand grasped this instrument of questionable usefulness, the other held a footstool,
newly covered and protected from the rain by old newspapers.

At last the sad trip ended at the door of the villa, an archi-
tecturally pleasant building at the top of a slight hill. Sauerbrand first helped Fräulein Woytich gallantly down from the
box, and then her sister, her companion, who went by the
title of Frau Justice. Her deceased husband, a state official,
had risen as high as imperial counsellor in the days of the
monarchy.

Fräulein Woytich hurried through the entrance and bellowed
into the garden, "Crescence! Crescence! Where is the creature! Don't, in the name of three devils, keep us waiting here!
We are melting like sugar!" A disgusted grumbling was
heard and after a while the creature appeared with measured
step, an angry looking maid of about forty-five. The things
which they had bought in the village were now unloaded and
brought into the house: a basket of apples; a second basket
of preserve jars and green vegetables; a dirty leather bag; two
loaves of white bread; a bottle of vinegar, a bag of salt and a
bag of sugar, and finally various packages containing candles,
cheap tinware, a box of matches, pipe tobacco, and several
novels from the circulating library. Fräulein Woytich divided
the burdens between her sister and Crescence; she herself
carried the footstool under her arm and turned to Sauerbrand
to settle the fare.

Hardly had he named the sum to be paid than she began

to scream, although, as Sauerbrand said quietly, she knew perfectly what the fare was—six hundred crowns. Soothingly he mentioned his usual excuses; the times were very hard; bread very dear; oats terribly high; and as for horseshoes—what one paid for them now would have kept the whole village, including the mayor, going for three days in the old times. But the old lady would not listen. She said she did not care anything about his old horseshoes and his oats, he could arrange that with old Rosinante; she called him a thief and a cutthroat, and with a wealth of big words and wild gestures swore that she would not pay a cent and moreover that she would report him to the law courts for pushing up prices. Sauerbrand scratched his head, looked at a loss and puzzled by the excited mien of his passenger. She, having given vent to her temper, pulled out a dirty, torn pocket-book, bent her short-sighted eyes upon it and took out bill after bill until the rain dripped through the holes in the umbrella on her yellow hands, handed one after the other to the grinning Sauerbrand, cursing softly as she did so, at the coined money, the paper money, the notes which were as unappetising and as unsuitable as everything else in these God-forsaken times. Sauerbrand, who had heard the old song often enough before, agreed with her and she disappeared into the house.

She hastened that nothing might be stolen of her purchases before she got them under lock and key. She could not trust the two in there, neither her sister nor Crescence. The former was always hungry; why should an old woman over sixty be hungry? One might take it for granted that she would steal like a raven when she could. Whom could one trust? Human society was just a gang of blood-suckers, cheats and idiots in upper circles, the washed and elegant, and in lower circles, the beggars and filthy.

But so far nothing had been stolen. Even the correct number of apples—twenty-four—was there. It's a wonder, thought Ulrika Woytich, and bit one apple in two and reached half of it to Anastasia. She found it too sour and threw it into the grate, at which Ulrika was indignant. Ulrika had finallly decided to invest in these luxuries because she was expecting a guest for the week-end, Anastasia's son, Philip Gentili, who attended to the money matters of his Aunt. Otherwise it was frugal living at the Villa Woytich. Malt coffee, potatoes and war-bread, and every bite fought for, for Ulrika thought that every expenditure of a crown spent for the satisfaction of the stomach cost a piece of one's life and peace.

She fetched her short English pipe out of the drawer of the mahogany table, stuffed it with cheap tobacco which she had brought, and as she lit it, began again a violent scolding over the fare they had paid the postwagon. It was a crime and a sin, she said. Her eyes gleamed. Her hair still untouched by grey, but stiff and lifeless fell in strands over her low forehead, in the heat of her speech. Her clever, vivid and passionate face, worn and lined fairly gleamed with wrath and from the corner of her mouth which held the pipe, a trickle of saliva dripped. Figures, figures, figures! Crescence stuck her head in at the door to see what the noise was about. Anastasia had slunk down in the corner of the sofa and listened, frightened.

Ciphers, ciphers, ciphers! Prices, nothing but prices. Curses upon any one who pushed up prices. She bellowed out with grim emphasis a long list of prices; prices of shoes, wood, tickets, rent, restaurant, butcher, and milk prices. A demonstration of unshamed caprice; an appeal to the justice of Heaven and scorn of any earthly justice; wringing of hands over the present-day rottenness and prophecies of evil ends; a wailing for happier days in the past and complaints that one had not ended one's days before this era of annihilation set in.

This lasted about half an hour. It seemed as if sterile humanity was expressing its disgust at itself and its despair over itself through this aged mouth.

Anastasia wondered how long she would rage. How long will she go on keeping up this senseless outcry? She is sixty-six now; how long will she go on heaping up her riches, multiplying her money and depriving us, me and the industrious Philip, who is simple enough to pull her chestnuts out of the fire for her? When will it all belong to us, the house and the furniture, the carpets and the clocks, the pictures and the china and silver? If one only knew where she had hidden her will, so one could be sure that it is all left to us, as she says. Nobody can believe her. How long will we have to wait? Perhaps she will outlive me. Perhaps she will even outlive Philip; people like Ulrika never die. What should she die of, anyway? She is as healthy as a fish. Franz is about to die. Severin lies in his grave. But Ulrika will live forever.

These were the not altogether sisterly reflections of the timid and humble Anastasia as she shivered in the corner of the sofa.

CHAPTER XXIV

THE WITCHES' MULTIPLICATION TABLE

ULRIKA had a fixed engagement with Philip Gentili to come once a month and spend Sunday with her, instruct her as to market quotations, and what investments he was making for her. The neighbours were always told that he was visiting his mother.

She always forbade him written communications. In the first place she never understood them properly. Prevailing and future values, set side by side, always confused her. Moreover, she suspected the postal officials, the postman, Crescence and Anastasia of secretly opening her letters.

She herself could only be persuaded to make a trip to town under the most urgent circumstances. Every step she took irritated her. People vexed her, surroundings vexed her, the weather vexed her, and as for hotel bills, they put her in a rage.

Therefore, it was always a great occasion when Philip came. The long weeks of waiting exhausted her. The question as to her fate fell from her lips with greedy vehemence whenever she saw him. Was one to breathe freely or was one's heart to stop short? The accounting, gloomier than any possible preconception of it, became a threatening reality. To her Philip was the guardian and preserver or enemy and destroyer of the Exchange. Hope or despair hung upon his smile or his shrug. In one instant it gave her thirty nights of bitterness or of rosy dreams.

Until a few years ago she had thought of her nephew as no better than a wind-bag. And with reason. He drifted about idly, with his moderately pretty face and the position she later gave him through her business connections was a sinecure to him. What he was openly waiting for, was to inherit from her, a circumstance that did not lessen her dislike of him, although she set against any demands upon her inheritance an iron silence, and planned like Uncle Clement to live to be as old as possible. She neither thought of death nor feared it.

But Philip Gentili belonged to those people whose talents were brought out by the excitement of the times, talents that might otherwise have been lost. The merry-go-round turned; the favourable moment suited one of the audience, he jumped on and whirled around with the rest. Once on, he studied the movements of the machine. It all seemed so simple. The little wheels obeyed the pressure of his hand. The fact that he did not know the hidden parts of the machinery gave him no scruples. The hand organ howled, the swift motion went to the heads of the passengers, and it was all a kind of drunken gaiety.

In the course of the year 1919 he had given his aunt a piece of advice, which she followed, hesitating and doubtful. Within a week the money she had invested with such doubt and trepidation, was doubled. And this changed her whole relation to Philip at one blow. She entrusted him with smaller and then larger sums; he worked carefully and cleverly; the results were simply dazzling.

Ulrika Woytich's delight knew no limit. Her thoughts were concerned with the single fact. And matters went beyond her boldest expectations. It was like magic. She could not understand it. She did know that even in quieter times, now and then, a man would reach great wealth, over night, by such methods, but she had never dared hope to take part in such a game; the risks were too great, the opportunity lacked, and she held what she possessed too convulsively tight to risk even the least of it.

With all her cleverness and cunning, her schemes were really of singular, almost peasant naïveté. Where did it come from? How should it be spent? How best could one hang onto it? Why were there fools who worked since it was possible to rake in heaps of money without taxing one's brain or labouring? She seemed to herself to be a member of a secret society, a money-makers' guild, and was always prepared to be dragged into a cave and made to take frightful oaths. As she did not in the least understand what was happening her imagination exaggerated possibilities, and her greed outran reason.

Philip wished a wider sphere for his newly discovered abilities, where he could act more freely. Ulrika exerted herself for him eagerly and turned to an old friend, a banker named Remschied, who had retired and left his business to a rather inexperienced son. Gentili was given a position and in a few months had reached an influential post, where he was able to reconstruct the old, reliable business and build a castle in the air, where formerly there had been a well-founded house. They submitted easily to him. No one seemed to resent it or ask explanations or say that he did not see the reality of the castle. On the contrary, they all ran after him and tried to get in on his deals.

Even Ulrika ran. She entrusted her entire fortune to the firm. This was managed with some difficulty as she had tied up a considerable portion of it in Berlin, namely, with Lothar Mylius, who paid her eight per cent interest. The bond between him and Ulrika had continued through the years; at times she had visited him in his princely home, and he had shown her, despite his notorious misanthropy, a certain careless fidelity. When she confided her decision to him, he warned her. As his summer vacation brought him into her neighborhood he invited her to Salzburg for a conference. She brought Philip Gentili with her. At first Mylius did not hide his vexation, but after a while he seemed really pleased with Ulrika's protegé. The cynical complacency of the thirty-year-old youth, his determination to make use of the disturbed conditions of the world, the cruelly pessimistic prophecies of what was yet to come, the official dryness of his manner, all this impressed Mylius, who was himself a cynic without the faintest trace of a heart. As he was in the habit, like most capitalists of Germany, of dividing up his money into various securities, and as these usually turned out favourably, he decided, on the same day that he gave over all Ulrika's savings, to invest a million and a half marks on his own account with Remschied and Company.

Ulrika triumphed. She believed Lothar Mylius to be a real genius in money matters. As Philip had succeeded in bringing him over to his side so quickly, he gained a very high place in her estimation and silenced all questionings. In order to show Philip her gratitude and also to spur him on, she took over from him all care of his mother, so that Anastasia had to eat the bread of charity from her. It was not very plentiful or very good bread and it mostly had to be eaten without butter.

The arrival of Gentili always set her in motion like quicksilver. By six o'clock in the morning she was up and on her feet. By nine o'clock she undertook a sort of general cleaning, as complicated as it was incomplete. At twelve o'clock she swallowed a couple of half-cooked potatoes, standing up, for her dinner. At four o'clock she dressed her hair, or made an effort at it, which usually ended in her using the curling irons to produce two very unbecoming curls on the right side of her forehead which were supposed to divert one's attention from the untidy twist on the top. At five o'clock she changed her worn-out slippers for a pair of high shoes in which her step was loud enough to have put a cannoneer to shame. Crescence was called first here and then there with noisy commands and avenged herself by a constant suppressed swearing. At seven o'clock one heard the carriage drive up to the door.

Then came greetings; the usual questions; the usual tales; the usual praise of life in the country by the guest; a little chatter and gossip; for instance, did she know that the Baroness Melander was living at her place at Eckern; yes, Ulrika had found it out; Crescence had brought the news. She made a grimace; the same one she always made when she heard that name.

Then came the question, shining in Ulrika's look from the first moment, which decided everything. Philip rubbed his hands; he seemed satisfied. He nodded contentedly and gaily patted his aunt on the back. It went to Ulrika's head like champagne and she chuckled joyously. She made a gesture of invitation, and while Anastasia set the supper table, they went off together into an upstairs room, like a pair of impatient lovers, who could no longer wait to be alone.

It was the so-called Italian room, all done in blue and gold, with graceful and slender chairs and tables, beautifully framed paintings, faïence and majolica ware, and a beautiful Siennese cupboard. To right and left were other rooms, the French room, the English, the real old-fashioned farm-house room, each one a museum of treasures, carved furniture and chests, china of the best period, brocaded hangings, lace covers, old church stalls and lights, books bound in parchment, crystal globes, bronze figures, and paintings by Munkaczy, Makart, Labery, Horwitz and Lenbach. The last room on the left was a small rotunda, in the middle of which on a six-cornered pedestal stood a great doll. The old English doll from Mylius's shop. With its foreign clothes, its hoop skirt, and its sphinx-like smile, the wax face looked like a secret house-idol in the dim light.

Philip Gentili never stepped over the threshold of this room without feeling a sort of devout shudder. Not that he was sensitive; not that a rich life, of unknown content to him, stimulated his imagination here, but because to his practical mind such things had a value beyond estimation. Therefore, he felt for his aunt that esteem which one feels only for people whose social opinions one must bow to; it was because of this that he bore with her moods and tempers and hesitated to contradict her; and this was not easy to him, though her tyrannical nature always subdued less strong characters.

He could not always escape fear and a certain secret fatalism —despite the wild confidence that was bound up with his success, the expression of which he wore on his face like a mask, when everything went wrong, here he would find shelter, this was his sheltering island, this gave him a background and an incentive. Every single object in this house greeted him as his future inheritance, and he already had all his plans made, as to how he would build on to the country house and make it into a lordly manor. His searching glance studied the old woman; he counted the years, noted her robust strength, her fine build, her smooth forehead, her picturesque clothing, in which she scorned the fashions of the day.

Still it was necessary to talk business. Ulrika could no longer rein in her impatience. Everything was going well, Philip Gentili assured her; the outlook was more favourable than ever. This was the historic moment; all one had to do was go ahead. Ulrika Woytich opened her eyes wide, her lips were parted, her hands clasped, and she drank in his every word breathlessly. He talked to her in a certain bank jargon which made her wild because she could not understand it, of the great favourite on the Exchange: the Polish mark, which the most careful investors guaranteed and which promised an unheard of, incomparable rise.

"What distorted Jewish Latin you are talking to me; speak German," groaned Ulrika. He laughed till he nearly burst and took pains to make the matter clear to her. The important thing was to buy cheap. The matter had been at a crisis eight days ago. He was so sure of her consent that he had bought at the right hour. He mentioned a sum that made Ulrika's knees give way. She had to hold on to something. Gentili lead her to a chair and made a ceremony of placing her in it; then he wiped off his eye glass and chuckled dryly. Ulrika was still gasping for air. She looked at him, with a mixture of astonishment, fright, suspicion and hope. She asked him about her gains for the past month. His answer brought peace to her disturbed countenance. As proof of his figures he showed her a page of his account book and explained to her, several times, the meaning of the figures. She stroked the enigmatic sheet with her knotty hand. A happy grin, that betrayed her all the more as she tried to hide it, lightened up her face. Purring like a cat she reached down into her yard-long pocket and drew out her pipe.

"Good," she said, benevolently, when she had lighted her pipe, "very good. Now I guess I can sleep a little while in peace. I need not be afraid that I will have to die on the pavement, in my old days. You seem to have managed very well, you clever rascal you. Well, well, it's the way of the world; one has the grain, and the other the empty bin. I never could understand the thing, it is all Greek to me, but perhaps it isn't important for an old woman to understand so much. Just let me make my little profits and that is enough."

She laughed and began to talk again in her loud voice. "I don't like it," she went on, half scolding, half jesting, "the adepts gets all the juicy bits from the dish and we stand by with our tongues hanging out. If I get a chance to stand near at hand they give me a bite; very good, but I never did like to look on. How does one go about making an anarchistic Sansculotte into a solid fat bourgeois? Do you know, my son? Give him a bank account."

Philip Gentili nodded enthusiastically and joined in her laughter.

"Of course, if you can make a hundred gulden out of a single one, you scoundrel," giggled Ulrika, "and make the credulous sheep believe that the hundredth part is as good as the whole, you can hardly be surprised if some day they rebel. But beware of the day when they refuse to give up their good coin for your false, while you still declare yourselves harmless and while you still give each other unclipped coupons. It is very mysterious, the poisonous drinks that you brew in your witches' kitchen, and the Chaldean oath formulas that you use." She rose up, put both hands on his shoulders, shook him a little, and while her clever, wicked face blinked and gleamed she said,

> " 'Make one out of ten,
> Let two slip then,
> Drop your third stitch
> And then you are rich.'

That is so, isn't it? Deny it if you dare!"

"It may be so," said Philip Gentili, who felt a bit uncomfortable and embarrassed by the old lady's rough familiarity, "but you, Aunt Ulrika, need never rely upon my magic arts. You have what is a thousand times better, you have money. You have things and what sort of things!" He pointed with an admiring look to the objects around them.

"Things, yes, things enough," growled Ulrika, suddenly put

out, and waved her hand as if she wanted to cut the thread of
his greedy glance. "Yes, they belong to me. The things belong to me. Or I belong to them. Can you understand the
difference, you witty gentleman? In these things my whole
life is hidden. For these things I deny myself. For these
things I do without bread and meat, and others will have to do
so too; I have arranged for that. They are my feet and hands,
my ears and eyes. They are my innermost self, do you understand that? Each one is a memorial, a piece of myself. But
what do you understand of that, you people of to-day, flitting
casually from place to place, without houses and without
homes!" She was shaking her fist and almost screaming in her
excitement. But Philip's humble manner reconciled her
quickly; she broke out into a gruff man's laugh, planted herself in all her gaunt length before him and recited with glowing
eyes—secretly somewhat amused by the embarrassment of her
nephew:

> " 'Lose your four
>   At the witches' door,
>   With seven and six
>   Know how to mix
>   Your nine and eight
>   And then you'll wait,
>   Till nine is won,
>   And ten is done.'

Yes, my dear fellow," she went on, and puffed smoke out of
her pipe, "I know the classics. I have my own traditions. I
did not come into the world through a chimney." She took
his arm and they went down to the table together.

CHAPTER XXV

THE WAX PEAR

ULRIKA WOYTICH bore the years heavily. It was not that she
denied them either to herself or others; there was no reason
to do that. Her retrospections satisfied her; she had gone
far, gone well, gone beautifully indeed. She felt a suitable,
pleasant, natural fatigue of the body. She would not have
liked to miss a step of the way; she could not have wished it
more peaceful, or richer in change and experience; she felt
no remorse, no shame, no grief, no belated wishes; she did not
philosophise over the past, nor find fault with it; she would
not have painted it more gaily, and as she looked back upon
it, she fell neither into bigotry nor into the outspread nets of
theosophy; she let it stand and looked at it as a painter
looks at his finished picture, needing no further stroke of the
brush, indeed unable to bear another.

She had missed nothing. Everything had happened at the
right time and in the right place, just as it should have happened; everything had been carried out just as circumstances
and Providence had ordained.

But it was past, once and for all, never to be lived through
again, and she could not get over that; she grieved over it,
sighed over it, and could not get over it. Nothing was ever
enough; such a pity that it was all over, and there were
hours when impatience and resentment broke barriers. The
blood became cooler and the senses slept, but her mind flamed
up still; the star of her life had long since gone out, the evening had become night, but she could not rest, she could not
forget. Yes; one drew the curtains, threw a couple of logs
on the fire, complained of the weather and the cold, and
pressed one's head deep in the cushions of the arm-chair and
dreamed: inadequate pleasure of old age, meagre shadow of
the past.

She crowded out of her memory the years of transition from the blossom-time to sterility, from the glow to the twilight, from the swarm and gaiety of the human press to loneliness and quiet; crowded them out because that was the beginning of her discontent. One true mirror she had never let drop from her hand: the mirror called Knowledge of Self. Nor would she wait until others made it cruelly noticeable to her, that she was one too many, with crow's feet around her eyes, and wrinkles around her throat, with teeth rattling in her mouth, and her knees giving as she walked; one who gave out queer, broken tones when she laughed and tried to make her five decades out to be only four and a half. No: she arose, holding herself erect, bowed politely to all sides, although with poison in her heart, and left the gala hall. And while the gay company still believed that she would come back to give a ridiculous twist to the played-out rôle, while they still wondered and asked about her (for the world likes to push you out, it does not like you to get up and leave), she went into her well-prepared hermitage, to live out to the end the remainder, the less joyous part of the programme. It was a thorny way to her and required resolution. For a time the noise still sounded in her ears; the monotonous days were heavy; she would start up and gnash her teeth; then finally quiet prevailed.

And she would say to herself: "You have lived, Ulrika Woytich! You have tasted and enjoyed: you have set the full cup to your lips and tipped up the cup until not a drop escaped you; you have driven, exulting through the cities, and with an eager, never-weary hand snatched at the gifts which were showered upon you; upon you and your youth, and your abilities, and your high spirits and your quick wits. That much is fixed. You have your trophies, too. You let nothing, nothing at all, escape you."

When with her rich booty, she had left the Mylius's house, she had already found the spring-board from which to plunge into the midst of life. She jumped, looked fearlessly about, saw a ladder and began to climb, round by round, neither too quickly nor too slowly. One after another, she was a

travelling chaperone, a reader, a companion, friendly guest of
two princesses, indispensable prop of a duchess, head of a
palace for a Russian prince of fabulous wealth, and then a
traveller for pleasure on her own account. But above all and
before all, she was a fine lady, a lady of position, wealth, and
influence; the daughter of a general (for her father had been
advanced rapidly since his death!), a favourite in aristocratic
circles, *persona grata* with every one, a significant and worth-
while figure in the world.

She always had recommendations as the most honoured
descendant of a great family. No door was closed to her.
If it did not open at the first knock, it did at the second;
if the key was not at hand she always picked the lock. No
porter could withstand her, no lackeys, no refusals, no exclu-
siveness. And once she was there, there was no longer any
doubt that she belonged. She knew all the forms, the
correct addresses, and in five minutes she was acclimatised
anywhere. She spoke Italian with Italians, French with the
French, English with the English and mastered all the languages to the furthest corners of their dialects, and even to the
most recent slang. She had the melody of each language in
her ear and its fine points at her finger-tips. She met all kinds
of people on their own grounds, the politician, the merchant,
the soldier, the sailor, the scholar, and the journalist. She combined things that belonged together like a soothsayer from
the most fleeting observation. She always knew the new
phrase before it became common and she drew upon an
inexhaustible memory. She knew whole careers by heart and
when she told about them people doubled up with laughter.
She knew five hundred anecdotes and told them; this
alone was enough to make her the centre of any social group.
When she told tales about family relationships or events in
her own circle, her audience giggled and trembled at the same
time. Her strange art of handling people consisted in a certain abrupt candour, in thoroughgoing flattery, in pretending
to be a child of nature and at the same time watching the
limits beyond which she might lose everything. The more
at home she became, the bolder was the mischief she plotted,

the intrigues she spun, the adventures into which she threw herself. She brought people together and parted them again, without their ever dreaming that she had a hand in it. She made marriages and destroyed them again; made and broke up friendships, sowed distrust everywhere and betrayed secrets that might have lain hidden forever. Then if the fatal results set in, discord, hatred, quarrels, she became the reconciler whom every one thanked and she washed her hands in innocency. A mere hint often sufficed her to brew her poison, a slyly-put question, to set ruin afoot. But she had to have movement, excitement, eruptions, developments. It was her special joy to get people upset and then to rub them up against each other, to rouse laziness, to use weakness and to try out her power.

The forms and activities of European society in the last blooming years of her maturity was as well known to her as a group of plants to a botanist who has devoted his whole life to them. She knew how it hung together, its members, its ways of life, its interests, vices and virtues, through and through; and how it desired no more than to riot and play, to dine and to dance, to meddle and to laugh, to dress and to confuse. She shared in its inclinations and its love-affairs, followed its fashions, worshipped its gods and its idols, served its vanities and strengthened it in its fashions and prejudices. She was a sort of sutler in the camp, truly and honestly suited to its methods, its outlook and its ways. She knew it, too; hence the storm, the racket, the wild chase. When everything stood on its head, the more quietly she stood on both feet and watched things. Nothing was hidden from her keen observation that these people, whom she both admired and scorned, did,—their business, their plans and their sins. When she betrayed one party to another, she first assured her own advantage and made herself as invisible as if she wore the tarn-cap. Little by little, she became an arbiter in all matters of taste and her easily roused enthusiasm, her Slav-Austrian adaptability and imagination, her inborn feeling for pictures, and sounds, and execution, and rhythm gave her recognition, a voice, and a following. Sometimes it was a painter, or a musician, or an actor she would take up; it did not reach very far or go very high but it gave her opportunity of playing the rôle of patroness and protector with charm and dignity; she worked, blew the trumpet, and cared for the purse and the renown of her favourites and so was celebrated by them as a modern Aspasia. She went to Weimar to see Liszt, to Bayreuth to see Wagner, to Vienna to become acquainted with Mackart, to London to meet Adelina Patti, and to Paris to visit Rodin. On the way there were always the minor and middling people, her "sparrows" she called them, whom she fed with crumbs and upon whom she always made the impression of being of the great world, an experienced person, a significant and telling personality.

How many unforgettable meetings, how many separations, flaming moments of mind and heart; what ambition and proud thoughts, lingering renunciations and youthful victories; what speeches and answers, and bold deeds and echoing words! How she had swept through the countries from city to city, and brought her shy desires to fulfilment; how, the clever creature, she always left a bit of herself behind and took a bit of something new with her, incredulously, as one accepts the imaginings of children, as if she intuitively knew that all this would go down and sink into nothingness with the passing of her own splendour.

She had dipped into everything and tasted the kernel, its sweetness and bitterness, its loveliness and losses. Sweetness and bitterness weighed against each other, exchanged their natures and took on the same flavour. Half dreaming, she could place herself in an imaginary mausoleum with niches in its walls, and in each one stood an urn with the ashes of an outlived passion. If one lifted the cover, a wave of decay came first, confusing one, and then followed figure after figure, face after face. Some came from far away, some were quite near, some glowed faintly, and some were all ready crusted over. They did not rush up, they had to be sought and did not always answer the call of memory. It was like a funeral service.

Nothing was a burden then. Pain and sorrow were not

to be found there, nor suffering of the soul, nor fruitless seeking. The hour passed. When the excitement was over, the joy of it had died. Happiness was only a joke; daring enterprises also; the enchantment was in multiplicity, and she was always mistress of the opportunity. Without danger and difficulty, no enjoyment; only none of the practical goods of life must ever be lost; wealth and possessions must grow, and to sharpen her instinct for this, to keep her mind and thought ever with cunning and calculations on this, gave her life a double excitement. There was a definite part in her life, somewhere between her twenty-eighth and thirty-sixth year, which was an unbroken series of romantic affairs; an intimate relation to two brothers, who were deadly enemies to each other; under the dazzled eyes of a newly married woman, whose closest friend she was, she had lured the husband into her net, and he refused to give her up, so that she had to fly, head over heels, to avoid the scandal. Mistress of a diplomat, and most gravely compromised, she had almost been suspected of having made way with certain important papers, in which difficulty she only saved herself by bewitching the son of the man in question and using him as a tool for her needs. For weeks she had made a wild dash over half of Europe with an opera singer, whom she had stolen away from a rabidly jealous countess; and in between there had been all kinds of trifling to fill up the empty days; complications without tragedies, lightly tied, easily loosed; one word could unite and a single look break again.

When she walked through her rooms, these rooms of memory, her eye was met by witnesses of the past, so inexorably lost. So many things, each one a guidepost to the past! Here was a silver bowl set in semi-precious stones; yes, that was the June night in Venice; Venice, all set in stars and glorious lights, a picture of the care-free century. Here was a portrait of a youth in furs; and she saw a sleigh speeding over the Russian steppes and a late evening arrival at the lighted manor house; the joyous barking of the watch dog, and the glittering snow caps on the fence palings, looking like crowns on winter elves. Here was a silver hand mirror to which the tenderest memories clung; there was a marble figure which had come from the South; here was an ivory letter case; a little decorated altar; a glass case with writing materials; a Greek lamp. And these were all little things, the minor harvest of before and after; but each told her something, each one warned her, in each one she felt herself. In such and such a way she had stood, or gone, or sat; in such and such faces she had looked; eyes were fixed upon her benevolently, expectantly, and she recognised them all, they were so shiningly dewy, so speaking. And she saw herself again dancing, being embraced, desired, commanding; or else in business activities, an energetic financier later, in those years when she was filling her storehouse.

That was what she had been, Ulrika Woytich, who now walked up and down her rooms and read the inventory of her treasures. Was she still herself? Who was it who kept looking back, peering and listening? Was she still Ulrika Woytich? This toothless old ruin, childless, friendless, sneaking around in rags: was that Ulrika Woytich? She shook her head. She almost doubted it.

It was certainly the logical inexorable course of nature. There was no fault to be found in what she had done or what had happened; there was nothing she would have wished different. She had satiated herself with life. She had worked hard and had been honourably dismissed with proper rewards. She owed no debts and had excused no debtors. She had caroused freely, paid the piper, and when she herself was hostess she had put a proper valuation upon everything. She had never asked too much, and had never wasted anything. Extravagance was a quality that she encouraged only in others. The storm of passions of every kind that had shaken her had never made a deep impression. She knew that she had to keep fresh to know what every morning would bring forth and to keep her people alert. She did not think highly of expressing one's feelings, indeed, she knew almost nothing about it. Fidelity to a feeling through years, that was a matter for little A B C pupils who were still reading from the primer. She knew that with a single piece of gold she could gild horse and rider.

To cling to the impulses of one's heart was both foolish and harmful. The thing that they called love, out there in the world, was a false coin, with which men were agreed to deceive each other, and in whose worth only a couple of romantics really believed. It was a lie, pretty, sometimes useful, sometimes uncomfortable, but always a silly lie. A trap for eyes and ears, an ape-like reflection, a snare. Ulrika Woytich knew this, and nothing could unsettle her conviction, no book, no example, no assurances.

She had a wax fruit, a pear, larger than her fist and so marvellously lifelike, so tempting in form and bloom and colour that many people had reached for it, wanting to eat it, only to put it back in its place again, frightened by its coldness and hardness. It lay upon a meissen plate in the French room, and sometimes it happened that Ulrika would take it up in her hand, look at it with her mocking, sophisticated smile, and take pleasure in the soft contours and golden glimmer of the dead fruit, as in a clever deception.

Her smile meant: "I never fell into the net; and thank God I never snapped at the bait."

CHAPTER XXVI

FANNY GOES WANDERING

When Philip Gentili left the Villa Woytich in the grey dawn of Monday morning, all the deceptive comfort and deceptive peace passed too. The first thing that Ulrika undertook was to look over the provisions, whereupon a frightful quarrel began between her and Crescence. Of the five bags of flour which on Saturday had filled the kitchen cupboard and which Ulrika had planned would carry them through the week, there was exactly three-fourths of a bag left. The sugar had gone, all but six lumps. The apple basket was empty. The preserve jars empty. The lard can empty. There was neither flour nor a kernel of rice there. The white bread was gone except for one stony crust. In her mouse-grey dressing gown Ulrika stood before the dishes, feeling around the still unwashed things. Finally she lifted up the empty vinegar bottle, held it close in front of the nose of Crescence, who was bursting with rage, and howled: "There must be somebody in the house who drinks vinegar! It is impossible for normal people to get away with a bottle of vinegar in two and a half days! We have not had salad on the table but once, one single time! Do you want to bring people to beggary? Who swallowed the vinegar?"

Crescence maintained a grim silence. And as Ulrika continued to scream and to paint her future poverty in the harshest colours, the maid tore the vinegar bottle from her and swung it like a battle-axe. At this moment, when blows seemed imminent, Anastasia appeared on the threshold, and Ulrika's bitterness suddenly turned on her. She missed an underbody out of her linen drawer; who had taken her underbody? If the garment was not brought to her at once she would send for the police. Crescence made a scornful face. "Good Heavens, Ulrika," said Anastasia, almost weeping, "your underbody was torn and I took it into my room to mend." Crescence impudently remarked that it was no wonder, that everything the Fräulein owned hung in rags until it was a shame and disgrace. Ulrika replied that she was lying, she had been wearing the underbody in perfect condition and doubtless certain people in the house took pleasure in wearing her linen. Thereupon Crescence stretched out her naked arm and hissed: "Get out! Get out at once!" And surprisingly enough, Ulrika obeyed the order of her maid. To show she was not retreating she continued to scold and abuse as she went up the stairs, while Crescence slammed the kitchen door. It was not long until she opened it again, as if she had used the interim to think over the insults which she had had to swallow; she stepped out on the threshold and began a very singular speech. She spoke neither angrily nor in an excited manner but in a restrained voice, a sort of nasal singsong; she made puzzling allusions to certain ladies who had better take care not to arouse simple folk in too proud a manner; certain ladies ought to be glad if one let things rest. They had better not threaten other people continually; it would be better for them to keep quiet and not row about the little amount of food that eked out the wages paid with so many complaints and grumblings, as if the eternal happiness of her poor, good-humoured servant hung upon her purse. As far as that purse went, a good deal might be told about it that was neither elevating nor Christian, if one decided to do it and one wanted to begin to gossip.

There she stood, her hands on her hips, her eyes glittering like a cat's, bowing from time to time ironically, and when she had finished, she marched back into her kitchen and broke out laughing. Ulrika had long since gone down into the living-room and drew Anastasia roughly into the room when she found her listening eagerly upon the threshold. "She steals, there is no doubt the creature steals," she whispered into her sister's ear. "Do you hear what she is saying down there?" Anastasia whispered again. Ulrika pretended that she heard nothing and could not make out anything. Then

Anastasia asked her shyly why she kept this person in the house; one really had reason to be afraid of her. Ulrika evaded the question sulkily, it would be hard to get anybody better, and as one had to deal with peasants, one might as well be content to have any one at all. But she is lazy, dirty, and inefficient, interrupted Anastasia, who was still trying to make out Crescence's words. This bothered Ulrika, as she was still speaking very noisily about the empty vinegar bottle, and she demanded loudly that Anastasia follow her into another room where the voice of the maid could not be heard; as she did not go quickly enough she drove her in front of her, clapping her hands. Ulrika's face expressed a cowardice and a fear that gave Anastasia a good deal to think about; and all that day she hardly left Anastasia's side, with the intention of preventing her being near Crescence; she treated her as if she were a jailor and followed her step by step wherever she went. To deceive her as to what she was doing, or else to interrupt her thoughts, she talked almost continuously of politics, jokes about the government, merciless criticism of the present bourgeois system, wailed over modern customs, abused the taxes, the officials, the weather, the craftsmen and workers of the day, and the whole rotten world, which was no more than a brew and steam of lies.

Anastasia, however, brooded over one thing only; why was it that Ulrika, who showed no one respect and was afraid of no one, humbled herself before a mean and common maidservant. There is something wrong about it, she thought, and she would have given her soul's salvation to have known what it was. Spying after the creature did no good; she had tried it often and gotten no results. It was not so much the hidden secret that enticed her; what excited her curiosity was that it was possible to silence Ulrika, the tyrannic, cold-hearted, unbending Ulrika, and bring her to a kind of humility. She wished that she had the secret, she who trembled day and night and humiliated herself for everything that she got, for every breath of fresh air, every glimpse of the sun, and every bite of bread.

Crescence's real vengeance came later and was certainly

unpleasant: she did not light the fire or cook anything. Ulrika, instead of objecting, fetched a tea-kettle into the living room and made tea on an alcohol lamp. This with a little sugar, a couple of slices of bread spread with lard, and the remainder of yesterday's potato salad had to do for both ladies' dinner. Anastasia swallowed it angrily but dared make no objection. Ulrika for her part seemed quite contented; it was a good way of saving, wood was saved, food was saved, and to Anastasia's rather bitter question as to what Fräulein Crescence would do all day, having withdrawn from her duties, Ulrika replied with a ghastly grin, that probably she had a lover somewhere whom she had to keep in a good humour, and for whom she packed up and sent away the stolen foodstuffs. Anastasia, who was a prude, and who objected to conversation such as this, was silent, but continued to wonder in secret. What was her surprise toward evening, as she was going out for a little and passed the kitchen door, to see Ulrika and Crescence sitting there not only in complete harmony but laughing and joking in the most familiar manner. There was no doubt that Ulrika could not rest until she had brought about a reconciliation with the angry maid, and condescended so far as to pay her compliments upon her fine appearance in the most flute-like voice Anastasia had ever heard from her—even to tease her with revolting allusions. Crescence, dressed in her Sunday best on a week day, had been off the entire afternoon and seemed to be very well disposed. Out in the garden, Anastasia folded her hands and looked appealingly toward heaven; she no longer doubted now that Ulrika had to protect herself against the maid, and that the maid knew of some dreadful weakness, or crime. Anastasia turned cold; all sorts of hopes and fears awoke in her grasping spirit and she determined to carry on her investigations with double zeal.

But although she was on the watch from morn till night, listened at doors, spied upon the ways of both her house companions, and secretly delved in all Ulrika's trunks and cupboards, reading her old letters, and split her head thinking about it through sleepless hours, she found no indication whatsoever, not even a hint, nothing to confirm her dark suspicions; perhaps the truth lay elsewhere. It was a very simple truth, yet in its simplicity pretty serious, and it is indispensable that we should know it, since the existence and soul of that not unimportant person, Ulrika Woytich, is the object of our study and consideration.

For fourteen years she had lived with Crescence. She had saved her when she was in the worst condition in which a feminine creature can be found. As Ulrika was coming back from the country place of a friendly family where she had spent the night, she had found this girl in a Croatian village, hungry, miserable, despised, left in the lurch with an epileptic child by a peasant boy who had lead her astray and then dropped her there to die. Ulrika had been moved, more by the devout humility of the outcast than by her abyss of misery, to take charge of her. Just at that time, Ulrika began to be very lonely, and was in need of some human being who would serve her in the ultimate meaning of the word; some one of whom she could say: This person I created, I lifted her out of the depths of a hopeless existence; she is completely subject to me, without conditions. For many years the relation remained as she had desired. For years she reigned over the willing and completely dumb creature. If she had commanded her to become a footstool for her feet the creature would have thrown herself down and become a footstool. Never a word, never a complaint, never a claim! And in the same measure as the world ceased to obey her, this creature whom she had lifted up and made her own, was obliged to submit herself and serve the more humbly. The power, which she lost in the outer world, or wisely laid aside before it was torn from her, she won in fourfold measure in her own four walls. And though she could only use it on a poor nonentity, hardly higher in rank than a dog or a starling, it was at least a compensation for what she had lost; at least she had power, she could say "yes" and "no," and there was some one with a credulous ear, a true echo, eyes that looked up to her. Here was gratitude that could never be paid off, a never ending debt, and the sight of her con-

tinuous service and devotion warmed Ulrika's heart. It would
have been unthinkable to be alone; but with a slave at hand
one was still linked to humanity and events; true, it was
with impatience, nagging, and all the heaped-up evils of old
age, that recur with every new day. Living at the cost of
others had ceased; and it was all the more important to
avoid expense. The more seldom an opportunity offered to
dine at other tables, the more economical her own became;
this alternation had been of extreme precision, showing the
relation between her miserliness and anxiety. But her slave
was there as witness; her slave was her living protest; her
slave was the bow that one stretched and set one's arrow
to, designed to wound the hideous, changed world; if she
hungered, hunger and deprivation were the law; if she suffered and broke down under injustice and tyranny, a bit of
the world suffered and broke down, and that helped one
along, aroused and excited one, filled up the time and gave
existence some savour.

Until once this happened: Ulrika was lying in bed. She
had kept the maid breathless all day, running hither and
yon on messages, carrying out capricious wishes and distrustful orders. Crescence had gone to bed dead tired, and
late at night was awakened by loud ringing; when she arrived, barefooted and in her nightgown, Ulrika ordered her
to go up into the attic and close a window that was creaking in the wind; the maid was very superstitious and terribly
afraid to go into the attic at night; however she obeyed after
a little silent hesitation, returning after a moment as pale
as death, to say that all the windows up there were locked
and that the gracious lady must be mistaken. Ulrika broke
out into a rage and poured out insults upon her. Crescence
stood silent there, went silently out, and Ulrika in a rage
shrieked at her to come back; she did come after a few
minutes with a strange fixed look on her face, stepped up to
Ulrika's bed, and raised her right arm: in her hand shone the
long, sharp, kitchen carving knife. She did not utter a word
but stood there with the knife raised, an alarming wickedness
and wildness glazing her eyes. Ulrika never moved. If she

had screamed perhaps it would have been the end of her. She stared at the woman and waited for the blow, and her astonishment was even greater than her fear. Then slowly Crescence's arm sank; she nodded once or twice and went out as silently as she had come in. The next morning she brought Ulrika's breakfast to the bedside, kissed her hand humbly, asked her if she had slept well, and behaved as if nothing at all had happened. Ulrika never said a word about it either that day or afterwards. In order not to bear the consequences and lose a person who was indispensable to her as air, she felt that she must spare this woman; she wished that this had never happened and so she erased it from her thoughts.

But from that day on her whole manner toward her maid changed. She took her into her confidence at times, treated her like an equal, or at any rate with a kind of consideration and care which, if it was not entirely sincere, could be recognised as something entirely different from her former harshness. She talked over the people in the village with her; she sat down in the kitchen with her and read her the newspapers; she told her little happenings out of her own life; in short she tried to erase the barrier that formerly she had built up with unyielding pride between them. At first the effect upon Crescence was only to make her shyer, more silent and withdrawn; but by degrees as Ulrika conciliated her, she gained courage to reply, to express her own opinions, and then it was not long until all this changed into boldness and impudence. Her timidity disappeared entirely and that was just what Ulrika wanted; there lay at the bottom of this an almost diabolical knowledge of human nature; she wanted to encourage in this downtrodden outcast whom she had learned to fear, a candid expression of her evil instincts. Words were not dangerous; words were weakening; the more freely words flowed, the weaker would the arm be for action. And that raised arm with the sharpened knife had given her the deepest fright that she had ever felt. Now she could rage and scold and give rein to her tempers and scatter suspicions around her and be

miserly with praise and with food. The house would echo
for a few hours with wild shrieks and rows, insults flew back
and forth, doors were banged and they were often at the
point of pulling each other's hair, and then the storm would
pass over; they growled and grumbled a little while, were
reconciled and made peace, until a new catastrophe turned
up. But the former crouching humility of the maid grew
less. Every time she allowed herself new freedom, she despised her mistress more; with every insult that she offered,
her hatred grew; a hatred that she nourished and kept as
if it were a beloved creature to which she clung and made
sacrifices. When she had seized the kitchen knife her strength
had come from despair; but at that time Ulrika Woytich was
a great personage to her; and perhaps it was only because
Ulrika had stepped down of her own free will from these
heights and made herself the equal of the lowest of human
creatures (for it was thus Crescence thought of herself), that
her hatred had grown so powerful.

And so these two lived together, strangely dependent upon
each other, strangely unlike each other, dwelt there in the
innocence and silence of beautiful nature, woods and mountains, meadows and brooks spread before their eyes and they,
both of them, felt nothing except its occasional ugliness and
harshness. For in the end, the maid Crescence had become a sort of shadow of the mistress Ulrika and knew
only the wishes and modes of thought of her mistress.
Ulrika hated nature, because it would not give her its fruits
for nothing; she hated trees, because they spread their
shadows over the peasant rather than over her. And as to
grass, flowers, the slender, soaring pine, the light glowing
around the tops of the mountains, and the shimmering of
stars—to Ulrika this was no more than a decoration, stage
scenery, a poor comfort. And nothing upset Ulrika more,
rousing her poisonous mockery, than to see city people spend
their holidays and vacations wandering through the country
and to hear their lying enthusiasm over sunsets and green
vegetables. If they were not lies at least they were stupidity,
or probably both; all the more they seemed to fit into this

thing which they called nature, which in Ulrika's eyes was a mixture of both lies and stupidity; they were empty as a stable, judging all human activity with the same measuring rod, whether it were that of a Michael Angelo or the village idiot. Unless men made nature bearable, by putting it in order, by building palaces, domes, and gardens, it was no better than a miserably painted canvas, even the famous heavens, in which simple-minded mankind had placed their philanthropic, dressed-up gods, and which was a sort of upper court of justice for their foolish deeds.

Ulrika believed in nothing and doubted everything. The only things she did not doubt were those that she could hold in her hands. She was so little of a Christian that at bottom she believed the principles of Christianity a thousand-year-old deceptive scheme of the priesthood, and every credulous Christian she thought affected and weak-minded. She had seen through things; she had learned life from the ground up; they could not paint black things white to her. She sat in her house, that was her temple, her fate, her earth and nature. That was all true; you could pick it up, feel it, count it, measure it, take care of it, treasure it. Outside was the primitive chaos, the yearly fair with its smell of sweat, noise of bargaining, its bad music, cheap wares, and false coin.

The day after the last reconciliation with Crescence, however, there was a terrible row, because she had dared to take out a plate of watery soup to a wretched looking boy who had cowered for some hours near the garden gate. Now next to the benevolent canvassing which took place amongst the people of the neighbourhood in the years after the war, Ulrika hated beggars. The sight of a beggar roused her rage, a sort of bilious fever, as if the sight of the poor people there debased her. She could not quiet herself; she scolded and rowed uninterruptedly from noon until late afternoon. Anastasia was silent and nodded servilely to all that she said. But as the litany never came to an end she dared to remark that after all it was only a child and perhaps very hungry. Ulrika asked harshly how that concerned her. She had no cure for it. No, thank God, her tears did not flow as easily as that. It was all one to her whether it was a child or an old man, a male or a female. Who had told beggars to go on bringing beggars into the world? If they would stop multiplying, the misery of the world would be much less. The blessed Malthus had proven that in his writings competently. "But what is the use of preaching?" she went on grimly. "The poor must be fruitful or else they will be trodden to death. Children ought to be killed who are born to become beggars or Social Democrats. And see how important they feel their children to be in these days; it is horrible to look at. In my day they brought them up with beatings and made real men of them; but now they pamper them and talk to them about equality and the dignity of humanity, and they all grow up to be thieves and swindlers."

"You would think differently if you had a child of your own," said Anastasia, not very pleasantly.

"Heaven forbid!" cried Ulrika, shaking herself. "A burden like that on my back would have been one too many. I would have hung my career on a nail and myself too. There are orphan asylums where it would have been better brought up than by me, but, thank Heavens, I was not built for productivity. I stand by myself. I believe the scholars call such people 'monads.'" She got up and took her stick to go out of doors, where she liked to look around for an hour in the vegetable garden. Anastasia followed her.

The sun was already dropping back of the western peaks and swarms of little gnats danced over the path. Ulrika threw back her Voltaire-like head, snuffed up the air, and felt inclined to praise the atmosphere. Suddenly she drew her brows together and pointed up towards the woods with her stick. "Hello, up there!" she cried, with all the power of her lungs. "What does this mean? This is private property. March, get out!"

It was a girl, who had run down from the top of the hill along the edge of the wood and now stood about two hundred feet away from the two women; in her eager chase of a squirrel she had come into the fenced-off property of Villa Woytich.

At the harsh call she stood still, frightened. She wore a little rose-coloured dress, just reaching to her knees, sandals on her bare feet, over her shoulder a green botanizing basket, and her broad-brimmed straw hat hung back over her neck. Her marvellous hair shone in the sun like a golden veil.

"Hello, who are you?" Ulrika went on, growling: "Where did you come from? What are you doing here? Why do you climb over strange people's fences? Is that allowed? Get out or you will suffer for it!" She threatened her with her stick.

The girl—it was Fanny Heinroth—looked once more at the trunk of the fir tree which the little squirrel had climbed and from which it was now looking down at her mockingly. She nodded up at him laughing, and then turned her rather frightened glance again to the scolding old woman. She looked uncertain whether she should take to flight or stand and talk. Her daily wanderings had brought her to this place for the first time. As usual she had escaped Fräulein Elizabeth's guardianship and was going her own way with fearless independence. She felt as if she were a discoverer of an unknown part of the earth and lived in prickling expectation of adventure. At the Eckern house they knew just so much of these wild wanderings as she chose to tell them; Fräulein Elizabeth would not complain of it, because she thought it would not be wise to try to control the child's passionate desire for freedom and also because she was afraid they would no longer entrust her with the care of Fanny if they knew of her wilful wanderings. She always followed her in the distance as well as she could, but always quickly lost sight of her.

After a moment of hesitation and consideration, Fanny went up to a huge oak tree which stood, one of six, as a sort of shield to the darker forest of pine trees. She stood by it and asked surprised: "Why do you scold so, you old woman? I am not going to steal any of your woods away from you."

Ulrika was speechless. She looked at Anastasia to find out what had been said. But if Ulrika was struck dumb how could Anastasia speak? They could only stand and wonder at such depravity. But there was a gleam of hidden joy in it, too, and Ulrika thought to herself: "Children and fools speak the truth."

As the child evidently belonged to the upper circles of society, Ulrika swallowed her anger for the moment and decided to examine the impudent little creature. A small runlet of water separated her from Fanny; shaking her head she stepped over the foot-bridge and stood beside her. "What is your name? Where do you live?" Fanny answered quietly and clearly, and could not help seeing that the name of her house made an impression on the bitter old woman. Ulrika measured the child from head to foot and, narrowing her eyes, she repeated thoughtfully: "Heinroth; so, so." The name seemed vaguely familiar to her; she had heard it somewhere and with renewed questions she tried to see if the child could not help her memory. But Fanny only knew that that was her name and as she was made uncomfortable by the fixed stare of the old woman she asked her what her name was. "What is your name?" She turned to Ulrika, who was so amazed at the unconcerned tone in which the child used the familiar address "thou," which she thought was the height of impertinence, that she answered only by an indignant shake of the head; she was mute with indignation. "Is that your house?" Fanny continued; and Ulrika, in her indignation, turned to Anastasia as if she called upon her to be a witness to such unheard conduct. Fanny either did not notice it or misunderstood it, for she did not really believe that any one could think ill of her; without any suspicion she began to chatter, becoming livelier every minute; and finally she laughed aloud.

She found it awfully jolly to wander around alone through the country. She told the ruses she used to escape Fräulein Elizabeth's eager watchfulness, and this aroused her liveliest gaiety. Nobody need worry about her, she declared, shrugging her shoulders; nobody would ever hurt her, and sometimes when people met her who did not look exactly friendly she always looked them straight in the eyes, so (she demonstrated how she opened her eyes wide, and standing close in front of Ulrika, fearless and laughing, she looked her straight in the face); the old lady nodded to her and let her go her way.

Was it then so awful that she had climbed over the fence, she wanted to know; she had not thought anything about it and did not suppose any one would scold her. It was all the squirrel's fault; you could not imagine how sly that animal was; it would run a little way and then turn its head toward her and look back as if it were inviting her to follow. She was silent then, looked around with an enraptured glance and said: "It is lovely here, wonderfully lovely. It is lovely too at the Frau Baroness's and we have a beautiful house there, bigger than this, but it is much wilder here; and I like it best where it is wild. Do a great many people live in your house? Are you also a Frau Baroness? Perhaps you know our Baroness Josephine?"

Ulrika answered only with a vaguely articulated growl. She had the strangest feeling about her. What sort of a face was that? What did it remind her of? Form, movement, glance and smile? It was something from the long past days; from a younger, gayer time. Those lightly-bowed lips, the nervous movement at the base of the nose—where did it come from? And how she stood there, graceful and yet full of childish pride, which is healthier and finer than any other kind of pride. How beautifully her limbs were joined to her body, and the hair on her forehead and neck, all of one shimmering colour; really she was astoundingly beautiful, a creature such as one rarely saw. And her voice! if she would only stop chattering, thought Ulrika; it is sorcery the way that voice makes one's spine shiver. How on earth did Josephine ever come by the child? Can one get such a thing by just being sympathetic and benevolent?

All these thoughts and feelings were mirrored in her restless face. Finally her glance fell to the ground; she drew a circle with her stick in the sand and said: "Since you have come this far, you imp, and the house excites your curiosity, come with me and see it. Then you can say you have been the guest of Ulrika Woytich," she added with a laugh. "That is a favour every one does not receive. You are politely invited, my dear Fanny, and if you are good I will show you something extraordinarily beautiful."

The invitation was not so very urgent and yet it was so un-expected to Anastasia that she stared at her sister, amazed. Fanny seemed to be thinking it over. She wore a small wrist watch, a present of Josephine's and she consulted it with gravity. "Oh, shall I? Isn't it too late?" she asked.

"Oh, no," said Ulrika, in a coaxing voice. "It has only just struck six o'clock. It is light now-a-days until eight o'clock, and you will be home long before that. I am not a baroness, to be sure, but I don't eat little girls." With these words she took Fanny's right hand in her left and started toward the house. "You can stay in the garden," she called back to Anastasia. "We two want to look into matters alone. Don't we, Fanny?"

It was an order, not a suggestion to Anastasia and her sur-prise grew. As she watched the strange pair, she could not suppress her evil presentiments.

CHAPTER XXVII

HOW DO YOU DO, MY LITTLE DARLING?

FROM the spot where they had met, to the second floor of the house, Ulrika had learned the chief events in Fanny's life history: the years in Geneva which she could hardly remember, except for blue water and white glaciers; the years in Yverdon where she lived with her teacher's family; the journey with her parents to Vienna and the miserable little room in the suburbs; her stay at Dornbach; and then the fairy-like change of destiny and her life in the house of the Baroness. Ulrika had only to turn her dull eyes upon her, and everything that she wanted to know, or at any rate, everything that the child herself knew, bubbled out fluently and gaily in perfect truth and freshness from her lovely mouth. And Ulrika listened, and thought, and combined, and yielded to the charm of the young voice.

They went past the rooms on the first floor and she led Fanny into the museum on the second. But the treasures there made little impression upon Fanny; she was used to such things; there was no lack of costly things in the Melander city house and in Eckern. Ulrika was disappointed. She had expected to make a greater impression with her treasures; she could not understand how it came about. As she had never in her life had anything to do with children, the narrowness of their circle of interest seemed strange to her; step by step, she had to remind herself whom she had with her and everything she said sounded uncertain and abrupt.

She opened a window that gave a wide outlook over the country. Even this view only elicited a passing comment of admiration from Fanny, who was already beginning to feel somewhat oppressed. She wanted to show that she appreciated the pains her hostess was taking for her and was trying to behave like a grown-up person. But the rooms did not please her; nothing about them pleased her; everything looked cold and unpleasant. Ulrika's last hope was the doll in the round cabinet; she had had it in her mind at the very beginning and was withholding it until the last. She smacked her lips as she brought Fanny to the threshold; she was still holding the little girl by the hand, thoughtlessly, and what happened surpassed her expectations.

Fanny gave a shout of surprise, pulled herself loose from Ulrika and rushed toward the doll. She raised her hands, clapped them together, laughed, stood up on tiptoe, threw aside her botanizing basket, stroked the arm of the doll, felt of the dress, devoured it with her eyes, asked the wildest questions, then stood breathless, pressing her hand to her heart; indeed she was quite beside herself.

Ulrika was frightened. Yes, just at first she was frightened. Such an outbreak of joy in its elemental freshness seemed mysterious to her. For an instant it seemed as if a dead veil rose from all the objects in the rooms, a veil which had lain upon them for decades, and they seemed to be freed thereby from a sort of disease. And it was like a dream to see the child, so enraptured, a strange unworldly vision, troubling her as nothing else ever had.

But the unexpected was not yet at an end.

Fanny embraced the doll as if it were a lost sister, newly found, and as the pedestal did not allow her to reach any higher than her waist, and Ulrika wanted to give her pleasure and make it more comfortable for her, she lifted the heavy thing down, which was none too easy. Fanny, with a lovely smile, first went all around the doll, touched it again and again, its hair, its shoulders, took one arm gently and raised it, then the other, pulled a fold of the dress to rights, saw a little slit in the shoulder and in this slit, on the body of the doll a little handle no bigger than a thumb. She looked questioningly at Ulrika and began to turn the handle. Ulrika was surprised, for she had not known of the existence of the handle.

Suddenly the doll began to move. She took a step and then another step. As if she had been singed by fire, Fanny drew her hand away and turned pale. But the doll walked. And after she had taken three steps with her right foot and three with her left she stopped and bowed. And when she came up again from the bow there came from inside of her a thin, strange, chirping, oddly-distant voice, which said the words: "How do you do, my little darling? Don't you think we might take a walk together?"

Then there was a whirr, the mechanism stood still and the doll stood stiffly in the room.

Ulrika was just as rigid. She had never dreamed of the doll's artistic abilities. She had owned it for forty years and although she knew it was a rarity, and had classified it and had heard that at that period in England walking and talking dolls were made, it had never occurred to her to investigate. Old Mylius had never mentioned anything about it. Very likely he did not even know it. Then time opened its dark abyss, the years rose grey from the labyrinth of the past, and there was nothing pleasant or agreeable to Ulrika in the fact that she had had to wait for this child to come with her spring-like joy and spring-like voice to rouse this homuncule to walk and speak. Shivering strangely Ulrika felt that these dead things had a kind of life, from the very fact of the years that they had left behind them, with which they still torment and deceive the minds of mankind; and in dark depression she listened to her own heart, as if this too were only a machine, dependent upon a handle to keep up its beating. Swift memory pictures and ruins; she fixed her glance upon Fanny who, in her nameless delight, had fallen upon her knees; her cheeks flamed up with joyous red, her eyes shone, and in her overwhelming pleasure she threw herself into Ulrika's arms; her surprise, astonishment, and gratitude dazed her and she covered the old woman's face with kisses.

"Now, now, now," said Ulrika, embarrassed and gruff, but the scent of the child's hair and skin had a strange effect upon her. She moved her arms carefully as if she were afraid that a quick motion might injure the tender little body.

"What did she say?" stammered Fanny. "What sort of a language was it? Please, please tell me what she said."

"It was English," explained Ulrika; "in German it would mean: 'How are you, my little darling? Don't you think we might take a walk together?' That is what it said."

"And can she say other words, too? Can she talk just as you and I do?"

"No, not that much, not that much," Ulrika replied, chuckling and freed herself from Fanny's embrace; the child now felt the impropriety of her actions and dropped her eyes ashamed. "But now it is time that you should stir your stumps, you imp," she went on, beginning to scold, "else your soup will be cold over there at Eckern and your Baroness won't know where you are."

Fanny realised it but could not tear herself away. She looked longingly at the doll.

"But this is not the evening of the last day," said Ulrika and patted her on the shoulder; "I don't mind if you come back again. Come again; you can come every day, to-morrow as far as I am concerned, but I advise you not to talk. Keep it quiet; keep it a secret. If they hear about it over there, they won't let you come back to me any more, I can tell you that much about it, little girl. There are reasons for it, you know, but they are old stories. As far as I am concerned the grass has grown over them, but over there I don't think any grass ever grows; they don't like grass to grow. So be clever; if you want to visit your aunt Ulrika Woytich in her bewitched castle, you must not even mention my name over there, or you will lose everything, and then good-bye to the doll, to the beautiful dress, to the lace cap, to the bow, and the 'how do you do.' Do you understand me?"

"Oh, yes, I understand very well," answered Fanny thoughtfully and, although the warning and the way in which it was given, troubled, almost frightened her, she resolved to obey, for she wanted to see the doll again at all costs, to live through again the rapturous magic of its walking and talking. She was so preoccupied and excited when she said good-bye that she forgot her botanizing basket, and Ulrika had to call her back to get it.

Standing at the window of the living room, Ulrika looked

in the direction that Fanny had gone. She stood there until with unbelievable swiftness the hurrying little figure disappeared in the turn of the road. Fiery glowing clouds swam in the heavens, and the wind that blew over the meadows bent the long stalks and turned the green into silver grey.

Ulrika lit her pipe and walked up and down in the room and puffed and thought. Suddenly she turned to the old desk, looked in one of the side drawers for a key, and when she had found it opened a middle drawer which was full of photographs. There were a number in tied-up packages; a certain order reigned, divided into decades and periods of her life. She took them out package by package and untied one of the last. There were pictures of Lex, Pillersdorf, Althann, Phillipsborn, Hartwich, Ittstein, and at last she brought to light one of Edward Melander, pale and time-worn like the others. With a hasty movement she tore it out, carried it to the window and looked at it.

It was the same face. The same lines, the same structure; the same forehead and mouth. That was a man, she thought, as if she herself had been the source of Melander's brilliant career; a darned clever fellow he was, who had gone far in life; mowed down everything that stood in the way, and grabbed everything that he wanted, and yet was honoured and praised by all. But she felt uncomfortable as she looked at the picture; she did not like to see the dead so near and so real; a cold shiver went down her spine and she threw the photograph back again into the drawer. Then she paced up and down again and brooded over the likeness and the confusing circumstance of the child's changed name, since she was undoubtedly Josephine's grandchild and did not in the least know it. Josephine had had no daughter, only one son. Perhaps she was an illegitimate child and did not know it. Since leaving the Mylius house, Ulrika had not concerned herself with Josephine's fate and she had never met Edward Melander again; their paths were widely separated, and like all sudden upstarts he had broken away from the witnesses and companions of his past. Now and then news had come to her ears, rumors of an unhappy marriage and quarrels with the son; but she had forgotten them.

When Anastasia came up from the garden it was quite dark. She had been gathering vetch and poppies, and was bringing in vases filled with water to put the flowers in. She turned on the light. Anastasia was a living chronicle of the events in the anterooms of those circles where she had once stood under Ulrika's protection. After her marriage her opportunities had been less, but out of a certain clinging dependence, and with the tickling curiosity of the empty-headed she had listened at cracks and key holes, and at least as far as her own home town went, she knew all the scandalous and compromising gossip of society, and got as much pleasure out of it as Ulrika out of her antiques. Ulrika knew this; she needed only to throw out a question as to whether the name Heinroth awaked any memories in her which connected it with the Melander house, and she would get full and detailed information.

Heinroth, certainly, Anna Heinroth: that was the little actress who had succeeded in marrying young Stephen Melander; in consequence of which he had to leave the military service and had had a complete break with his mother; he was a rotten youth, too; all sorts of scandals about him. He had been talked about a good deal ten years ago and after that had disappeared from the picture. What had become of him she could not say.

Ulrika sat in the arm chair, with her spotted coffee-brown shawl around her shoulders, for no summer evening was so warm that her bones were not cold; her red-striped stockings hung down over her low shoes. "Queer stuff," she mumbled. "How can one grasp it. Heinroth. And he married her. And the child is named after the mother. Did the donkey give up his beautiful title, or did he compensate himself by using her name, when she, the clever baggage, had decided to wear the trousers. And Lothar never told me anything about it. But all the Mylius people were secretive; always; it was in their blood."

Anastasia had already grasped the matter and expressed it

in her own way. "The girl is a Melander, of course," she said dryly, pleased with herself; "I think it is this way: Stephen got into some sort of disgrace. The Baroness Josephine undertook to bring up the child, probably paid off the mother, but does not want the child to pass as her grandchild, because she wants no claim from that side. Stephen had to change his name, I remember that quite distinctly. So the child had to remain a Heinroth for quite definite reasons."

"What definite reasons?"

"Well, one hears that the Baroness Josephine has left her entire private fortune to her institutions."

"What?" Ulrika jumped up and her teeth chattered. "Are you speaking seriously? Who told you any such tale as that? Do you mean seriously that the untold millions of the Mylius family and the other millions, too, for Edward must have made a stately addition to them, do you mean that all those millions are to be given to her sentimental tomfoolery? Do you think that is possible?"

"It is what everybody says, my dear Ulrika. You ought to pay a little attention to what is happening in the world."

Ulrika breathed heavily. "It is enough to make one's hair stand on end!" she cried out, beating on the table with her fists. "And such a thing has to be allowed? It is a crime a crime before Heaven. Of course, Josephine was a complete fool from childhood up, and one can believe the maddest things of her. But why should this child have to bear the penalty, I ask. Why should that innocent thing be cut off from her natural, inherited rights, I ask. Let her do as much mischief as she likes with her exaggerated charities, but everything has a limit, and the good creature is deceiving herself as she is sure to find out."

"I don't see why you are so hot about it," Anastasia remarked, suspicious as always when money was talked about. "No outsider can mix into that, as I had better warn you."

"Keep your warnings to yourself," Ulrika growled, sitting down again and dragging her right stocking up over her leg with an angry jerk: "We will see. We will keep our eyes open; 'mouth shut and eyes open,' that is one of the best proverbs.

Now I am going to eat. I am as hungry as a wolf." She pulled open the door, and bellowed in stentorian tones, "Crescence! Supper!"

"Supper," scorned Anastasia inwardly, "ten potatoes and six spoonfuls of rice." She had hallucinations of roast meat like an Arctic explorer.

At the table Ulrika did not stop complaining. The Mylius and Melander millions had grown to something gigantic. She calculated, and the sums that she named grew bolder and bolder; she had images of gold mines and treasure rooms under the earth, and her excitement grew with her description. Anastasia interrupted sceptically that like so many others, the Melander fortune, as it consisted chiefly in stocks and bonds, had probably diminished and that all the Crœsuses of yesterday were on the way to becoming the proletariat of to-morrow, a remark which kept Ulrika with her mouth full while, with angry eloquence, she tried to consider this strange case.

"They have kept something back," she said angrily; "they have foreign investments, as sure as I sit here. They are not so foolish as to let themselves be dragged to the ground by this cracked Republic, and in the end they could put a stack of poor spungers like us in their sack. I readily believe that they howl, and their teeth chatter, and that they cry 'murder'; that has been their business ever since Adam's time, but one has to be a stupid goose like you, to be taken in by it."

Anastasia swallowed the insult and was silent.

"Just look at Lothar Mylius," Ulrika continued; "he eats oysters and lobster every day and drinks French brandy, and has only a fourth of what Josephine Melander has." Her head was burning, she waved her arms in the air, and when Crescence came to clear the table she called her to her suddenly. She had a real healthy human understanding, she told the maid, and she must know, as did the whole village, the Sanitarium and Baths and the entire neighbourhood, about what the fortune of the Melanders amounted to; and there sat Frau Anastasia Gentili who had the face to say that those people were no better off than the average wood and vegetable hagglers; isn't that enough to make anybody laugh?

Anastasia pressed her thin lips together and said sharply that Crescence's opinion was all the same to her. Crescence shrugged her shoulders and replied roughly that the gracious Fräulein was too excited to-day and she had better take her purgative again. Ulrika, flattered by so much attention, broke out in a loud stable-man's laugh and began to tell how Fanny had found the machinery for the doll in the cabinet up-stairs. "And just think," she ended pathetically, her eyes bulging, "the century-old thing began to walk and to speak (you can try it yourself to-morrow), actually spoke English, 'How do you do, my little darling,' and bowed, a real bow such as they make at dancing school." She mimicked the bow and the walk of the doll, and her two listeners laughed incredulously, and then when she told them how the child fell upon her neck and kissed her in her joy, yes, honestly kissed her, Anastasia shook her head troubled, and Crescence, the serving tray under her naked arm, giggled sarcastically.

It was a real Dutch picture.

I would like to know if the brat will really come again to-morrow, Ulrika thought more than ten times in the course of the evening. And more than ten times she ran to the barometer to see what the weather would be, something she never did otherwise: if it rains or is cloudy, she will not come, she decided; then too one cannot know whether she will not tell the whole story; she will show it in her manner and they will insist until she tells it. Then they will watch like the devil, for I am to the Frau Baroness, what a red rag is to a bull. All I can do is sit here and wait.

In case she never comes again, she considered further (a thought that made her blood boil), who will stand between her and the caprices of that Josephine? Who will unearth the deceit? Who will save her millions and millions for her? Who will prevent them from being transformed into soup-kitchens for the poor, a sop here and a sop there, poor student scholarships, and dowries for clerks' daughters? Then the little blond creature will have to whistle for her money. There is nothing doing, good people, nothing doing—Ulrika Woytich is here and

she won't stand for it; she will take the little blond creature
under her wing.

Restlessly she wandered through the house like a big black
bird. When Anastasia, puzzled by her sister's manner, retired, Ulrika went into the kitchen and confided her cares and
fears to Crescence and they must have sounded very odd to
the maid. The things that Anastasia had told as gossip and
suspicion were already a certainty to Ulrika, for why should
not one always believe the worst, since one never saw or heard
anything else. And so she confided to the listening Crescence
in what danger the Melander millions stood. The window
was wide open and her resounding voice sounded through the
quiet woods and came back as an empty echo. At the end
she asked Crescence eagerly if she had looked at the little
blond creature.

Crescence said: "What has the stranger child and stranger
money to do with you? So far as I know you have never
cared for children, and as to the money, you are living well
enough, I think, even if our stomachs do rumble most of the
time. When a Jew has no trouble, he makes some, they say.
When fire burns me I don't blow on it."

They sat mute for a while and Crescence began to tell in
uncouth phrases a coarse story of adultery down in the village, just to liven up the conversation a little. Ulrika, to
keep her intimate and in good spirits and because she liked
to hear such things anyhow, made a few obscene jokes which
elicited noisy approval from her maid. Love affairs of man
and woman, she looked down upon them from the heights with
cold scorn and biting irony and called the thing by its right
name unadorned; these things gave her real enjoyment.

She lay restlessly in her bed, turning from side to side, and
could not sleep. She sighed as morning came and went on
asking: What is the matter with me? What is it I want? She
had not been in such a state for years. It was as if a glimmering spark of an old fire were burning up. But where did it get
nourishment? Who had set the match to it? She wondered
gloomily about herself. She looked back for something like it

in the past. But there was nothing there. She decided that old people, in time, forgot their own natures. That made her anxious.

The noon hours crept by with leaden feet. She went into the garden. She walked into the wood to pick up underbrush. Every five minutes she looked up to the sky. A cloudy veil was rising in the west; she swore and cursed to herself. The clouds broke and she began to hum. It sounded like the crackling of leaves. The costume in which she was working excited even Crescence's anger, and Anastasia, who always looked as if she had just come out of an egg shell, turned her glance indignantly from her. Only after dinner she decided upon a less filthy covering. She sent Anastasia down into the village to buy two cakes of chocolate. Anastasia could not believe her own ears; chocolate; it was a word she had never heard since she had been in the house. But she obeyed, although it took her two and a half hours to go and come.

Ulrika sat at the window and darned stockings. Black, yellow, blue stockings, all darned with bright green wool as she had no other at hand. By five o'clock she could not restrain her impatience any longer; she went to the cupboard and fetched an old opera glass, went up to the balcony and began to look over the entire country. When the heavens began to cloud over again she shook her fist, embittered. Some cottage children, coming out of the wood, ran over the edge of her land; at first her breath stopped short in her throat, her pupils grew big, then she recognised her mistake and she screamed at the little group angrily so that they fled through the meadows in a panic.

It was six o'clock, half-past six, and when the village clock of Riednau struck seven she picked up one of her potted plants and threw it angrily to the earth and broke it. She went back into her room looking for something to let out her spleen upon, and came across Anastasia; she began to scold at her and asked where she had been so long. Anastasia replied that she had been to church; to-morrow was Corpus Christi day and there was a special service. Oh, think of it, in church, Ulrika mocked her poisonously; a service, just think of that; added to everything else she was going to become mendicant sister; since when? Anastasia turned sharply upon her and asked her what she meant by saying: "added to everything else"? Had she not always lived in the holy faith and said her prayers every night? Did Ulrika in her heretic's rage want to call every pious person a hypocrite? Little inclined to explain, Ulrika continued to abuse her, and Anastasia, foregoing any replies, sat down and burst into tears dramatically. Ulrika burst out laughing and left the room. She was thirsty; she turned on the spigot of the water pipe and put her mouth down to the pipe. The water tasted bitter as gall.

During supper she did not speak a word. It was raining out of doors. She stared gloomily at her plate. Then she lit her pipe, fetched a torn French novel from the bookcase and sat down in her arm chair, but she did not read a single word. She sat there and brooded until two o'clock at night. For a long time her thoughts ran round in a circle: the rain; the lost fortune; the vain watching for the child; and then again the rain; how long was it going to last; the misused millions, withheld from the child; herself as the great defender of right; the long, vain wait.

And the millions, they sang in her ear like an organ tone.

Then she began to make plans. She was oppressed and full of anger over what she was undertaking, but also full of foresight and cunning. First she would have to get full information about Eckern; who lived there, how they lived and with whom she would have to deal. Then she would write some letters to her former friends and acquaintances who could tell her something about the present circumstances of the Baroness, her connections, her business, her inclinations and her servants. And the wheel began to spin again; the hopeless rain; the millions like a cloud-burst of golden ingots, which she had to stem; and the child, and then of a sudden she was asleep and in her dreams she felt the child hanging around her neck and kissing her; it gave her a strange voluptuous feeling as if she were holding a warm kitten against her icy breast. "Ugh," she cried, "don't kiss me."

Only with the first chirp of the birds she went to bed and

was up again early. In the night she had heard a dripping from one of the roof gutters. Crescence had to drag out a ladder and go up from the balcony and look after it. The gutter leaked. She sent for the tinner. Damage to the house upset her more than wounds on her own body. Nothing must ever happen to the house. All the tenderness and care of which she was capable went to the house. The tinner did not come until nearly eleven o'clock. While she was talking to him down in the lower floor and quarrelling over the price that he asked for the repairs, the entrance door opened. A joyous greeting reached her ears. And there stood Fanny with the triumphant smile of one who has overcome obstacles and reached the goal, waving her hand to her. Ulrika had to steady herself against the banisters and when she was certain that it was no illusion, broken lights flashed over her wrinkled face and she called out in her rough voice: "There you are, you little will-o'-the-wisp, there you are." And she blinked as she added: "How do you do, my little darling?"

CHAPTER XXVIII

THE GUEST AT ECKERN

WHEN the first step was taken upon the impulse of the moment which found her weaponless, and the words which she addressed to the child had been accepted, Josephine waited further developments with all her inborn anxiety. As every crushing-down of anxiety had meant to her a deception either from outside or inside, she was doubly watchful, and always hesitated to trust what she saw and heard.

She always smiled pleasantly when she talked to Fanny, but she listened to every tone and half tone of the child's voice; yes, she listened to the voice suspiciously even after it had ceased. Manners, bearing, walk, and posture could not have undergone a more thorough test than she undertook, and she was as stern toward herself and the honesty of her observations as she was inexorable toward the child.

She was painfully sensitive toward anything shallow; the slightest hint of it gave her positive bodily pain. She had found so few sincere people; everybody was besmirched up to the very eyes by egotism and untruth; it was difficult for her to believe in anything. Often the most innocent things had proved disfigured by the rust of lies; so often, when advantage beckoned, she knew the hands were smirched and played a false game; hands whose cleanliness she had not dared to question; but she had kept silence and had been content to be the scorned sacrifice, rather than to disclose the cunning nets, or shame those who had woven them.

With the same friendly smile toward liars and cheats she had grown grey. All her experiences had been bitter. And such a child, so lovely to look upon, what might it not bear in itself of the world's poison? One knew nothing of the rooms in which it had dwelt, or the faces it had seen, or the words it had heard. Souls are like sponges; they suck up the hideous things in life and when the fist of destiny squeezes them, the pestlike lye spurts forth. She had already experienced it. The most unexpected things had happened at times.

But as she followed Fanny's comings and goings, carefully but always secretly, she found nothing evil about her. It was always the same picture of joyous activity that she offered, a little unfolding soul asking, wondering, full of joy and beautiful motion. In the city she had been given a little room to herself and the joy that she expressed over it had moved Josephine despite herself, like a flood of unknown music. She took up every object in her hand, was astonished at everything, and talked to these lifeless objects tenderly, looked round again and again as if overwhelmed, and in the evening when she lay in her little bed she seized Elizabeth's hand and asked if she believed it was all true. What was one to answer? Was it true because it was objectively real? Or was it illusion because only for this little child it signified so much? Josephine wondered as she stood at the door, her head bowed.

The child was kindly to all the people in the house and talked to them quite naturally, from the dignified Casimir to the dirty little scullery maid. She did not understand the difference between masters and servants, and when she noticed it was always surprised and never applied it to herself. This trait, carried to an exquisite point, exercised a most winning charm; the result was that everybody in the house praised her from the first day on, and from the second day on they loved her, and from the third day on they spoiled her and tried to foresee and grant her every wish. It seemed to them, since she had come, that light had broken into the dark halls, and as if the closed rooms had all been thrown open and the banqueting lights lit. It was enough that in these solemn rooms a little creature ran around laughing, laughing with voice and heart and that the heaviness of a place which threatened to smother them gave way for the present to these unwonted sounds and echoes.

But Josephine's distrust remained. No one noticed it, not even Elizabeth; perhaps Fanny sometimes felt it vaguely; an

uncertain glimmering in the child's glance showed it, and
often when Fanny turned to talk to her she seemed a little
more timid than she did with others. Josephine could not
forget and could not overcome it; the misery lay in her memory
like a lasting sickness; she could not turn aside from it; she
sought the features of the father and the grandfather in the
little face, and the fear of a confirmation of her fear affected
her so physically that she had violent headaches for days, before she was able to make the journey to Eckern. The
thought constantly bored into her consciousness: Is it possible
that the bad. blood, born· in· her should not pass on to the
third and fourth generation? Can· Melander's blood throw
aside its taint, extinguish or transform it, or is this only a deceptive temptation that leads one to believe it?

She· would have liked to have faced the Lord God himself
with the question; she would have liked to have torn open the
heavens to have gotten her answer; for men could tell her
nothing.

Then something happened that upset her dreadfully, though
the cause was slight. It was late one morning; the doctor
had been there as her headache was almost unbearable.
Elizabeth was creeping around the room, the curtains
were close drawn, and deep twilight reigned there; Elizabeth
asked if the Frau Baroness wanted anything more and if she
felt easier. Josephine had closed her eyes and her pale hands
were spread lifelessly upon the blue satin counterpane. "Tell
Ilka out there, not to make such a noise with the dusting,"
she whispered; "if she could only be a little quieter."

"I have told her a hundred times, Frau Baroness. I will
go and tell her to stop work now."

This was a dialogue that had taken place in exactly the
same words for three days and Elizabeth went to stop the
noise which was hardly greater than the creeping of a mouse.
A short time after she had left the dark, restful room, another hand opened the door and there stood Fanny. She
opened her eyes and looked around and could hardly distinguish anything in the dark but she crept up to the bed, on
her tiptoes, to soften her footstep even on that thick carpet.

Then she sat down on a stool and was silent. Silently she sat there and held her folded hands in her lap. Josephine was only aware of her after some little time, for although she lay with her head quite high, she had her eyes shut and the child had appeared without making a sound. "Good morning, Fanny," she whispered. "Good morning, Frau Baroness," answered the child. "Do you want anything? Who sent you?" asked Josephine in a strained voice, for each word gave her a separate pain. "No one," came the bright reply, "I only wanted to see how you were getting along, Frau Baroness." Josephine smiled a little for the child's familiar address of "thou" in connection with her title sounded very odd. She had not allowed them to correct her; she wanted to avoid all corrections for the present and wait and see how the child's nature adapted itself to its environment. That seemed the best way.

A few minutes passed and Fanny began to tell her little experiences about the house, quite as if she were talking to herself, in a sad little voice, taking the greatest care not to make any undue noise. She described a conversation with Casimir; then her first lesson with the teacher that they had gotten for her and who pleased her because he knew so many stories; then a funny little quarrel with Elizabeth, who had asserted that she could not look at her for ten minutes straight into her eyes, without laughing; she had almost burst after the first half-minute and had had to press her lips together tight; and then about a dog that she had known in Yverdon who not only knew how to open all the doors in the house, but also knew how to fasten them again; then what she thought about when she lay in bed at night and could not go to sleep right off; she usually made shadow pictures on the wall, for instance she knew how to make a camel with a hump and a goose with its bill open; and she often wondered what it would be like when one was dead; whether the world would be there or not there; she used to think that each dead person got a star out of heaven to take with him into the grave and that the evening star was only a great big mirror of all the stars in the graves on earth.

She asked no questions, in her care and consideration; evidently she wanted to distract the invalid and therefore never stayed long on one subject It was just a bright chattering, careless and disconnected, as if one were emptying out a basket of all sorts of gay little flowers, and her tale pulsed with life, feeling and observation. It was a well-ordered, well-ruled little miniature world with its experiences all at first hand, and each word came out as fresh and new as if it had never been used by human lips before. When she said heaven, it was really like the infinite heavens, and when she said dreams, the word was all full of secret significance and there was nothing worn or shabby about the thing. How beautiful and innocent it all was, how close was the word to its meaning and its picture!

And as Josephine listened and listened, the strain on her nerves yielded bit by bit; the iron pressure on her forehead lessened, and the martyrising rumbling in her ears passed away. A happy, dumb wondering possessed her; she breathed more lightly; she raised herself a little on her pillows, rested her head on her arm and listened, and listened; and as she opened her eyes to this vision, her heart opened too. From this hour on Fanny was another creature to her; from this hour she began to love her.

And that was something she could neither comprehend nor describe. It fell upon her like a destructive force. It was like the awakening of the seven sleepers, who found the world changed, speaking a language they could not understand. One had heard of such things, read of them, known them; one had accepted them as one of the innumerable formulas out of the sphere of coincidence, but it was an unknown joy, long since despaired of, actually to share and feel them. So many people believed in the existence of this thing called love, and so many people in one way or another filled their life with it, that she had also believed in it somewhat; but it had been nothing more than that. At eighteen years old she had lost her mother, the only human being whom she had ever loved. But the Josephine who wept over her mother's coffin was quite another person from the one who had loved her. She had kept nothing of her youth, had saved nothing but this wandering shadow of a body. For three and a half decades she had gone the appointed way; doing without feeling, bearing her burden, dragging the torment, devastation, and illimitable loneliness of her life. She had quite forgotten that there was such a thing as love. The vase of love had broken, the contents had spilled out, and the fragments had been destroyed by the juggernaut of the years. Neither man nor woman had ever received love from her, or offered her love, or felt any wish or impulse to do so; no sad bereaved image of love hung in the rooms through which she wandered; the sterility of fruitless days and the fright of grief-spent nights stretched behind her.

And now all at once love was there. A manna fallen from heaven. A magic spring opened in the rock. But the receptive part of Josephine's nature had been so deeply wounded and distorted in her innermost parts, that she no longer dared to stand upright, and she contented herself with looking on in a sort of dazed and fruitless way. Only to make no sign; never to betray herself; for any reaching out after the truth might mean disappointment. To shut herself up and turn away and hide; and never let her hand reach out or her eye glow. This was the stern command that Josephine had given herself and she would break it for no blossom, no flame, no sudden appearance. Behind all this lay fear; the awfulness of the world she had known and experienced; a fear of a returned feeling, an equal fear of one not returned; a fear of tenderness and a fear of uncertainty; a fear of the past and a fear of the future. She was so bound she could not be free.

But she surrounded this child with every care. Elizabeth, who was conscious of every change in the relation between them, was satisfied. She showed it, and it made Josephine nervous and she became more than ever restrained when Elizabeth seemed eager to have her say a kind word about Fanny.

When they moved over to Eckern, Fanny was uncontrollably gay. The innumerable chests and trunks excited her admiration, the disturbance in the house seemed to her very festive and the eagerness and excitement in her little face, from morning till evening, was as if she were living through the surprising end of a fairy tale.   During the trip she could not see enough of the landscape and she chattered untiringly. Late in the afternoon when they arrived at Eckern, she went about as if dazed with happiness through all the spacious house, looked through the stables, the stalls, the tennis court, the flower garden, the hills and woods and when in the evening Elizabeth came to say good night to her she said blushing, as if she were asking forgiveness for the wrong she had done: "I never believed that Eckern and all this was here really; I thought you just talked that way about it."   Five minutes later she was asleep and the expression on the sleeping face seemed so beautiful to Elizabeth that she called the Baroness in to look at her.   Josephine complied but went away immediately; but when Elizabeth had left the room she came back and stood gazing a long time at the sleeping face.   Then finally she folded the little hands.

Valerian de Groot was expected at the end of the week. He had let himself be persuaded to give two concerts and had played in Berlin and Amsterdam.   On the third day after Josephine's arrival, while they were still in the midst of unpacking and putting in order, his Excellency Herbst, whom Josephine had invited to spend the summer in Eckern, had arrived.   He was one of the few friends she possessed, a slenderly-built little old man, known for his high culture and unstained character.   A heavy fate had weighed upon him and broken up his life, and every one, even Josephine, had shown him sympathy.   But the usual surroundings in the city, the sight of sympathetic and curious faces, had become unbearable to him and Josephine had urged him, until he had finally accepted her offer, to make Eckern a shelter and asylum.

The actual happening as it was seen from the outside and as it was told in more or less veiled form in the newspapers was this.   He was division chief in the ministry for foreign affairs, living in the happiest family relations, with a bright, clever wife, and two children, a son and a daughter.   In the last year of the war, he lost his son.   After the overthrow of the government, he resigned his post, in obedience to his convictions.   He had saved nothing.   From moderate prosperity

he fell into most abject poverty, through the general catastrophe. He bore all this with dignity, the loss of his son, the
loss of his office, the loss of his fortune. Then came the final
blow. The daughter, a lovely nineteen-year-old girl, Marie
Helen, got a secretarial position in a moving picture company, and helped with her salary to lighten the burden of the
little household. But she fell under the influence of a worthless fellow, always out of work, a former movie actor, named
Rutowsky, who won a fatal influence over her, destroyed her
whole nature and, in a short time, transformed her into a hussy
and a criminal. He had been four years at the front and had
been heavily wounded and once shot in the head. Wild and at
odds with God and man, he returned from the war, a loafer, an
enemy to all established standards, determined upon evil.
Marie Helen became acquainted with him in the office when
he came to ask for work. In some inexplicable way she fell,
unresisting, under his influence. Her whole nature was
changed; her resolution turned into melancholy; her gaiety
into dull sorrow, her candour into stubbornness and deceit-
fulness. Her father, overwhelmed and anxious, tried to investigate the cause; but it remained hidden. He forbade her
to see Rutowsky and she refused to obey. Her mother begged
and plead with her; but she would not listen. She remained
away from home for weeks and when they reproached her she
raved. She stole from her parents and paying no attention to
their horror, she packed up all her possessions and went to
live in Rutowsky's room in the suburbs. She became his mistress and his servant. She lost her position and in order to
earn something she ran the streets until her feet were sore. Her
necessities became ever more pressing. Rutowsky forced her
upon the streets. When she refused he beat her, and when he
had beaten her until she was half conscious she would fall at
his feet and kiss his hand. All this had been learned from
witnesses. She learned that he had been in prison for robbery.
Even this did not break down her devotion. He became one
of a set of professional burglars and had laid a plan to break
into a jeweller's shop. Marie Helen was to be the outside
guard. She did not dare resist and when the time came for

the deed, she was by his side. But the police had been fore-warned and while she kept watch outside the door, he was arrested inside. But she remained at his side. She obeyed the prearranged system of denial, planned in case of arrest. She never wavered by a breath or a look; indeed behaved like the most experienced aider and abettor of thieves.

For four months she was under arrest. The court was seeking witnesses and proofs. The general opinion, that the greater part of the guilt lay at her door, wavered and Rutowsky's past brought constantly new crimes to light. People talked a great deal about hypnotism and criminal influence, and many pens were busy making much of the happening and giving it a sensational twist, which was very characteristic of the times and the general decay of all moral consciousness, even in the best circles. But no description and no criticism threw a ray into the secret of this fallen soul, which had broken with custom and decency, upbringing and inheritance, for the sake of a man who was the dregs of his kind. She showed no repentance, could not be brought to any confession, and it seemed as if she had lost all memory of her former sheltered existence.

The mother did not outlive the disgrace. She broke under it. When they brought the news to Marie Helen, she never winked an eyelash. The old man, who had greatly loved his daughter, the late fruit of his marriage, wanted to visit her in prison, but she refused to see him. The public trial was set for the twenty-fifth of June; and this above all else had moved him to come to Eckern, and to hide there until he was summoned as witness to the trial. He had given his last cent to a clever lawyer to defend her and now he was waiting.

In Eckern he hardly left his room. Sometimes in the evening Josephine would persuade him to take a little walk. As they wandered through the meadows slowly, they would talk in short phrases with long pauses about the past. Josephine went to the station to meet Valerian de Groot, in order to tell him about his housemates and the table guests at Eckern. But she was so little able to give a clear account that de Groot, always upset at the prospect of new faces and strange meetings, made a scene in the carriage. He said she had promised him peace and solitude, and instead she explained the necessity of adapting himself to tragic figures and interesting children. That was not what he had wanted, he was tired of it, he had said good-bye to the world's whirl before he came. He would therefore leave, in order not to offend an old friend, in three days. He behaved like a naughty child and, despite her surprise, Josephine had to smile. However, when, still sulky and angry, he saw the wide meadows and the landscape crowned by the stately house behind its wall of great trees; when he entered the room prepared for him with its gay furniture and hangings; when he saw all his chests of books that had already arrived; when Elizabeth hastened up to greet him shyly and behind her a lovely, tender little figure; when Josephine, standing before him, with down-cast eyes, begged for absolution, he broke out into good-humoured laughter, seized Josephine by both hands and said, as he shook them, that she had exaggerated the difficulties in a very dilettante way and that, for his part, he could see only the charms.

His presence alone brought a new rhythm into life on the estate. Every one bowed down to him, and submitted to his opinions. He saw things very keenly and very quickly and expressed his opinions without reserve, but he did not always express himself and then they were afraid of what he suppressed. He was in the habit of listening to others with polite, almost over-polite attention, while his keen glance rested on the speaker's eyes; Josephine was often so alarmed by it that she would lose the thread of what she was saying and stare back at him in confusion. That flattered him, for he was a domineering person; but it also awakened his love of mockery.

The story of the old Excellency he listened to, when Josephine told it with visible emotion, but he said nothing. Josephine had gone up to his room to help him unpack his books, a work to which he devoted thorough and pedantic care. They had to put up another shelf as there were some three hundred volumes. When Josephine told him that she did not see why he brought so many books, since there was already a library in the house, he replied arrogantly that in the first place, books furnished an atmosphere in which a man of brains felt comfortable; it was not necessary to read them all, or to have read them all, but one must know their faces like the faces of good comrades; ten or twenty were not enough, but as in good landscape the trees should make an impression of plenty, so with books, one must get an impression not only of plenty, but of actual extravagance. Fanny, sitting opposite him, watched him with her mouth open and he bowed to her as if she were a grown lady; the irony behind his earnestness was hardly noticeable.

Now he crouched on the floor with his legs folded under him like a Turk, sorted out the volumes, set them up in rows around him, and the sun touched his silver-grey mane. While Josephine talked he let his hands fall quietly and watched her with the eager look of a child. "Of course, we cannot speak before him of anything that concerns him; we even keep the newspapers from him, that he shall not hear the results of the trial too soon. It is a misfortune that he has to appear as a witness. He will, of course, deny the accusations, but imagine what it means to him to stand with her there before the bar."

De Groot's head sank and he was silent.

"It were better never to have children than to have them like that," murmured Josephine. Then he looked at her with a strange look and shook his head slowly.

"Don't you think so?" asked Josephine, and an anxious wave of colour passed over her face. He jumped to his feet. "My opinion?" he scolded and shrugged his shoulders up to his ears. "What use is my opinion in this world of murderers. That I should praise death because it may spare me some trouble is asking too much. To have children is to have the way open before one; one lives in eternity; one's roots are in the ground, even if at the top one fades and loses leaves. Let it come as it may, with disgrace, and sorrow, and trouble that eats the heart out, anything is better than to stare into the black night called Death."

"Forgive me, dear friend," whispered Josephine.

He stood still before her and looked searchingly at her. She evaded his look and went on: "Yes; I beg pardon, but not because your words convince me. Experience has taught me differently. In fact, just the opposite. I could not—no, I never could bring myself to feel so. There were times when my deepest wish was—only that one thing— Do you understand—" She stopped, pressing her hands together.

Valerian knew only the general outline of Josephine's story, mere hints and echoes from those who lived about her; he had never tried to find out and never demanded anything; closer sympathy had been arrested because his friend had never wanted to burden him with her sorrows, she was too proud, too silent, too ashamed and humiliated; and he, in his royal egoism had never seen or felt what simple sympathy would have felt. He had no inkling of the life-long, hidden grief; but now it sprung up before him like a flame.

He was touched and asked with unusual severity: "And would you have taken all the responsibility upon yourself, if you had by chance had the power to fulfil your wish?"

"It is not the same creature who wishes and who does," Josephine replied. Then: "Yes, I would have taken it—" She hesitated. In a low voice she added: "To-day I should have been poorer than I am." And at his questioning look she said softly, making a gesture toward the outside: "The child."

He continued to question her without words. She walked up and down in front of him, her eyes fixed upon the ground. She would have liked to turn her head away from him and to have spoken to the walls. She did not tell him her whole past; she would not and could not. But she explained the presence of the child and the circumstances that had brought her. She was still in doubt as to whether she was doing right in denying her her right name and her family. She wanted to know what he thought about it. She explained her reasons. One was that she wished to make no claim upon the child, either a claim upon her feelings or upon the possession of her; she wanted to give her no bias for the future; she wanted her to grow up untrammelled, unburdened, and inwardly free and self-possessed. The important thing was, however, that Josephine denied herself a claim upon the heart, the feeling of possession; and she showed it in her confused words. And Valerian recognized that it was a kind of asceticism that she practised. In her fear of life, filled with timid superstitutions, that made her afraid of happiness, she found a spring of disaster whenever she opened her feelings to any one. She did not want to escape a duty or a burden but she wanted to lift and carry them for others. He found it hard to put himself into her world; by nature he was sympathetic and here he met under a veil of gentleness the most immovable stubbornness and she went so far as to assert with sorrowful resolution that she would send the child out of her house if ever it learned of its blood relationship to her. "Before all else, I always remember that the name Melander bears a curse with it, and any one bearing the name can neither have, nor give happiness."

Valerian was too astonished to contradict. After a pause he asked if Fanny never enquired for her parents and had said nothing of their disappearance. Josephine said, No, she had never uttered a syllable about either father or mother. It was astonishing for it implied that some definite resolution lay beneath, and one could only take it for granted that the child was more developed than she appeared. Elizabeth believed that she had been entirely indifferent to her parents, which, of course, was possible, when one remembered the neglect she had suffered. She herself believed that Fanny was silent out of offended pride and that she had some idea of what sort of people her parents were. She kept it all to herself and it was wonderful how a child, who had grown up without love or tenderness, could have grown to be what this child was.

Valerian said thoughtfully: "Many people think that the love of parents is like a chain around the feet of a child and a wall around its heart. It is possible. It is even probable. In the past epoch of apparent humanitarianism, several thousand people in the cities of Europe apparently overweighted the scales of feeling. It softened our world and distorted it. Now destiny and history are avenging themselves and everything is transformed into bestiality."

CHAPTER XXIX

ULRIKA APPEARS

FROM that day on, Valerian paid quite a little attention to
Fanny. At the table he often spoke to her politely and listened
earnestly with bent head, to her replies, and when on her side
she turned to him with a question or a request, he showed the
utmost willingness and friendliness. Their relation took on a
quite extraordinary aspect, since Fanny always addressed him
familiarly as "Du," while he addressed her with the utmost
dignity and formality. No one could forego a smile, even the
sad face of his Excellency showed a ray of amusement. Fanny
had learned that de Groot was a famous violinist; and this in-
spired her with a great respect, for by a violinist she understood a man who played in Beer Gardens and City Squares
to amuse the people. Quite unabashed she asked him to play
to her, and when he looked down mockingly from his Olym-
pus at her, she promised that if he would she would sing;
she knew a great many pretty songs. "Well, first you must
give us a proof of your art," said Valerian. She did not wait
to be asked twice but rose from the table, placed her hands
lightly on her hips and sang with surprising expression and a
flexible, rich, alto voice the Swiss romantic song: *Son tre mesi
che fo il soldato.*

"Good heavens, she has music in her body!" cried Valerian,
applauding as she ended, and Josephine, whose heart fairly
sobbed at the lovely appearance and voice of the child, dared
neither to move nor to raise her eyes.

When Fanny repeated her request that he should play to
her, he answered her roughly and went out of the room. Josephine tried to make her understand who this man was and
what his playing meant; but she did not understand it and
only wondered about it. But from that time on she left him in

peace even when she was in his room and saw his violins lying in two costly lined cases, which he had not as yet touched. Satisfied with her restraint, he tried to make up to her by showing her the globes he had brought with him and the telescope that stood on a rotating metallic stand in the bay window with the great glass windows as its walls. If she wanted she might come up some evening to him and he would let her see the stars through the telescope.

Meanwhile Elizabeth was greatly troubled. It had been very difficult for her to hide Fanny's independent wanderings. It had all come about so suddenly; the girl had coaxed and persuaded her with flattery and caresses so that she was quite weaponless. The first day when they took their walk together she had escaped. Elizabeth sat restlessly on a bench by the road, and looked eagerly in the direction from which Fanny must come. At last she appeared, grateful and beaming. It gave her, as she was never tired of saying, the greatest rapture to go out alone on an unknown way, here and there, up hill and down dale, and she made Elizabeth promise not to tell the Frau Baroness; if she would do her this favour she would love her forever, she promised, and do anything for her. But what would happen if the Baroness knew it; she would probably forbid it and one would have to obey; the Frau Baroness was old and easily frightened, but she, Fanny was neither old nor frightened. Elizabeth could not withstand the honey-tongued pleading; she only made the condition that Fanny should come back at a stated time. They arranged a place where Elizabeth should wait for her, either in the morning or afternoon, whichever time was fixed for Josephine's drives. Then Fanny would press a kiss on the cheek of her bribed guardian and disappear. Elizabeth always trembled for her, although the neighbourhood was famed for its safety; sometimes she even followed her for a while secretly, but soon gave it up, for the child flew like a bird. As soon as the first hour was over she began to count the minutes, watched eagerly and reproached herself because she was deceiving her mistress, whose constantly growing affection for Fanny she noticed with joy. However, when Fanny came back safe and sound, delighted with all her little experiences and discoveries, Elizabeth's anxiety quickly disappeared and she laughed with the laughing child. The whole landscape was transformed by Fanny; the wood was more mysterious, the meadows were deeper, the sky was bluer and the clouds more fantastically grouped. And Elizabeth herself was transformed; her heart was no longer a desert.

Now, however, one evening Fanny came back in a mood that was different from that of the other days, as one could see at a glance. She was excited, but it was not the same sort of excitement; she chattered indeed, but there was something false about it, and after a while she became perfectly silent. Elizabeth enquired but the child shook her head. She asked more urgently, but Fanny evaded her questions and looked away with an embarrassed manner. She threatened to stop these lonely wanderings; but Fanny plead with folded hands. "Later," promised the child, "but to-day I can't tell you. To-day I can't tell a thing. But you must keep it to yourself and not spoil the splendid thing for me."

During supper she remained in the same state of excitement. Josephine did not notice it as her thoughts were with his Excellency Herbst. He had received his summons as a witness and was to leave the next morning, although the trial was not to be for ten days. He had not appeared at the table and Josephine spoke to Valerian of his pitiable condition. Fanny had no appetite; Elizabeth did not wait until the last course, but took her out of the room and put her to bed. Then she began to enquire more urgently than ever, relying upon the lovely twilight hour when the violence and excitement of children begins to soften, and Fanny told her. She told about the doll; almost feverish, her eyes shining and both little hands up against Elizabeth's cheek. How she came to the house; how they took her in; and the doll, and how the doll quite unexpectedly had walked and talked. Elizabeth listened in astonishment; but when she heard the name Ulrika Woytich she was frightened. And when she learned that the old lady had told the child to keep absolute silence about it at home, she was even more frightened. She knew that between

the Villa Woytich over in Ried and the Eckern estate there
was irreconcilable enmity, this she knew through casual utterances of the Baroness and common hearsay. Casimir had
only a few days ago spoken about it more in detail, and what
he said about the Woytich woman had certainly not sounded
very respectful.

Elizabeth was in no doubt as to her duty and was unwise
enough to speak of it before the child. The child pushed her
away and hid her face in the pillows. Elizabeth wanted to
correct her mistake and talked tenderly to her. But she
shook her head wildly and clenched her fists. Elizabeth said
possibly the Frau Baroness would give her permission to go
and see the doll. But Fanny asked what they were to do
if they told her and she did not give her permission? The
doll's old aunt had certainly said that she would not be allowed to come if she told; then what was she to do? She
would get up and run away through the night and the mist,
she would run away.

The child showed a violence of nature that Elizabeth had
not dreamed she was capable of. Her lips trembled, she was
all aglow, will and desire shone in her beautiful face. That
doll seemed to her the goal of all human striving; all the
magic of life for her lay in that talking doll. To quiet her
Elizabeth promised to keep silent at least to-day and to-
morrow. Fanny embraced her stormily and made her promise
again and again; at last she was content, and Elizabeth sat on
the side of her bed until she had fallen asleep. She sat there
wondering how to get out of the net. She vaguely felt the
danger rather than knew it, but the child's pleading and the
memory of it, the sweet sound in her ear, the happiness of
making this elf-like creature happy kept her still in a state of
uncertainty, so that she involved herself worse than ever in
guilt. The next morning she succeeded in keeping Fanny
back; she read fairy tales to her, played ball with her, and
took her in the woods to the place where the wild strawberries
grew; in the afternoon the weather was unsettled, and she
could hope silently that with the passing of time the picture
would fade and the wild wish become fainter. But here she

deceived herself, for the next morning as the sun shone, Fanny demanded as soon as they went out that they should take the road toward Ried. What Elizabeth wanted to arrange was that Fanny would let her get into the immediate neighbourhood of Villa Woytich. She said she would wait for her in the woods, but had to promise very solemnly that she would not let herself be seen.

So it happened, and the third day likewise, and in the course of the next ten days it happened four times. And Elizabeth kept up the deception, although it depressed her. She felt that she was not acting in the interests of her mistress. And she found also, from time to time, a change in Fanny that made her very thoughtful. The fever of excitement was, indeed, not the same, it was even greater, so that her face and hands flamed and the eyes shone in their blue depths, but it was not the same joyousness as at the beginning. It seemed to weigh upon the child. Often she walked along the way home perfectly dumb, by Elizabeth's side, which disturbed her as the sudden stopping of a clock might disturb a man, accustomed to its faithful ticking; and when Fanny answered Elizabeth's questions her answers sounded dull and confused. Then Josephine noticed the thoughtfulness and trouble and spoke about it to Elizabeth, who let it pass with a few embarrassed evasions. Finally, driven into the corner, she began to speak seriously to Fanny about it.

First, Fanny thought it over; for a long time she looked thoughtfully in front of her, she really seemed not to know what Elizabeth meant, seemed not to know that she herself had changed since she went to the Villa Woytich. Elizabeth was patient and loving with her; and then Fanny, with a light shiver of her shoulders, said: "To tell the truth I am afraid of Aunt Ulrika."

For the present that was all. "Aunt Ulrika," the title, did not please Elizabeth; a complete stranger. She let it pass, however, and only asked gently the reason for it. But Fanny either could not or would not tell, and when Elizabeth, seizing both her hands, said to her that the simplest thing would be to stop the visits, Fanny shook her head and replied with strange determination that she could not, she had to go there, it was too thrilling when the doll walked and bowed and spoke English words.

But she was not telling the whole truth. It was just as exciting to her, as she expressed it, to see the old lady, and sometimes the interest in the doll dropped into the background as against her attraction for this person who filled her both with fear and restless curiosity. She was always received by Ulrika Woytich like an important guest and greeted with all sorts of fine titles. Then when the doll had played her part, Fräulein Woytich would have Fanny sit down beside her and would tell her stories. And she would laugh aloud and make jests and ask for Fanny's father and mother and enquire most searchingly about the Frau Baroness; what she did and said and what kind of people were at Eckern, and what kind of food they had on the table. If Fanny hesitated with an answer or only partly answered she grew angry and muttered; then again she would pat her on the cheek and hair and say ten times, one after the other: "You poor child." But the worst of it all was, and she would not have confessed this to Elizabeth for anything, that she always began to speak of the Baroness in contemptuous terms and made harmful allusions to her. Fanny would sit motionless and stare at her, but Fräulein Ulrika was not in the least disturbed by her horror and went on saying worse and worse things. This confused Fanny unspeakably and saddened her. Ever since she had first seen the Baroness she had considered her the person most to be honoured in the whole world, high above all other people so that not even her shadow might be touched by anything unworthy; so that to be treasured and loved by her was to be noble oneself. Now the light that had lit up everything for her was covered. She could not understand why. It was very painful. What was it the Baroness had done? Why was it that one should love her, if she was as bad as the old woman said? And the power of this old woman: how she grabbed one and stared at one and commanded, so that one had to come back to her. And she went again and would have gone again even if the doll had not been there. But why?

It was as if she were poisoned. One evening, as she lay with·a troubled heart in her bed and Elizabeth was trying to persuade her and plead with her, words escaped her that fairly frightened Elizabeth. She had long understood that the little tender creature had become subject to a dangerous influence, but what she now became aware of, although in the vaguest outline, opened her eyes to the depth of the injury. In anxiety and repentance she made the determination which perhaps was now too late. When Fanny was asleep she went across the floor and knocked at the Baroness's door. Josephine was sitting by the open balcony looking into the blue-lighted night. The lamp burned in the middle of the room. Elizabeth asked to be heard about a difficulty that was very pressing and probably had come about through her own fault. Josephine turned to her, frightened and surprised. Not specially gifted in explaining things clearly Elizabeth's sentences became confused and she stammered rather than spoke. But Josephine understood at once. The unhappy creature was not near the end of her story when Josephine rose with a suppressed groan. She stood before Elizabeth looking frightfully pale. "Go on, go on," she said and leaned against her arm-chair. Elizabeth had never seen her so overcome. With a trembling voice she brought her story to an end.

A long silence followed. Josephine did not move. The pallor made her face look almost corpse-like. At last she said: "You have done a great wrong, Elizabeth, a great wrong, both to me and to the child. Only your utter ignorance can lessen the guilt. Leave me alone now, I want to think what can be done."

Elizabeth burst into tears, kissed her mistress's hand and went out. And Josephine was alone.

There it was again, the horror. This was the fulfilment of her life-long terror. It was repetition and constant return. This was what one had to expect from fate, as soon as one dared to breathe freely, in the very first bloom of a new hope, the thundering No of destiny; one could never escape that Argus eye and that threatening call and if one seemed to see the smallest pathway out of the gloom, there was the mischief maker again, the destroyer of all dreams.

How should one escape? The first thing that Josephine thought of was to leave. But against that stood her duties as hostess and friend and her horror of the outside world. The next thing was to send the child away. But where? To whom could she trust her? And how could she make her understand so that the ruling should not seem like punishment? Hardly had she made herself at home in her nest, the first real home of her orphaned existence, and now she was to be thrown out again? She was innocent; she had only submitted to the enticements of the Rat-Catcher * as a whole army of the bewitched had done before.

If there were only some one whose advice she could ask, some one wise and merciful, who could measure and understand the fear she felt of this infernal creature, the antagonist God had set before her. But each had his burden to bear, and all were too reasonable or too cold to understand this phantom of destiny, though she raged over the hills at night with trumpet blasts. She was reaching out greedy hands for Fanny; but in the tormenting intensity, born of her new feeling of love, almost like a higher kind of jealousy, Josephine was aware of passionate, greedy cunning and sinfulness; here again was repetition and return, a memory of the laws of blood, a knocking at the doors of fate. What could be more important than to save Fanny from the reach of this devil. Josephine did not suffer for a moment the thought of giving up the child. She knew she could no longer do that.

It happened that she went at night to Fanny's bedside and blew out the candle that she brought with her. She did not want to turn on the electric light, and even the candle seemed superfluous for the full moon stood in the sky and lit up the whole room. She sat a long time on a chair by the bed lost in contemplation of the sleeping girl. She thought she

---

* A famous legendary figure who bewitches people and animals; the Pied Piper of Hamelin is an example.—Translator's Note.

had never seen anything quite so beautiful. The face was as pure and peaceful as nature outside. Her soul was like a stream flowing noiselessly and powerfully, in a supernatural sphere, drawing into its depths this unstained figure of life. Suddenly the child awoke, just as Josephine had wished; and like most young people when their sleep is broken naturally, she awoke without the slightest confusion and as she saw her protectress sitting beside her so unexpectedly in the bright moonlight, she smiled, astonished. And then Josephine found words that she would never have found by day; she was master of a profound eloquence; motherly care mixed with reflective warnings; there was no reproach, no demand for explanations, and all the ugly and painful part remained hidden.

She won the child entirely and gained her complete confidence, and Josephine herself grew in power and assurance. The few questions she asked were answered without any hesitation. And again the doll came up like a ghostly symbol, binding together in a mysterious way early youth and late age. Evelyn was the name of the doll; so Fräulein Woytich had said, and she wore a wide hoop-skirt of pale green silk with edging and on her head a lace cap and round her throat several rows of little pearls, and she had rings on her fingers and morocco shoes with green silk stockings.

The description was most enthusiastic.

Then Josephine demanded of Fanny that never again, under any circumstances, led away by any promises, should she go into Fräulein Woytich's house. Fanny's eyes grew big and a veil of trouble fell over her face. But she laid her tiny hand in Josephine's and her voice was very solemn as she promised. She understood from what she had heard, that this was no grown person's caprice but that it really meant something to the Baroness for her to obey.

"I know that it is hard for you," said Josephine, "and that you may understand that I prize your obedience I will also try to do something difficult for you. I will see if I can buy the doll for you. I will try to buy it from Fräulein Woytich."

"Oh, Frau Baroness, you are too good!" Fanny called out, pressing both hands to her heart and turning pale with joy and surprise. "No one was ever so good to me before."

Josephine smiled. "Of course we don't know yet whether we shall succeed. It is even quite improbable," said she.

"That is nothing," said Fanny; "it is that you wanted to do it! That you wanted to!"

"Now go to sleep again, my little heart," said Josephine, kissing the child's forehead. "Sleep well."

The next morning Josephine sent for Elizabeth and said: "I am not going to scold you, Elizabeth, for the mistake you have made. Let it be forgiven and forgotten. But I have a very delicate task for you, and if you carry it through cleverly, you will earn praise."

"I hope the Frau Baroness does not doubt that I would go through fire for her," Elizabeth hastened to assure her. Fanny had already told her of the last night's conversation, and she was excited and eager to make amends.

"I won't give you as hard a test as that," Josephine went on. "Let each man do as well as he can what is demanded of him; that is sufficient. Go to Fräulein Woytich's. Let it appear as if in passing you wanted to make a casual visit. Say you have heard of the treasures in her house and gradually lead the subject to the doll and then find out very cautiously if it can be bought. Don't let the price count at all. Don't mention my name. Don't let her find out that you have been sent. You are simply a lady interested in antiques. Of course Fräulein Woytich will see through it and know who and what is behind it. But you must deny it and be indignant at the suspicion that you do not come on your own account. Your chief object must be to arouse the old lady's love of money. Pay no attention to anything she tells you and say it does not concern you. She will probably tell you dreadful things but do not dispute them. Do you understand? You know, don't you, what it is all about?"

"Certainly, Frau Baroness, I understand perfectly and will act exactly according to your directions," Elizabeth replied, proud of her mission and convinced of success.

It was eleven o'clock when she started out; at half-past twelve she was back again in a most perturbed frame of mind. At the moment Josephine was consulting with a tenant about some meadow lands. Elizabeth could hardly wait until he had gone. Then, breathlessly, her face flushed, she told indignantly what had happened.

Fräulein Woytich had received her amiably, though somewhat distrustfully, and had allowed her to talk quietly for a time while she listened. Suddenly her glance became fixed upon Elizabeth and she asked directly: "So the little tattle-tale talked out of school; did she?" Elizabeth pretended to be astonished but the old lady, now that she had made her spring, went on: "Is she coming here or isn't she, the false little toad? That is what I want to know and nothing else. Have they forbidden her to come to poor old Ulrika Woytich or not?" Elizabeth, according to directions, pretended not to understand. Then Fräulein Woytich laughed an evil laugh and cried out that they need not take her for a fool or believe that she crept around on liquid glue; if others were already snoring in their feather beds, she was standing firm in her shoes; they need not make any pretences to her, nor would she let herself in for any such bargaining, she was no Jew haggler and she did not keep a rubbish shop. She was not like the nobility, who gathered everything together that came under their hands; she was always content with what she had, and they would never get the best of her by juggling. Let them keep guard over the child and she would keep guard of the doll, and the Frau Baroness would have to make the best of it; but they would never get anything out of her, now or ever, not for all the Melander money. She went on in this way for a while, becoming more and more excited, talking now of Fanny and now of the doll, calling Fanny a tricky little villain and threatening to burn up the doll, "the sweet Evelyn," as she mockingly called her; she was wild with anger; she crowed angrily and then broke into strange expressions of tenderness, as if she wanted to conjure the child, as if she had suffered the bitterest wrongs from Fanny and was complaining of her. Then she planted herself directly in front of Elizabeth, looked at her with her violet eyes sharply (Elizabeth insisted earnestly that she had violet eyes), and asked if it was definitely, irrevocably settled that Fanny could not visit her any more. Elizabeth, who had now given up all attempt at pretending, as she saw there was no use in it, said "yes." Then Fräulein Woytich, suddenly self-possessed, sent her greetings to the Frau Baroness and a message that she might have the doll; yes, she might have the dead Evelyn she said, grinning at Elizabeth's surprised movement, but only in exchange for the living Fanny; let them tell that to the Frau Baroness from her former friend and obedient servant. At these words Elizabeth left in silent indignation.

Josephine shrugged her shoulders in resignation. "That is all a sad farce and theatricality," she said. "I thank you, Elizabeth; you have done all that could be done."

The next afternoon, a few minutes after five o'clock, Josephine's maid came to her room where she was resting on the sofa, and said timidly: "There is a lady down in the conservatory who wishes to speak to the Baroness."

"Who is it? Did she give her name?" Josephine asked, full of presentiments.

"Yes, she did; Fräulein Woytich."

It fell upon Josephine like a blow. She needed all her self-control to keep her countenance before the maid. She answered in a hardly audible voice: "I am not at home. I beg that any business, if there is any, should be communicated to me in writing. But first of all go to Fräulein Schönholz and tell her she must not leave the room with Fanny. Don't stop to wonder; there are good reasons."

When the maid left the room she pressed her hand against her breast, but her hand involuntarily doubled up into a fist and a purple flush covered her forehead and cheeks.

"God protect and give me strength," she murmured.

CHAPTER XXX

ALL SORTS OF LETTERS AND WRITINGS

MEANWHILE Ulrika Woytich had made herself comfortable in a big arm-chair in the conservatory, not without some groaning, for the long walk through the hot sun had tired her. First she walked all around the house but finding none of the servants, had begun a loud fussing and fuming. This awakened the distrust of the watch dog, who rushed out of the stables, a handsome brownish black Dobermann,* and began to bark at her. Naturally this roused her wrath, and she fought with the dog and abused him until the maid reappeared and called the dog off. In the meantime Ulrika had gone into the open drawing room and when the maid followed her she said: "My pretty child, first of all bring me a glass of water and some bread and butter; if you don't you will have a corpse on your hands."

"Whom am I to announce?" the maid asked stiffly, pretending not to have heard the extraordinary order.

"First go and get what I ordered," Ulrika hissed, "and then go to the Frau Baroness and tell her Fräulein Woytich is here."

The intimidated maid disappeared and in a few moments a second maid appeared with a tray, a glass of water and a bit of pastry. At the same moment the first maid reappeared with Josephine's message. It did not seem to upset Ulrika at all. She drank the glass of water at a gulp, nibbled at the pastry with all the pleasure of a person that had not tasted it for years. She was dressed in an old mantilla, formerly used for state occasions, covered with rusty spangles and other superfluous ornaments, showing her complete scorn of the fashions. On her head she wore a strange mongrel

* A kind of German pointer.—Translator's note.

362

affair made of steel thread covered with various coloured trimmings and metal beads. The maid stood in front of her and looked at her unpleasantly. Ulrika had given no answer to the message, evidently wanting to gain time. Then loud steps were heard, a shadow fell across the threshold, and Valerian entered in his white linen costume, slender, deliberate, a cigarette between his lips. He was passing through, as it was the quickest way to his own rooms, but stopped short when he saw the strange guest and bowed politely. Ulrika rose with every manifestation of reverence and joy. "Herr de Groot, if I do not mistake," she said, stepping up to him. He bowed again not less polite and cool. The maid stood hesitating and Ulrika swamped de Groot in a flood of words, to which he listened without moving; of course she had heard of the presence of the celebrated man at Eckern; the event had made a sensation in the whole neighbourhood; she herself was a glowing devotee of music, oh, a bred-in-the-bone fool over it, and in the course of her long life she had become acquainted with all the virtuosi of the piano, the violin, the orchestra, and even the conductors and she herself considered it the greatest honour to greet this famous artist face to face.

"With whom am I sharing this advantage?" Valerian asked icily.

She gave her name, and she concluded that he recognised it from a quick frown and jerk of his head. But he recovered himself with a low bow. He asked her to sit down and sat down himself opposite her, somewhat at a loss to know what to do. The conversation which began now was entirely one-sided; de Groot contented himself with nodding approval or disapproval but after a while he found himself thoroughly amused and laughed aloud. With quick skill she had touched upon this subject and that, dropping them again until she found ground of common interest, mentioned a name that he knew well, went on to a second and a third and in a short time she had flung out that great social net from which no one can escape who has lived in the outer world. She needed only to freshen up her memory, her knowledge of relationships, friendships, connections, and so forth. A malicious remark here, a naughty aside there, now a little double meaning, then a deliberate coarseness, and her tasty ragout was ready. She was in her element; she had forgotten nothing. To be sure, it was only the left-overs of day before yesterday but they served their purpose still and she was used to dusty things. She watched his eyes and saw just how far she dared to go, where the danger line lay, and she rattled skeletons instead of using rods upon living people, turned away at just the right moment and was doubly witty, hypocritical, and apparently candid.

Despite his amusement Valerian felt very uncomfortable in the situation. He looked at the slovenly figure, the faded face, the impossible costume, the play of expression with its lightning flashes of wit, scurrility, and slyness on the surface, and an unnamable something of unrest and fury beneath; the rattling teeth and the violent gestures; she was like a hobgoblin, ugly, comic, and frightful all at once. Suddenly the figure from the distant past arose before him; it had been erased long ago, but now he saw her, and strangely enough not as she then was, but old and rotten and grotesque; it was on the tip of his tongue to say: "Do you remember the little boy in the Dorothea Street, Ulrika Woytich?" and then to enjoy her embarrassment. But it seemed unworthy of him and he let it pass; but he began to feel more and more violent physical disgust that spread to his finger tips and his toes.

He was asking himself what had brought her here and whom she was waiting for. It surprised him that she should sit there so long and that Josephine did not come. But when he tried to imagine Josephine coming in and talking to her he was even more astonished. Still he paid her compliments on her lively sense of fact, as he expressed it, and her youthful fire. She sighed and replied that she was a bit of a Bengal light left over; unfortunately people no longer used them. He assured her that she could hold her own with a dozen men in their prime. She giggled frivolously and said there had been a time when she could hold her own bravely with a dozen. He said she was none the worse for wear and offered her a cigarette. She replied, sighing as she lighted her cigarette, that she had had her own troubles. "But I hope," he comforted her impudently, "you have not failed to fill the larder."

"I did pretty well," she answered, crossing one leg over the other. "What more could one ask, honoured Master," she added with an impudent grin, *"ce que vient de la flute, s'en retourne au tambour."*

Then they both laughed and Valerian's horror and disgust grew unbearable, while Ulrika went into details about her miserable fate, buried alive as she was in a neighbourhood where all the cats said good-night to each other and amongst people who were too bad even for the devil. Tricksters, drunkards, worthless idlers; no peasant who could plough his field properly, no shopkeeper who would sell his wares for less than five hundred per cent more than their value; no craftsman who could do his work or knew good materials when he saw them; if they could not plunder you they did not want to work at all; all the working people spent their money in taverns; and the ruination began with the children and the old people followed them shamefully into the gutter; in short, it was the horror of the Apocalypse.

Valerian had lost patience and rose. Ulrika rose too and said casually, as if it were not the real object of her coming and waiting: "Now I should like to say good-day to my little Fanny, as the Baroness is not gracious enough to receive me. Perhaps, dear Master, you will be so kind as to send the child to me for a moment, just for a moment." Valerian said good-bye ceremoniously. He met Elizabeth in the hall and gave her Ulrika's message. Elizabeth opened her eyes wide with fright and rushed to Josephine. Josephine smiled a little scornful smile as answer and gave the maid orders to say to Fräulein Woytich that Fanny had gone out with the Frau Baroness and then to show her the door politely. Ulrika stared the messenger in the face and said, raging: "I hope you will choke over that lie, you little cat"; then she grabbed up her stick and tottered off. She turned round on the garden path and called back: "You will hear from me yet, depend upon it."

She turned in the direction of Riednau. She did not want to go home; she did not know why. As she walked along she muttered constantly to herself. She walked first on the left and then on the right side of the path so that seen from a distance she gave the impression of a drunken person. Once she stood still and yelled an Italian oath out into the woods. Why Italian it was not quite clear. An old peasant greeted her and she did not reply. She lost her handkerchief, a coarse blue calico rag and did not notice it. She stumbled over a root but never once interrupted her muttering.

In Riednau she went into the Inn, sat down in the empty, damp-smelling room in a corner and ordered corn whiskey and letter paper. "Do you expect me to write with my fingers, you sloven?" she snapped at the peasant girl who brought her the paper without pen and ink.

She wrote in her big straggling handwriting: "To the High-born Baroness Melander. In case that sweet little angel Fanny should come into her proper title and her fortune—" She stopped, tore up the paper and began on a new sheet: "To the High-born Baroness von Melander. No harm ever came to that sweet little angel Fanny in my house, nor was she subjected to any danger there other than that of a desirable explanation of her rights, which—" Once more she tore up the paper, bit her lips, chewed the pen holder, screamed for another glass of brandy and after reflecting began a third time: "High-born Baroness! That sweet little angel Fanny came of her own free will to my house. Nothing was done there to harm her but, on the contrary, everything to give her pleasure. To rob this extraordinary child of her innocent pleasure in the doll, I consider just as cruel as robbing her of certain other things for which it would be very easy to demand an accounting. The law still appoints guardians and we still have orphans' courts. As I have no infectious disease, nor is my modest home a vicious place, I demand your consent that Fanny Heinroth, rightly named Fanny Melander, shall be allowed to come again to her motherly and loving friend, and I call your attention to my former faithful services to you ——— which in this ungrateful world seem to have been in vain—and I sign myself with respectful humility, Ulrika Woytich."

This seemed satisfactory. She sealed the letter, paid her bill and started out. The host, hostess, errand boy, and waitress all stared after her. On the village street she hailed a boy and bade him carry the letter to Eckern, for which she gave him an unrecognisably crumpled bank note.

It was evening. She should have been at home long ago. Again she went in another direction. It was a side pathway to Eckern. She was very tired but she was impelled to follow this path. What did she want? She did not herself know. A dull anger raged in her that drove her along the road to Eckern. She imagined that she might see Fanny if she could only get near to the Eckern estate. Good; but what could she gain from seeing Fanny? She did not know. Only a dull driving impulse pushed her.

When she reached the top of the hill, for she had to cross two, she realised that a storm was brewing. Blue-black clouds rolled up heavy and threatening from the west, surrounded by dark scarlet and above broken by gold-red lightnings. The bushes rustled, the pine trees crashed, and the wind whizzed by as if it were rising from a hot shaft. Ulrika stumbled, she looked around and went on. After a quarter of an hour she saw the Eckern house lights shining through the bushes. The thunder muttered. Only some of the windows were lighted. Ulrika approached. Heavy drops were falling. She sought shelter under the broad spreading linden tree. Her figure was indistinguishable in the darkness.

Behind which window was Fanny? What was Fanny doing and who was with her? Was she afraid of the storm? Was she thinking of the old Ulrika? Why should she think of the old Ulrika? What was an old woman to her white-blossoming youth, her joyous laugh, her merry eyes? A nothing, a nothing, blown across the garden of her thoughts. Ah, but you imp, did you not fall on the old woman's neck and kiss her? Kiss this old, leather, wrinkled cheek? Was that all pretence? And the pleading chatter of the little voice with Aunt Ulrika here, and Aunt Ulrika there, and the little folded hands

and the sweet upturned eyes, all pretence? Such a thing could
not be, it could not be, one can't believe it, come down and
tell me so to my face, you elf, you wild little chatterbox, you
naughty little kid—

She screamed out the last words into the thunder. It was
raining torrents and she was wet through to her skin, the mantilla, the hat, skirt, stockings, even her chemise, everything
was wet. She looked up at the windows, covering her eyes
when the lightning flashed, and shuddered at the thunder claps
that fell like blows on a gigantic threshing floor, and she
trembled with the wet and with the immeasurable hatred of all
the people in this house except the one little creature for
whom she was to save the millions of the Melander family—
she thought this and believed herself appointed to the task.

She thought of nothing else, or if she did, she hid it in insane anxiety. A shudder went through her to her very roots
and to the upper nerves of her brain, and in her midst something burst as a vessel bursts over the fire, but she would not
understand it. An outlived life drained to the very dregs,
what was there left to her but the scattered fragments; what
was to come? The blind cannot see again, no fruit can grow
out of a stone, and yet a picture of exquisite loveliness,
strange unworldliness, mocked her empty days.

At last in the storm and the black night torn by vivid
lightning, she took her homeward way. Crescence met her
with a lantern on the crest of Riednau. She crossed herself
at the sight of her mistress and threw over her the water-
proof coat that she had brought. It was half-past ten. Anastasia stood wailing at the door. Ulrika answered no questions.
She stamped up into·her bedroom, took off her dripping garments and reappeared shortly in a grey dressing gown in the
living room. Frightfully hungry, she swallowed her warmed-
up supper. As she sat there dumb, Anastasia withdrew offended. "Creep into your own nest," Ulrika growled at Crescence and when she was alone she sat down at her writing table.

On a quarto sheet she wrote the following words: "In case
of my decease, I leave to Fanny Heinroth, rightly named Me-

lander, my entire fortune, together with all my furniture, my house in Riednau on the Ried, upon two conditions: First, that she be reinstated into all her natural rights by her grandmother, the Baroness Josephine von Melander, and that she be not prevented, but on the contrary encouraged, to visit me as often as I desire her companionship. Written in Ried, being of sound mind, on the twenty-seventh day of June, 1921."

This document she intended to send the next day to Eckern. Then they would not hold out any longer, then they would come at her call. They could not turn away from such a bait as that. They would come and thank her respectfully and bring the lovely Fanny with ready willingness. And while she was still looking down at the writing her eyelids dropped from exhaustion and she fell asleep. But as luck would have it, Anastasia, who was disturbed, and moreover had news to give her, came back into the room and seeing her sister asleep at her desk she crept up cautiously. She saw the written sheet and bent down and read it over Ulrika's shoulder; she read it, and a scream sounded through the room. "So, it is thus," stammered Anastasia, and pointed with a convulsive motion to the sheet; "that is the thanks I get. That is what you do to your nearest blood relations, you secretive creature; it is for that I sit here in prison and waste my life and go half hungry; it is for that poor Philip gives his services; that is our thanks. That is our reward."

"Rot," said Ulrika crossly, "don't get so excited; that is only a mouse-trap. Can't you smell the bacon?" The reference to Philip made her uncomfortable and her uneasy conscience made her yielding.

But Anastasia was not to be quieted. Standing straight in a real prima-donna pose, for all the Woytichs were dramatic when they were angry, she accused Ulrika of her sins, all the sins that she had committed against her and still committed, the scarcity of food, the unheated or ill-heated rooms in autumn and winter, the lack of any social intercourse, the familiarity with the stupid and common maid, and all these accusations flowed out bitterly while Ulrika listened, bored. "If you had

only given me enough money for travelling I would have gone
to brother Franz," Anastasia ended, weeping; "I might have
nursed him and made death easier."

"People don't die any easier because you are there, don't
imagine it," was the reply; "but perhaps you wanted to inherit something there? But there was not anything. Three
pairs of socks and a dozen ribbons that his orders had been
sewed on. He had pawned the medallions themselves long
since. And his Casanova, which he had in all the various editions, was there."

"It is like you, in the cruelty of your heart, to make little of
your own brother," said Anastasia.

"Rubbish," muttered Ulrika; "get down off your perch.
Why declaim, when there is no one to hear you?"

"Since I am talking of Philip," said Anastasia, "he wrote
me to-day. He says he can not come to us this month. Business is tying him down. Business isn't going very well anyhow. There is a panic on the Exchange. Some firms are
totally ruined. I am not very pleased with the letter. It
sounds so confused, but he sends you greetings."

Ulrika followed her sister slowly and put her hand on her
shoulder. "What is the matter?" she asked with a searching
look. "Since when is he writing to you and not to me?"

"Well, I guess he can write to me sometimes," Anastasia
answered.

Ulrika demanded the letter. Anastasia drew it out of her
pocket and gave it to her. Ulrika read it again and again,
gave it back, stroked her forehead which had suddenly become
moist.

"Do you think anything has happened?" she brought out.
"Do you think there is any danger? Tell me openly without
any reservations—"

"You can rely upon Philip as you can upon yourself," said
Anastasia with the pride of a mother, who knew nothing of her
son except that he was her son.

Serious and thoughtful, Ulrika went to bed with a heavy
heart. She was tired and was afraid to go to sleep. She
was shattered in her innermost being and brooded over the

news from the Exchange. A devouring heat shook her and then again she froze to the very marrow of her bones. An angelic little face seemed turned toward her, and she trembled for her possessions and her wealth. She reached out for a soaring figure, but her greedy hands clasped only bank notes. Full of horror she weighed the possibility of losing her money, her idolised money, and a little, gentle voice mocked her and enticed her.

It was dark, she grasped her head with both hands and spoke aloud, terrified: "Have you lost your mind, Ulrika Woytich?"

CHAPTER XXXI

OBEDIENCE

THE same day Excellency Herbst and Josephine had exchanged telegrams. The trial had ended with an acquittal for Marie Helen, while Rutowsky was sentenced to eight years in prison. The unexpected verdict was attributed to the fact that Marie Helen had given up her stubborn denial and had flung an accusation against her tempter and destroyer, such as had never been heard in the court-room before.

Josephine heard the fact at once. After the first telegram a second came, in which his Excellency Herbst announced that he would start with Marie Helen at once. For this event, which he had weighed as the last, almost impossible chance he had arranged with the Protestant pastor of the Baths with whom he had long been friendly. The pastor had declared himself ready to offer an asylum in his house to the unfortunate girl where she might gather her forces in absolute quiet for her new life amongst men; for it was not advisable to expose her to the eyes of the curious, who were not lacking even in Eckern; she did not wish even to see Josephine, while the shelter of the pastor, it appeared, would have a softening effect upon her in every way. He was an unusual man, a naturalist and philosopher as well as a spiritual leader. The suggestion had originally come from Josephine; at that time his Excellency had only listened to it with an incredulous shake of his head, but had afterwards resolved to speak to the pastor about it.

The pastor and Josephine both went that evening to the station; the storm raged with all possible violence when his Excellency Herbst and Marie Helen arrived. Very little was said. The heavily veiled young girl was taken by the pastor to a carriage outside, in which Josephine and his Excellency

also took seats. At the door of the rectory they were awaited
by the pastor's wife. As Marie Helen got out she turned
faint and fell upon her knees on the steps. She got up immediately, refused all help and followed the pastor's wife to her
room. Josephine invited the pastor to accompany them to the
Eckern manor for a cup of tea, saying the carriage would then
bring him back again. He bowed silently and went on with
them.

The table was set in the library. The window was open
and the leaves rustled in the rain, a smell of wet plants blew
in, the lightning flashed still, and the thunder died away in
the distance. Elizabeth was pouring out tea, but she left at
a slight sign from Josephine. His Excellency Herbst was
leaning his small, thin face upon his arm; after a heavy silence
that followed the few necessary words with which they met
each other, he said with a long sigh: "I will tell you how it
all was. I hope that I am in a condition to do it. It is better
for me to do it to-day, for who knows, to-morrow it may all
be less vivid, or I may not be able to force myself to it. It
is better too that you should learn it from me than from the
misrepresentations you will hear elsewhere. Oh, God in
heaven, what an hour that was!"

He folded his hands and his eyes were full of terror, a repetition of the terror he had lived through in that hour. He was
about to begin, when the door opened and Valerian came in.
He started and asked politely if he were disturbing them.
Josephine pointed him to a chair and he obeyed, strangely
shaken. His Excellency Herbst let a few moments pass; the
new arrival, although he honoured and liked him, embarrassed
him at first.

"The room was full to bursting in spite of the broiling
summer heat," he began in his deep restrained voice, "all the
halls and even the corridors and staircases were crowded with
people, elbow to elbow. There were a good many suspicious-
looking faces; especially upon the witness bench there was a
gallery of real gallows physiognomies; people to whom this
place meant nothing at all, and who laughed when they were
reminded of the dignity of the court-room, and this the presid-

ing judge was obliged to do more than once. Rutowsky's hearing brought out nothing new. He denied all his former crimes. The crime for which he stood before the jury he denied also. At every accusation he referred, shrugging his shoulders, to the testimony of Marie Helen. I could hardly sit through it. I can only say that never before had I seen such a creature. Try to imagine something half Apache and half reprobate. There was something indescribably cold and smooth about him, something indescribably low and yet powerful. His red-brown hair was oiled and brushed back smooth; his forehead was very narrow and high with two large knobs of intelligence over the eyebrows; he wore tortoise-shell spectacles that made him look like a hoot-owl; his face was dried-up and shrunken like a mask, and yet strangely gay, with a self-sufficient little smile around the lips; his whole appearance was very striking, rather like a comedian's; and every time he answered a question he would whisk a speck of dust off the arm of his coat and look out of the window as if he were bored. Whenever they spoke of Marie Helen, he would look in her direction and rub his chin, smiling. That was the most horrible thing he did, that rubbing of his chin. Well, I won't linger over this. Marie Helen was called. She stepped up to the bar, her head dropped low. She gave her name, the date of her birth, named her father and mother; you can imagine how I felt then. The room had become absolutely still. She was asked if she confessed herself guilty. She reflected; she raised her head; she looked all around the room; her glance fell upon me; I could not even guess what was going on in her mind; she turned pale and swayed; I stood up, I don't know now why I did it but I had to; she stretched out her arms to me; the judge repeated his question; she answered with a clear, loud, 'yes.' A shudder went through the courtroom. Requested to give an account of what had happened she did it. There were hardly more than ten sentences. Asked about the mysterious nature of her relation to Rutowsky, she replied that she would tell about it, but only face to face with him. She was confronted by the accused. He noticed at once the changed situation and stared at her, raging and pale.

His look was trying to overpower her, and thus they struggled opposite each other for a time, while the silence in the room was almost breathless. Then she began to speak. It is difficult to repeat it. I do not think any one could do it. Try to imagine a cry out of the darkest depths of nature, the monstrous attempt of a corrupted and debased creature trying to win her soul again, before herself and humanity; to tell the madness of the unexplained mystery, as to how, step by step, she had been dragged down. The criminal was one of those moral incendiaries with whom the world seethes to-day, endowed, moreover, with eloquence and wide experience. She, with all her senses and her blood at a point of crisis, sliding with all the rest of us down the steep precipice, saw him falling and grasped at him to save him. She had given herself to a desperate man, and was herself already desperate. She had nothing to hold by; she confessed that; everything about her was decay and waste and filth, wherever she went and wherever she looked; and she had experienced what the whole youth of this generation has, the frightful downfall of the gods. Why should we talk about that? She held out her hand to this man, because he had the damned courage of the fall, because he had stamped into bits her father and mother and upbringing, her home, her friends, her God, and the Divine Power, and the whole body of society; and because this seemed possible, and because there was no hope anywhere, and because self-destruction seemed only a hastening of the end, and crime an act of vengeance, she gloried in it. We know all about that. We have lived through it and suffered. She believed the whole world as lost as she was. She was too innocent and too pure, at bottom, to look upon the darkness which had come over her life as other than evidence of the general explosion. She believed too much and that was why she fell so deep. She had loved the world and mankind too much, and that was why she tore herself so cruelly free from them. This is the fate of those who have loved and believed to-day. Kingdoms and nations cannot be destroyed without cutting away all the props. We have a great deal on our consciences that we have looked at silently and in other days, without remonstrance. How

false were all our thoughts, how deceitful our easy consola-
tions, how short-sighted our look into the future. But perhaps all this does not belong here. I cannot even dimly hint
how Marie Helen's tormented and yet wonderfully released
words, gripped the people, without her knowing it, and how
the gentlemen of the jury felt it, and the judge, and the spec-
tators, and the lawyers, and pleaders; a human being stood
up there, struggling for her own soul, not only against her
accusers but against them all there, and against. all humanity outside, and against me, for I was perhaps the most guilty
because the blindest. And when they asked her why she had
denied and kept silence heretofore, she cried out: 'Because I
have lain in his arms!' and when the judge asked her how she
could ever bring herself, even at his command, to go out into
the streets, she cried out again: 'Because evil was my good, and
because, as his beloved, I could find nothing wickeder to do!'
And then before any one could prevent it, she had flung herself on his neck as if she wished to drag him away into some
other existence, with all her power and all her pain, where her
deception and her infatuation should be justified; he, however,
pushed her back till she reeled, and at the same moment people
stood up from among the witnesses, surrounded the girl, strode
up to the jury's table, their fists closed, and from the benches
in the room, where apparently comrades of Rutowsky's were,
came calls and wild threats; it was a devil's uproar, and I
knew where they were steering. There is no tender-hearted-
ness left in the world, there is not a heart that can be touched
anywhere, that is it. Then the room was cleared; the verdict,
'Not Guilty,' was given, and with difficulty and the help of the
police I managed to get Marie Helen home, and all night she
lay in a sort of cataleptic state. The next morning, however, I was able to talk to her, and she consented to whatever
I suggested. And now we must spare her, spare her."

The old man covered his eyes with his hand and was silent.

After a long pause the pastor spoke: "I believe that in the
name of us all, I may tell our friend with what reverence we
have received his trustful confidence, and that we know how

to honour the great-hearted way in which he has accepted his fate. Certainly he has given me the feeling of how frightful our destiny is. I have spent thirty-one years here in my office, happily and willingly. But the way things have gone outside is enough to tear one's heart out, that is true. It often reminds me of the prophet's curse of the great whore of Babylon. Has not the whole world become a Babylon? In my narrow circle of influence as the Protestant priest I stand outside of much of it, but there is devastation everywhere, the spirit of decay and denial. Those who would build, only destroy; no one honours the convictions of others; faith is a public derision, or else an excuse for hatred, and the poisoning of the spring of politics has brought forth a new kind of plague. No life is worth while any more, nothing holy is inviolable, no sacrifice is valid, no eyes look heavenward. What has happened to us? Why are we so forsaken? Why is the whole world diseased?"

For the first time Valerian raised his head, looked around the circle dreamily and said: "It's the stars, pastor. There is disorder in the cosmos. If science had only gone a little further we could give the causes and explain the results. Changes have taken place in the path of the constellations; somewhere in eternity there is chaos and this causes a seething catastrophe in our world. I often feel it in the depths of the nights. If only a man can force himself to listen, in absolute stillness, he will feel it, as if a ghostly sigh shivered along the edge of the firmament. And can we not conceive that this planet should tremble in the universal calamity and that the poor, lost, swarming souls upon it should sicken of an unknown disease? The universe is all one, is it not?"

The pastor shook his white head. "That seems to me too irresponsible," he said gently; "I would not like to make it so easy for humanity to excuse itself, although I do not deny the possibility of such things and the range of thought that they give. But when harm comes to my own house, I must try to mend it, and cannot call upon astral influences."

Valerian's face darkened; he could ill brook contradiction.

Josephine, however, with a glance at his Excellency Herbst, put an end to the discussion and they got up as it was now past midnight.

When Josephine came to her room, she found Ulrika Woytich's note, which had been brought in during her absence. She read it with involuntary disgust. It did not disturb her, because it was all too low. As was her nightly custom before going to bed, she went into Fanny's room to see if she were sleeping quietly, if the window was open and chiefly to watch, undisturbed, that beautiful face. The things that she had heard and lived through this day still troubled her, but when she looked at the child's slumbers a smile lighted her face, everything was smoothed out and there was no more bitterness in her. She felt devout again, devout as she was in her girlish time, but it was all simpler and quieter now.

This was so strange and new. After the storms, whose beginning was lost in time—quiet and confidence. The dove had come back after the flood. Thanks, dove, for the flight and the message. Love, though it had come late, was a gift she accepted in silent humility, prepared, however, for fate to snatch it out of her hand at any moment. Not counting those, who perhaps at any moment might make their natural claims, either because of their real feeling or because they hoped to reap advantage from it, she had to reckon upon the unknown, which might stretch eager arms out of the past, again, for this living good.

But Josephine was prepared. She would watch. She would measure the strength of her own heart against the rage of destiny. She wanted to try to be more obedient and higher than the demons who drew their swords against her.

The next day a profound calm fell upon her mind. It showed so plainly in her face that Fanny, who was spending a rainy day in her room, looked at her several times in surprise. She had called the child to her to give her a little gold chain because she had had to tell her that the plan about the doll had fallen through. But Fanny did not want to accept the chain; it was a little feeling of pride that made her resist; she felt that it was a kind of compensation for her, and she told Josephine, with a smiling glance that had in it something of the understanding of woman to woman, that she really did not need anything, she had quite gotten over the doll and had almost forgotten it. Between them stood the open case from which Josephine had taken the little chain, and there Fanny saw a gold-framed miniature of the Baron Edward Melander. It had lain so many years in this case that Josephine was not aware that it was there. It dated back to the time when she was a bride, and she remembered that then it had been to her the symbol of all misery, humiliation, and loss of self-respect. She was frightened when she saw Fanny's glance fixed upon it and wanted to hide it. In the city house and also in Eckern she had put away all the pictures of the Baron when she took the child in; and now this rose out of the past. Fanny noticed her hasty movement and asked: "Who is that beautiful man?" And before Josephine could prevent it she had taken the little picture up in her hands and looked at it attentively. Josephine was silent. "Do you know, Frau Baroness, that looks just like my father," said Fanny, astonished. This was the first time she had ever spoken of her father. Her brows were drawn together and a strange shadow of grief fell over her face. As Josephine looked at her, and her glance then fell upon the picture, she saw how like it the girl herself was and she shivered in face of this evidence of nature, and did not dare to deny it before the questioning clear eyes of the child. She recognized the law and bowed to it obediently. "This man is a near relative of yours," she said in a low voice, "but it is not time yet to tell you about it. Have patience, dear little heart." And Fanny was content.

It was toward evening, and Fanny rushed into Josephine's room pointing to the mountain peaks in the east, that were all in flame. "Look, Frau Baroness, look!" she cried out breathlessly. She was trembling from head to foot in joy and admiration, and Josephine, troubled by the violence of her feeling, lifted her into her lap. And so they sat dumb for a time looking at the glowing rocks, and Josephine's happiness was almost pain when she felt the child so near her.

It had never happened to her before: to hold a human body in loving embrace. Fanny talked, her head leaning against Josephine's shoulder, with shivering curiosity and imaginative longing which were so marked in her when she was receiving a lively impression, and she said that her greatest desire was to climb such a mountain, if possible all alone. She talked about it as if it were a voyage to heaven and her expectation of it was so immediate that Josephine felt anxious about destroying it. Everything to this little soul was possible, and everything was still a dream. And Josephine bent over her obedient to the word, obedient to the image.

It was obedience again when she was called to town, by the upset conditions of her Institutions and she gave way to necessity. The journey had long been threatening, the existence of many people hung upon it, difficult matters stood before her, material exertion of an almost insuperable kind; but she did not hesitate to do her duty. She wanted to serve because of her new happiness, as formerly she had served to prevent her misery from breaking her altogether. If fate desired to put her to greater tests, she would have the strength to try everything, perhaps to win everything. After she had most carefully told Elizabeth what to do she went quietly about her preparations for an absence of from ten to fourteen days and took a painful leave of Fanny, even though outwardly she smiled.

CHAPTER XXXII

A SHORT INTERLUDE

ALTHOUGH Anastasia pretended that Ulrika had quieted her, the incident of the will made her very thoughtful. She realised, indeed, that such a document was not binding and was ambiguous, that the way it was written could hardly amount to danger; also Ulrika made no resistance the next day when she demanded its destruction and threw it in the fire before her eyes as if she realised herself the foolishness of her undertaking.

But the fact that it had ever been written made Anastasia anxious. Ulrika's fortune was Anastasia's fortune, Philip's fortune, the Woytich inheritance. No stranger dared have one farthing of it and no one who did not belong to the family was to enjoy it. Her painful astonishment then, was perfectly explicable when in so unexpected a manner this little sprig of a Melander jumped up as an heir to be afraid of. It was wanton of Ulrika even to play with the thought of it; who could tell if some day this ridiculous whim might not bear fearful fruit? By degrees Ulrika was showing her age and she became constantly more capricious in words and deeds.

Anastasia wanted to go to the bottom of the matter. The attraction which the child had exercised over Ulrika had disturbed both her and Crescence greatly and unawares Anastasia had gained a confederate where formerly she had had an enemy, for the investigation of this matter. Crescence was so sure of her dominance over Ulrika that the very thought that it might pass over to another threw her into a paroxysm of rage. She declared that she was ready of her own free will to help Anastasia and that together they would watch Ulrika and consult about her actions. Crescence showed more real understanding of what went on in her mistress's mind than

Anastasia did; she saw only the strangeness of the happening without understanding it; she thought it was one of those cases of foolish stubbornness that one often noticed in Ulrika, or a sort of superstition or a secret interest.

Both watchers admitted, shaking their heads, that Ulrika hardly ate or slept any more; that when one asked her questions or spoke to her, she gave quite distorted answers; that she would stand for half hours at a time at the windows and look in the same direction as if she were bewitched; that she would light her pipe and then let it go out again; and night after night she would stride through the rooms aimlessly or sit at her writing-table and write letters which she would tear into a thousand pieces in the morning; that she would prepare herself with great care for a long trip and turn back again as soon as she came to the wood, muttering angrily to herself and then take up her usual occupations. It was impossible to insinuate oneself into Ulrika's confidence especially when one had an object to gain. Having an object made her highly distrustful and stubborn. They had to be contented with listening, spying, and consulting. Anastasia had heard the conversation between Elizabeth and Ulrika from behind the door and thus understood that the little Fanny was not allowed to come to visit them. It was difficult for Ulrika to get into the neighbourhood of Eckern except on a casual walk. If Ulrika really suffered when she could not see the child then the cause was discovered. Anastasia, driven by sympathy, turned the conversation one evening to this subject. She said that if Ulrika would like her to, she would gladlly carry the child a message, since she was entirely unknown up there; and no one could forbid her the roads. She waited to see what impression these words would make upon Ulrika. At first she was disappointed; for Ulrika was silent, but after a time she asked if Anastasia was really willing to undertake such messages. Anastasia said yes, energetically. It was nothing very important, said Ulrika, after some hesitation, except to find out now and then what was going on or to take a casual message; she would like to keep *au courant* and would like to know daily what the little creature was doing and would like to meet her somewhere. She had made up her mind, she said, to save the millions for that little girl, just as years ago she had made old Mylius turn his millions out of his safe. If Anastasia could manage that, could see and speak to the little creature, she would not mind giving her a big present; she would give her flat silver enough for twelve people, which she had so long wanted.

A blush of surprise covered Anastasia's face. Silver for twelve people—surely she was not deaf—that was a prize for which one would kneel down in the dust, for it would be worth a full million to-day.

In covetousness she was Ulrika's own sister, although cut after a smaller pattern. She said she would think the whole matter over carefully; she was very gentle and considerate for by degrees she began to see light. She told Crescence about the conversation, naturally without mentioning the silver. Crescence was of the opinion that Anastasia should set to work immediately, and this would give her the best opportunity to gain influence over the little imp, and cure her of all thoughts of the doll, of Ulrika, and of the inheritance; one would not need much time for that and then afterwards when Ulrika saw this little apple of her eye, she would be much surprised by the change which had taken place in her. That, and no other way was the way to go to work. Moreover, she was well acquainted with the gardener and his family at Eckern; the gardener Pohl was the one who in winter supplied Villa Woytich with vegetables from his hot houses; they had a fifteen-year-old daughter who was lame in both legs; she was the happiest of people when any one gave her books or illustrated magazines and there was a mass of such stuff about the house.

The next day Anastasia came back with two important pieces of news. One was that the Baroness had gone back to the city; the other, that Fanny played a great deal with the lame daughter of the gardener. She had been at the Pohls' house and had known how to win over the family. The gardener was very learned in his own line; he loved to talk about how to grow roses and his were famous in the entire neighbourhood. It was with much art and pains that he won these marvellous specimens from the sterile earth, and as Anastasia showed extraordinary interest in his art, he, on his side, showed her every honour that a guest of rank could demand, and delighted in her daily visits.

And so Anastasia went to work.

CHAPTER XXXIII

THE CYCLE OF TIME

ELIZABETH saw with satisfaction that Fanny expressed not the slightest desire for her lonely walks. She knew indeed that the Baroness had made her promise not to leave the house alone and she was sure of her honour. But there was a new cause for watchfulness since Fräulein Woytich had been in Eckern; Casimir asserted that on the evening of the great storm he had seen her in the neighbourhood of the manor house. Elizabeth decided to be upon her guard, and she never went out to walk with Fanny without scanning the landscape with her short-sighted eyes.

Fanny made fun of her anxious zeal at first, indeed she seldom lost an opportunity to laugh melodiously over the weaknesses of her care-taker. She was always wondering over these big people, the so-called grown-ups, who moved so stiffly and said such serious things, got vexed over everything, and could not even see what lay right in front of their noses. She knew better than Elizabeth where to look, to take care of herself, and because it seemed to her a kind of deception to keep silence, she ceased to make fun of Elizabeth. It was useless for a child to be cleverer than grown people, for then they feel a little wounded in their honour; she did not want to hurt these helpless, though in many ways superior creatures and make them ashamed of themselves.

But there were other reasons which influenced her to hold back. There was no good chattering, especially when threats were attached to any breaking of the silence. One must manage for one's self, one must show that one really was reasonable, and not run and complain at once to the powerful grown people.

Her second reason was that the departure of the Baroness grieved her. It was a vague feeling rather than conscious-

ness. She understood naturally enough that the powerful
adults had business that could not be put off; they seemed
never to have any time; and never thought of the really important things; only such things as seemed important to them
in their imaginations. Well, now let them be punished and see
for themselves, where their important things lead. She nourished a little wounded sense of vengeance in her breast. She
was so devoted to the Frau Baroness; she loved to sit by her
and talk pleasantly with her; she liked to look at her big
eyes and ask herself why they were so sad; she liked to put
her little hand in the Baroness's soft, cool hand; it was like
fluttering to a lovely shelter and feeling suddenly safe from
all dangers; it was nice, too, to listen to the soft, slow voice,
and nice to think: "Frau Baroness"; it seemed to her the
tenderest word in the language. Why did she go away? If
she were more childish, she would have wept. But no, she
would not weep.

She let out nothing at all of what happened between her
and Anastasia; she did not betray her constant presence at the
gardener's house. It never occurred to Elizabeth to investigate or suspect Fanny's visit to Pohl's; the lame Rosine was
a good-natured, friendly creature whom the Baroness loved,
and the distance Fanny had to go was not more than a hundred yards. And so Anastasia developed her plans unhindered,
and threw out her net. It was a coarse-meshed net, doubtless; clumsily made, and clumsily used; but perhaps the very
finest and most skilful schemes would have been less suited to
catch this little victim. Dull instruments are often useful
where sharp instruments fail.

It was easy enough to draw the child aside. Pohl's wife was
in the kitchen and he out at his work. It was easy enough to
intimidate Fanny and make her believe that her silence was of
greatest importance. It amused Anastasia to see the child look
at her with great, frightened eyes, and to see all the feelings of
her inmost heart betrayed on mouth and cheek. It was a satisfaction that Fanny came and came again, charmed like
a little animal that stares at the hand reaching for it. It was
quite in order that one should suppress her a little bit, Anas-

tasia told herself, filled with the measureless envy of small natures. "Everything goes too easily with her here; it is all skipping and singing; she ought not to have things so easy."

She gave her news of Ulrika, and news of Evelyn. That was the beginning of it all. The old Ulrika was grieved over the ingratitude that had been shown her and poor Evelyn missed her faithless little playmate. At this last Fanny shrugged her shoulders; although the messages made her restless, she despised them. She knew very well how to distinguish between the fairy tales that one spins dreamily for oneself, and the lies that these grown people told with so little shame and understanding.

Each time the agreeable longing messages were woven together with something evil, at any rate in the beginning. Ulrika and Evelyn—it seemed as if they were one—although one had to ask how it came about that two such utterly different people were so united. The result of this was that Evelyn fell in Fanny's estimation and lost ground in her heart like some one who has been guilty of an underhanded action. She did not want to think of the enchanting creature any more, if she had to think of her in such a connection. The picture floated about her and became troubled so that her mind turned from it even in her idle hours, her dreamy hours, and a strange thing happened, namely, that Fanny really felt only a shuddering discomfort over the matter upon looking back at it, with the passing of time. It was a revulsion to which she had not before confessed, and in the innate politeness of her nature she had tried to withstand. Now it shivered through her when she remembered the hours she had spent with Ulrika; her breath failed her when she remembered the snarling voice, the whining, snuffling, bellowing, smacking, and pawing, and the violence of all her actions and words and the secretive ugliness and loneliness that was all about her. The more Josephine's figure penetrated her innermost feelings, the icier her thought became of the other one, and she had a feeling of something inimical, like the eternal play of the elements, whose stage is the world of men.

She could not understand why Frau Gentili came, making

so many pretty speeches and giving no end of messages and greetings, and asking questions. And it did not remain at that. She brought presents with her; silver coins from Ulrika; old Roman coins, and a Maria Theresa thaler; then she brought a turquoise ring from Evelyn's wax hand, and it had something sad about it to Fanny, like all very old things. What were all these coins and this ring for? Anastasia bade her hide them. She said great misfortune might come if any one knew of the presents. She said they were all magic, each one a talisman, a protection against bad dreams, evil looks, poverty and disease. Ulrika had conjured them all; Ulrika had power over dreams, people, and fate itself. Fanny's look was veiled and Anastasia saw that she had known how to awaken fright in her.

The fifteen-year-old Rosine was in many ways like a six-year-old child. Her joy was unbounded when Fanny brought her a couple of coloured ribbons, or a dish of strawberries she had picked herself, but her greatest joy was over a box of coloured stones that Fanny had gathered in Yverdon. She poured them out over the covering of her lounge, let them glide through her fingers, and would play with them thus for hours while Fanny and Anastasia sat near her. Anastasia could talk to Fanny then without the girl's noticing her and she never missed the opportunity. Fanny wished that she were a swallow and could fly away out of the window, over the peaks of the mountains into the blue sky. Instead she had to sit still and listen; and she had to come whenever Anastasia was there, for if she stayed away, her imagination of the fright became a reality, and Anastasia's whisperings of Ulrika's mysterious powers became near and real. By degrees Elizabeth found the frequent visits to the garden house odd, and persuaded Fanny to go on little walks with her. How Fanny wanted to go! Elizabeth did not see or understand the pleading look that Fanny turned upon her, nor could she read those searching, shining eyes. She had a great deal to do, during Josephine's absence, with the household, and was obliged to leave the child to herself for part of the day. She felt vaguely that something was happening to Fanny, she noticed her de-

pression, her eagerness, her timidity, her excitability, and her
loss of appetite; she attributed it to the sultry heat, or to the
long rains, or to the fact that the Baroness was away, for she
had gained an insight into the child's devotion to Josephine.
As Ulrika Woytich seemed to have moved quite out of their
circle and no one spoke of her any more she felt that she had
nothing to fear. She was a sanguine nature and events always took her by surprise, without her being able to draw
profit from them. Fanny wondered at Elizabeth's ignorance
and lack of penetration. But this belonged to the general
riddle of the ways of the powerful grown-ups; they always
complained when anything dreadful happened but never took
the trouble to foresee and forestall it. She wondered that the
Baroness could stay so long and began to doubt her affection,
in which she felt so sheltered. She was inwardly wounded; if
she had not been she would perhaps have sat down and
written to the Baroness: "If you love me even a little, Frau
Baroness, come soon." She thought over it often in the quiet
of her sleeping hours, but then such a step seemed too bold,
so day by day she became more and more ensnared, and
lost her way in the darkness.

Lead by her evil instincts which reached an almost clairvoy-
ant power under the pressure of circumstances, Anastasia
began one day to talk to Fanny about her mother. The child
shuddered as if she had been stabbed in the back. Then Anastasia knew that she was on the right path, and immediately
made up a story of a secret understanding between Ulrika and
Fanny's mother. To tell the story, absolutely undisturbed, she
drew the child into the corner by the stove; she had to wait a
little while for Frau Pohl came and began to work around the
room; during this time Fanny, who had grown white down to
her very throat, never took her eyes from her.

Her mother! A tragic knowledge of the low, worthless,
and shameless; she had never experienced anything from her
but scornful indifference, nagging blame, unjust reproaches,
hateful abuse. The child had always been in her way, was
always costing money, always expecting things that were un-
justifiable. She felt herself an object of eternal scolding

and quarrelling between her mother and father and for the latter she felt a glimmer of love in her heart; it was her mother who had thrown her out from the home shelter, her mother, through whom she was accursed. It was only since she had lived in happier surroundings that she knew this really; formerly she had used every power of her gay nature to withstand it. She remembered all the gaiety and rioting of that evening when Elizabeth had come and taken her from the forsaken dwelling. Her mother had gone! Well, that meant that punishment had gone, disapproval had gone, scorn and wounds and darkness had gone. It had hurt her, even through her wildest pranks, and yet again she felt something light about her heart. But the secret fear and suffering had left a kernel of melancholy in her nature that never disappeared, however golden the path of life stretched before her.

Anastasia told her, what Fanny had already observed adequately, that an old, old hatred reigned between the Baroness and Ulrika. And one just as old and just as irreconcilable between the Baroness and Fanny's mother. It was impossible for her, she said, to tell her anything more about it; it had its own reasons and some day Fanny would know and understand them. When Fanny came into the Baroness's home Ulrika had learned it and had written at once to Fanny's mother, whose address she knew, as she knew everything that most people did not. Her mother had been very angry and gone at once to Vienna to get Fanny out of the Melander house, and then when she found Fanny no longer there she had written an angry letter to the Baroness and demanded that Fanny should be brought at once to Ulrika, of whom she thought a great deal and whom she wished to have Fanny. Thereupon the Baroness had gone at once to Vienna to persuade Fanny's mother, and this had been the real reason for her trip. (Fanny sighed deeply here; it threw a halo around the Baroness, and inwardly in her heart she begged her pardon for her doubt and anger.) The person who had started all this was Ulrika and only Ulrika, Anastasia added, as she finished her story, nodding grimly, for she had no other goal in view than that the Baroness should give Fanny to her.

"But why?   But why?" whispered Fanny.

"What are you asking?" Anastasia answered, giggling. "If you must know, you little imp, it is because she loves you."

This word, love uttered, in such connection and with laughter, made Fanny turn cold all over. She thought and thought; an anxious presentiment filled her heart. Toward evening she slipped off to an out-of-the-way part of the park and buried the coins and Evelyn's ring as deep in the earth as she could get them. When she was through she threw the little shovel away that she had carried with her, clasped her hands at the back of her neck, looked with longing eyes to the peaks in the west, which had so often fired her imagination, and said out of the depths of her heart: "Oh, you mountain, you mountain!"

In the meantime Ulrika was getting more and more impatient, and with anger that was almost insanity she demanded of Anastasia that she should show some results of her running about and her efforts. She, Ulrika, wanted to see the little creature, wanted to talk to her, the time was getting too long and she could not afford so many preparations, and if this was all she could do she would not give her a single silver spoon, much less a complete silver service. She wanted to see the little creature every day, at least once a day; she had a right to, a perfectly natural claim. She would show that proud, wooden Josephine who Ulrika Woytich was, in case she should have forgotten, and who she had once been, in case she had lost the habit of remembering. She might as well remember that when the deceased Baron had come as a hungry student to Vienna he had been her lover, her creature, and if he owed his baronetcy and his money and his position to any one, it was to her, Ulrika Woytich, and to no one else on earth.

So she raved until she lost all control over herself. Cold and decided, Anastasia said that if she would give her the silver she had promised to-day, she would arrange a meeting with Fanny to-morrow; and she would arrange it this way: She would tell Fanny that she had something very important to communicate to her and lure her into the Pohls' best room; Ulrika was to be at the house beforehand and when Anastasia came to the window and knocked on the window pane, that

would be the sign for Ulrika to come in. Ulrika asked eagerly
if the little creature was sure to be there; Anastasia said that
there was not the slightest doubt, and she felt very sure of
what she said, for she had brought the child to the point of appalling fright. Fanny always wanted to hear, always wanted
to hear something new, even when her heart fainted at hearing.

The sisters discussed the matter for a while and finally
Ulrika gave in; with sighs and groans and last attempts to
gain time, she dragged out the big trunk and opened it. Anastasia was dazzled by the sight; in her uncontrollable delight
she kissed the hand of the gloomy, staring Ulrika and then
carried her treasure off to safety.

Fanny dreamed that night of spiders. Innumerable yellow
spiders that gathered together in a sort of coil, and she knew
with sorrow and disgust that it was hatred that had called out
these monstrosities. Hatred; this word had an awful meaning
since Anastasia had spoken it to her; yes, she had never known
it till then. People hated each other: unbelievable! It was so
much harder to live than she had thought; what good was it
that one was happy at times if people hated each other? And
then, in the dream two figures appeared, constantly alternating,
two that were yet one: Her mother, but with Ulrika's face;
Ulrika, but with her mother's face. Everything was mixed
up, far and near, outside and inside, obedience and disobedience, memory and presentiments, the world and feeling, everything was coiled around together like the yellow spiders.

When Elizabeth appeared the next morning by Fanny's bed
with her chocolate, she started and asked if anything was the
matter. The morning gaiety of the child, which had so often
delighted her, had given way to tired thoughtfulness. Her
eyes had dark circles. Fanny said that nothing was the matter. She got up, washed and dressed; outside the sun shone,
the cock crowed, the throstle called longingly, the linden trees
breathed out their odour, and all nature had something festive
and careless about it, but it made no impression upon Fanny;
she could neither see nor feel it. She hardly touched her
breakfast, and at noon she only nibbled at her food, and
Elizabeth watched her anxiously and asked her what it was,

again and again. After dinner she stood a long time by the well-trough in front of the stables and looked at the trout that swam round and round stupidly in the basin. Then she went to the gardener's house, driven by unconquerable restlessness, commanded by her dream, warned by her waking senses, wavering between a tormenting curiosity and a tormenting repulsion.

At the back of the Pohls' house, hidden from sight by currant bushes, Ulrika walked up and down like a soldier on guard. Her hat had fallen back over her head; it was the one trimmed with hen's feathers; her hair fluttered in the light wind around the passionate, faded face, and her hands gripped her clothes now here, now there. She had already waited a long time; she had begun to doubt furiously whether the meeting would come off, and brooded feverishly over what she would do and what she would say when she saw the child. The things she had intended and planned in the beginning did not hold good; to tell the whole deception and her relationship to Josephine might cut both ways; for if the child learned that the Baroness was her grandmother, there was the danger that the child would consider her claim and duty paramount, and this was a thing that up to the present moment she had not had to fear from Fanny. It would be best to think of nothing and plan nothing and trust to the moment. At bottom it was true that Ulrika had not the slightest notion what was to happen, nor why she had brought about and so hotly desired this meeting. It was impulse; a dark, brooding, undirected impulse.

Then came the knocking on the window-pane. She went through the narrow entrance, Anastasia thrust her over the threshold and disappeared. There before her stood Fanny, trembling like an aspen leaf and staring at her with wide open eyes. Her gold hair hung round her head and shoulders, down to her hips, and her dumb amazement gave her face a nobly helpless look, so that Ulrika turned almost faint and was herself frightened, and for the first time understood what was going on in her and what moved her. "Now, greetings, you little grasshopper, God greet you!" she cried in her hoarse voice and stretched out her arms. "Is that the way to meet a good old friend? To have to arrange secret meetings in order to see you at all? Aren't you ashamed, you miserable little trickster? Come here and kiss me this minute! Will you come? Will you hurry?"

Fanny never budged. And then a horrible thing happened: Ulrika Woytich, who had lived sixty-seven years without having wept, burst into tears. The tears flowed down from her jet black eyes, over her brown wrinkled cheeks, and inarticulate sounds choked her; she rushed upon Fanny, caught her in her arms as in a vice, and as she embraced the slender little body—all this incarnate glow and fragrance—something that verged upon madness possessed her, a desire to kill, a kind of tender intoxication. She fell upon her knees, stroked the silky gold hair with her hands over and over again, bit her lips and stammered, begged, cursed until the saliva ran out of the corners of her mouth; in her breast was a ceaseless cry: To possess her! to possess her! to possess her! This was the fundamental word of her language, of her whole being, which now in her madness and bitterness was driving her to the very point of insanity.

Nothing, nothing that had ever happened, in a nightmare or in nightly imaginings, had ever brought Fanny to this point of horror. At first she folded her hands, pleading and resisting. Then she wept softly and tried to escape the embrace, everything from the alarming outburst of tears of the old woman, to her physical nearness, the smell of tobacco and decay of her clothes, the hot, unclean breath, the distorted features, the incomprehensible, threatening, boring, drivelling, caressing words, everything was so frightful that her very soul died and there seemed to be a yellow spotted blackness all around her, as she shut her eyes. Like lightning it came over her that all the story about her mother was a lie; and all the more horrible was this real sound and image, this touching and being touched. She did not scream, she gave way; she felt a feverish desire to get to the surface as if she were struggling under water. And this increased her strength tenfold; she disentangled herself with a deep breath that came from her whole body, white in the face as if she had been covered with chalk. And while Ulrika still kneeled upon the ground blubbering to herself: "I've got jewels for you, diamonds for you, I brought them with me, wait a minute, they are here in my pocket; listen, you little grasshopper, I am going to save your millions for you, stay here, stay here—" but Fanny had flown in a wild flaming rush from the room.

She ran, ran, ran. Horror drove her like a storm. She ran through the woods like a deer and saw the peasants mowing the meadows. She changed her direction. Then she saw tourists and turned round. After a time she saw the Eckern manor house close before her. She had run in a circle. Without being noticed, she slipped into the door, went up the stairs into the attic. She threw herself down in the corner on a straw bag, her face downward. Her heart almost stifled her with its beating. The whole space seemed filled with the voice of the old woman, she felt her damp clothes around her like spiders' webs, her eyelids burned, the woman's shoulder still pressed against her as though she were in a barrel, she trembled and shook all over and cold shivers went up and down her spine. Yesterday, an hour ago even, what a lovely life it had been; in despite of everything she had her little silent joys and pleasant expectations; and now everything was different and the whole world lay before her like a dead fish. Her horror would not pass, nor the shame; it bored into her heart with the sharpness of a knife and every thought was fear and disgust. She sobbed into the straw and the sobs made her little body leap as if she were a rubber ball; she bit her hair; she longed with all the power of her soul for a hiding place where no one could find her; for the sorrow that she felt robbed her alike of people, and animals, and dreams, and games, and left her in utter loneliness and guilt, with a feeling of having been mastered, and a feeling of unspeakable fear.

The stalks of straw, pushing through the bag, pricked her, and she turned to lie on her back. She lay that way a long time and did not move, and then her glance fell through the attic window at the end of the room, right upon the mountain, her mountain, which rose up to the very heavens in a blaze of sunshine, and looked like the bearded face of an old man of noble beauty and divine, gigantic form. Her eyes rested upon it, and the uproar in her heart became quieter. She thought that the mountain was gracious toward her and would be kind to her and care for her if there were no other way of escape; she would like to go to it and tell it her sorrow, and it would show her one of its hidden, magic caves, and there she would live enchanted like a princess, and only come back amongst people again when the frightful thing was no longer to be feared, perhaps in a hundred years. She would climb to the highest peak right near to the secret spirit that lived there, and there she would be safe. And she was penetrated by the friendly feeling of the mountain, so that her spirit threw off part of its burden, although she was still sad at the thought that she must leave the Baroness.

Suddenly she heard soft music, marvellous tones reached her from the house below. She stood up and listened. The sounds were more and more beautiful, sweeter and sweeter. She stepped out of the attic door on her tiptoes that she might hear it better. Led irresistibly by a strange, devout curiosity, she went step by step along the hall, stood at Valerian's door and listened entranced, with an enchanting cherub smile, for she had never heard anything like this before; she opened the door involuntarily, slipped in, shut the door without a sound and stood motionless, with the enchanting smile upon her lips.

Valerian's back was turned toward her. The windows were closed, the blinds were lowered on account of the heat and a sort of sultry afternoon twilight reigned in the room. On the floor an enormous map of the heavens was spread out and around it books were heaped up and on the map lay a compass and a carpenter's square. As he turned his head Valerian became aware of the child at the door and stopped short. Letting the bow in his right arm fall, and the violin in his left, he went up to Fanny and looked at her severely. "Who gave you permission to come in here, Fräulein Fanny?" he asked sternly, and he added: "You look dishevelled enough. Where have you been? And you look as if you had been crying. Why have you been crying?"

Fanny dropped her head with shame and was silent. If he only would play again, she thought inwardly, with such intensity that it seemed as if her whole future happiness depended upon this wish: if he would only play again!

But de Groot laid the instrument down on the table, began to whistle softly to himself and crouched down upon the carpet. "There is reason enough to cry," he said, as he picked up the compasses and stuck the needle into a point in the map, "many and sufficient reasons. But see, my child, here is a world," he pointed to the map again, "whose investigation moves man to beneficial wondering, and wonder, note that, wonder is a heal-all. These two things save us from despair: the starry heavens and art."

His jesting mode of speech made Fanny uncertain again. She did not understand what he was saying, she only knew that he had been angry because she had disturbed him and listened, and that he was dressing up his anger in grave, bitter turns of speech, and he was not the less angry because it was a child who was the guilty one. And Fanny prayed with inward devotion: "Dear God, make him play again, and that shall be a sign to me that everything will come right."

"Come here, Fanny," Valerian commanded. She stepped up obediently to the edge of the map as to the border of a blue lake. "That is a picture of a constellation, Lyra," he said; "and this is a constellation, Cygnus, the swan. Neighbours, as you see, and though they seem to walk over the firmament, these two, arm in arm, the sparks in the eyes of the swan and the lightning in the strings of Lyra are a chain of millions of years apart. The suns there, and the suns here are not brother suns, and the call and light of the one to another dies in the icy night of eternity. Do you understand? No? Too bad. You see me lying here? And I cover up the whole heavens from Virgo to Andromeda and the Fish. A worm spreading itself over the universe and trying to possess it."

He laughed Homerically and shook his mane. Fanny looked at him, pleading, bent her knee slightly and in a low voice said: "Please, please play something on the violin, please, please."

He arose, serious suddenly, looked at Fanny surprised, and as if he wanted to answer something when some one knocked at the door. Elizabeth opened it and rushed in, crying out to Fanny. "There you are, there you are, God be thanked!" she cried with a strange sort of exaltation. "For three hours I have been in the most frightful anxiety about you." Fanny stood with her head sunk down. Valerian cleared his throat and, seeing his disturbed manner, Elizabeth begged him, with many confused words, to excuse her. Then she turned again to Fanny, to question her, and then to de Groot to beg him to tell her what had happened.

About five o'clock she had gone down to Pohl's to fetch Fanny and order the carriage for the Frau Baroness. The Frau Baroness had telephoned that she would be in about nine o'clock. Fanny was not at the Pohls'. The gardener, who was drinking his coffee, remarked casually that she had probably gone off with Fräulein Woytich. "What, for heaven's sake, Fräulein Woytich here at your house?" Elizabeth had called out. The gardener was surprised at her excitement and said that he had seen Fräulein Woytich there shortly before four o'clock and had supposed that she was waiting for her sister. Then Elizabeth learned, with sorrow and fright, of Anastasia's regular visits. She overwhelmed the couple with reproaches, unable to explain to them why, and left them quite overcome when she went to find Fanny. She wandered all over the place, called everywhere in the house for her, hurried through all the rooms and finally, in her excitement, decided to go to Ried. It was half-past six when she arrived there. Down in the garden she saw Frau Gentili busy planting a bed. Elizabeth, ready to drop, asked after Fanny. Anastasia, though visibly of an evil conscience, replied snippily that no Fanny was there. Suddenly a window was thrown open above, Fräulein Woytich's head appeared and she waved a paper in her hand. But she was not able to get a sound out of her throat. It was evident that she had lost her mind. Elizabeth thought that it must be a telegram; the telegraph messenger had just gone down toward the Villa with Elizabeth. Then Fräulein Woytich screamed in a voice that would have wakened the dead: "Your Philip has killed himself." Anastasia dropped her shovel and stood as if turned to stone. Elizabeth stood there and did not know what to do. After a while the maid rushed out of the house and called to Anastasia: "Fräulein Ulrika is going to Vienna to-night and you must go with her. Hurry up. I always thought that that Philip would come to a bad end. And now we have the proof." Frau Gentili staggered into the house, Elizabeth turned to the maid and demanded that she tell her if she knew anything of Fanny, or had seen Fanny. The maid shrugged her shoulders and answered roughly, while a strange howling sounded from the room above, that this was too much; she used a coarse expression and said that if she hung around here any longer asking pert questions it would go ill with her; she wanted nothing to do with strangers' children and fortunately had none of her own. Then Elizabeth, in despair, had turned homeward. "I don't know how I ever got back," she said, pressing Fanny in her arms, "and as Herr de Groot's room was the only one that I had not searched through I took the liberty of coming in."

Valerian had not been able to turn his eyes from Fanny all this time. He could not make out what it was that fascinated him so in that face. Rarely had he seen the mobility of a soul mirror itself so eloquently in a face. At the words of the maid, in the tale: "Fräulein Ulrika is starting to Vienna to-night," a smile of happiness spread over her face that moved him like a powerful melody. There was a complete transformation; the puzzling contradiction between the news of sudden death and this strange, innocent joy, made him thoughtful, and yet he felt no desire to question her: that was not his way.

At supper Elizabeth told numberless details about her adventure, and her volubility bored de Groot. Especially the ways and conduct of the maid she described fully and said that so wicked a creature had never before come under her eyes and that she feared her as a veritable witch.

"I think you exaggerate there," Excellency Herbst commented. "Most so-called bad people are stupid, simply stupid."

"If that is a mitigation, it is also devastating," said Valerian. "You are always talking of Majesty! Reverence! reverence! Make way for her Majesty, STUPIDITY, the mightiest of all potentates. No one has ever won a war against this ruler who taxes us all and holds us all in subjection, and she does not care a hang whether we make music or calculate the way of a comet or measure the depths of the ocean or write 'The Brothers Karamazow'; she crushes us like flies if we become insistent over these things; she grins shabbily at us even if we labour unremittingly; that is, if she takes any notice of us at all, which would be peculiar, too. Your health, your Excellency, your health, Fräulein Fanny." He raised his glass.

When the meal was over he offered his arm formally to Fanny. She laughed up at him. She looked very aristocratic in her yellow muslin frock, which left the slender, stem-like throat free, and she moved with gentle grace. It seemed to Valerian that she had grown gentler recently.

They walked up and down the pebble-strewn terrace. An electric lamp burned in a metal stand. It had been one of those days when Nature seemed full of sultry, suppressed threats; it showed itself in the flight of the birds and in the form of clouds, and seemed to want to unburden itself like the gases from an overheated kettle. In fact, the salt-workers who came down from the mountain, Fanny's mountain, reported that the south peak of the massive mound had broken in the early afternoon, and thrown itself like a huge avalanche down into the valley, toward the river-bed, bending the woods over as if they had been grass blades and burying them. The people said the cause perhaps was that during the recent heavy rains the old Roman props inside the mountain had crumbled so that the rocks had no foundation.

This was the cause of the heavy grumbling that Valerian and Fanny heard from time to time which was quite different from thunder. The mountain was not yet at rest. Several times they stood and listened. Valerian, looking up at the first glimmering stars, said the Heavens were clouding over and the absolute hush below signified severe currents above. Suddenly Fanny gave a light cry of pain; Valerian asked what the matter was and she laughed to herself as she replied: "My shadow knocked against that tree." De Groot laid both hands on her shoulders and looked at her astonished, without saying a word. And as her eyes still had the same pleading request, that urgent request, which it was impossible to misunderstand, he shook his head like a person who gives way because he sees nothing to do but to yield. He took her up into his work-room, told her to sit still in the corner, took his violin and bow out of the case and began to play, in the dark.

Fanny, her chin upon her breast, her hands folded in her lap, sat like a statue; she sat there silent, a little speck of light in the dark room. Now everything would come right again, she thought happily.

Outside in the hall, all the people in the house had gathered. Even Josephine, who had just gotten down from the carriage, despite her fatigue, joined the others and listened.

And as he had played a generation ago for an old man, when he was a child, so now as an old man he played to a child.

The return of the cycle was written in the stars; and he obeyed.

CHAPTER XXXIV

A VAIN OBLATION

ULRIKA and Anastasia travelled third class in the passenger train, packed like sardines in a box. Tourists, peasants, workmen, people who had been out buying provisions in the country, butter, eggs, lard, and meal, or had made exchanges and were returning to the city with their filled-up bags, sat in the dull light of a flickering oil lamp, with trunks, bags, cans, cloaks, sticks, and umbrellas, above and below them, laughing fighting, smoking, singing, discussing politics, and telling each other stories. Only after midnight a little quiet prevailed, heads sank drunk with sleep on neighbouring shoulders, and from every side snores in all the different keys were heard as the train rattled on from station to station.

The sisters sat at an open window opposite each other. They had not exchanged a word. Both faces were pale, Anastasia's dried up like a mummy's, and she stared at Ulrika in depressed, reined-in anxiety. Anastia was still trying to keep up the appearance of a lady; at intervals she murmured the Lord's Prayer to herself. Ulrika, when any change at all drew over her features, ground her under jaw like a cow chewing cud.

Not for a moment did her anxiety give way. Burning up with impatience, raging under the pressure of uncertainty, cursing inwardly at the slowness of the train, she wished a death by torment for the officials, the conductors, the guards and the passengers getting out and in, as tormenting as this night of uncertainty was to her.

She had heard nothing of Philip Gentili's suicide. The telegram had told nothing but the mere fact. What frightful thing hid behind it was still to be learned. But perhaps there was no further misfortune, perhaps he had done the deed because of some love-affair. Perhaps he had overworked and his nerves had given way; perhaps a disgust of life had gripped him; young people to-day were apt to make a short shrift of things and they did not cling with mulish strength to the general splendour of living. All this was possible; one might hope any of these things; it would be all right; she would go to his funeral and have a good-looking headstone made for the grave, with an inscription something like this: "Philip Gentili, beloved of his friends and honoured by all." She had seen that once in the cemetery of Turin and it pleased her.

But why were all these harmless possibilities so unbelievable; what was it about them that made them seem so scornfully unbelievable? At bottom she really knew; it was that. Even in sceptical natures there is a feeling of the inexorableness of fate, and hope and consolation burst like water bubbles before it.

The night passed; the goal was reached. The sisters drove to Philip's house; the body had already been carried out. At nine o'clock they arrived and at half-past Ulrika knew that her entire fortune was lost.

She threw herself on the floor and tore her hair. She shrieked like a jaguar. She went into convulsions and threatened to throttle any one who came near her. She threw open the window and tried to throw herself out. Several people had to hold her and force her back upon the sofa. Her voice outdid itself and no one could make out what she was saying. She took a glass of water and broke it between her two hands till they were covered with blood. She cursed life—all life, those born and unborn, she blasphemed God, she seemed to plead with some invisible being that stood before her, for mercy, she tore great wounds in her neck, and the undisciplined violence of her nature showed itself in an alarming, frightful way.

Frightened by her wild cries, a number of people living in the house and passers-by rushed up to the floor. The door had been left open; the old couple from whom Philip Gentili rented tried in vain to stem the tide of people pushing in, and they turned them away explaining as well as they could what had happened. But more and more came; there were about twenty in the room, an attorney's secretary, a young lady typist, a clerk from the fur business below, a fat lady in a red-striped dress, some girls from a dancing school, a student with a blue cap on, a dentist's assistant, an official with a great slash on his face. These were the first to reach the scene of action, but there were others on the stairs.

Ulrika, her arms waving in the air, escaped the soothing words of Anastasia and lay on the floor, raging, screaming to the crowd that pressed in: "There is nothing to stare at here. Go to the circus if you want to stare. This is not a circus. This is a mad-house. This is a place where people go mad. This is a criminal's cave. Where are your judges? your law books? Bring them here! And when you have them burn them up, burn them up! They are worth nothing any more. You are a thieving crowd! A thieving people! A thieving state! Yes, open your mouths! And stare at me, yes, yes, yes! I have saved for forty years, saved a dollar at a time, spent nothing, wasted nothing, always gay, always industrious, always the first up and at it, and what have I now? What is this woman, from whom a damned dog has stolen all her possessions and all her fortune, and then thrown himself down in the dust and spit out his filthy soul? What is she, hey? What is she in your broken-down world."

The faces around her were stretched in broad grins. They managed to bring the mad creature into the room. When she had become a little quieter, she wandered ceaselessly up and down, her hands clasped to her face as if she were tortured by tooth-ache, groaning monotonously. Anastasia cowered on the sofa, her elbows in her lap and wailed: "If you have not your money any more at least you have your house. You can sell your furniture, and live a half year off each piece, but I, what have I? Everything gone. No woman who works by the day is as poor as I. My only son, brought up honestly and ending as an embezzler. Disgrace upon disgrace. You have your furniture, you have your house. But I, what have I?"

"Shut up, you empty-headed fool," growled Ulrika and began to groan again.

An hour later a comrade of Philip's arrived and told Anastasia that three days before Gentili's adventurous speculations with falling stock and the failure of the Remschied bank, Lothar Mylius had drawn his entire capital out of the business. Ulrika listened. She asked a number of confused questions, all turned toward a definite end, and in a minute she had decided to go to Berlin. She imagined suddenly that Mylius must have used this opportunity to save her money, too, or at any rate, a considerable portion of it. She clung with all her powers to this hope and nothing could rob her of it. "The sly fox," she babbled to herself, excitedly, "he knew it beforehand; he did not tell me anything because he wanted to impress me with his genius; but he thought of his old friend, that is certain, that is quite certain, and if I don't stir my stumps at once, a second misfortune may happen, or he will forget about it, or he will cheat me out of it; what can one tell in this dogs' day, in such a dogs' world; safety is safety."

All her energy awakened. Before noon the next day she had summoned a whole army of helpful passports and visées. She learned that Lothar Mylius was still in Berlin, from young Remschied, who had talked to her that morning over the telephone. In the afternoon she drove to the station. As she took the cheapest possible route, she was thirty-two hours on the way, but she felt no fatigue. She sat motionless in the crowded trains, she stood for hours waiting at stations, she paid no attention to the teasing formalities at the boundaries; now and then she ate a piece of bread and took a swallow of water, she carried her own suit-case, avoided conversation, and stared into the void with tightly closed lips. Worn out, dirty, dusty, she reached the Mylius house in the evening, dragging herself to it on foot, though it lay in the neighbourhood of the Potsdam Square.

He was not at home. They told her he would hardly be home before midnight as he was at a party. She decided to wait. They knew her and took her into his work-room. She was too restless to sit down. The deathly stillness of the house made her nervous. She went from room to room and turned all the electric lights on. She did it in a mixture of curiosity, fear, and excitement. She knew the house well. But never before had its fantastic decadence so depressed her. Moreover, there were a great many new things there (the war had heaped up many new things everywhere), and he had submitted to the mad fashions of the day, to its morbid moods, and with cold calculation had supported the feverish productions of the newest currents in art.

There were primitive, roughly-painted pictures of gods, there were foreign war masks, and masks to frighten you, African headdresses, and carvings from New Zealand. The place was covered with grotesque toys; dwarfish marionettes, hunters cut out of wood and made into nut-crackers, stuffed monkeys hanging on rubber strings between the door posts. In the Italian faïence pots grew horrible, luxuriant, numberless kinds of cacti, and between them one saw little erotic objects made out of porcelain, women's legs, women with lace petticoats on, thrown backwards, obsequious soldiers, with sturdy legs and impudent little cupids; there were animal figures, and caricatures of animals made out of jade, soapstone, ivory, clay, bronze and ebony. There were numbers of snuff-boxes, some made out of foreign nuts, Japanese and Chinese, with indecent pictures on them, smelling bottles ornamented with rhinestones and painted with heroically sentimental landscapes, showing behind their trick covers some shameless picture. There were red lacquered cupboards set with mirrors and sconces; they held ruby glasses, Bernstein glasses, cut and etched goblets, that dated from the seventeenth and eighteenth centuries, great blue Delft imitations of Chinese vases and ebony pedestals. There were Empire furniture, Aubusson carpets, laces, embroideries, English table silver, baskets, plates, carafes, salt-cellars and tea-caddies of all shapes and kinds and watches of every period and style. In one corner stood two life-sized gilt bears carved out of wood, who could open their jaws and roll their eyes, and in another were two gilt caryatids bearing torches, that had come from an old French castle. In the dining room hung an enormously costly Meissen sconce, and metal lamps bought from churches and temples stood about. The walls were covered with pictures of the most mannered school, all painfully glaring, and hideously distorted; on the dressing tables and the wardrobes in the bedrooms voluptuous scenes were painted and on the tiles of the bathrooms and on the tub steps were hundreds of coloured cockle-shells and strangely perverse toys.

Ulrika pushed her under jaw further and further forward and wandered joylessly. She felt as if she had entered a tropical swamp full of rank, luxuriant vegetation. All these overwrought, glaring, shrieking, disproportionate, ghastly objects looked to her as if a satyr in grim cynicism had gathered together and thrown in a heap beauty and ugliness, propriety and impropriety, heaven and hell. It aroused a feeling of icy loneliness, and she felt strange and depressed. Taken together they seemed to her like a face, an unhappy, worn-out face, with a hypocritical smile, thickly made up to hide its age, denying its decay, scornfully and weakly: The Face of the Times. Suddenly she knew that her journey was a silly and futile undertaking, and that she had nothing to hope, and that she might as well have relied upon the Javanese idols there by the door as upon the master of this house; she knew that she was a beggar.

She collapsed into an arm chair. Perhaps in the exhaustion which now became apparent, she dreamed this; or perhaps it was a waking vision: she stood on gold green moss in the woods and at her feet rustled a little brook. She could plainly hear the silver splashing of the water and when she listened more carefully, she believed she heard distinct words coming up from the brook. Have I grown childish? she thought. It was a human voice, there was no doubt about that. The thing that had driven her to the water was thirst, a thirst that she had been feeling for a long time past, but of which she could not be quite sure; it was no ordinary thirst that shows itself in a desire to drink, but it was a longing that filled her whole being, a deep, tormenting yearning, that she had never been able to satisfy and of whose presence she was only now, at this moment, really distinctly aware. At first she thought that the peace that flowed through her, came from the contrast between the dark, unholy, shadowy splendour of the Mylius house and the innocence and sweetness of nature, but there was something else in it, for the devouring, burning, thirsty longing was not to be stilled, not even when she bent down and drank of the crystal waters. For strangely enough the water tasted bitter and the burning grew intenser and when she looked down again she saw two little naked arms reaching out to her, suddenly dragged back again by the waters and disappearing.

She shuddered and opened her eyes. "Fools' games," she scolded crossly; "may the devil take such fancies." Then she heard a little human voice saying: "Give it to me, give it to me again. How can I believe you if you don't give it to me?"

She looked around shyly. Her face darkened. Poverty—that was the lot that from childhood up she had feared. Every motion, every thought, every step, every deed of her whole life had been to avoid this. How comfortable it is to possess! How royal to be able to say: I possess. Not only what life's market offers and what will shelter us from need; for things are a mere outward expression. The reality was something other, that mysterious, holy element, awakening and commanding reverence, which is called Money. In her memory like a flaming guidepost was the picture of old Mylius, wrestling with death and crying out: My Money! It was unforgettable, that My! It was the summing up of all joy and pride and anxiety and power: mine! mine! From that time on it seemed as if she had drawn her strength from the power of that "Mine," to strive and to keep, and fate had thrown things constantly into her lap, which were worth possessing.

And now: loss—emptiness—nothing—despair.

But whence came this thirst in her body, it was becoming worse from hour to hour and it stifled the despair, so that that seemed hardly anything in comparison. She had missed something, that was what it was. Somehow she had missed something great. But she could find no word, or concept, or support. It must be in her blood, or deeper yet. Like snow under the plough it broke up and bared the hidden roots and fibres. And out of the emptiness soared a little spirit chirping, "Give it to me, give it to me!" With an anxious movement she struck her breast and murmured in agony: "Is it you, Fanny?" And the little voice continued to say: "Give it to me, give it to me!"

Ulrika stared in front of her for a long time and then said with a faint smile: "Yes, you shall have it. Rest easy, you shall have it."

A finger tapped upon her shoulder and some one said sulkily: "Now, Ulrika, how did you get here?"

Before her stood Lothar Mylius, in his dress coat, in a negligent attitude, not in the least curious, smacking his voluptuous lips together, turning his fixed glance of a sleepy roué to one side, for it was always difficult for him to look one in the eye. He was a very pale man, with a sponge-like, cheesy skin, very fat and very dark. A man who had to overcome himself, even to speak a single sentence to the end, because he begrudged his kind the pleasure of hearing a complete thought from him. He was a man who was too lazy and too proud to speak to his inferiors, or to offer his spongy hand to his friends. A man of secret undertakings and of blood-sucking, perverse vices. A man who despised women as if they were poisonous animals, who showed his contempt by paying them. A man who was too rich to look at outside needs and too satiated to feel anything other than disgust: disgust of the flesh and disgust of the spirit. A man more celebrated for his excesses than for his luxury and riches and whose cynicism was more to be feared than his hardness. A scornful profiteer of the ruins and sorrows of a nation, the great figure, whose wealth was the glory of an epoch, the last of a race of industrious citizens, whose simple ideals of life in his flabby hands had become symbols of murder and destruction.

Ulrika could hardly bring herself back into reality. "I have been looking around a little in your Sardanapalus palace," she said. "It is overwhelming. In former days we did not make so much noise about our things and yet could be greater lords. To-day I grant you we have to knock

people on their heads with our fists to make them see anything. Give me something to eat, I am hungry, and then I
will tell you why I am here."

Mylius ill-humouredly brought what he could find at this
late hour, chocolate, cakes, fruit, liqueurs, and wine. Ulrika
swallowed everything eagerly and drank until her head was
aglow. Mylius waited in lazy silence. When she was finished
and told him of her misfortune, his face never changed. He
asked sleepily after the amount of her loss. She counted it
up: three hundred English pounds, four thousand dollars,
twenty thousand Swiss francs and more than two million
crowns. With a flicker of pity, Mylius turned his head to
the left and shrugged his shoulders. Ulrika did not even
need to ask the question which had been the cause of her
journey; one look at this man was sufficient. She sat there
motionless.

Lothar Mylius yawned and spoke between short pauses
that emphasised his feeling of the costliness of words: "Always overrated the boy. Pitiful fool. People think if they
have a single cow in the stall they can give milk to the whole
province. Foolish. Manœuvred without any covering. Deserved licking. Too bad; shot himself." His other oracular
comments were lost in a yawn.

"But you smelled a rat; you took your money away,"
Ulrika grumbled.

"I did," he answered, and looked with fixed attention at
a negro's shield on the wall. "Meant to warn you. Forgot.
Too much doing at the moment."

Ulrika got up with difficulty. Leaning on the arm of her
chair for support, she let out: "You scoundrel." Mylius
looked at her surprised.

"You miserable scoundrel," Ulrika said in her rough voice.

A hateful smile spread over Lothar Mylius's face. He
looked as if he felt flattered. He patted Ulrika's bony hand
with two of his soft white fingers and said: "You ought to
have indulged yourself a little. Put all your eggs in same
basket. Why? Stupid. Now you repent. A man must
enjoy. You always wanted to enjoy at others' expense. Great

lack of heart. Man with heart shows it by spending money.
Look at me. It runs out of my pockets. And everything bows
down, bows down. So I can only see backs, only backs. Most
amusing."

"Very likely," Ulrika answered bitterly; "faces are often
troubling. One need only look at you."

He patted Ulrika's hand again and continued: "Understand your pain. Who knows to-day or to-morrow—everything's the same. To-morrow it may be my turn. Everybody's turn comes. The downward grade, my good old Ulrika,
the great slide." He bleated softly. His voice was a little
squeak. "Want to go down into the cellar? You will hear
the foundations cracking. Very impressive. Word of honour.
Hear it everywhere in Berlin. Every cellar. Pure music.
Music of the great slide. Pretty, what?" He was undoubtedly pleased, as far as he was capable of being. "Moreover,"
he added, suddenly staring again sleepily at the negro shield,
"if you are in difficulties I may be able to use some of your
furniture. No fear. Stand at your service."

Ulrika shook her head senilely. A new species, she thought,
a new species of the genus Man; he ran quicker than I. I
could not keep up with him.

"You have, for instance, the English doll," said Mylius in
a casual tone; "I'd be willing to buy it. Worth a bit of
money, that thing. I'll take it."

Ulrika was startled. Hastily, in a shrill voice, she replied:
"You'll take it? Ei, ei. That is not bad, Herr Mylius, not
bad. But getting it, that is the important thing, and you
will never get it."

"Why not?" Mylius asked harmlessly. "Can I get it for
a hundred thousand marks? That would be lovely. Hope
you will think over the matter."

Ulrika held her balled-up fist close in front of his nose
and said with strange violence: "Not for ten hundred thousand, nor for twenty! There. Now you know. She is not
for sale, and you may know it; there are things that are not for
sale; and though you were to open your pocket-book as wide
as your mouth you won't get it."

Lothar bleated. He understood nothing. He took Ulrika to a guest room. Lying there in bed, she turned from side to side. Suddenly she said aloud: "You shall have it; be still, child, you shall have it."

The next morning she went home. She rode dumb, sunk in herself, through the German country that showed its wounded breast and torn face to its own children and to strangers; through the German life, which was like a body without any skin to cover it. She did not see it. The second evening she reached home. As she had done in the cities so here she dragged her own suit-case for an hour and a half along the road. From time to time she said crossly, half as if she were trying to justify herself: "Be still, you shall have it."

In her own house she fell into brooding. She did not even notice when Crescence grumbled at her silence. Toward midnight the maid stepped up to her bed and asked: "What is going to happen?"

"I don't know what is going to happen," Ulrika answered and looked at the wall.

"Butter costs four hundred and fifty crowns; next week it will be five hundred," said Crescence, like a Cassandra.

"Men can live without butter," Ulrika replied.

"Shall I stay with you, or are you going to throw me out?" asked Crescence masterfully.

Ulrika sat up then and stared at her. "You stupid sloven," she muttered. That was enough for Crescence. She nodded and went. Ulrika stared at the wall.

The next evening, about seven o'clock, she carried the doll Evelyn from its pedestal upstairs into her bedroom. She took up a letter, which she had written beforehand, folded it and tied it with a rose-coloured ribbon onto the thumb of the wax hand so that it looked as if the doll were holding the letter, and handing it out.

The letter ran:

"My sweet little Fanny: now you have her. You have your Evelyn. The old Ulrika makes you a present of it.

And she asks for no other thanks from you than that you will think of her sometimes with a shadow of the kindness, with which she writes this to you. Evelyn comes to greet you and to tell you that the poor old Ulrika is always waiting with open arms for her sweet little Fanny. Always, always, always, waiting."

She wrapped up the doll in a piece of coarse linen, carried it, groaning, to the front of the house, fetched a little cart, which stood in the tool house, loaded the burden on the little wagon, took up the handles and began to pull. Crescence leaned out of the kitchen window. "What are you doing there?" she asked distrustfully.

Ulrika did not answer. She looked at her and was silent.

Three-quarters of an hour later she arrived at Eckern. She hid the little wagon under a bush and crept cautiously toward the house. It was already dark. At the kitchen entrance she stood quiet. She knew, that a short time ago the Baroness had taken a girl from Riednau as an assistant in the kitchen; Ulrika knew this girl and she was waiting for a moment when it would be possible to call her out. It was quite a long time before she could beckon to her without being noticed. The girl, whose name was Romana, came. Ulrika led her to the bush where the little wagon was and said she would give her a petticoat if she would do something for her. Romana wanted to know what it was. Ulrika explained in whispers that during the night, when every one was asleep, she should carry the doll into Fanny's room and stand it up beside the child's bed. Nothing more. There was no danger in it and she would be doing no wrong. It was to be a surprise, that was all. Despite this Romana hesitated, in a kind of shy uncertainty, as the whole way of the old woman seemed queer to her. Then Ulrika added to the petticoat, a red peasants' head cloth; she had brought both with her, with forethought. Romana could no longer resist and declared that she was willing to do what Ulrika wished. "But don't wake the child," warned Ulrika, after she had already turned to go; "don't wake her out of her sleep. She isn't to see it until morning, not until morning." She threw a glance up to the windows and then disappeared into the darkness.

It happened that Fanny woke at half-past five in the morning, because the rays of the sun fell upon her face. Elizabeth had forgotten to draw the curtains. Her first glance fell upon the doll who stood there three steps from her bed. Her eyes grew round as wheels. She believed, at first, that she was dreaming and felt of one hand with the other. When she was convinced that she was really awake a shiver ran over her whole body.

For a long time the doll had not been a real thing in itself. It was the image of her persecutor. In the doll, she saw Ulrika and Anastasia and her mother and the false enticements and lies. But above all she saw Ulrika, above all else. If Evelyn were there, Ulrika could not be far away; that was Fanny's first frightened thought. She sprang out of bed. She raised her hands, pleading. She fled trembling into a corner. She looked about her, in terror.

No, it would do no good to call. No one could help her. No one had the power to prevent the appearance of her who was behind the doll or perhaps even in her. There it was again, the fright, the touching and being touched, the feverish desire to get to the surface, as if she were being strangled in water. It must not happen again, or she would die of shame and fear and pain and guilt, oh, heavens, no. No one had the power, not even the Frau Baroness, and that the doll stood here in the room was proof of it. It was a proof that she was forsaken, and that she was to be handed over to them, and that she would have to manage to get on with her mother and Anastasia and Ulrika and that she would never again find shelter, and need expect none.

Her fear almost robbed her of her senses. Murmuring disjointed words, turning her look as much as possible away from the doll, she slipped into her clothes, gathered together her coat, her hat, and her little bag, put her sandals into it, reassured herself that no one was in the way, ran to the staircase, down the stairs, through the hall to the door, and unseen she made for the open.

CHAPTER XXXV

THE MOUNTAIN

ABOUT eight o'clock Elizabeth gave the alarm. Her voice sounded so shrill that everybody ran up. Elizabeth wrung her hands and stammered only: "Fanny—the doll—Fanny—the doll." When she discovered that the child was not in her bed she searched the entire house and asked all the servants. She had received a complete confession from Romana of how she had been bribed by Ulrika, but that did not make the disappearance of the child any clearer.

Josephine kept her self-control and admonished Elizabeth to calm her excited bearing. She noticed the letter which the doll carried, tore it open and read it. She was very thoughtful; there was something unexpected in the letter but it did not lessen her anxiety. She ordered a number of people to be sent out to search through the neighbourhood. It was important to send some one to the Villa Woytich, who would not be frightened by Ulrika, but who, in case of necessity, would know how to intimidate her. Casimir was entrusted with this mission. He came back in an hour, and told her that Ulrika Woytich had shown so real a consternation at the news that Fanny was lost, that there could be no possible doubt of her innocence. After all sorts of incomprehensible speeches she had said that she would come over herself. Josephine turned to her people standing about her and said in a severe tone: "Once and for all, any one who lets this woman pass over my threshold is dismissed from my service."

They acted upon the order. A half hour later Casimir had a sharp controversy with Ulrika in front of the conservatory; she refused to be turned away and after a good deal of abuse and angry, wailing excuses she went her way. But all day long it was reported that she was on the outlying grounds or in the neighbourhood of the house, and that she

stopped and questioned all the messengers who were sent out
and came back again.

The morning passed, and it became midday. Fanny did
not return; no one had found her or seen her. Josephine's
painful unrest grew every hour. She could not think or
make any plans. Valerian encouraged her. Unfortunately it
occurred to him to tell her how strangely the child had behaved when Elizabeth brought in the news of Ulrika's
nephew's suicide. He only wanted to show her how strangely
endowed Fanny was and what a conscious life was developing
in her, so that one need not be too anxious about her, but
Josephine only saw from the tale that something had been
hidden from her, and that secrecy had worked harmfully upon
the child, and her anxiety could no longer be assuaged. Although Valerian took pains to treat Fanny's disappearance
as a harmless joke, he got up after dinner himself and went
out to scour a part of the woods, while his Excellency Herbst
hunted through another part. Both returned about four
o'clock bringing no news. Elizabeth, the maid, the gardener
Pohl, the assistant gardener, and various other house-servants
and peasants hunted with as little result. The police in the
Baths and in Riednau had been notified before noon. Josephine had announced that she would give twenty thousand
crowns to any one who found the child or would bring news
of her that led to finding her. Search was instituted in every
house, barn, inn of the neighbourhood, bicyclists were sent out
along the main roads, all the nearby stations were telephoned
to, and in Eckern no one went about his business but dedi-
cated himself to the search. In vain. Evening came without
a trace of the child being discovered.

Josephine sat at her table in her work-room, like a figure
cut out of wood. She wanted to thrash out the whole matter
in her mind. But causes and connections were lacking. With
hallucinating power she peered into the hidden past, and what
escaped her reason, her intuitions solved. Elizabeth, broken
by the excitement of the day, was called in to her mistress
to consult, and had at last told her of the unfortunate incident of the meeting with Anastasia; Frau Pohl and Rosine

had been able to explain many things afterwards, so that
now the wanton game was fairly clear. But not what had
happened in the child's mind; there something appallingly
hidden was lost in unfathomable depths, in which Josephine
looked for her own negligence, and searched for her own
guilt, and once again faced her demoniacal persecutor who
no longer bore a name or could be singled out, or bore living
features. It seemed to her that never before had she stood,
with all her activities and being, before the forum of the
spirit world, and that now she must make a decision which
would be finally effective and control the future.

It was eleven o'clock when she heard excited talking outside of her door. After a hasty knock Elizabeth came in,
bringing a man, a young peasant whom Josephine knew. His
name was Justler. Elizabeth was no longer able to tell what
she had heard from him; she dropped at Josephine's feet and
pointed at Justler. He reported that at noon, as he was
picking Alpine roses, he had seen a child on the mountain,
the upper half of the western grazing pasture. She had on
a brown dress with white dots, a big straw hat, sandals and
a bag slung on her back. He had been surprised and had
called to the child; she had turned around, looked at him
for a moment and then gone on. In a few moments she was
lost from sight and he thought no more about it; children
often climbed up to the pasture to get flowers and berries;
only this time he had been astonished that one should climb
as high as the ridge, in these days when everything was in
dangerous motion up there. But by that time it was too late
to reach her. He told about it at home that evening; his
two brothers had looked at each other thoughtfully and exclaimed that it was undoubtedly the little girl from Eckern
who was being looked for everywhere, and they had immediately lighted lanterns and started out on the way to earn
the reward. And he had come over to tell the Frau Baroness
about it.

Josephine rose, considered for a few minutes and then
asked the man: "Can you take me to-night up the mountain?" Elizabeth looked horrified. Justler scratched his head

and reflected. Josephine turned to Elizabeth: "There is no use sitting here eating my heart out; I can't think of sleeping; I would rather act, or at least persuade myself that I am acting. You shan't lose anything by it," she turned to Justler; "but if you are too tired I will find some one else." Justler turned aside the allusion to the reward, somewhat ashamed, and declared that he would take the Baroness. Elizabeth, pale with excitement, declared eagerly that she would go too; if the Frau Baroness went without her it might be her death. Josephine shook her head impatiently, begged her not to make a scene but remain quietly at home; Justler's care would be sufficient for her, and having Elizabeth along would make things so much the harder.

"But if the Frau Baroness exhausts herself too much and breaks down, not being used to such exertion—" wailed Elizabeth. Josephine paid no attention, told Justler to wait for her downstairs, and gave Elizabeth orders as to the clothing she needed. Elizabeth listened, weeping quietly to herself. "It is all my fault," she moaned softly, as she helped Josephine to change her clothes. "I was blind, I was negligent, it is all my fault." Josephine replied: "It is no one's fault, Elizabeth; let us not even speak of fault."

Before Josephine started Elizabeth got provisions from the kitchen and gave them to Justler. She asked if the huts on the Alm were still occupied. He replied that those on the west side were still safe, but the others had been destroyed by the avalanche and lay buried under the rocks; but there was shelter everywhere. Elizabeth enquired whether accidents were to be feared from the avalanche. He laughed soothingly and said that he knew the way. "Even at night?" Elizabeth asked anxiously. He replied that the sun would be up long before he had brought the Baroness through the woods. Then having been made talkative by a glass of wine, he told her that outside the edge of the park he had been waylaid by Fräulein Woytich; she was sitting there on a bench and looked as if she had lost her mind. He had to tell her in detail all he knew, and he had hardly ended before she had gotten up and rushed off like the devil. He laughed in a good-humoured, knowing way, that with which the people in the neighbourhood laughed at Ulrika Woytich. Then Josephine came downstairs and he lit his lantern, he walked on ahead and Josephine followed; first painfully, but by degrees all her muscles and joints became freer. Neither spoke. It was a warm August night. The moon had climbed the eastern peak, but now slipped behind the mist. A heavy silver edge enwreathed the lower clouds and drew itself up in manifold shining rays into the higher lying strata. For an hour the way led up and down through the meadows. All colour was blotted out, trees and tree-trunks stood black, the brooks ran silently, and the mountains stood in a wide semicircle around the sleeping valleys and woods. Toward one o'clock the really steep ascent began; Josephine leaned heavily on her stick. Sometimes a shimmer of moonlight broke through, but the clouds were getting heavier and heavier and finally covered the sky completely. At the top of the ridge which they had just climbed, the way turned into the wood. Josephine had to rest and sat down on some recently cut wood that spread about a sharp odour of vegetation. A little screech owl called monotonously through the woods. Justler said: "The mountain is still in motion." Josephine answered: "Yes, I have felt for a long time that something was happening up there." And she thought of Valerian's assertion, that the crash of the mountain, as he called it, had been brought about by catastrophes in the orbits of the stars.

Then they marched on. Justler kept nearer to Josephine and raised the lantern high in his outstretched arm, for the darkness was so dense under the trees that one felt as if one could cut it with one's finger, and the path, which was hardly a foot broad, went up and down between powerful tree-trunks and close-grown underbrush; here and there it was covered with stones, or broken by swampy mudpuddles, or led over heavy roots, or was laid over with lathes which had become as slippery as soap in the dampness. And there seemed to be no end to it. Hour after hour they went on until the last of the path turned sharply to a steep ascent. Josephine stood still for a moment frightened. A scarlet glow shone through

the trees. Justler told her: "That is the sunrise." And Josephine sat down to rest in the moss and closed her eyes.
When she opened them again the grey daylight was creeping
through the peaks.

After they had climbed for a while, the woods stopped
short. They were cut off from the valley beneath by the wide
bed which the avalanche had covered. On the banks of this
horrible stone stream lay hundreds of corpses of pines, spruce,
firs, and larches, splintered, broken up in fragments, bent into
woven branches like basket work, and everywhere the black-
brown mould clung round the bared roots, and the thrown-up
stone street showed on its entire length not a trace of life,
not even dead life; the brook which had flowed here was
gone, no animal, no blade of grass, no moss, nothing but the
bristling brown and yellow distorted rocks were to be seen.
Gigantic blocks and slabs had followed the crash that dragged
them valley-wards, and where the pressure had been from the
middle out toward the sides, the most powerful ruins had
been ground into sand and dust. A hardly recognisable path
lead along the edge with innumerable windings, formerly used
by the peasants who took their cattle up to graze in the pasture. It would have been possible to climb the mountain
from the other side, Justler told Josephine, but one would
have been obliged to take a fourfold longer way to reach the
spot where the child was last seen. The place lay, indeed,
fairly far from the peak that had been broken, but from this
side where they were the avalanche had turned sidewise from
the mountain top, and one had only a little way to go, to
reach the place, and from there one could see the whole picture of the disaster.

Josephine looked up with a feeling of unspeakable impo-
tence. She thought of Fanny lost in this desert of rock,
unconscious of the dangers of this wholly discouraging scene,
nature turned to stone; she thought of her trembling back
from the abysses, or clinging frightened to the steep walls
and her blood froze and she needed all her will-power to put
one foot before the other. Justler was helping her now at
every step, for the way was very difficult, and an exhaustion

overcame her that she hardly knew how to cope with. Justler asked if she would not take something; she refused; he advised a swallow of cherry brandy from his flask, but she refused it. The sun, high up in the southeast, broke through the mist and over the southern mountains, white and gigantic, stood the enormous glacier; they had slowly encircled the first peak and were nearing the destroyed one, when they heard loud calls. Justler listened. "My brothers," he murmured, and then stood still and looked about attentively. He returned the call, and his voice broke the crystal silence so sharply that Josephine's heart began to beat rapidly. "If the Frau Baroness can keep on for five minutes," said Justler, "we will reach the herdsmen's huts; one of those huts is still standing, only a piece of the roof has blown off. There the Frau Baroness can rest, until I return. Yes, my brothers are there; they must have seen us from above and I will see why they are calling."

Josephine, leaning on his arm, dragged herself almost fainting to the huts. He brought her water to drink and put a little luncheon down before her. Mechanically she ate and drank, and then for a little while she saw and heard nothing. About a half an hour had passed and heavy steps were heard coming through the mountain stillness. A man appeared in the frame of the door. He looked around. A second followed him with a burden in his arms. It was a human being; it was Fanny's body.

Her hair, blood-stained and clotted, fell to one side over the arm of the man carrying her, her little limp legs, with her insufficient shoes in rags, hung over the other. Blood trickled from her forehead and rushed from her mouth. Her eyes were closed. Josephine stood upright as a candle in the wind. She wanted to stretch out her hands; she could not; she wanted to force a question from her throat; she could not. The first arrival took an armful of hay from the corner and spread it over the bench, the other laid the child carefully down upon it. He told Josephine that the child was not dead, only unconscious; the other told her that they had found the child on the north peak; he could

not make out how she had gotten there, every step meant the
end for an inexperienced person there. There was a sort of
noble consideration in his words, which is native to these
people in every time of trial. They handled the child skilfully; no nursing sisters could have dealt more tenderly with
the wounded. They had bandages with them; and Josephine's
guide came now, bringing water to wash the wounds; when
Josephine roused from her rigidity, Fanny's head was already
bound. Her face was white as snow. She was still breathing,
though irregularly, a short, sharp panting. "It is not dangerous, Frau Baroness," Justler, the guide, assured her,
touched by the sight of the extraordinarily beautiful creature. "People like us know when it is dangerous."

Little by little, Josephine gathered her senses together and
became quiet. She listened to the heart. It was beating. She
felt the breast. It was warm. She said: "Go down at once
to Riednau. It is the nearest village. Fetch a doctor and
a stretcher. If you are tired send others. I will not let her
be moved without the help of a doctor. It would be easy
to make another mistake that could not be remedied. I beg
you, hurry as much as you can. I don't need you here. I
need no one. There is plenty of water, that is good. But I
beg you for Christ's sake, hurry, hurry with all your hearts.
Remember, that I am waiting up here in torment. I will
thank you all later."

They hesitated a little as to whether they should all go
but understood the feeling that the Baroness wished to be
alone. Nothing could happen to her and there was little
help to be given. So they went. It was ten o'clock. They
believed that they could be back by five in the afternoon.
Soon their steps and their voices faded away.

From time to time Josephine renewed the bandages. In
the pauses between she sat on a wooden bench, bending far
over, her head pressed between her hands. Sometimes a shiver
went over Fanny's body. Josephine laid a wet cloth over her
chest. When she saw the wonderful skin that looked like
foaming blossom petals, she could hardly restrain a sob.
"What was it you did, Fanny?" she whispered. "What was

if you did, soul of my soul?" And again: "Why, oh, why did you do it?" The blood had ceased to flow from her forehead and as the cold water always brought a little sigh and gentle wail, Josephine left the bandages on a longer time. She cowered on the wooden bench, her head between her hands, not moving, suddenly very old, and listened with all her power to the marvellous silence of the mountains.

Two hours must have passed when a shadow fell across the threshold and she heard a heavy, tired, step. When Josephine looked up Ulrika Woytich was standing before her. Her face looked like a piece of the rock outside, it was so grey and worn; her skirt was torn, her shoes full of holes, her hands wounded, and she was staggering. In her toilsome hours of climbing she had run across the brothers Justler and they had told her how they had found Fanny and pointed out the direction and the way to her. Moreover in earlier years she had been well acquainted with this mountain.

She leaned against the wooden wall, exhausted. Josephine, her face turned toward her, looked at her dumbly. A railing ran along the wall about the height of a seat and Ulrika worn out dropped down upon it and fixed her faded eyes upon the bench where Fanny lay. The two women sat silently opposite each other, like two she-wolves who meet upon the steppes.

Then Ulrika said in a hoarse voice: "Give her to me, that little creature; you must give the little creature to me, Josephine."

Josephine answered tonelessly: "Some one is speaking whom I do not know."

Ulrika said: "Give me the child, Josephine. Your pride and your stubbornness will not help you now. The child shall not stay with you."

"The person who is speaking has evidently lost her mind," said Josephine grimly.

"With her mind or without her mind, you will have to give up the little creature," Ulrika insisted in quiet fury.

Then Josephine answered with icy bitterness: "First give me back my life again, Ulrika Woytich."

Ulrika stared without understanding and then laughed shrilly. It was a frightful laugh. Laughter reveals men and shows their nobility or their meanness.

Josephine continued with sullen composure: "My life; it is that that I demand of you. My life that you trod upon, threw down in the mud, sold to hell, and covered with all the disgrace that the world of man contains. Try to see if you can give it back again now, close before the great portal through which we must both step soon. And if you know no answer it would be better and more humane for you to keep silence, Ulrika; keep silence until death."

"I don't understand a syllable," murmured Ulrika; "or are you trying to say that the well-meant arrangement of a marriage between the Demoiselle Mylius and the late Sir Melander was such a misfortune? Rubbish. I can hardly think so. That is only the relighted ash of a burned-out cigar. What are you talking to me about? Only one thing matters to me, Lord in heaven, only one thing." The last words she shrieked out with fanatical wildness and covered her eyes with her hands.

Josephine pointed warningly to Fanny's bed. She rose, looked into the child's face in alarm, and then sat down again. "You never think of it now, I believe you," she began without looking up and in a voice as if she were speaking only to herself. "I know that you have not thought of it for a long time, no living creature thinks of it. But it still lives on and works and sends its black waves even to this hour. We are in a strange loneliness, Ulrika Woytich, and nearer to God's throne, if you will, than we two ever were before, or than men often are. And there lies the most precious and most costly treasure that fate has entrusted to me, since ever I have felt the breath of fate in my heart and consciousness. We cannot know yet, we can only hope, that this new, this bleeding disaster is not a last sacrifice that I must make, in expiation. The last; after that there could be no more. And for this reason, Ulrika, because I know what has happened to you and what is happening, I am willing to do what I have never done before, and to speak of things that have never passed my lips. Perhaps you will understand then. Perhaps then you will begin to think about it."

Ulrika never moved. Struck by the nobility in Josephine's voice and manner, she listened, with a wrinkled forehead.

Josephine continued: "You were the originator of it all. You were proud of your work. And now I want you to hear what came of it, your work. It was you, Ulrika Woytich, that discovered that man of steel and wax, who could make himself into anything that he needed to be. If the most inimical and irreconcilable life powers had plotted at my birth the best way to cut me, Josephine Mylius, most surely off from all joy and happiness, and destroy me most completely, they would have brought me to this man and made me this man's companion. It was a slow recognition, step by step. When I despaired that I had lost my mother and my mother's love and I gave my consent, I had only a vague idea of what I was doing; the realisation of it came in the slow, deadly continuation. And what did I become aware of? What did I see? I saw lies personified. The slippery, inaccessible, unmalleable, unprovable lie, idolising itself and never recognised by the world. A friend of the people? Lies. An honest servant of his state? Lies. A decent citizen? Lies. A considerate master? Lies. A model husband and father? Lies. He had only one thing, one unconquerable aid, one helper that made all his lies seem sincere and upright and that hid his true nature so that it could never be found out, and that was his smile. There never was such a smile. I don't think anything like it ever existed before, a smile that was so welcoming, so friendly, so intellectual, so tender, so full of understanding, so sympathetic, so gentle, according as he needed these qualities; but I saw his face without the smile. There are people of whom one says that their most devoted followers and humble friends would be frightened to the very marrow of their bones if they saw them naked. I saw Edward Melander without his smile. And then the truth was written plainly on his face, his brutality without shame, his contempt for all morality, the coldness of his nature, his determination to reach the goal, his reckless self-indulgence, his glowing hatred of all rivals, and his complete ignorance of, and turning from, divine things. How did I feel then? How all my senses faded and the colour of the world disappeared and I myself became a mere shadow! But that was only the beginning of things. To live with such a man means to live through hours and days; and the processes of experience are tormentingly weary. Deception after deception, bitterness upon bitterness, blow upon blow. From seeing to knowing and from knowing to the final image that can no longer possibly deceive one, until the noblest part of one's strength is spent and the ways, that hope and despair first thought possible, are all confused. A marriage such as mine makes a woman the loneliest creature in existence. She is secure, rich, honoured, envied; who would think or believe that she is the most outcast of her race, betrayed and lost to the very inmost kernel of her body and her soul? Not to be saved, with her only life lost. And he? What did he know about me, except my name? Perhaps only one other thing, that I knew him without his smile. And he never forgave that. To oppose me in everything was a law to him, the law of his nature. And little by little he unclothed himself before me and showed himself just as he was. As if I were not already sufficiently initiated, he wanted to leave me no illusions. The good that I wanted, he cheapened and if he gave in to it, it was only to work against me in secret. The generosity that he made a show of before the world, changed in his own four walls to calculating, scornful miserliness. The honour, which he always showed me before others, became icy mockery when I was alone with him. The people whom I had reason to honour he calumniated so skilfully that disgust seized me in their presence. Anything that I admired was a horror to him, anything that I bowed down to he spat upon and besmirched and everything that I clung to he undermined so that it ripped loose when I tried to hold by it. The ideals for which he pretended to fight and which in public he spoke for with pathos and passion were a joke and a derision to him when he was with me, and when he wanted to humiliate me he undermined the whole machinery of the world sarcastically—

that world which he had flattered and conquered. He spared
no one, no one went unpunished and unsuspected, and where
he seemed most trustful, he really scorned most deeply. His
politics were a gambling game, his patriotism a business, his
religion a deception of the masses, his friendship a joke, and
yet all these things he hung with the disguise of loyalty, self-
sacrifice, faith, honour, manliness, and dignified propriety,
and at the same time before my pained eyes he would shell
off the hulls and show me the worm-eaten kernels. Only
before me, he did it for my eyes alone. He seemed strangely
moved, more and more with the years, to drop every sense of
shame and shyness before me; perhaps it was to bring me to
the last stage of retribution, and punish me because I was not
blind like his other creatures, those he deceived; and because
I could not be blind, and because now, once and for all, it
had happened that I had lifted the edge of the veil with
which he hid himself. He made life hell for me as long as I
was childless, and he made it arch-hell when I had borne
him a son. He ignored this son, as long as he was what he
called a toy for women, and when he grew up to be a criminal,
he ceased to bother about him. He said that the continuation of the Melander name would be very likely to trouble
the picture of his own personality and therefore went against
his interests. For he held himself as a representative of his
time; he considered himself the last and most important
member of a modern development and after him he said, let
the deluge come. This gave him his strength, his hardness
and his unexampled lack of scruples. He had pictures painted
of himself, and statues carved and was never tired, and all
these pictures and statues had the same bewitching smile, the
same winning, kindly look. Up to my eighteenth year, I
had believed myself to be under God's particular protection,
and that I should be indissolubly bound to a man who had
never heard of God except when he undertook to be sponsor
for a church lottery, and who otherwise built his own world
of things and senses capriciously, and as he thought well, and
who broke my faith as he had already broken my soul by
his mere existence, I early learned to think of as a decree

of God. I said: indissolubly bound; for if he had given me my freedom (and he never thought of it because my fortune was as indispensable to him as my knowledge of his person and secret intentions and activities were dangerous to him); or if I had tried to force it, he would have hindered me with every possible means and power, and avenged himself with merciless persecutions: what good would that freedom have been to me then? How could I use it? What was I worth to myself any more? Can any one lead two lives, one after the other? I had only one, and this one was destroyed on the day when I walked to the altar on his arm, and the night when I bit my pillow with my teeth. Experiences either eat their way into the blood and spirit or else they never existed. One cannot do anything one wants, if one has learned to do only one thing and that has been forbidden; to yield oneself and serve consciously. And so it came that I lived through days, months and years, with a lie at my side, a complete, impressive, unrecognised devilish lie, and the deceived and befooled world lay before me and sin and degradation within me and it went on until he died. He died in the arms of a prostitute; he had gone off with her after a banquet of the Ethical Society, whose founder and honourary president he was. It was all hushed up and he remained still in death the beloved and praised of all, the pattern of virtue, and benefactor of his nation. And then again I lived through days and months and years and decades, and the lie still remained at my side, and the deceived world before my eyes, and the sin in my breast. For death takes nothing away, it only makes the form final and what he left behind him in my life were lies, lies of life, of deed and of seed."

She was silent. Outside they heard a falling rock. A finch twittered frightened, on the eaves of the broken roof.

After an eternal silence Ulrika rose and stammered, grinding her jaw with a hateful cunning look: "Those are old stories. Old stories of past things."

Josephine made no answer.

Ulrika made a motion to go toward the bench and stretched out her hand saying: "But there—that—the child—is that nothing? Is that no compensation? Can you wish that out of the world?"

Josephine barred the way for her and said threateningly: "Here you will never go! Just because that is worth while! Because nothing else matters! Not another step! For once in your life you shall leave something holy and unspotted, Ulrika Woytich!"

Ulrika's eyes glimmered and her head fell from side to side like an idiot's and she gurgled: "Let me go to the little creature! Get out of my way, Josephine, or something will happen. Let me go to the little creature!"

"What for?" asked Josephine, standing upright.

"What for?" asked Ulrika beside herself. "I think you will suffer for this. You will rob her of her name and her inheritance; I know that is what you have in your mind."

Josephine smiled. And the smile had in it such an expression of surprised pity that Ulrika's head sank as if she had been struck. Then the unhappy passion came over her again and she went up to Josephine as if she intended to tear her from the spot where she stood.

"What do you want?" Josephine asked again.

"I want to kiss the sweet little Fanny!" Ulrika shrieked.

"You shall not get a breath nearer her!" Josephine replied, rigid as an arch-angel.

"But I love my sweet little Fanny," howled Ulrika as if she had lost her senses; "I love her and I want her to love me."

"And will you try to force it?" cried Josephine with flaming eyes; "always and always force things? Have you not understood that one cannot force things? Love cannot be won, nor bought, nor gained by flattery, nor paid for. It is grace. And don't you know that yet, you corrupter, you destroyer?"

With shaking knees, her mouth half open, her stiff stray hairs wandering over her cheeks and forehead, Ulrika stood there before Josephine, before the wooden bench as before a door where she was denied admittance. She turned around and looked into the clashing, mid-day waste of the mountain outside; she raised her head and looked through the broken roof to the sky; she rocked herself strangely on her hips and whispered questioningly, so one could hardly hear it: "Grace, what is grace? Just one of your wishy-washy pieties: grace? What is grace?"

Josephine nodded emphatically and repeated: "Yes, grace. All loving and all being loved is grace. But people have forgotten it, or have unlearned it. And you have separated yourself from it. See, Ulrika, how things have gone with you. Look back, a single look. Tumult and haste and noise, these have been your life. You have always been willing, and you have always been striving. Doing, doing, doing, and you knew nothing else, but where have you been? Where was your real being all this time? You haven't been anywhere. You never have been. Your desires, yes, they have been, and your greed, and your cunning, and your illusions and your tireless striving; your anxiety about things, your idolatry of your things, these have been, but you yourself have never been at all. And after all this you come here in an hour of crisis and want to take a human being, a soul, a heart, and love it? Love never possesses, love just is."

Ulrika pressed her lips together. Her hands trembled. "And if she decides herself, the little creature, herself decides between you and me?" She asked it with a frightful, comfortless leer in her look.

Josephine looked at her and recognised that their words did not meet, that they were worlds apart. It seemed to her that she was looking down into a bottomless abyss. But as she turned shudderingly away pity for the creature seized her and she hid her face. But there was a movement behind her, and as she turned, Fanny lay there with big, wide-open eyes and smiled at her as if she were still tired and dazed. She bent down involuntarily and the child threw her arms about her neck with utter abandon and pressed her joyous trembling body closer and closer to her breast.

When Ulrika saw this she turned away quietly and went.

The powerful mountain sun dazzled her and instead of taking the path downwards, by which she had come, she turned her straggling steps up into the wilderness. When she had climbed some distance she sat down on a stump and stared motionless in front of her. It was hours before she got up again to wander on. She wandered amongst the rocks and looked with the astonishment of an animal into the measure-less ruins, the clefts in the rocks, the yellow gold roll of the brooks, the icy-grey granite needles, the whole torn skin of the mountain. Still wandering aimlessly she left the region of horror and resting under a withered larch tree she opened her eyes unexpectedly over the depth and width of the coun-try. There lay the valley before her with its gradations, its peaceful roads, its houses, its churches with their steeples, all its green and blue and red and grey, its trees and water, and life and death, and all the sadness and joyousness of the darkening world.

THE END